A PATH OF BLOOD AND AMBER

SILVERBLOOD RAVEN SERIES

NIKKI McCORMACK

ISBN: 978-1-7367938-1-7
First Edition 2022

Published by
Elysium Books
Seattle, WA

Written by Nikki McCormack (https://nikkimccormack.com/)
Cover Design by Robert Crescenzio (https://robertcrescenzio.artstation.com/)
Typesetting and Design by Brian C. Short

•

After the isolation of the pandemic,
I dedicate this book to everyone who
is figuring out
how to be social again or, like Raven,
for the first time.

•

Raven froze, standing as still as the tree next to her. Her breathing was soft and steady. Her Silverblood enhanced eyesight quickly picked a hare out of the underbrush despite the changing light of approaching dusk. Slowly, smoothly, she raised her bow, nocking an arrow in the same motion.

She focused on her breathing and waited a few seconds, watching the unsuspecting animal. The brush next to it shifted, and another hare hopped cautiously out into the open to join the first. Raven drew the string back until the end of the arrow was alongside her cheek, in front of one pointed ear. The bow had belonged to her father. It was too long for her, but she adapted her style to it. These days, she rarely missed. That mattered because the animal wouldn't suffer as long as her aim was true.

Drawing in a steadying breath, she let the arrow fly. The hare went down with a slight squeal. The second animal had an instant to react, spinning to leap away. Another arrow sank into its side, dropping it a few inches away from the first. The poor creature was no match for half-elven reflexes enhanced by Silverblood magic and years of rigorous training.

The dense canopy of leaves overhead cast flickering shadows on the ground as the sun sank on the horizon.

Raven worked quickly, putting away her bow and going to collect the hares. They were healthy animals. A good kill. She tied the hind feet of each hare to either end of a leather strap.

For a few seconds, she remained crouched there, listening for the sounds of predators lured by the cry of the hare and the scent of death. Hearing nothing, she stood, lifting her kill with her. The two animals swung from the leather strap. That lifeless weight made something uncomfortable stir in the dark recesses of her mind.

How could the memory still be so vivid? It had happened such a long time ago. She had been a child. Yet, somehow, every creature she killed to keep food on the table, no matter the size, had the same dead weight when she first went to pick it up as her mother's lifeless arm clutched in her eight-year-old hands.

•

The stenches of charred flesh and fresh blood filled her nose. Her mother's eyes turned black, then silver blossomed from the pupil, filling them to the edges. Blood trickled from her mouth as she murmured her last words—an apology and strange words in a language Raven didn't recognize— before her hand went limp in Raven's grasp. No declaration of love. No goodbye. Raven screamed at her to stay, but it did no good. Her father's burned body lay silent behind her. Her parents were gone.

Then heat filled Raven, burning through her as if her blood had caught fire. Not with the same literal flames that killed her father. This was something different. It raced through every part of her: muscle, bone, and sinew. All of her burned as she was agonizingly remade with magic. Silverblood magic.

A mother's act of magic to protect her daughter. An

act of love. A curse that would mark Raven forever.

•

She shook herself and blinked back tears, her hand closing into a tight fist around the leather strap. Deft fingers tied it to her belt alongside a pouch full of mushrooms she had collected that would add a musky flavor to the gamy meat.

A hawk lit in the tree above her, cocking its head to the side to consider her kills.

"Would you steal my hunt from me, hawk?" She gave the bird a challenging look.

It tilted its head to eye her now, assessing the threat she posed.

Raven grinned at it, pleased to have a diversion from memories it seemed would plague her all her life. "Not today, my friend. Although, should you follow me home, you might find scraps out in the midden heap by morning."

The bird tilted its head the other way, the intensity of its gaze giving her the sense that it was trying to understand her. She often fancied, foolish as the notion was, that she should be able to communicate with the creatures of these woods. She had grown up her entire life among them. They were much less peculiar to her than the rare human or elf she spotted if she wandered closer to the wagon tracks. Jaecar scolded her when she ventured near those places where someone might see her. When she was younger, it was something of a game trying to sneak out there without getting caught. Now that he watched her less closely, she itched to go even farther. He could not intend for her to spend her entire life in these woods with only a cranky old warrior for company.

Raven turned toward the keep. A steady, tireless

jog had the crumbling heights of the old west tower visible through the treetops within twenty minutes. The tower itself was no longer safe, though she remembered playing in it as a child, practicing sword forms up and down the now-collapsed staircase. At twelve, Jaecar assured her she was faster with a blade than he had ever been. Nowadays, he insisted she was a better warrior and hunter than any student he had trained before her. He probably exaggerated, though his praise still made her beam now as much as it had when she was a child.

She passed over the rubble of the courtyard wall, leaping from one block of stone to another with a sure-footedness Jaecar spent endless hours drilling into her. What else was there for them to do here, living alone in an abandoned keep in the woods? Jaecar had been a soldier somewhere before coming here. He never told her what army he fought for or where, but he did say that he had been a combat instructor for many years. He had no experience raising children, only soldiers. So that was how he raised her after her parents died, more like a recruit than a child. Not that she minded much. She was a Silverblood. Those magic enhancements were of little use without the proper training.

Raven smiled at the flicker of light from the study window, one of five usable rooms in the keep. He was rarely in there at this time of day, so the light would be a candle he had forgotten again. Jaecar taught her to read all the books he kept there. Books he had collected on war, weapons, and history, along with practical books on subjects like herbology and alchemy that had belonged to her parents. Her favorites were a small batch of made-up stories. Tales of love, adventure, and distant places she would never see. Stories about things she would never experience because her mother remade her.

Her gaze flickered toward the hillside that flanked the keep. Her parents were buried on that hillside, a tree planted between them where its roots could claim them and make them part of its life. That tree was now tall, healthy, and strong. Memory and emotion granted physical form.

The familiar sound of stone on metal greeted her when she opened the front door. Shadows hid dust and cobwebs in the high corners of the big room. Massive threadbare rugs that whispered of former glory lay in the entry and before the large fireplace. Jaecar, becoming himself another relic of the past, sat before a crackling fire with his back to the door. The muscles in his broad shoulders worked as he ran a sharpening stone along whatever blade—a sword judging from the length of the strokes—rested in his lap. He wore his grey hair bound into a loose tail at the nape of his neck, wayward strands escaping and twisting away in myriad directions.

Raven kicked her boots off alongside the door before tugging each of her socks off by pinning the toes to the ground with the other foot. A childhood behavior she never outgrew. Her bow and quiver, she leaned against the wall before padding over. Where the aging rugs didn't cover, cool, timeworn stone soothed her tired feet.

When she moved between Jaecar and the fire, he finally looked up. There were more lines on his face now. Most of the time, she didn't notice, but something in the way he regarded her today made him seem much older. A twist of icy anxiety sparked in her, contrasted by the comforting warmth of the fire at her back.

What would she do when he was gone?

"What are you working on?" she asked, pushing down her fear.

His dark-eyed gaze drifted first to the hares she still carried, then sank to her bare feet, lingering a moment as a hint of a smirk curved his lips. After a few seconds, he met her eyes, his hazel ones staring deep into her. He made no room for timidity in his world, and his stern gaze was the initiation into that domain.

"You need a blade that better suits your size."

Excitement sparked in her. She stepped closer to look at the weapon resting across his legs. The slender blade had a gentle curve, inscribed near the top with elven writing. She could make out about half of it. Her mother had been teaching her elvish. That early education in the language might have faded if Jaecar had not asked her to teach him. He also insisted that she read her mother's elven books. Most unfamiliar words she managed to puzzle out through context. A few, she still had to skip.

"What does it say?" She asked.

His silence and stern gaze said he wouldn't tell her until she tried to figure it out herself.

Raven set her jaw and pointed to the finely etched script. "That's justice. And that's mercy." Jaecar nodded as she considered the whole. "So this says 'Wield in justice.' I'm not sure about the second part. 'Don't in mercy'?"

"Withhold in mercy," he offered.

"Wield in justice. Withhold in mercy." As she said the words, the weight of them sank over her.

He nodded. "This is a weapon meant for killing. How you use it matters." He gestured to a smaller blade resting on the end of the bench, as elegant and refined as the sword. "There's a matching dagger. You know why I'm giving you these?"

Raven swallowed, fighting the tightening in her throat. Her lungs squeezed tight as well, making it hard to breathe normally.

"It's my birthday tomorrow," she managed.

It wasn't her actual birthday. Neither of them knew when that was. Tomorrow was the anniversary of her parents' deaths. The fourteenth anniversary. Her day of rebirth, as Jaecar called it. The day her world fell apart.

Silverblood. Since the Brotherhood consisted entirely of human men, Raven could never pass herself off as legitimate. She hadn't chosen this, but, as Jaecar often reminded her, she would be judged on sight, and that judgment was unlikely to be kind. Being half-elven and a female was challenging enough without that working against her.

She swallowed the sour taste of fear. "I don't know anything about the world outside of this place. I don't know how to talk to…" She trailed off when he gave her arm a reassuring squeeze.

"You won't be out there alone." His tone promised her protection. "I have some documents hidden in an old chest under stones at the bottom of the tower. We'll go over them after your birthday and begin planning our departure. You should be familiar with their contents in case anything happens to me on the road."

That cautious wave of giddy excitement that started to rise at the idea of taking on this adventure with him crashed against a rocky shore of reality. If something happened to him? Then she would be alone out there. How could she hope to survive alone?

She focused on the less scary part of what he had said. "What kind of documents?"

Sorrow lingered in his eyes, but he forced a smile. "One is the deed to the lands I mentioned. Don't worry about the rest tonight. Let's dress these hares and have some supper."

She answered with a firm nod, determined to push away the ill-feeling spreading in her gut. "I picked mushrooms too."

This time, his smile came easier. He put an arm around her shoulders and steered her toward the kitchen. "You take good care of us."

CHAPTER TWO

For Raven's birthday, Jaecar took her on a day-long outing up higher in the mountains to gather some of the hard-to-find sweet roots she loved. It provided a welcome distraction from the memories the day dredged up. Another year come and gone. Perhaps the last one at the keep.

Tonight, they would start planning a new future. She wanted to bring back something better than another hare for supper. If she could catch a deer or mountain goat, they would spend much of the evening dressing the kill, but it would provide food for several days. Then they could focus their attention on planning the journey. Some of the meat could also be dried to make travel rations. Now that Jaecar suggested going out into the world with her, she could hardly wait to get started.

The trail she followed was fresh enough to be promising. The deer, probably a doe, stepped light on the forest floor, not a heavy animal she would have trouble carrying on the long walk home. And it was going to be a long walk. Her hunt brought her closer to the wagon tracks than she intended, but the game went where the game went. She couldn't do much about that.

The sounds of several birds taking flight from the trees ahead drew her attention. Raven stopped and peered in that direction, her giddy optimism vanishing.

Another bird took to wing, and she heard something large – more than one something – moving through the brush.

She sprinted to the nearest big tree and leapt up, grabbing hold of one of the lower branches. It took a few seconds to pull herself up and climb through the branches to find a good, stable vantage point. Once settled, she drew up the hood of her green cloak to hide her face in its shadows. Then she waited.

"I'm sure it was over this way." The voice was male and too loud for a hunter, at least an experienced one.

"That was how many days ago?" This voice was also male, but deeper and more robust, the softer tone not intended to carry, so she had to listen more intently to hear his words.

Raven's pulse raced. What strangers had wandered into her woods today? What were they looking for? Would they come close enough for her to see them? Would they drop something that she could add to her collection?

"I know what you're trying to imply." This was the first speaker, stumbling over a branch as he stomped into view, staring back at whoever followed. He was young and light-skinned with a mop of blond hair that curled slightly upon his head. He glowered at the branch as if it, and not his inattention, were to blame for the stumble. "However, doesn't it make sense to start searching where last I saw it?"

Two more men walked into view. One wore a long black cloak embroidered with subtle silver designs around the edges. With his hood up, all she could see was that he carried a substantial two-handed sword in a sheath on his back. When a branch caught the side of his cloak, she got a glimpse of the crossbow at his hip and black leather armor also accented with silver. The third man, more simply dressed, walked with a measured stride that kept him behind the other two. He watched the man in the cloak warily whenever he wasn't casting exasperated glances at the younger man in the lead.

The cloaked man stopped, bringing his hands up to push back the hood. Dark blond hair hung down almost even with his jawline. He was handsome, at least so far as she could tell from the strong lines of his profile and based upon her own admittedly lacking experience. A trimmed beard followed the line of his jaw to join with an equally well-trimmed mustache under a nose that was a hint crooked, as though it might have been broken at some point.

He looked away from her hiding spot at first, then gradually rotated toward her, scanning the area. When he turned her way fully, she sucked in a breath, tucking herself closer to the tree's trunk when he looked up at the sound. Her heart was pounding now, the possibility of being spotted shooting arrows of fear through her. What she thought she had glimpsed at first was confirmed when he looked more precisely in her direction. This man was a Silverblood. His eyes gleamed with metallic silver, marking him as like her, only not. Like her, his eyesight and hearing would be sharper than an average person's. His reflexes faster. His strength greater. He was different, however, because he would have been made following the accepted rules that governed the creation of their kind

She kept her breathing shallow and soft, pleading with the forest not to let him see her. The other two men watched him for several minutes as he looked at her tree, cocking his head to listen and sniffing at the air a few times.

The younger man began to shift with impatience. "See anything, Adept Marek," the youth finally prompted, still speaking much louder than necessary given their proximity.

The Silverblood, Marek, turned a deep scowl on the other man. "Only a bird. We'll be lucky to find anything with all the noise you're making." He glanced around at her tree once more, and a faint smirk curved his lips before he turned away, pulling his hood up. "I told you, your beast isn't out this way anymore. We should head back toward the wagon track."

Once they were out of sight, Raven sank back on the branch, trembling so hard she didn't trust herself to climb down yet. Hiding from humans was easy enough. She had grown up in these trees, and her elven blood, along with the Silverblood enhancements, gave her some advantages. But Marek was an unknown quantity. She'd never seen another like her. When he'd looked at her tree, she had been sure he knew she was there. For whatever reason, he chose not to call her out.

According to Jaecar and the many books she read, the Silverblood Brotherhood maintained strict control of that magic. Anyone outside of the Brotherhood Priests caught making more of them would be turned over to the Brotherhood, who meted out death as punishment. Interestingly, Brotherhood doctrine taught that women, children, and elves could not be made Silverblood. The magic was too strong and would always kill them the way it did many of the human men who tried to use it. She gave the lie to all three of those points as a half-elven female who had survived being made a Silverblood at the age of eight. Jaecar told her that her existence would threaten the Brotherhood's control of that magic. That made Marek, and others like him, the most dangerous thing she could encounter in these woods.

She made herself take several deep, steady breaths, staring up through the foliage at small patches of blue sky.

How had her mother known that magic? Why would an elven female – one who had been little more than a servant before fleeing into the woods with her human lover – have knowledge of magic that was jealously guarded by a brotherhood of men? Jaecar couldn't answer that question. He insisted that nothing in her parents' home when he went through it had offered any insight. Since her mother was dead, Raven would never know how she knew that magic any more than she would ever understand why she had chosen to use it that day. It did give Raven greatly enhanced abilities, but it marked her in a way that made it impossible for her to join normal society.

Then again, maybe that was her mother's plan. She had found a way from beyond the grave to force Raven to stay hidden from those who might hurt her simply because she was a half-elf and a female. A way that also gave Raven the skills to hopefully deal with anyone who did find her. If her mother's goal had been to keep her isolated for her own safety, it was working out well. For her sanity, however, it didn't promise to be a tenable long-term arrangement.

No longer trembling badly, Raven climbed down from the tree and struck out in the opposite direction from that the men had taken. She would have to find some other game to track. That particular deer was out of her reach now.

She stopped.

Something shifted in the brush close by. She heard a low growling off to her left. It wasn't a warning growl. It was too soft. A sound most people wouldn't have heard. This creature was growling to itself as it prepared to attack its prey. She had an uncomfortable feeling that she knew what prey it was after.

Walking slow and steady, she angled her path away from the creature. She drew her blade, hoping it would be intelligent enough to recognize the weapon as a threat and search for easier prey. She could hear it moving now, slow, calculated movements. It was tracking her.

Looking for the right moment to attack. The hope that it would give up faded.

Precisely what kind of beast had the Silverblood and his companions been hunting?

Raven took another step slightly away. The creature moved fast, lunging from the bushes. Its size startled her enough that its front claws managed to brush the edge of her shirt sleeve before she leapt to one side. Agile like a cat, the beast twisted almost entirely around before making contact with the ground. It was vaguely canid in appearance but larger than a bear. When it rose on its back legs, standing at least three feet taller than her, her gut screamed at her to run.

The beast let out a roar, saliva spraying past its deadly canines, and a new fear twisted in her. The sound was more than loud enough to reach Marek and his group. If they came running back this way, she would have a few minutes to get out of here before they found her.

Raven didn't wait. She sheathed her sword and leapt up, catching hold of a tree branch. The beast roared again as it lunged for her, missing her feet by a few inches as she pulled herself up into the tree. She leapt to another branch and then another. Something caught her pant leg. Suddenly she was falling. She twisted, grabbing for her dagger as she tried to catch sight of the beast. Had it pulled her down, or had she merely caught herself on some branch she overlooked?

As she twisted around to land on her feet, the beast landed next to her, answering the question of what had caught her pant leg. It lunged. She ducked one swinging paw, bringing the dagger around to bury it deep in the creature's ribs. It let out a cry. The other big paw struck her, sending her flying back.

She hit the ground hard, her only ready weapon still in the beast's side, wedged solidly between two ribs. She was half-sitting on her sheathed sword, so she grabbed the bow that had fallen off her back with one hand, reaching for an arrow with the other.

A crossbow bolt appeared in the creature's shoulder as it poised to strike. It roared again, twisting around to face the three men that had arrived at the edge of the clearing. Casting one mournful glance at her lost dagger, Raven scrambled to her feet and ran. They would have to get past the beast to get to her, and now they had its full attention.

"Wait!" It was Marek's voice that yelled after her. Then the beast roared again, and he cursed.

Raven kept running.

It was midafternoon before she found another doe, taking it down fast with a single well-placed arrow. The earlier encounter left her shaky and feeling sick, but she had work to do. Jaecar would be waiting to help dress her kill and show her these crucial documents that would set off their adventure.

She realized now why the Silverblood opted not to call her out at the tree. Instead, he chose to bait her out, drawing his companions away and letting her walk into the beast he had to have known was lurking nearby. They were tracking the beast, and he was Silverblood. No human could track better than a Silverblood. She should have considered that. If he had come that far in his search of the creature, then he must have known which direction it had gone. Since she was hiding from them, he would have expected her to head away from them after they left. He had trapped her, and she had gone right along with it. Now her dagger was gone, but at least she had gotten away with her life and no more injury than some bruises and a torn pant cuff.

Raven hoisted the deer over one shoulder. It was a smaller animal but still a burden even with her enhanced strength. It would be easier if she started dressing it now, bleeding it out, and gutting it before carrying it. Still, the blood and some organs could be useful. Given their plans to travel soon, it made sense to bring everything back today.

She would have to tell Jaecar about the Silverblood. There was always a chance the man would try to find her, though she was confident that he hadn't seen enough to know what she was. To them, she was only some hooded figure they had encountered in the woods. Once Marek had his pay for taking down the beast and a new elven dagger courtesy of her brief scuffle with the creature, he would have little reason to dig deeper.

For a time, anger and shame over the lost dagger boosted her pace, but the weight of the deer dragged her back down. She eventually made her way up a familiar sparsely wooded hilltop, catching a view of the distant keep. She dropped the deer, panic burning through her with the force and speed of a wildfire.

In the distance, smoke rose from the main keep, billowing and dark. Not the smoke of an ordinary fire burning in the hearth. This was much more. Something was very wrong.

The deer forgotten, Raven ran. She was no longer a clumsy eight-year-old child, stumbling through dense woods as she ran to get Jaecar's help for her parents, but the memories of that day pummeled her as she sprinted through the trees. She knew these woods well, but tears began to blur her vision. Somewhere behind her, her parents once again suffered the torture of their attackers while she ran – too slow on short legs – to find Jaecar. Branches she should have easily avoided smacked her in the face, scratching at her cheeks.

She wiped roughly at the tears, trying to focus on the present. This was not that day. This time, she didn't need Jaecar's help. She needed to help him. And she was an adult now, her legs strong and fast. Brushing away her tears, she made herself run faster, fighting the fatigue of a long day.

Jaecar might not be home. He might have gone out, and something had happened in his absence. Odds were against it, though. He didn't leave the keep grounds without her often except to take occasional trips into the nearest town. He always told her about those beforehand since he was sometimes gone a day or more. That meant he was there, so if the keep was on fire, something must have happened to prevent him from controlling it.

She was still some distance off when she came to the next vantage point. It allowed her to pause and catch her breath as she took stock of the scene. The smoke billowing up from the central part of the keep was thicker and blacker now. She counted seven horses in front of the crumbled wall around the courtyard. Five men were there, mounted on four horses, two of them riding double on one animal. The other three animals had bodies tossed over the saddles and strapped in place. She couldn't distinguish many identifying features from this distance, except that one of the dead had long graying hair dangling down below the horse's belly. The sinking in her gut told her the rest.

It might be futile now, but she started running again. The riders in the distance were urging their mounts away from the keep. They moved quickly up to a trot, and one of the horses being led bucked a few times, irritated by the dead weight on its back. It straightened out quickly at a sharp jerk on the lead. She would never be able to catch up with them. It didn't matter. She had to get down there and see if anything could be salvaged. She had to see for herself that Jaecar was gone.

After leaping through the remains of the collapsed wall with the speed and accuracy of a mountain goat, Raven sprinted for the portion of the keep they had made their home. The building was constructed of stone, but the materials used in some of the framing and other structural elements would burn well enough, as would most of the contents. Most of the dark smoke came from the windows of the study. With so many books, that room would burn the fastest and was probably where the fire had started. That meant she might have a chance of getting inside to grab a few things from the main room.

She threw off her bow, quiver, and then the cloak before kicking open the door. Heat and smoke boiled out at her. She dropped low, trying to duck beneath the assault. Even so, she found herself coughing within seconds and pulled part of her threadbare shirt up over her nose and mouth. Crouching low, she entered the building, the smoke stinging her eyes. She couldn't see much. After so many years, the layout was familiar enough that, even changed by smoke and heat and the flames that licked out the doorway of the study, she could move through with relative confidence.

The study was too close to the sleeping quarters for her to get in there. She never owned a lot, but what she did own was mostly gone now. Nearer the fireplace in the main room, which, ironically, had a small fire burning in it, she saw the pack that Jaecar kept there. It was sized for him, but she didn't need to fill it to capacity. She snatched it on the way past, moving in her awkward crouch-walk, and went for the kitchen where she threw dried meat, nuts, and other more lasting provisions into the bag, along with a few fresher items—some bread and cheese—that she could eat sooner. She also grabbed a couple of full water skins, hoping they held actual water rather than the bitter mead Jaecar favored.

The fire was scaling the wall outside the study and had caught the edge of one old rug. The heat intensified, making the skin tighten on her face and hands. The fire on the rug began to race across it, some flames lingering to start climbing the leg of a bench near the wall. The larger rug that sat inside the entry burst into flame before the onslaught of severe heat, and Raven knew her time was up. She sprinted for the door, stopping in the small armory to the left of it to grab an extra pair of worn boots, a thick leather jacket she wore when sparring, a couple of daggers, including the one Jaecar used to gut and skin his kills when he dressed them in the field, and a handful of arrows to add to those in her quiver.

The flame raced across the rug behind her, and smoke made it hard to breathe. Coughing, she sprinted for the door and ran out into the open air. For a few minutes, all she could do was stand there bent over with her hands on her knees, coughing so hard it hurt her ribs. Her throat was raw as if some beast had raked their claws down it. Her gaze moved over the courtyard, picking out several places where considerable amounts of blood were still soaking into the dry dirt. The ground had been disturbed by many booted feet engaged in a bloody fight.

The image of the body hanging over the saddle with its long gray hair flashed in her mind. A sob choked out of her.

"Jaecar," she rasped.

At least he had taken a couple of them with him. Considering he faced seven men, that was no small accomplishment. There was a little comfort in that. Very little.

"What do I do now?"

It was foolish to ask. No one was there to answer. She couldn't stay here. That much was certain. The fire would grow. It was too far along for her to do anything to stop it. It could spread to the surrounding forest, though the buffer of land devoid of trees might slow it down if it made it past the crumbled wall. Regardless, it would attract attention. She also had to remember the possibility that Adept Marek would come looking, following her trail, or drawn by the fire if he and his party hadn't already taken their quarry and left the area.

Exhausted, she tucked the arrows in her quiver and one of the daggers into her belt. She arranged the rest of the items in the pack, then donned the jacket and cloak since daylight was starting to fade. She eyed the stable, considering the trove of treasures she'd collected from passing travelers. Those things were meaningless now and would only add weight she shouldn't waste energy carrying.

Grabbing her things, she walked over to the crumbling tower and climbed through the rubble, searching for where Jaecar had hidden his chest of documents. It was a surprisingly quick process. Knowing they were there made it easier to pick out the most likely hiding places. The chest was small, tucked away in a corner under a pile of rocks. It had a lock, but the latch was broken. She opened it and pulled out a treated leather case. A quick peek inside the case ensured that the documents were within before she sealed it back up and stuffed it into her larger pack. A pouch full of coins was also in the chest. She'd never needed money, but that was about to change, so she tossed that in the pack as well.

She had no one to go to for help, so she would go north the way the riders had gone. The way Jaecar had planned to go. At some point, she would have to interact with someone, but she would figure that out later. For now, she had to get away from here.

Raven walked to the hill where her parents were buried. She stood there for a few minutes, watching smoke rise in front of the slowly setting sun. Flames poured out all the windows now, reaching hungrily upward. Almost nothing would be left of the keep but a pile of stones by morning.

She turned the way the riders had gone. With her eyesight, it wouldn't be that hard to track seven horses, even in the dark. She would have to rest soon, though.

"I won't see you again," she said to the tree that had come to represent her lost parents. "Don't worry, though. Jaecar taught me well. I will avenge him. I promise."

It wasn't until the eve of the fifth day that the real pain of a lifetime of isolation made itself known. She followed the path the riders had taken to the wagon track, where they had met up with three others. Then three had gone their own way, though not the same three, judging by the hoof prints. One from the group that killed Jaecar had gone with the smaller group back toward Andel, and one of theirs continued north with the group that killed Jaecar. Perhaps a business deal of some kind, though it was beyond her to puzzle out precisely what.

She continued to track the larger group over the following days, only leaving the cover of the trees when the intersection of another road or track forced her to confirm their direction. She hunted small game and avoided areas where she found signs of predators, though they seemed to stay farther from the roadways. Each day, she changed her boots around midday, hanging the morning pair off her pack by their laces to dry from the morning dew. At night, she slept secured on a large branch in some tree where she was less likely to be stumbled upon by predators or people, the latter being arguably worse.

There were few other travelers, even after their tracks merged onto a more established roadway. One large wagon laden with barrels that she passed from within the trees captured her imagination for a few hours. What might be in those barrels to make the heavy draft animals strain against their traces? The answer was likely ale or mead, though she amused herself by trying to come up with more exciting options.

On the fourth day, her hunt brought her to a town. The road met up with the Link River, a slow, wide, and deep river that served as a primary trade route for many of the cities in the region. It continued on the left bank, following the river in both directions. Getting across was the first significant challenge. There was a ferry at the crossing, but she would have to talk to someone to get passage the usual way. Swimming was a poor idea. She'd read enough about it to know that there were creatures in the river large enough to make a meal out of her.

Instead, she doubled back and pulled a small log into the road. Then she waited for the wagon to get there. While they removed the obstacle, she slipped into the back and hid under some empty burlap sacks.

It was an uncomfortable passage. She barely dared to breathe, waiting with trembling hands near her blades for the moment they would discover her. The burlap stank of something she couldn't place, but the smell helped encourage shallow breathing. To her relief, the wagon's owners and the ferrymen showed no interest in the wagon's contents, using the slow, tedious crossing as a chance to discuss the local economy and weather. Once they were over, she slipped out the back as quiet as a fox and waited until they were gone to search for the tracks she was following.

Their route curved north, meandering along between the river on the left and a steep mountainside on the right, which made hiding in the trees more challenging. Then, on the evening of the fifth day, as the road curved around the side of the mountain, she spotted the end of an empty dock reaching out into the river ahead. It gave her sufficient warning to slip into the narrow band of trees between the road and the river and advance far enough to confirm that she was coming to a small town. She stayed hidden there until after dark.

The town was a problem, albeit one she'd known she would encounter eventually. She could possibly swim across the river, though the same dangers lurked in the dark waters here that she would have faced further south. The land on the far side looked marshy and difficult, making that prospect even less appealing. Such terrain made for poor hunting and provided a haven for nasty creatures from biting marsh flies and mosquitoes to larger predators that lurked in muddy pools. Besides, this was where the riders had gone. She needed to figure out if they stopped here or continued, and in which direction if so, preferably without entering the town proper.

If she worked her way around the town's perimeter, she might be able to find their tracks on a road heading out. Those tracks were getting harder to pick out with the passage of time and other traffic on the solidly packed dirt road. It didn't help that she had fallen well behind. She was on foot. Their mounts could cover ground more quickly, and she'd been delayed at the river crossing. Enhanced or not, she was only a half-elf on her own two legs. The brisk pace she had kept up on this hunt was much more demanding than the typical day spent casually hunting dinner in the forest.

She waited until dark when her cloak and caution would help her avoid being seen, then she followed the road around the bend and considered the town. Several smaller boats were tied along the less substantial docks further up. The nearest dock was much bigger, intended to accommodate larger vessels with more cargo. A few people were out on the docks even at this hour. One appeared to be making rounds, a lantern in one hand and lance in the other. A guard, perhaps, acting on his constable's orders. From her reading, she knew about constables and other officials who enforced the local laws. Laws like not stealing, killing, or using Silverblood magic outside the Brotherhood. She needed to avoid such individuals at all costs.

She glanced at her hand, holding it up so that the moonlight caught the silvery sheen of her fingernails. The magic had done that, the same way it changed her eyes and gave a silvery sheen to her black hair. She could not hide what she was.

Her thoughts wandered back to Marek. He was a Silverblood. His eyes made that obvious, but she hadn't noticed any silvery sheen to his hair. Perhaps it didn't show as much with the lighter color? Or did her being a female and half-elven result in different effects from the magic? There was no information regarding how women, elves, or children reacted to the magic beyond the assertion that, according to the Brotherhood, none of them could survive the initial making.

A fat lot they knew.

She smirked at her fingernails and turned her attention back to the town.

On the eastern edge, opposite the river, the land rose steeply, though not as steeply as it did along the road. A bluff overlooked the town on which a small manor stood, surrounded by a high wooden fence. She began to make her way in that direction along the near side of town, navigating the rocky hillside that wrapped this part of it carefully. A better vantage from the rocks revealed a building toward the center with light spilling out the open door and a few people wandering in or out that she suspected was a tavern. Light was visible through some windows on other buildings around the town, but few people were out. The high wooden fence that enclosed the manor continued around to the river to the north and east, separating the town from the old forest beyond. A few watch towers reached up at intervals along that fence, built of a mix of wood and stone.

Raven started to move, intending to traverse up and around the outside of the manor to search for the road's continuation. She ducked back into the shadows at the sound of someone knocking on the door of a rundown little shack below her vantage point. Fear and excitement burned in her as she carefully shifted position, angling for a better look at who was there.

When the door opened, spilling dim candlelight into the muddy roadway, she was surprised to see a male with the slender features and pointed ears of an elf standing there. So few elves came into her woods that it was oddly comforting to see someone else with ears more like her own. His hair appeared dark brown, though it was hard to be sure in the dim flickering light. He wore a bow and quiver of arrows on his back and carried a haunch of a deer over one shoulder.

"Eamon," a woman's voice greeted from within the house. She sounded pleased to see him.

The elf's answering smile had the tightness of unease to it. "I had a good hunt today. This should help keep you and the children fed for a few days."

He passed the haunch to the woman.

"Would you care to come inside? I don't have much to offer, but..." she trailed off at a slight shake of his head.

"No. Thank you. I've got a few more stops to make this evening." He lifted a sack sitting by his feet.

"You're too good to us. Thank you."

The elf—Eamon, she had called him—nodded and turned away, heading off to whatever other stops he had to make. The light from inside cast the woman's shadow in the space he had left for a few seconds before she shut the door and turned the street dark again.

Raven watched the elf carry his burden down the street. He stuck to the shadows, which struck her as curious. Was there something wrong with what he had done? If anything, it appeared to be an act of generosity. Then again, what did she know of their world in reality? The books she read were far from an exhaustive resource.

Perhaps it was because he was an elf? She knew many places treated elves as lower-class citizens. The woman in the house had been hidden from her view. She could have been human or elven as far as Raven knew. If she were human, such interactions might be frowned upon.

Raven shook herself and refocused on the climb up to the level of the manor. If she remained outside the fence, she should be able to move around the outskirts of the town unnoticed. There were the towers, but their torches offered little illumination beyond the immediate area. The guards wouldn't see far in the dark, especially if they were human.

It took a few hours to work her way up and around the perimeter of the fence to the river on the north side. She didn't run into any people, though she found footprints on some game trails. The more significant concern now was that there were only game trails. The foliage around those was dense enough to be virtually impassable on horseback. No other road or even a wagon track headed out of the town. The only way in and out on a proper road was the way she had come in. No hoof prints left the town anywhere. If Jaecar's killers continued north, they had to have gone by boat, which didn't bode well for tracking them.

It was also possible that they were still in town. She hadn't seen much sign of horses in the town, though a small one or two-horse stable stood alongside the tavern. There also appeared to be a small stable alongside what she thought might be the barracks or jail—possibly both—that she had spotted from high up in a tree on the northeastern side. What she didn't see were any hoof prints or droppings in the dirt streets. There were no large compost piles outside of one communal one on the north side that the small population of livestock in that area could easily account for.

From what little regional geography she learned in her books, she believed this was the last settlement on the northern edge of the kingdom of Andioch along the Link River, though she couldn't recall the name. Labeled a smaller town by those better traveled than she, which had to be about everyone. She tried using that as a comfort, reminding herself repeatedly that it was small and there couldn't be that many people here. Still, when she considered entering the town, her muscles started to seize up, and she had to wage war with herself to keep from fleeing to the familiar forest she'd left behind.

There was an alternative. These people couldn't spend all their time within the town proper. They had to leave to hunt, considering how little livestock she saw, even in the area near the river where several homes were trying to raise cattle, goats, and pigs in mucky little paddocks. Those homes were outside the main fence, though another more recently constructed fence with spiked posts stretched around that section. One portion nearer to the river looked newer, as if the expansion had been recently repaired.

If she timed her approach in the shadowy hours of dusk or dawn, the poor lighting would make it easier to keep her features hidden in the shadows of her cloak. Whoever she spoke to would hopefully be able to provide some information about the men she was following. In such a small place, their passage couldn't have gone unnoticed. Then she could decide what to do next. For tonight, she would find a big, high branch in one of the massive trees and settle into sleep.

Finding a suitable branch was easy. Resting proved more of a problem. With the town so close, she couldn't keep her eyes shut. Every sound was someone about to discover her hiding place. Every breeze, the passing of an arrow meant to shoot her down. Although, the distractions from sleep weren't all bad. She spent a great deal of time gazing down at the lights of night candles burning in the windows of the houses. There were enough that she could imagine the stars of a fallen constellation were trapped behind those wooden doors.

By the time predawn light crept in, her head ached, and she yearned for a moment's rest. She had a purpose, though. One she meant to fulfill. The men who took Jaecar had been at least a full day ahead of her, possibly two, by the time she reached this town at the end of the road. If she didn't pick up their trail soon, she might never track them down. For Jaecar, she would make herself talk to someone.

She left her pack up in the hidden reaches of the tree and climbed down with only her weapons and some coin. With the hood of her cloak pulled forward, she found a lower perch between the two northernmost gates and watched for a promising subject.

The first to come out was a trio of loud men carrying woodcutter's axes. She already trembled, on the verge of throwing up the meager breakfast she'd eaten, at the thought of speaking to anyone. Three loud, burly, distinctly human woodcutters were about as unattractive an option as she could get. She bolted higher into the trees after that, watching from a distance as the occasional citizen or guard wandered briefly beyond the safety of their fences.

It was easy to come up with reasons each of them would be a bad choice. The guards were no question. It was too likely that they would demand to see her face and turn her over to the Brotherhood. The others were all human men. How many times had Jaecar told her that, despite her human father, she could pass as a full-blooded elf? Knowing that and how rampant discrimination against elves was in some areas, she couldn't bring herself to approach them.

Time ticked by, and Raven grew increasingly restless.

Aldrich Darrenton walked out into the manor courtyard feeling hopeful. He hadn't expected them to find his brother this fast. Assuming this was his brother. They had encountered a few false trails, one of which led to the murder of someone who looked a lot like his brother. That debacle required some quick thinking and careful silencing of witnesses. This time, a feeling of confidence accompanied him out to inspect the recent catch. He attributed that to his extraordinary ability to sense how things would go well before they happened.

Of the five men waiting in the courtyard, four were his soldiers. The fifth was a Silverblood adept. Aldrich took note of that and offered the stranger a nod before glancing over the three horses with bodies draped across the saddles. Two he recognized as his men without needing to see their faces. It was the third he was interested in. The fact that their catch had taken out two of them was encouraging. All his older brother ever cared about was combat. If they had taken him down too quickly, Aldrich would doubt this was him.

He walked to the waiting horse and grabbed a handful of the long graying hair. He pulled the head back and bent over, tilting his own head at an odd angle to get a better look. The bruised face that looked back at him was clearly an older version of the brother he had once known.

"Didn't age well, did he?" He stood up and faced the group's leader, his guard captain Karth. "You said he was living alone in a crumbling keep in the woods?"

Karth nodded.

"Always running away from responsibility, eh Jaecar," Aldrich muttered, letting his brother's head fall back down. "You found the deed?"

Karth stood at perfect attention, ever the soldier. "No, milord. We couldn't find the deed, but–"

Aldrich silenced him with a quick gesture. "No need. His death is enough to nullify the deed. We'll hold a funeral. Make it all official." He eyed the Silverblood then, noting the man's lean build under the black and silver Brotherhood armor and the many weapons he wore. The adept stared boldly back at him with those odd eyes, the irises as silver as the steel of his sword, rimmed in a jagged border of black. "Perhaps you could introduce me to your new companion."

The Silverblood didn't allow Karth to make the introductions. He took a step forward and inclined his head in what appeared to be the maximum deference he would offer in recognition of Aldrich's rank. "I'm Silverblood Adept Marek."

Aldrich gave a slight nod, suddenly feeling less motivated to respect the Silverblood's rank.

"We thought he might be able to help us clear out the Amberwood area," Karth stated. He gave Marek an uneasy glance and added, "For a price."

Quaint how they doubted themselves. His own warriors were already recruiting aid for a job they hadn't seen yet. Aldrich barely contained his sneer. "I don't think that will be necessary. An ambitious group of former residents and their new friends have gone into Amberwood to try to reclaim it for themselves. I say let them do the heavy lifting for now. We can deal with them when they're done. I'll reconsider if it takes too long, but I appreciate your coming all this way, Adept Marek. I trust you won't have trouble finding other work in the city."

The Silverblood looked like he meant to speak, but Karth shifted and cleared his throat. Aldrich drew in a deep breath and exhaled heavily. Whatever Karth wanted to say, he could already tell it was going to irritate him. He needed to maintain his temper. This was, ultimately, an exceptionally good morning.

"What is it, Karth?"

"We learned of a ship full of supplies heading to the squatters in Amberwood. We may have told the constable in Manderly they were moving stolen cargo."

Aldrich clenched his teeth. He wasn't going to show his temper. Not in front of the Silverblood. "That could slow down their progress. Don't you think so, Karth?"

Karth shifted his feet again and averted his gaze, now staring to the left of Aldrich. "Yes, milord."

Aldrich turned back to the adept. "I may require you after all. I would like you to return to Manderly and ensure that ship makes it to Amberwood. Look around when you get to Amberwood, then report back here to tell me what you saw there. How many there are and what they have in the way of fighters."

Marek cocked his head to one side, his eerie eyes somehow making the gesture seem less human. "Perhaps we can go inside to discuss what you need and what it will cost you."

"Perhaps we can." Aldrich glanced around at the others. "See that the bodies are taken care of. Jaecar's needs to be prepared for proper burial in the family tomb. Father will turn over in his grave, but we must make it look good if we're going to avoid questions about his death."

The others moved to do his bidding, and he turned to walk inside, all too aware of the man following behind him. A dangerous creature to turn one's back on. He didn't trust the Silverbloods and their death cult they called the Brotherhood, but he also didn't believe in accidents. His soldiers had been inclined to invite the adept here because they thought he might be useful to them. As far as Aldrich was concerned, that meant the man had a part to play in this. He intended to take advantage of his skills, even if they did tend to have a steep price.

Aldrich led Marek to the first-floor study, calling to a servant to bring them wine along the way. As they walked, he explained. "The Amberwood lands have lain empty for many years. Long enough to become infested with all manner of foul creatures."

"I presume you're not referring to the folks trying to move in there now."

Aldrich sneered over his shoulder. "No. Not yet, anyhow. I'm hoping they prove useful in clearing the grounds. After that, if they are amenable to the idea of new leadership, I may let them stay." He opened the door to the study and walked in, leaving the other man to follow.

"How gracious of you," Marek commented dryly.

Aldrich gave him a sharp look, trying to determine if the man genuinely disapproved of his methods or was simply making commentary for the sake of something to say. The Silverblood's expression remained vexingly neutral. He took his seat behind a big, polished bloodwood desk. The adept removed the sheath that held a two-handed sword on his back and set it against the wall inside the door. Aldrich noted how he held the weapon as if it weighed almost nothing. Marek appeared lean, not overly muscular, but the magic enhancements made him stronger than an ordinary man without the need for bulk.

He sat across from Aldrich, not waiting for the invitation to do so. An invitation that had been deliberately withheld to see if the man would respect the rules of etiquette. It was a test Aldrich often put his guests to. In this case, it served little purpose. He wasn't likely to take any direct or indirect actions to punish this man's lack of politeness. The Brotherhood was much too powerful to risk angering. Not to mention, this man could almost certainly take out most of his guards with relatively little effort.

"What I need from you is to first fix the problem my men created and see that these people get their supplies. Then, I want you to spend a little time in Amberwood. Not enough to seem suspicious, but enough to..."

He trailed off when the servant entered with two goblets of wine and a decanter. When the man had placed a filled goblet before each of them, he left the room, shutting the door behind him and Aldrich continued.

"Enough to take stock of their weaponry, numbers, and skills, not only in combat but also in building, smithing, anything that might be useful to me going forward."

Marek gave another nod, ignoring his wine. "May I inquire as to why you now want these lands that were bequeathed to your brother and abandoned for so many years?"

Aldrich smiled and steepled his fingers in front of him. "Resources, of course. The Amberwood forest alone will become a veritable gold mine with the growing popularity of that bi-colored wood among the nobility. And that's just scratching the surface. I see no reason to let those resources go on being wasted."

Marek offered no reaction. No glimmer of greed. No hungry smile or disapproving frown. Absolutely nothing. It was maddening, but Aldrich drew in a breath and refused to let it bother him. When the man was gone, he could go out to the courtyard and take that pent-up frustration out on a practice dummy. Or a servant.

"It won't be cheap." Marek's tone was flat, discouraging negotiation before a price was even named.

Aldrich held his smile through force of will. The fact that he couldn't read anything from this man made him want to punch something. It was going to make any attempt at bartering harder than usual. Buying himself a minute to soothe his frustration, he lifted his goblet and sipped from it, holding eye contact with those strange eyes. He swirled the wine. "I'm sure we can come to an arrangement."

Despite the pressure of knowing the men she hunted were getting farther away, it wasn't until the morning of the third day that someone Raven could convince herself to approach emerged from the town. The elven male she had seen the first night came out the gate closest to the river on the north side, a bow slung over one shoulder and a weary old mule scuffing along behind. In the morning light, she saw that his mid-length hair was red, not brown, and his clothes were a bit worn, though not as tattered as her own.

"Good hunting, Eamon," someone called from the tower alongside the gate as it closed behind him.

If she read the situation right that first night, which was debatable given her lack of experience with people, he seemed like a generous individual. From what she could see, his bow was his only weapon, though she wouldn't be surprised if he had at least one dagger on him for dressing kills. That didn't matter much. She was confident she could defeat him in single combat if it came to that. It was the idea of talking to him that made her legs turn into pillars of gooey mud, threatening to collapse beneath her. Doing her best to ignore the sensation, she made her way through the trees and heavy underbrush in search of an interception point out of sight of the towers.

She watched, hidden in the underbrush, to see which of the few available paths he would choose. Once she was sure of his direction, she crawled low through the bushes to a spot near the trail and waited. It wasn't long before he passed her hiding place. His footsteps were remarkably quiet, but the dragging strides of the mule were easy to track. The mule balked halfheartedly when they passed her position, catching her scent. A light tug on the rope had it moving again. Raven slipped into the path behind them, stopping in the deeper shade.

"You can't give up on me now, friend," Eamon said, glancing around at the reluctant animal. His mouth opened again, but whatever else he meant to say died on his lips. His hand went to a dagger hidden beneath his jacket.

She didn't move, keeping her gaze slightly down so her features would remain hidden in the shadows of the cloak. The fact that he didn't draw the dagger as he turned the rest of the way around was encouraging. He did step to the side to place the mule solidly between them.

"I didn't see you there." He glanced around as though expecting others to come out of the trees.

It wasn't an unreasonable concern, she supposed. She wanted to assure him she was alone, that this wasn't an ambush, but she found she couldn't bring herself to speak. The words, the very air needed to create them, had become stuck fast in her chest.

His brow furrowed after several long seconds of silence. Concern overcame caution, and he maneuvered the mule to the side to take a few steps closer. "Are you all right?"

He reached out toward her, and she nearly fell over her own feet backing away from him. To her relief, he instantly withdrew his hand and retreated a few steps.

He held both hands up then, the mule's rope

hanging loosely between the thumb and forefinger of one. "I won't hurt you."

"I..." That was a start, albeit a weak one. "I... need a road."

Raven wanted to smack herself in the head. She could see by his expression that he now thought she might be simpleminded. The furrows in his brow deepened briefly, a glimmer of early sun highlighting the autumn red of his shoulder-length hair. Then he offered her a gentle smile, slouching a touch to seem less intimidating. Her chest started to ache with a strange sense of longing.

"Please, excuse me." Putting a few sensible words together boosted her confidence. She made herself take one wary step closer. "I'm tracking some riders. I followed them here."

His expression hardened, though she didn't feel that that instant of darker emotion was directed at her. "Lord Darrenton's men? They headed north on a river galley the same day they arrived. What could you possibly want with them?"

He was curious now, leaning slightly to the side to peer into her cloak.

Raven shifted her stance, determined to thwart his efforts. Anger steadied her voice. "They killed my father and took his body. I want it back. I need a way to follow them."

The way pity and sorrow warred across his features as she spoke brought the unexpected sting of tears to her eyes. She clung to the anger she harbored for those men, determined not to become a weeping mess in front of this stranger. Why did his pity make her loss so much more poignant?

"I'm sorry about your father." The way he bowed his head added sincerity to his words. "I would advise against going after them, but if you must, then the only way north from here is up the river. There should be another passenger ship through in a couple of weeks."

Despair swept through her. She had lost too much time already. She peered past him at the forest as if she might see another way to follow. When he took a step to the side in another effort to look into her hood again, she dropped a few steps back and turned her face into the shadows.

"If I wait that long, I'll never find them."

"I dare say it might not be as hard as you think." His tone was soft now, matching the gentle smile that had returned.

She recognized the look in his eyes, the way he moved, slow and deliberate. Bent ever-so-slightly at the knees and hips to make himself smaller. It was how one moved when approaching a frightened animal, like the fox that had gotten tangled in a pile of rope in the keep's courtyard once. She'd watched Jaecar spend over an hour inching his way up to the animal on his knees, tossing it morsels of meat and murmuring soft words until he was close enough to grab hold of it and set it free.

"What do you mean?"

"I mean, they were Lord Darrenton's men. I imagine they went to his estate in Pellanth."

The name sounded vaguely familiar, though talking to him had disabled her ability to think clearly. "Pellanth?"

He titled his head slightly, looking puzzled. "The capital of Habarin."

"Oh."

Not just a large city, but a *very* large city. A city of that size would have a Silverblood Brotherhood and hundreds of people. A massive population center like that was the worst possible place for her.

Her shoulders sank, and she lowered her head, defeat opening the door to the sorrow she had been beating back. "Thank you for your help," she murmured.

Jaecar told her once that it was polite to thank someone for helping her. He'd found it amusing when she started thanking him for her almost daily, grueling training sessions after that.

Jaecar. She had failed him. Not only had she failed him, she now had no place to go, no purpose. She started to turn away, intending to return to the tree where she'd left her things.

"I'm Eamon."

It was all she could do not to visibly startle when he spoke. Somehow, despite the terror that filled her at approaching a stranger, she had dismissed him from her mind. There was a devastating power to defeat. She made herself turn back toward him, but she couldn't think of anything to say. What point was there in offering her name? She wouldn't see him again.

"Other ships stop here," he offered. "Some are willing to take passengers. I can help you find a room in town if you want to wait for one."

Panic burned through her chest at the thought of entering the town. She shook her head so violently that she almost threw her hood off. Grabbing the edge to keep it in place, she turned and bolted into the forest, ignoring his attempts to call her back.

Karsima picked up another yellow flower and began to weave it into the delicate circlet she was making. The small blond girl sitting closest to her, Deyva, the youngest of the nine children and one of two elves in the group, took a matching flower from their shared supply and began weaving it into her circlet. Karsima's hair had been that blond when she was young, though it had darkened considerably since. Being elven, Deyva's beautiful locks would probably hold their color most of her life.

Karsima smiled and looked around at all the kids sitting in the sunshine weaving circlets. They laughed and played and joked with one another. Before they arrived in Amberwood, there had been a lot fewer smiles. Many of their families struggled, so there hadn't been time for such frivolous activities before. Changing that was one of the reasons they were here.

"You know," she raised her voice so they would all hear, "when I was seven, me and some of the other kids who lived in town would race to the creek over there some afternoons when our chores were done." She pointed down the hill. "We used to build little wooden boats to race down to the river. Whoever lost the race had to buy sweet rolls in the market for the rest of us."

"What if the one who lost couldn't afford them?"

She glanced at Braden. It wasn't hard to understand why he was quick to ask that question. He was almost the oldest among them at twelve. His family lived on the streets begging for scraps before they came here.

Karsima picked up a blue flower and began weaving it into the circlet, delighting in the fact that Deyva grabbed a matching flower for hers. "Well, Braden, that did happen sometimes. But we had one young elven boy in our group whose father was the best bowyer in town. No one else could make a bow so fine, and he made a good living selling them. As such, his son always had a little extra coin. So, if whoever lost the race couldn't afford the rolls, he would sneak them the coin so they could pretend they'd had it all along and wouldn't be embarrassed."

Braden frowned. He wasn't going to let it go with that. "If he was sneaking them the coin, how'd you know about it?"

Karsima glanced up at the trees. The memory was so strong that she could almost see that young elven boy up in the branches now, waiting for her to come out with the other kids in the afternoons. He might not have been as social as she was, but he assigned himself the task of looking after them all.

"I know because he was my best friend, and we told each other everything. Do you want to know who it was?" Several children looked up and nodded at her, open curiosity in their wide young eyes. "Phendaril."

"No." Deyva wrinkled her nose.

Karsima leaned close, looking her in the eyes. "Why no?"

"He's scary."

She sat back and laughed. "He can come across a bit severe, but he's got a very kind heart when you get past that prickly exterior."

"Look!" Deyva pointed excitedly at a yellow and

violet butterfly as it landed on their supply of flowers.

Karsima grinned. "Perhaps it wants to help."

"I want one on my flowers," another of the children declared.

"Well, if you're quiet while you work, one might come to visit you too." She watched with a smug grin as the children fell silent, focusing on their circlets and watching their flower piles for winged visitors.

"Milady," a familiar voice called from behind her.

She sighed softly. Jenner's penchant for calling her milady was starting to spread. He even had some of the elves doing it now.

She set the circlet in her lap and turned to look at Jael as he came to the edge of the circle. He offered a slight bow, his black hair tied back in a tail to keep it from getting in his way. Many of them were starting to need haircuts, but it wasn't worth fussing about when a hairband served well enough. Besides, the elves all had such lovely hair. She liked the fact that they were letting it grow.

"What is it, Jael? And please don't call me milady again."

The way his lips twitched up told her his adoption of the honorific was intended to tease her. "Veylin's party brought back some more maps for you. I thought you might want to take a look."

Duty always called. She glanced around at the children. Deyva and a few others put on dramatic pouts as they protested the fact that they weren't finished yet. She looked up at Jael. "I don't suppose you'd take over here. Someone has to finish my circlet." She held the growing band of grass and flowers up to him.

Jael chuckled. "I'm not sure who's getting the better deal here," he answered, accepting the proffered item.

"I'm sure it will look lovely on you," Karsima teased as she switched places with him.

She started to walk away, then paused to listen as he began to impart some elven grass weaving knowledge upon the children that would undoubtedly improve on her own design. They moved in closer to him, eager to learn. They were in good hands.

Several minutes later, Karsima spread another roughly drawn map on the table. The one she had lain it on top of showed where a pack of wolves had turned an old overgrown stable yard into their home turf. The animals had a den dug under the floorboards of a collapsed barn that was disappearing into the foliage. Her scout said he'd seen at least three new pups playing king of the mountain on what appeared to be an overturned trough that the grass had grown over. She wasn't worried about them yet. That location was removed enough from town that they could let the wolves roam for now and wait to devise a plan to relocate them if it became an issue.

This new map showed something less pleasant. The original human inhabitants of the area had built crypts, digging a maze of tunnels through the pliable earth. Those passages were now infested with corpse eaters—foul beasts that fed on the flesh of rotting corpses. Most of the food in those crypts had likely been consumed by now. Unfortunately, they appeared to have made nests in the overlapping mine tunnels, one of which a section of crypt passage had collapsed into. They brought their fresh kills back there to let them rot until they were ripe enough to eat. They could use smoke to drive them back into the mine and collapse the passage behind them to keep them out of the crypts for a time, but they would have to be dealt with more permanently at some point.

To make matters worse, a drake or wyvern had been spotted flying above the trees a little farther south. That scout insisted she'd seen it hunting from a distance, and the creatures it appeared to be hunting looked like "nasty old harpies," as she had put it. Karsima hoped it wasn't an accurate description, though knowing the scout was an elf made her more inclined to take it as such. Elves simply had better eyesight than humans. Old harpies tended to be much more temperamental than their younger brethren, like any old crone who'd had enough of young ones making a mess of things.

Karsima smiled wryly to herself and shifted the map to match up the edges as best she could with others.

Harpies. Drakes. Corpse eaters. Wolves. Giant wasps.

Everywhere they scouted, they found some unpleasant creature or another that had made its home on the abandoned lands. Even if they managed to clear away the many beasts, they still had to tear down old structures to make way for the new. It didn't look like many of the old materials would be reusable in what had been the more impoverished parts of the old town. It was starting to feel like they would be better off finding new lands. Of course, for many of them, this land had been home once before. The lords who destroyed it in their war to resolve the question of whose land it was left it to crumble away and become infested with all manner of creatures.

Why? Why bother fighting so fiercely over it if they didn't plan to use the land for something? Was it merely to prove a point? Hundreds of people were killed and displaced for nothing.

She scowled death at a beetle marching across the table and reached for her dagger. The cloth hanging over the doorway of the rough-built round hut pulled aside, letting in a spray of sunlight. The beetle opened its back shell to set free luminescent gold wings. Karsima watched those wings catch the light and reflect it around the room in a tiny but beautiful display. She set down the dagger, suddenly glad she hadn't killed the insect.

The man who entered strode halfway across the room to her before he came to a stuttering halt and removed his hat, mussing his unkempt brown hair in the process. He half-turned and glanced back toward the door.

She leaned on the table, giving him a look that was hopefully stern enough without being too cold. "You've come this far, Jenner. You might as well finish as boldly as you started."

"Sorry, milady, I keep forgetting these are your private quarters too." He crushed the hat in his nervous hands now.

"Don't we all," she muttered under her breath.

She didn't enjoy all the deferential treatment. If she'd known being their elected leader came with a mantle of bows, milady's, and distance from old friends, she might have been less willing to take on the role. Her vision was to gather a community that would rebuild Amberwood together. That community wanted someone to take charge, though, and since she and Phendaril started the project, it made some sense that the burden became hers.

A little louder, she said. "You clearly had some purpose. Please feel free to speak openly."

"I just came up the river from Manderly." A light flush swept up his cheeks. "I mean, you knew that. You sent me south. But some of Lord Darrenton's men were on the ship I caught coming back. They were boasting about telling the town constable an elven galley was coming north with stolen goods on it. Laughed up a storm about all the trouble those 'pointies' would have getting past the town."

She grabbed the dagger and stabbed it through the maps, driving it deep into the old wood of the table.

Jenner jumped, hands tightening convulsively on his hat.

"What do you want to bet that ours is the next elven galley coming through?"

"I've no doubt, milady. They were almost ready to

start loading the ship before I left Chadhurst. They may be in Manderly by now or close to it."

She gripped the side of the table. It was made of junk wood they had managed to salvage from some of the destroyed buildings on the north edge of the old town. They'd used the same wood to build some of the structures here, in what would hopefully be a short-term camp, while they began dealing with the challenges standing between them and where they planned to start rebuilding the town. The salvaged wood had an earthy yet slightly sweet scent that took her back to her childhood, running through these forests and learning all about the flora and fauna from her best friend. That smell made her more determined to make this work.

"They had three bodies with them," Jenner added after several seconds of silence.

That caught her attention. If they were carrying bodies with them, the dead were companions or essential to them in some other way. "Anyone you recognized?"

He shook his head. "Sorry, milady."

"Don't worry about it. Can you send Phendaril in? He should be up in one of the trees on watch if he isn't down by a fire pit talking to his scouts."

"Yes..."

"Don't call me..."

"...milady." He flushed more brightly this time and hurried out through the doorway.

Karsima gave a slight shake of her head and watched him go. Jenner wasn't the worst. Many she had known for years, human and elf alike, treated her as though her new leadership had turned her into some powerful noblewoman. There were also a few who resented her. A smaller group, to be sure, or she wouldn't have been the one chosen. They watched her and whispered and smiled with false politeness to her face. She wasn't sure which she liked less, the change in her friends or the discovery of a few enemies.

It only took a few minutes to become engrossed in the maps again. Enough so that she wasn't sure how long Phendaril stood there, absolutely still, a few steps inside the curtain over the doorway before she noticed him. From this side, his features were perfect. Strong, lean, and unnervingly hard to read. Every line that might be too intensely defined, from the faintly hawkish ridge of his nose to the sharpness of his jawline, came together in a harmony that made him rakishly handsome. Flowing dark auburn hair, though it lengthened the lines of his features, enhanced that unexpected allure. If he didn't have that brooding edge, intensified by a scar cutting along the inside of his right eye down to where it pulled slightly at his upper lip, he would have the attention of many willing partners. Something about the darkness that resided in him—a darkness that had appeared in their years apart—kept even the most determined admirers at a distance.

For the briefest of moments, she forgot her woes, and a smile tugged at her lips. "How long have you been standing there, my friend?"

He shifted to face her without leaving his spot. "Long enough to think I might need to assign you a guard detail."

She waved him over. "I don't think that's necessary, but I trust your judgment. I do have a couple of enemies now."

He walked to the table, his dark eyes picking over the maps, undoubtedly marking the dangerous areas. Each threat would be a puzzle for him to work on. A challenge. When he met her eyes, there was a hint of anticipation in his expression.

Karsima shook her head. "I wish these problems excited me as much as they do you."

He schooled his expression, subduing it for her sake.

"Jenner said you needed my help."

"You may never realize how much I appreciate you not calling me, milady." She offered a grateful smile. She didn't wait to see if he would respond, though his gaze softened a fraction. "Jenner overheard some of Darrenton's men on the ship north bragging about telling the constable in Manderly that an elven galley full of stolen goods was coming up the river. I need you to take a small group down to Manderly and make sure our crew and supplies don't get stuck there."

He started to shake his head.

"Phen, I'll be fine. I need someone I can trust to do this, and you and your scouts are the only ones I trust who have the skills to get them out of there if there is a problem. I have a whole unit of Stonebreakers coming to protect me."

The slight permanent sneer the scar gave him intensified. "The Stonebreakers are good fighters. They're better masons and smiths. And who knows when..."

He had the decency not to finish his thought when she put her back to him. She didn't want to contemplate how long it could be before Alayne arrived with the Stonebreakers. She walked to the table that sat next to what passed for a bed, though it was little more than a rough wooden cot. It was better than most people had. She didn't like that her quarters, though spare, were much nicer than almost everyone else's. It encouraged the animosity of those who resented her sudden rise in station.

Next to the table was a small chest. She grabbed a coin pouch off the table and counted some coins from the chest into it. Then she tightened the strings and tossed it to him as she turned around.

He snatched it from the air with a frustrated shake of his head. "You aren't going to listen, are you?"

She made herself smile, though his concern was a sobering reminder of all the dangers that lurked here. "Not any more than you would in my shoes. Besides, you know I'm not helpless. How many times have I fought at your side?"

"Recently?"

She wanted to punch the taunting look off his face. Unfortunately, the table between them was too wide. She stood a little straighter and placed one fist firmly on her hip. "I am the authority here. I believe even you voted in my favor." She gave him a stern look, daring him to claim otherwise. "So, you will take a small boat south and get me my people and my supplies. The sooner you go, the sooner you'll be back."

He didn't appear impressed by her attempted show of power. He hefted the pouch in his hand and raised a brow at her.

She shrugged in response. "You might need to bribe someone."

He tucked the coin pouch into his pack. "We'll be gone by morning."

"Hurry back," she said firmly. Then, so he wouldn't think her too worried about him, she added, "I need your help figuring out how to address this mess." She gestured to the maps on the table.

Phendaril gave a quick nod, though a faint gleam of amusement lit his eyes now. With a toss of his head, he cast a few locks of dark hair out of his face and walked out. Karsima heaved a sigh as she watched him disappear. She knew what had broken the happiness in him, and she couldn't do anything to fix it.

The rage that filled Raven after fleeing Eamon had no basis in logic. She was angry with herself, mostly, for being so rattled by talking to a stranger that she couldn't think clearly and calmly. Everyone in the world now was a stranger. Somehow, she had to find a way to deal with that.

She climbed through the trees a little deeper in the forest, spending several hours scaling the soaring giants until her arms trembled with exhaustion and the reckless rage burned itself out. Then she made her way back to the tree where her belongings waited and used the little energy she had left to climb up and secure herself there.

She stared at the sky, remembering how her mother's eyes changed as she lay dying, putting her last few moments into a spell that would permanently alter Raven's life. Maybe making her a Silverblood really hadn't been an act of love intended to protect her. Perhaps it had been an act of control. A way for her mother to force Raven to stay hidden from the cruel world even after her death. Had she known it would bring her daughter so much misery when she did it?

She cried then, for her parents, for Jaecar, and for herself.

Raven woke later in the day and watched the town for a while. After dark, she foraged for something to eat, returning to her branch above to sit and stare at the sky, lost in memories of Jaecar and her parents before him. Had her parents meant to hide from the world forever? It was easy enough to blame Jaecar for teaching her to survive alone, but not how to do so around others. Would her parents have done anything differently?

She sat awake until the dawn when she saw Eamon head out from the gates again with his mule plodding behind him. He peered about him more today as if searching for strange females hidden in the bushes. The thought made her laugh for a moment, then she cried again, pointless tears streaming down her cheeks as she watched him disappear into the woods. Deciding it must be the lack of sleep, she settled back in her perch and closed her eyes.

It was mid-afternoon when she woke from a restless slumber. Her eyes were puffy, and the dried salt of her tears made the skin of her cheeks feel stiff. She sat up and pulled out some nuts to soothe the growling in her gut while she stared at the river that bordered one side of the town.

Her options were limited. If not for her conspicuous features, she might have taken Eamon up on his offer to find a place in the town for a few days. But what was the point in risking problems here when she couldn't go to Pellanth anyhow? A city that big would be a death trap for her, especially with no one to help her. All she had to her name, other than her weapons, were Jaecar's documents. She didn't even know what was in them yet. Since she was now stuck, this seemed like a good time to investigate.

Pulling her pack onto her lap, she drew out the treated case and opened it. There were several folded documents inside. Securing the case between her knees, she pulled one out. The broken seal on the outside had a raptor under a crown pressed into red wax. She unfolded the parchment and stared at the words that greeted her gaze, dully surprised that she could feel any more disappointed in this day. The characters on the page offered no clarity. It was written in a language she didn't recognize at all. The symbols bore no semblance to elven writing or Thedan, the region's most common written and spoken language. This might be the deed. Several people had signed it and stamped it with some official-looking seals.

If it was the deed, not that she could prove such herself, what were all these other pages?

She tucked it back in the case and pulled out each of the other papers one at a time, looking at them long enough to confirm that they were all written in the same unfamiliar text. All three bore signatures and seals that provided little insight. For several seconds, she considered the merits of building a fire somewhere and burning them. Then she contemplated something simpler. She could tear them up and throw the pieces in the river. She went so far as to line them up in her hands and grip them, ready to pull in opposite directions and put an end to them.

The pages were useless. Right now, they meant nothing at all to her.

She hesitated.

Not quite nothing.

She lowered her hands and set the pages in her lap, slowly smoothing them out and folding them to return to the case.

This was Jaecar's legacy. These pages she could quickly destroy. Whatever land he owned, where he hoped to build a community with her, at least one of these documents made that land his. He was dead now, though, so didn't that forfeit his claim? Yet, there was more here than just one deed. Whatever the other papers were, didn't she owe it to him to at least find out? There might still be something to his legacy here.

Raven closed the case and put it back in her bag. She sat for a while, watching people in the town go about their business. Some appeared busy, wandering to the market or going about various chores. Plenty interrupted their days, stopping to chat with others in the streets. Did they all know each other? Were they friends? She spotted children running in the mucky roads nearer the river and in the relatively empty town square near the tavern. Surprisingly few even went close to the gates leaving town.

That struck her as odd. Why wouldn't they wander out in this magnificent forest rather than confine themselves to the filthy, pungent streets? And they were pungent. When the breeze blew her way, she almost abandoned her perch to get away from the stink. That was from a distance. How awful must they smell up close? How did one get used to such a stink?

A movement caught her eye. She got up, climbing further along the branch to get a better look at the river galley coming into view around the mountainside that loomed over the south part of town. It was a long, sleek ship. The crew moved with expert teamwork, easing the craft close enough to the dock that two agile members were able to make the leap across. The boat was large enough to carry a good load, and she was relatively sure she caught the ends of pointed elven ears peeking through the hair of the two males who'd jumped ashore. They had to have room for one passenger on such a vessel.

Raven watched them docking for a few minutes, admiring the easy camaraderie in the crew's actions. Then she gathered her things in her pack and secured it in the branches before climbing down the tree. She wasn't ready to try going into town, but Eamon might still be in the woods. She could head him off and ask him to investigate the ship for her. Inquiring about the captain's willingness to take on passengers on her behalf wasn't that much to ask. She could offer to pay him if necessary, though she had no idea what a fair price would be or how much she had with her in Jaecar's coin pouch.

Trying hard not to think about how she had fled earlier and the impression that might have left him with, Raven struck out toward the last place she had seen Eamon. Once she reached the game trail, she waited in the bushes for several minutes, listening and watching for anyone nearby. When she was confident no one was around, she moved out on the trail and began searching for the tracks of the mule. She found them quickly. It didn't take long to confirm by the presence of a fresher set that they had already returned to town. The mule's hoof prints were distinct enough that, if she waited a few more hours until after dark, she could still track him to his home with little effort. That meant going inside the fence, but there were a few places where it could be crossed. Given the rough workmanship of the fence, she thought she could free climb over. There were also spots where tree branches hung down upon it. Crossing at one of those points would be even easier. As barriers went, it wasn't an impressive one.

Her stomach growled as she wandered the nearby woods, making her difficult way through some heavy undergrowth. It was next to impossible to sneak up on any decent prey in the thick foliage. Sneaking up on a few edible plants, however, wasn't so hard. In a wet area closer to the river, she found a virtual field of a ground cover distantly related to lettuce. She chewed on several handfuls of leaves while she hunted around for something else to soothe her hunger. After snacking on the leaves and some berries, she noticed the light was beginning to fade. She found an edible woody vine and cut a few pieces of that to chew on while she made her way back toward the town.

This forest was full of life. From a distance, she spotted massive reptiles as big as horses trundling about on all fours. She encountered more insects than she cared to count, some of which were distinctly less pleasant than others. With her clothes and cloak covering much of her bare skin, she avoided too many bites. The worst swarmed closer to the river near the hulking lizards, so she made a mental note to avoid the area.

There were a few large cats here as well. Cats that were skilled climbers, judging from the frequent disappearance of their tracks and the claw marks on many of the trees. Knowing they were out there, she would need to be a little more careful exploring the forest heights.

She stumbled upon a creek in her wandering, the water there much clearer than the river it flowed into. It tasted clean and crisp. Good enough that she filled the skin she had been conservatively drinking from. She would have to come back with the other skin, which she had discovered amidst much surprised choking was full of mead. A glance at her reflection convinced her to dedicate a few minutes to scrubbing away dirt from her travels and the salt of her earlier tears.

It was near full dark when she reached the fence at the point she intended to try crossing. A thick branch hung low and heavy over the structure on the river side of the path she had met Eamon on. It would put her inside, close to the gate he'd gone through. From there, she shouldn't have to go far to pick up the mule's trail, considering that most of the livestock in the town seemed to belong to the houses on this side near the river. Odds were that he lived close to where she would be crossing the fence, assuming the mule was his and not an animal he borrowed.

She tossed that concern aside and leapt up into the tree. Her bow she had left with the rest of her things, but her elven sword and Jaecar's hunter dagger came with her. She would never go inside that fence without protection. She crouched on a branch that would take her over and waited, watching and listening for any sound or movement that might indicate she had been spotted.

Then she saw him. Eamon was coming through the gate in the older wall that separated this section of town from the rest. He carried the sack she'd seen him with the first night, but now it was empty, his deliveries made. She crept a little farther out on the branch and watched him. There was a weary hang to his shoulders and head, casting his autumn red hair into his face. Whatever weighed upon him, it had his full attention. He didn't look up from his path. She waited until she was sure which structure he was heading toward. A glimpse of the mule in the tiny paddock next to the building confirmed it.

After glancing around once, she crept further out, then took hold of the branch and lowered herself until she was hanging from it. She dropped down next to one of the houses. The landing was almost perfectly silent, but she made a point of moving away from the spot quickly in case anyone did hear or see anything. Sticking to the darkest shadows alongside the buildings, she began to sneak around between the houses and the fence. The stink here wasn't too unpleasant. The stench of animals partially overpowered the nastier smells that crept out from the inner town.

As she came around the side of the next house, she startled a goat that had been standing in the corner, half-asleep. The surprised animal bleated and took two bounding leaps to the other side of the small pen. Raven ducked down in the darkness when someone from inside pounded on the wall of the building.

"Shut up, ye daft bastard," a woman's voice shouted.

The goat stared at Raven, wide, surprised eyes slowly shrinking back to normal size. When she made no aggressive moves, it took only a few more seconds for the animal to lose interest in her entirely. She listened for any further signs of involvement from within the house. Two people now engaged in a mundane conversation about a shortage of feed for the livestock. From what she could see, that consisted of the goat and a pig laying against the house that had barely lifted its head to acknowledge the goat's moment of panic. Then a smell that wasn't at all unpleasant wafted through the window, and she found herself salivating.

Then, she hurried away from the hut and made her way behind the one Eamon had gone to. She hoped to do some spying first, to see if he was alone and what weapons or lack thereof there might be within, but the single window on the back was securely shuttered. She would have to take her chances and go to the front door.

She worked her way back around the same way she'd come, avoiding the side where the mule was penned in case it, like the goat, felt the need to announce her arrival. When she got to the door, she stared at it for a minute, uneasy at being out in the open but reluctant to proceed. She'd never had a need to knock on a stranger's door before. What might he think of a young female coming to his door at this hour?

She raised her hand.

This was ridiculous. What would she do if she could get passage on the ship? She'd decided that she couldn't go to Pellanth. The city would be much too dangerous.

Her legs started to feel like they were made of soft mud again. She tugged at the sides of her hood, determined not to be recognized for what she was.

Maybe Eamon could read the documents she had.

Though she would have to trust him with them and their contents to find out. He was a stranger, and she hadn't brought them with her anyhow.

This was absurd.

Raven was about to turn away when the door opened. Eamon, holding up a lantern, almost stepped into her before leaping back in surprise, reaching for his belt dagger. Raven got to her sword first, then checked herself, stopping short of drawing it.

W ait!" She held up one hand, the other still on her sword hilt.

Eamon hesitated, peering past the lantern at her, his eyes narrowing as he moved his hand away from the dagger. "You're the girl from the woods yesterday." He set down the lantern on a wooden table near the door. Given the size of the house, the table seemed to be near everything. "I'm sorry if I frightened you."

Raven almost laughed at that. She'd sent him jumping back into his house, grabbing at his dagger in alarm, but he was worried about possibly having frightened her. "I need your help."

"I suspected as much." He nodded, taking a step back and to one side. When she continued to stand there, he gestured with one hand for her to enter.

Raven found herself rooted to the spot. The building was so small, so enclosed. Not much more than a cage. There was no room to keep her distance from him. No space to fight in. She glanced up at him, finding it hard to believe he expected her to enter.

His breath caught, and his eyes widened. "You need more help than I expected, and I'm not sure I can offer it."

She jerked her gaze away, blocking out the candlelight that had brightened the shadows of her hood. She had let him see her face. Her eyes. Raven spun away, ready to bolt. He caught her arm, and she twisted back around, jerking free of his grip. Fury at her own carelessness warred with her fear of this world she didn't know. She half-drew her sword. He held his hands up in a quick gesture to show he meant no harm.

"Please. Come inside." He retreated into the small building. "I'll help you if I can."

Keeping her hand on her sword hilt, Raven glanced around the interior again, then took one cautious step through the doorway. Eamon continued to back away, moving around the other side of the table. She didn't get the sense that he was afraid of her, although he had taken note of her sword with a quick glance, but more that he was trying to keep from spooking her. Again, he treated her like a wild animal. As much as she wanted to be offended by that, it was a fair analogy, even as she let him slowly lure her inside with his calculated retreat.

He took a seat on a bench on the far side of the table. Once she was fully inside, he gestured to the door. "I suspect you'll want that closed. We don't want to attract curious neighbors."

She watched him as she reached behind her and shut the door. He nodded slightly, then gestured to the bench across from him.

"Sit."

She glanced around the room at the few burning candles and the small assortment of chopped vegetables and meat on a counter near the warm blaze of a cooking fire. A bed against the wall behind him had some clothes hanging off the foot and a few threadbare blankets strewn haphazardly across it. His bow and a quiver of arrows leaned against the wall by the bed. Herbs hung from hooks in the ceiling in the corner behind her, offering their aromas to help mask the town's smell that clung to some other items.

"It's not much." A hint of self-consciousness showed through in his shrug.

She had no idea how to make small talk, so she jumped ahead to the reason for her visit. "There's a ship at the dock."

"You're a Silverblood," he shook his head, a touch of breathy awe in his voice, "and female."

His appraisal left her feeling uncomfortably exposed. "I'm happy you noticed," she snapped.

Eamon chuckled. "Which part?"

There wasn't much point in trying to hide now, so she lowered her hood to let him get a full helping of her glower. It didn't have the intended effect. His expression sobered, but something in it made her instantly uneasy. His gaze flickered to her hands, watching her fingers for a moment. The silver cast to her fingernails and hair had caught his attention.

"A very strong Silverblood and an elf as well," he murmured. "I've never seen anything so beautiful."

Raven expected a lot of reactions, but this she was unprepared for. Her throat tightened, and tears stung her eyes. This wasn't hatred or fear. This was awe and admiration. She yearned for more like this. For acceptance. For welcome. For someone to tell her she wouldn't be alone forever now that Jaecar was gone. She lowered her gaze, staring hard at a strange metal piece on the table.

He reached out to touch it, bringing his hand into her vision. A long scar ran across the back of it. "It's a compass. Humans have to use such things to find their way because the woods don't talk to them," he offered.

"I'm only half-elven," she blurted, bracing for the disgust, the rejection that Jaecar told her she might encounter. Now it would come.

Eamon's smile was warm and disarming. "Half perfect is better than not at all." He started to stand, hesitating when she tensed. "I haven't eaten. Can I offer you some supper?"

Her stomach growled then, and he breathed a soft laugh at her flush. "That's a yes then?"

Raven slid to the end of the bench closest to the door and straddled it so she could keep an eye on him as he moved around into the cooking area. He began collecting and chopping more of the items that were already prepared and added to the piles. He spoke while he worked, apologizing that his cooking was nothing exceptional, then rambling about the town. The center of town was primarily human, though there were a few elven merchants, including a family that lived on the edge of the market. The wife was a seamstress and her husband a cobbler. They had two children who had made friends among the other elves who lived on the town's outskirts closer to the fence.

None of it mattered. She recognized that he was trying to help them both relax.

"Since I'm cooking for you, perhaps it's time I knew your name." He turned to regard her, reclining his lean frame against the counter while a collection of meat and herbs boiled over the fire.

She stared at him for a moment, running through their exchanges in her head. That was basic etiquette, wasn't it? Every introduction she had ever read included the sharing of names. He had given her his yesterday morning, and she still hadn't offered her own. It wasn't going to be easy getting the hang of interacting with strangers. At least he wasn't trying to kill her or turn her over to the authorities like she had been raised to expect.

"Raven."

His brow furrowed ever so slightly. "That isn't your birth name, is it?"

She bristled. Not that he was wrong, but Raven was

what her parents and Jaecar called her by. She only ever heard her birth name when Jaecar used it to get her attention during training. That name was too personal to offer up to a stranger.

"Why? There's nothing wrong with Raven."

His smile banished her defensive anger. "Nothing at all. I like it. It's just... unusual, quite like the lady who bears it."

Her face heated, and she pressed back against the wall as if she might somehow inch her way out through it. The faintest shine of laughter brightened his eyes. She wasn't sure whether to be offended or share in his amusement. She was entirely out of her depth.

"Where are you from?"

"South."

"Around here, that's just about the only option if you didn't come on a boat." He picked up a ladle and stirred the contents of the pot. "I was hoping for something a little more specific."

Without his gaze on her, she dared to let herself admire him. Something about his profile struck her as distinctly pleasing when he looked to the side to inspect the food. "I didn't choose to be this way," she stated, relenting to a growing need to have him think well of her.

He glanced at her, one eyebrow rising in a little arc. "I didn't think you had. You'd have to be mad to choose to be that way. Your very existence violates Brotherhood law and, according to their doctrine, shouldn't even be possible."

Raven liked the way he regarded her. Curiosity burned in his gaze and something else she couldn't quite place, but it was gratifying. She had the strange temptation to relax in his presence. His good-natured manner and kindness put her off her guard. It made her want to trust him, though she wouldn't allow herself to.

She wasn't going to be a fool.

Realizing she had shifted forward on the bench, she pushed herself back into the wall again. "I need to go north."

He added the vegetables to the pot, set a kettle on the grate over the fire, then returned to his seat across from her. "I can't get you on that ship. The crew was arrested as soon as they disembarked. Something about stolen merchandise from what little I heard. Besides, a few days on the confines of a galley with other folks and you're certain to be discovered for what you are."

He wasn't wrong, and yet... "You don't seem that bothered by what I am."

"Well, you're not exactly a menacing figure, are you?"

Raven glowered at him.

"Except when you do that," he teased, though his expression quickly turned serious again. "I get the sense that you haven't been out in the world much."

Her throat tightened at the idea of admitting how right he was. She was ignorant of the world he took for granted in many ways. Her parents and Jaecar had seen to that. To protect her, perhaps, but it left her flailing in the dark now. She didn't want him to think her a witless child, though he had apparently caught on to that already.

"It's not meant as an insult," he added soothingly, calming the wild beast again. "You can't expect the same treatment you've gotten from me from others. Most people . . ." He got up, a dark expression clouding his features. "I'll just say that I've encountered a great deal more cruelty in this world than I have kindness." He didn't look at her as he went to stir the pot.

Another aroma had begun to fill the air. A sweet and spicy scent rose under the growing savory bouquet of the stew. Her stomach growled again, and she put a hand over it, willing it to be quiet.

"Why do you take meat to the family on the other side of town?" The piercing look he turned on her then told her she had erred somehow. "I saw you the other night when I was making my way around the edge of town."

"I didn't see you."

"I was up above."

His expression changed, something different in the way he regarded her then. It reminded her of how two predators might consider one another with wary respect. She preferred the previous look. The one that said he liked what he saw when he looked at her. Though she would take the respect as well. She just didn't want to have to trade one for the other.

Growing up with stern, quiet Jaecar as her father figure, mentor, and only companion left her unprepared in ways she couldn't have imagined. Eamon was kind and attractive. The way he spoke to and looked at her made her hungry for more. She barely knew him, and still, she wanted to trust him and linger in his company. Raven had no idea what to do with these feelings. All she knew was that, as she watched him walk around the room, she struggled with an utterly ludicrous urge to move closer to him.

Seemingly unaware of her inner conflict, Eamon collected two mugs from a cupboard and poured the steaming liquid from the kettle into them. It was that liquid that smelled so delicious. A little like the sweet root she loved back home, only with that intriguing hint of spice. He brought the mugs over, set one in front of her, and then took his seat with the other.

"A woman lives there with her five children. Their father fell ill last winter and died. I've been helping them out for a while. I also bring food to an elven widow on the edge of town. Her husband chopped her foot off with a wood axe for trying to run away when he was beating her. She cut more than his foot off after that. Now she has a difficult time getting around and has no one to look after her, so I do what I can to help."

"I thought so." Raven took a sip of the warm drink. The spice perfectly balanced the sweetness, the flavors dancing across her tongue in delicious harmony. She closed her eyes and breathed in the aromatic steam. Then she remembered where she was and snapped her eyes open again. The fondness in Eamon's regard from across the table left her confused and adrift. She averted her gaze.

"What did you think?" he asked. As he waited for her answer, he took a drink from his mug, holding the liquid in his mouth a few seconds before swallowing with a contented smile.

"I thought you were doing something kind for her. It's part of why I chose you to speak to." She took a longer drink this time, savoring the way it warmed her as it slid down her throat to settle cozily in her stomach.

His head tilted to the side, a shrewd look sharpening his features. "You've never ventured away from home before, have you?"

Her throat seized, and the swallow she had just taken got caught halfway down. Her expression was apparently enough of an answer.

"Why now? What drove you to risk being discovered like this?"

Raven forced a painful swallow. Though she tried hard to fight it, several big tears splashed down her cheeks. She set the mug on the table and wiped brusquely at them. Eamon stood and walked over to the pot, allowing her a moment of privacy as he tended the food. It took her a few minutes to stop the minor breach and dry her cheeks again. When she managed to compose herself, he topped off her mug and set a bowl in front of her, returning to his seat with his own.

He gestured to her bowl with one hand. "Have something to eat. We can talk about that some other time."

She watched him for a minute as he turned his attention to his meal. His words promised her more of his time. That was somehow both frightening and exceedingly comforting.

Raven jerked awake, panic setting her nerves ablaze. This wasn't the tree she was sleeping on. She sat up, becoming aware of two things simultaneously. First, she had a blazing headache, and second, she was still in Eamon's house. The sudden change to upright sent both her head and stomach spinning uncomfortably. Violently enough that she couldn't do anything more than sit there for a moment, gripping the edge of the bed.

What had he done to her?

She glanced around the room, noting a blanket and balled-up pile of clothes that served as a pillow on the floor. Eamon appeared to have given her the bed and taken the floor for himself. She didn't remember going to sleep, though she vaguely recalled feeling dizzy and Eamon telling her that she ought to lay down for a minute. There was some apology in there for something, though she couldn't recall what it had been.

A few things did stick out firmly in her mind now. One was that Eamon knew what she was and had reacted to that revelation with patience and kindness. He also was a better cook than Jaecar had been, though all food sounded distinctly unappetizing now. The thing that struck her most powerfully was that she had enjoyed being around him.

And he was gone. It wasn't as if he could hide

anywhere in the tiny house. Pulling up the hood of her cloak, she walked to the shuttered window and yanked one side open, startling a spider that reared back, lifting its front legs as if it meant to fight her. Despite how the creeping light of predawn made her head hurt more, she found a faint smile for the bold little creature.

"Sorry," she murmured, closing the shutter carefully so as not to hurt it.

Raven collected her sword and dagger that had found their way to a resting place near the bed. Then she left the house, hurrying to a spot along the fence that the branches and other houses hid from view. She scaled it with a little less than her customary grace, receiving a few annoying slivers in the process. Her landing back on the other side ended in a stumble. Whatever made her head ache was messing with her equilibrium and strength.

It also lessened her awareness. She had barely crossed the path to head back to her tree when one of the woodcutters she'd seen before caught sight of her before she noticed them.

"Where you headed, lass?"

Raven turned, checking that her hood was pulled well forward as she did so. Two of the men were there, coming down the path. The third...

She heard rustling in the bushes back and to her left. One of the two in front of her let his gaze briefly dart that way. The hint of recognition in his expression told her what she needed to know. She took several wary side steps back into the path where it was more open. These were not warriors. That much was evident in how they held their axes, but they did have axes.

The man outside of her field of vision was closing in. She could hear every sound he made. Even with the headache, or perhaps more so because of it. He would be within distance to lunge for her in about three more strides.

"Go on your way," she warned.

One of the men laughed and came forward, his companion following a few strides behind. As he moved, he pointed at her with his ax. "You one of them pointy bitches. That why yer hiding in that cloak?"

"Pointy? Do you mean elves? I don't see why that should matter."

The man behind her had stopped at three strides. She could almost feel him there, breathing too hard for the lack of exertion.

"A pointy out in the woods likely knows where to find bloodwood. That's the rich stuff. You'll take us there."

"I can't," she answered with relative honesty. Technically, she probably could find bloodwood, or whatever else they were hunting for, given time to wander the forest. Still, she didn't currently know where any was. This wasn't her forest.

"Lying bitch," the man in the back growled. "I told you there's no point talking to them."

The man in front gave a nod, his gaze shifting to the man flanking her. Raven twisted to the side. The man's hand brushed her shoulder as he lunged past. She had her sword out before she finished her turn and caught him in the back of the head with the hilt. He staggered into one of the other two, who had both rushed forward. Raven adjusted her stance to face the third. He came at her with his axe raised. She caught it with her blade under the axe head, then kicked him in the gut and jerked back, sending the axe flying into the bushes behind her while he doubled over.

The other man shoved his companion off and was coming at her when an arrow skimmed past his ear, sinking deep into a tree alongside the path. The men turned. Eamon was jogging toward them, his bow drawn and another arrow nocked.

"I never miss, Darrin. You know that," Eamon warned.

The man Raven had disarmed held his hands up. The other two stepped back.

"We were just having a little chat," Darrin defended.

"The more you talk, the more tired my fingers get of holding this bowstring back. I suggest you just move on."

Raven stepped back and watched them hurry off, Darrin grabbing his axe from the bushes on the way. She sheathed her sword. After they were gone, Eamon put away the bow and arrow, coming to collect the other arrow from the tree.

"I see you can look after yourself," he commented with an approving nod to her sword.

Her head was pounding harder now. "I don't usually have to. I'm not normally one to let people sneak up on me, but I don't quite feel myself this morning."

"About that." He averted his gaze and cleared his throat. "I'm guessing you don't have much experience with alcohol."

Everything clicked together suddenly. Jaecar had offered her a drink now and then, but she didn't like the taste of the alcohol he drank. As a result, though she'd read about what it could do to one's body and mind, she'd never experienced it firsthand.

She drew her hood back some to look at him. "That sweet drink with all the spices, that was alcohol?"

"Mmhm. Sorry. It didn't occur to me that you might be that inexperienced. You did seem to sleep well, though." He held up a water skin. "This is a little something I mixed up. It'll help with the headache and nausea."

Raven took the skin, pulled the cork, and sniffed at the contents. She gave him a suspicious look. He chuckled and gestured for her to drink it. The same kindness rose in his green eyes that had helped her feel safe speaking with him last night. His manner was more relaxed now as if he no longer felt the need to treat her like an animal that might flee at any moment. Had something changed between them last night? Was it this easy to find someone trustworthy, or had she gotten exceptionally lucky?

Raven glanced after the three men. The dense forest had hidden them from sight. "That's what you meant when you said I couldn't expect from others the same treatment I was getting from you."

He moved up beside her now, close enough that she expected to be uncomfortable with it, but somehow, it didn't bother her. "One example, yes. Though it appears you've been trained by someone with some fighting skill."

"Fighting and hunting are all I've been trained in," she answered, wishing she didn't feel resentment toward her parents and Jaecar for that. It felt wrong to be angry with them. She knew they had wanted to protect her. Now, all that protection put her at a disadvantage in confronting a world she didn't know how to interact with. Although – she glanced over at Eamon – it wasn't going as poorly as she had expected.

He turned to look at her at the same time, and a hint of color touched his cheeks. "What?"

She averted her gaze. "Nothing."

"Well, since you have all this training in hunting, perhaps you'd be willing to join me for my hunt today. I'd love to show you the nicer side of Manderly."

She gave him a tentative smile, surprised that she was already starting to feel better. "I take it that side of Manderly is all outside the fence?"

Eamon laughed. "You catch on quickly." He held a hand out for the skin. "Can I have some of that?"

After she retrieved her bow, they spent the rest of the day wandering the forest together. He was easy to be around, though not necessarily easy to talk to. She wasn't ready to talk much. When he asked questions, she evaded or simply declined to answer many of them until he settled into telling her more about the region and his experiences. She hoped to learn how to talk easily with strangers by observing how he did it with her, but the details of her life were still something she wasn't prepared to share with someone she barely knew.

Eamon showed her areas to avoid, where dangerous creatures had nests, dens, or favorite hunting grounds. He took her to places he went to find many of the wild herbs and roots he used to liven up his cooking. Raven took a little time in these places to collect some herbs and mushrooms she was familiar with. Around midday, they stopped in a meadow that was full in bloom with a carpet of yellow, white, and red wildflowers that cast their glorious aroma into the air. They sat there for a time, sharing fresh berries and other foods they had gathered during their explorations along with a surprisingly comfortable silence.

After that, Eamon showed her some of his most productive hunting grounds. He watched with open admiration as she brought down a hare they might share for dinner with her first arrow. She took a small deer they could split up to take to the family and the crippled female he was looking after with her second. She helped him dress them and carry them most of the way back, then left him to enter the town alone. After dark, she climbed the wall again and returned to his home to cook him supper in return for the meal he'd made her.

She drank lightly of the spiced wine and shared tales of hunting adventures. They seemed a safe way to start telling him about herself. She didn't talk of who had taught her to hunt and fight. Jaecar was still a piece of her broken heart that she would keep to herself, as were her parents. Then she left him and went to sleep in the tree, where she drifted off thinking of the way he made her feel like she might be able to be happy again someday.

The following day, Raven woke with a sense of almost giddy anticipation. She hurried down the tree and went to wait for Eamon by the path. He came along a short time later, a little earlier than he'd come out the past two days. When she stepped out from behind a tree, his smile lifted her mood into the soaring embrace of the treetops. She smiled back, and the resulting gleam of delight in his eyes filled her with a powerful desire to be closer to him.

How did ordinary people deal with these inclinations?

Raven turned away, peering into the forest. "Where today?"

He walked up beside her, and her pulse quickened. "I have another place I'd like to show you today." He looked at her then, his gaze moving over her in a way that made warmth spread through her body. "Come."

The pressure of his gaze disappeared when he turned away, and she could breathe again. She followed. He was quiet this morning once they started moving. The barrage of questions she had mostly dodged from the day before didn't begin again today as she expected. He appeared to be on a single-minded quest to take her somewhere, so she followed, appreciating how he moved skillfully through the thick undergrowth.

Eventually, they came up alongside one of the broader creeks. They followed it deeper into the woods until they reached a large crystalline pool at the foot of a waterfall cascading down stair steps of pale stone carved out by centuries of erosion. The same stone surrounded the deep pool, along with a plethora of ferns that spread their leaves gracefully over small patches of dirt that filled cracks between the rocks. Violet flowers sprouted up from the center of the ferns, nodding in the light breeze created by the waterfall.

"This," Eamon said, spreading his hands to encompass the scene, "is my favorite place in the forest."

Raven smiled and removed her bow and quiver. He glanced over at her, raising one eyebrow curiously. She took off her sword, dagger, cloak, and boots and set them aside. Then she stepped to the edge of the pool, peering down into the clear water for a moment before diving in. As she finished surfacing, there was a splash alongside her. Raven dove back under before he came up and swam over to emerge under the falls. She stayed there a moment, closing her eyes and letting the water pound down over her. When she opened her eyes, Eamon was less than a foot away, watching her intently.

Raven's chest tightened, and her pulse sped up again as it had earlier. He was looking in her eyes, searching her face for something. She had read a little about romantic relationships but had no personal experience. No idea how this was supposed to work. The thought of being touched by him terrified her as much as it excited her. Perhaps he saw that in her eyes because he moved back another foot, giving her room to come out if she wished.

Raven closed her eyes again for a quick moment. Part of her wanted him to come closer. Wanted him to take on the burden of that choice, but he didn't. She opened her eyes again and swam forward, putting them closer together once more, though not uncomfortably so. She tilted her head back and bobbed underwater for a second to get her hair out of her face. He was still watching her when she came up.

"You've never been..." he hesitated, perhaps trying to choose the right words, "in love?"

She held his gaze and shook her head, unable to make herself tell him that she had never met someone she might fall in love with. In his eyes, she could see that he wanted to touch her. This was the moment that she should move toward him. Their lips would meet, and he would kiss her, holding her close as if she were the most important thing in his world, like in a few of the stories she had read. She wanted to feel that.

Raven dove back under the water, swimming to the edge of the pool, where she pulled herself out. She didn't look at him, saying over her shoulder, "I'll be right back."

She heard the splashing of him climbing out as she slipped behind some trees and brush where she was out of sight. Then she pulled off her clothes one piece at a time to wring them out and put them back on. When she returned, he was standing beside the pool, wringing out his shirt. She watched the muscles move in his arms and back as he twisted the garment, noticing a long scar that ran down the side of his ribs.

He glanced over his shoulder and smiled at her. If her abrupt departure had upset him, he didn't show it. Raven walked to where she had left her things. As she bent down, she caught a sound from the forest beyond Eamon. The soft creak of leather. More than one set of light footsteps.

"Someone's coming," she hissed, grabbing her things. "Elven, I think."

Eamon nodded and pulled on his shirt. "Hide."

Raven ducked into the trees and pulled her cloak on over her damp clothes. She tucked her sword, dagger, and boots in the brush at the base of a tree and climbed up with her bow and quiver slung over one shoulder. Settling on a nicely hidden perch, she pulled up her hood to watch. Four well-armed elves, wearing leather armor with a distinct elven style and quality, emerged from the forest. There was one female among them, armed and armored like the males.

Three of them had their bows drawn, and they

trained them on Eamon. Raven's stomach twisted into knots. The fourth in the front didn't touch his weapons. He had an air of authority about him. His long hair, a dark auburn that edged toward black, was pulled back in a loose tie at the base of his neck, strands of slightly shorter hair around his face hanging free to frame strong features. A scar cutting down the side of his nose near one eye gave a particular ferocity to his appearance. Raven trained her bow on him.

Eamon held his hands up. His bow still lay on the ground, though he had put on the belt with his dagger.

"You're new to these woods." His tone was far more casual than she felt the situation called for.

The leader took another step forward, Raven tracking his movement with her bow. "And we would be pleased to benefit from your knowledge of the area, should your companion choose to lower their weapon." The leader glanced up at her hiding place.

A jolt of surprise went through her. It was disconcerting that he had spotted her so quickly, though perhaps he had seen her climbing up before they emerged from the trees. Or maybe there were more than four of them.

She scanned the trees.

"Perhaps, if you were to lower yours..." Eamon countered.

The leader gestured to his companions, who lowered their bows. Raven spotted a fifth elf, another female, in a tree off to their left. She shot an arrow into the trunk a foot below her. The female startled and grabbed a branch to keep from losing her perch.

"That one too," Eamon added.

The leader smirked, looking almost amused, and

cast another glance at her hiding spot. Then he gestured to the elf in the tree, and she lowered her bow. After one more quick scan of the trees, Raven followed suit, lowering her bow, though she kept the arrow nocked.

"I'm Phendaril," the leader offered.

"Eamon."

Phendaril responded with a respectful nod. "You're from Manderly?"

"I am."

"Then we could use your help." Phendaril made another subtle gesture, and the three elves with him put away their bows. Like Raven, the one in the tree kept her bow lowered but ready. "Our galley was supposed to come through Manderly. It..." She couldn't see Eamon's expression, but the leader trailed off, a scowl darkening his features. "I see you already know something."

"The galley was detained, and the crew taken into custody," Eamon answered. "Something about stolen cargo."

Phendaril looked as if he might spit venom for a second, and Raven almost raised her bow again. Then he shook his head, his expression stilling like the calm before a storm. "We'd heard Lord Darrenton's men spread a rumor to that effect. We were hoping it wasn't true."

"That sounds like something they would do." A hint of sympathetic anger came across in Eamon's tone.

The elf in the tree put away her bow. She was looking in Raven's direction as she did so. This was a complicated game, but Raven recognized it was her turn. She hesitantly put her bow and the arrow away. The situation was unbalanced. If they decided to attack Eamon, she would be unable to save him. She could, and would, shoot some down, but there were too many for her to stop them all before they got to him. Now she had to rely on the not unreasonable assumption that they didn't want to hurt him.

"Those supplies were legally obtained and are much needed by the people in Amberwood," Phendaril explained.

Eamon had shifted his stance enough that she could see a little of the surprise in his face. "Amberwood? I thought that area was abandoned and overrun with beasts."

"It is," Phendaril replied. "A group of us who used to live there, and a few new friends, have come back to rebuild the town. We need those supplies, however. We don't have a lot of coin to toss at replacing them. I know the local constable isn't known for his generosity toward elves, but perhaps, being local, you could get us some more information on the situation. What is he planning to do with the crew? Is the cargo still on the ship?"

"You want me to run reconnaissance so you can decide whether to try to negotiate for their release or break them out and take the galley."

Phendaril didn't disagree. Instead, he hefted a pouch at his belt. "I can compensate you for your time and risk. I can also offer you and your companion a place in Amberwood, should you be weary of living in this backward shithole."

"I'll look into it," Eamon answered, and Raven itched to ask why he didn't follow up on the offer of compensation or a new home. "My companion, however, will have no part in any of this."

Raven bristled. As always, someone else was making her decisions for her, to protect her. What gave him that right? At least her parents and Jaecar had started doing that when she was too young to make her own choices. When did that change? When did she get to start deciding things for herself? Perhaps this should be that day.

The elf in the other tree was making her way down. Raven moved to do the same. She would walk out there and offer to help. Suppose she continued spending time with Eamon. She couldn't let him start controlling her life the way everyone before him had, even if he did have far more worldly experience than her. She would learn nothing that way.

Her gaze moved to the other elves below. To Phendaril, who was glancing up at her tree again, that scar standing out white against his pale skin. His dark eyes were critical and penetrating. He wore his weapons as comfortably as he wore his leadership of the others. To make her statement here, she would have to walk up to him and speak to him as though she had spoken her mind to many an intimidating stranger.

She wasn't ready for that yet. She could talk to Eamon about it when they were alone. Maybe it was better to take this one small step at a time.

"It will take a little time. I don't exactly have the constable's ear," Eamon said then. "Give me until tomorrow afternoon to see what I can learn?"

Phendaril nodded. "We'll meet here again. By two o'clock."

The two shook on it, and Raven dropped down the branches to the ground, grabbing her things as Eamon turned his back on the strangers and collected his bow. She met up with him a short distance into the woods, far enough away that they could no longer see the other elves. Eamon did not appear pleased. A look of relief eased some of the tension coming from him when he saw her, but his smile was troubled.

"Thank you for your support."

"Why did you tell them I wouldn't help? Isn't that for me to decide?" She instantly regretted the anger in her tone that brought hurt to his eyes.

"I was only trying to keep you safe. They may be elves, but they are clearly no strangers to combat, and I don't know them. I don't know if they might be dangerous to you given…" He only had to glance down at her fingernails to finish the thought.

He was right, and she hated the fact. "I can't hide behind the protection of others for the rest of my life. I must be able to take care of myself. What if I end up…" She couldn't bring herself to say the word. Alone was painful. Alone meant losing someone she had only just found. Hadn't she lost enough?

Eamon stopped walking and caught her arm, drawing her around to face him. He leaned in close to her, meeting her eyes and holding them with the intensity of his gaze. He placed a hand on her cheek, and she drew a sharp breath of surprise.

"I don't plan to see you alone if you'll let me have a say in that, but I promise," he leaned a little closer, "I promise I will help you take control of your life so you can confidently make your own decisions."

She thought he might kiss her then, but she didn't honestly know him. The part of her that wanted him to was fierce, passionate, and much more vulnerable than the part that had long been a solitary hunter and fighter. This part was so new she didn't know if she could trust it.

He seemed to sense the war inside her, for he drew a deep breath and backed away. "Come on. Let's get out of these wet clothes. Do you have something else to wear?"

She shook her head.

"I'll see if I can find you something when I go into town. You can borrow some of my clothes if you wish. They'll only be a little big. You're also welcome to stay at the house if you want to while I'm information gathering."

She still wanted to do something to help. To show that she wasn't useless. "Do you need to hunt?"

His smile was affectionate, but pain showed through in the tightening around his eyes. "No. They should have enough to last a few days, as should I. Come on."

Raven suspected that, while he might be telling the truth, he was also trying to keep her safe again. If she went out hunting, she could run into those other elves, the ones he didn't know if he could trust. Figuring out how to interact with strangers would be an ongoing process. Each one a little different than the last. Running into Eamon first was extraordinary luck. Taking time to learn what she could from him might be the wise thing to do before she pushed things.

When they neared the town fence, Raven slipped over using the tree. With the guards' attention taken by Eamon as he went through, she didn't have to worry about them. The other people out in this small partition of the town were a different problem. She patiently timed her drop when no one was looking and made her way back to the house.

When Eamon walked in, she had the fire burning. None of the houses in this part of town had locks. Most couldn't afford them. As Eamon pointed out, the fence limited the pool of suspects enough that they were respectful of one another's belongings. Since they were all elves, most of the town's occupants assumed they didn't have anything worth stealing, which wasn't entirely wrong.

She watched that he kept his back to her as she changed hastily into some of his clothes so they could hang her damp ones near the fire to dry. When she was done, she turned her back to him while he changed. Then he left her there, going out to see what he could learn about the galley and its crew.

Not wanting to make her way out again in the daylight, Raven spent some time reflecting on the day. Then she started digging around the house, arranging things the way she always had at the keep. Jaecar liked orderly but only enforced that in the study. Everywhere else, he was negligent, so she had tended to organize things. It was one of many chores she gave herself to keep occupied when she wasn't training, hunting, or reading.

Under the bed, she discovered a locked chest and a partially carved longbow. The part that was finished was beautiful. In the open cupboards, she found containers full of dry spices and herbs. Some she recognized, most she didn't. She took the time to tidy those, organizing them primarily by what she thought they would be suitable for based on smell. A few she set aside, figuring she could use them for supper.

When he returned about two hours after dark, she was struggling her way through an elven book she'd stumbled upon. A bit of early history of one of the elven forest cities. A stew was simmering over the fire. He had a bruise around one eye and a cut on his forehead. Raven sat up from where she was reclined on the bed and set the book aside.

He glanced around, and his lip twisted in an amused smirk. "I see you got bored."

She stood and walked over to him. "You're hurt."

He shook his head. "This is nothing. Just a brute at the inn looking to fight everyone who got within three feet of him. They kicked him out as soon as they gathered enough muscle to drag his ass outside."

She got the feeling he wasn't telling her the whole truth, or he was merely dodging her concern. It didn't seem worth the effort to press him on it. "Did you learn anything?"

"Not much, but I have a few leads I can follow up on tomorrow morning." He sniffed the air. "That smells delicious." He lifted his pack. "I found some clothes for you. You like dresses, right?"

Raven stared at him in horror. Unless her mother had put her in a dress when she was incredibly young, she was confident she had never worn one in her life. She wasn't about to start now. They weren't made for hunting or fighting.

A smile broke through his serious expression, and he started laughing. "I would never have bought you a dress unless you expressly asked for one."

Raven tried to glare at him, but an irresistible smile tugged up the corners of her mouth. "Begging for a second black eye, I see." She took the pack and set it on the table. "I should at least wipe the blood off your face. Sit."

She collected the cloth and got it damp before realizing she was acting like she always had with Jaecar. She had helped him tend his wounds, and he had seen to hers when she couldn't do it herself. Together, through training and hunting, they both had their share of injuries. This was good, though. Something from her old life could help her interact with others.

She turned to look at Eamon sitting on the bench, at the blood on his face, and realized this wasn't the same. She was about to touch the face of the male she had contemplated kissing more than once that day. Raven sat facing him on the bench, straddling it the way he had. She paused for a second there. The teasing about dresses was a reminder of how unladylike she was. Sitting like this was glaring proof of that.

She met his eyes and saw that the intensity from earlier had returned. He didn't appear to care how ladylike she was or wasn't. She wiped gingerly at the blood from the cut, cleaning it away until she could see that the wound was minor and no longer bleeding.

"It's not so bad," she said softly, trying not to get caught up in his gaze.

She stood and went to rinse the cloth. Eamon walked up next to her and placed a hand on her arm.

"I'll clean that and get some food served up. You try

on the clothes. They won't fit perfectly, but they should be close."

The fluttering in her chest went wild as though a hummingbird had become trapped there. She turned, but not away from him, toward the table where the pack waited. Instead, she turned toward him, so they were looking at one another, a few inches apart. She glanced down at his lips, then met his eyes.

She whispered, "If I wanted you to, would you kiss me?"

His breath caught, and his hesitation made her fear for a second that she had misread him. Then he slid his hand up her arm to touch her cheek lightly. "I can think of nothing I would be happier to do. If you also wanted it."

Raven's nerves danced like lightning had struck them as she nodded. "I do."

There was a slight tremble in his touch as he leaned in and pressed his lips to hers. The kiss was gentle and sweet. His lips were soft and warm against hers. She closed her eyes and breathed him in. Every part of her yearned to move closer to him, but she couldn't bring herself to do so before he drew away. He rested his forehead against hers for a moment, his eyes closed. They were both breathing a little faster, and she yearned to kiss him again, but this was something she truly knew nothing about. She would follow his lead, even if her body did have ideas of its own.

Eamon did not kiss her again that night. She tried on the clothes he had gotten her, which fit passably well and were far less threadbare than those she'd been wearing. She didn't drink much of the sweet wine and, despite his assurances that he would be happy to bed down on the floor again, she declined his offer of the bed and went out to sleep in her tree. She wanted to make sure her things were undisturbed and think through her new experiences without him there to influence her emotions.

The next morning, she spent wandering the wooded areas away from the waterfall. Something about Phendaril she found highly intimidating. She had no desire to run into him alone. Especially not knowing how he and his companions would react if they learned what she was. So, she retraced some areas Eamon had shown her the previous day, reflecting on how he made her feel and the kiss they had shared.

When it came time for him to meet Phendaril, she found a tree near the path she knew he would take and waited for him there. He appeared around when she expected him to. The way he peered into the woods around the path told her he was expecting her to be there. She waited for him to pass before climbing down and creeping up behind him.

"Eamon," she whispered.

He spun and gave her a mock scolding look. "You startled me."

She grinned. "What kind of elf are you, anyhow? Letting me sneak up on you like that."

"A preoccupied one, who was being stalked by a Silverblood half-elf," he returned lightheartedly, though there was a certain unease to his manner today that the bruises on his face added weight to. He stepped closer and took her hands in his. "I'm going to meet with Phendaril. I shouldn't be long, but I must ask you not to follow me. I know you're more than capable of doing so without me knowing, but please don't."

She saw how important it was to him through the pleading in his eyes and the firmness of his grip and made herself nod.

He stepped closer, and the flutter in her chest went wild. One hand came to rest on her shoulder, his thumb brushing the skin of her neck as he leaned in to kiss her. An exquisite fire followed in the wake of his touch, sending a shiver through her. His lips were soft and warm against hers. She was short of breath and a little woozy when he drew away. Longing burned bright in his eyes, his hand lingering on her shoulder.

He smiled. "Thank you. I'll be back soon."

Raven watched him disappear into the woods. She wanted to do as he asked, and yet... Eamon standing in front of Phendaril with four archers aiming their bows at him popped to the fore of her mind. She touched her lips, savoring the sensation of his gentle kiss. The skin on her neck still tingled where he had caressed it. He was being slow and careful. As naive as she was, he could take advantage of her without much trouble, but he wasn't doing that. She wasn't ready to chance losing him, and she didn't trust the strange elves not to put him in danger. His injuries suggested they had already done so.

She heard the gate from town opening and darted into the bushes, finding a spot to hide. A few minutes later, fear swept through her as a man she had encountered before came up the path. His hood wasn't pulled forward enough to hide his features and his silver eyes.

Marek paused in line with where she was hiding and glanced around. Raven's elven dagger she had left in the beast in the woods was sheathed at his belt. She barely let herself breathe until he continued to where Eamon had turned from the path. He examined the ground there for a few seconds, then he too went off the trail in that direction. Raven followed.

The effortlessness with which Marek kept to Eamon's trail left her feeling ill-at-ease. He had to be close to catching up with the elf at this pace. He paused a few times, usually to glance behind him like someone who thought they were being followed, whether he was confident of it or not. It appeared that Eamon's trail was his priority, however. They reached the falls fast enough that she suspected Eamon and Phendaril wouldn't have had time to say much. Marek didn't hesitate before walking out into the opening near the pool. As she climbed a tree that would give her a good vantage, she was surprised to hear Eamon greet him.

She climbed onto a sturdy branch and peered into the clearing next to the waterfall pool. She drew her bow and got an arrow ready. Marek had walked up beside Eamon and drawn his hood back. The others weren't there yet. Or, they weren't obviously there, though she spotted a hint of movement in the trees ahead. The way Marek narrowed his gaze at those same trees suggested he had also caught the movement there.

"Things have changed," Marek stated, not looking at Eamon as he spoke.

"How?"

Marek held up a hand, and Eamon waited. After a

few seconds, Phendaril and his three archers emerged from the forest shadows. The fourth, she spotted scaling a tree on the other side to get a vantage like her own.

"I see you brought a friend," Phendaril stated, casting an icy gaze on Marek.

Eamon took a step forward. "You said you were willing to pay. Adept Marek has agreed to help for a price. The constable sent a man back to Chadhurst to verify the legality of the cargo. If a Silverblood vouches for it, he may be willing to let the galley and the crew continue north now without waiting for his man to return."

"Actually," Marek stepped forward, placing himself a little closer to Phendaril and the others than Eamon was, his position demanding attention, "it may not be that easy anymore."

All of them looked at him. Phendaril tilted his head to one side and narrowed his eyes in as clear a statement of distrust as he could get without words. Whether it was because Marek was human or Silverblood or both of those things, she couldn't say, but it was apparent the elven leader didn't like him.

Marek offered a tight, sour smile in response to the look. "As I was leaving town, I overheard one of the guards talking about armed elves spotted in the woods. Apparently, the constable thinks you're here to break out your companions and steal the ship, which confirms, in his mind, that the cargo is stolen. He's planning to have the crew taken to the gallows at sundown today."

Phendaril snarled an elven curse under his breath. "How did they find out so quickly?" He cast a glance at Marek, then at Eamon. "Perhaps your companion from yesterday?"

Eamon scoffed at him. "I can guarantee you she spoke to no one."

A flicker of curiosity lit Phendaril's eyes at Eamon's response, but he had other things to concern him.

"We'll have to move to get the others now then," the female elf flanking him stated.

The other two males nodded their agreement. The one in the tree slung her bow over one shoulder and started to descend. Raven heard footsteps back the way they had come at the exact moment that Marek's attention turned that way. He didn't say a word before stalking off in that direction, drawing his heavy blade as he moved. Two of the elves with Phendaril also drew their swords, heading after Marek with noticeably more caution. Phendaril drew a beautiful, curved blade much like the one Raven carried, though his was longer, more appropriate to his height. He didn't follow them, remaining behind with the other elf.

Eamon glanced up into the tree she'd hidden in the day before, then he drew his bow and started after Marek and the first two elves. Raven would have followed, but the sound of several arrows releasing from the direction of the waterfall sent a jagged blade of fear through her. The female elf in the tree made almost no sound as she fell, hitting the ground hard with an arrow driven deep into the soft tissue above where her collarbones met. Raven heard the unmistakable sound of more arrows hitting flesh. Someone cried out. Her mother, tied to a post for target practice, flashed through her mind, freezing her in place for an instant. When her vision cleared, she saw Eamon collapsing. Battle cries wrenched her attention back to where Phendaril and the other elf were.

She could hear steel clashing in the direction Marek and the other two had gone. Four Manderly guards charged from the trees behind Phendaril and his companion. The elven leader dodged the first attack, whirling around to take the man out with a sword through his low back. He kicked him out of the way as he fell. The other elf had fallen back a few yards to the left, now engaged with two of the guards. The fourth man dodged around Phendaril and came at him from the side nearer to her hiding spot.

Raven wasn't going to be able to get to Eamon with the fighting, so she nocked an arrow and aimed for the guard's back. As she readied to fire, motion in the woods caught her eye. Two more guards were emerging from the trees behind Phendaril. The elven leader was focused on the man in front of him. He didn't appear to be aware yet of the others.

Phendaril disarmed the man before him and drove his blade through his chest. The two behind him were closing fast. She grabbed a second arrow, then aimed to one side of Phendaril's head and let the first fly, nocking and sending the other immediately after it to the opposite side. As he started to turn toward the guards, the arrows zipped past him, one on either side of his head in quick succession. Both hit their marks, plunging deep into the throats of the two men. The elven leader saw them go down and whipped around, his sharp gaze homing in on her perch.

Marek and the other two elves were already coming back into the clearing, their weapons bloodied. The elf with Phendaril finished off the second of his opponents. He turned, glancing with raised brows at the two men lying behind the elven leader with arrows in their throats. Marek noticed them as well and was now peering in her direction.

Raven tossed her bow over her shoulder and dropped several branches to the forest floor. She pulled her hood far forward and sprinted for Eamon. He lay on his side, two arrows sunk in his chest. She fell to her knees next to him. Choking on a sob, she rolled him carefully onto his back. His moan turned into a wet cough, spraying a mist of blood across his lips. The sound tore through her, sending her to a different time when an eight-year-old child clung helplessly to her dying mother's hand.

Marek strode toward them, and she could hear someone else walking up behind them. She wanted to be strong and tell Eamon it would be all right, but she knew it wouldn't be. Her tears were already telling him that.

"Raven." His strained whisper forced her closer. "Marek is... a danger to you. Run from this place... and don't... look back."

She could hear how much effort each word cost him. That he would waste his last breath trying to warn her only worsened the pain in her chest.

"I will not leave you," she answered softly.

His eyes squeezed shut as he coughed some more, his face contorted with pain. She took his hand, trying hard not to remember the last time she had been in this position. Marek stopped next to them, gazing down in silence. There was little to say. He had to know Eamon's wounds were fatal as well as she did. Phendaril moved into her peripheral vision, carrying the elven female who had been shot from the tree. He laid her out near the pool, not far from Eamon, and crouched there, gazing at her in silence.

"I wish... I had gotten to know you... better," Eamon rasped.

Raven wanted to say something to reassure him. She wanted to say that she loved him. Wasn't that what he would like to hear? Yet, she didn't know what that kind of love was. Was it what she felt when he kissed her? Or was it something else entirely?

"I'm sorry," Marek offered, his tone respectful. The careful tone reserved for those who had suffered a loss.

She wanted to yell at him that Eamon wasn't dead yet, but it was no longer true. His strained breathing had stopped while she struggled with what to say to him. Raven bent over him, fighting back sobs that tore at her throat and crushed her chest. Her parents, Jaecar, and now Eamon. Would she ever find someone else as accepting of her as he was? Had this been her one chance to have something good in the cold world outside her forest? Maybe she simply wasn't meant for those things.

Phendaril brushed the elven woman's eyes closed and stood up. He turned to Raven. "I am grateful for your skill with a bow. You're welcome to come with us, but we must go now, or more of our people will die today."

Raven swallowed hard, keeping her head tilted down within the hood, and willed her voice to work. "Shouldn't we bury them?"

"They're elves," he snapped, the hint of kindness in his tone a few seconds ago vanishing. "Do not dishonor them with human burial customs. The forest will reclaim them as it's meant to."

Raven cringed at his words.

Was it dishonor for an elf to be buried? Had Jaecar dishonored her mother by burying her along with Raven's father?

He stalked over to one of the dead men and shoved him with a foot. "The only shame is sharing the forest with these bastards."

One of the other elves quietly set Raven's two arrows on the ground next to her. She had wiped the worst of the blood off them.

Eamon had told Raven to run. Marek was a danger to her. That much was true if he discovered what she was. But where was she going to run to? She still didn't know what Jaecar's collection of documents were. Her home had been burned, and the only family she had murdered. Now her brief hope of someplace new to belong, someone new to belong with, was also gone.

She looked into Eamon's green eyes, glazed over in death, and gently brushed them closed. Her control almost broke when she leaned down and kissed his forehead, but she fought the pain back, harnessing it to a new purpose.

Taking a deep breath, she picked up the arrows and stood, dropping them into her quiver. She kept herself turned slightly away from them all as she spoke. "If I help you free the ship and crew, you'll take me north?"

She heard Phendaril move. A low glance at his feet told her he had turned to face her again.

"As far as Amberwood," he answered.

She didn't know where Amberwood was, but it wasn't here. "Good enough."

Marek took a step toward her, and she stepped back. He stopped, not pressing the issue.

"They're down several guards with their losses here. A town this size won't have that many more to spare. If she comes with me as ranged back up," Marek suggested, "the two of us can free the crew, but you need to have that ship ready and leaving the dock by the time we get there. Can you do that with just the four of you?"

"Yes," Phendaril answered.

Raven admired his confidence. She glanced over at the two men she had killed. She had never killed anyone before. If she did this with these strangers, she might have to do so again before the night was out. She glanced back over at Eamon and quickly decided she didn't care. The men she killed were part of the group that had taken him from her. The men they were going to face to save the elven crew would also be part of that group.

"Can you do that?" Marek took a step toward her again.

Raven realized he must have been talking to her. She took another step away from him, maintaining her boundary. "Do what?"

"I need you to enter the city. I need you to stay

hidden and be ready to back me up when they bring the crew out to the gallows. Can you do that?"

"I can. I need to gather my things first."

"Fine. Just make sure you're there. We don't have much time." His voice had a hint of an impatient growl to it now. "And try not to kill anyone else. Just disable them enough for me to get the crew out."

Raven answered with a curt nod and started to walk away.

Phendaril called after her, "What's your name?"

"You haven't earned that yet," she snapped back, and broke into a jog.

aven crouched in one of the trees near the fence. When the time was right, a moment she hoped she would recognize, she would drop down one branch lower and head over the fence. She watched, for now, waiting for the crew to be brought out into the square where the gallows were.

She had snuck back to Eamon's home and wept while she broke into the locked chest under his bed. A small pouch of coins was tucked in with a woman's necklace, a worn dress, and a pair of well-made gloves. There was also a set of child's shoes. All part of a story of his past she would never know, though she could make some guesses. A letter in elven signed by him referred to the recipient as his beloved wife and mentioned their son. Perhaps they were dead now, or there had been some other parting of ways. She suspected the former, given that the letter he had written to her resided among his things. These items had been special to him, but they were not part of how she had known him in their brief time together. She left everything but the money and the gloves.

The gloves she put on. They were a decent fit and would hide the silver sheen on her nails. The coin she took to the house of the crippled widow he had been helping. It was in this same part of town, so she deemed it safe enough to make the quick visit. She had no way to safely reach the family he had been caring for in the time she had. Instead, she hid her face and asked the elf to share the coin with that family if she would. After that, it was up to the elven widow's generosity or lack thereof to decide. She hadn't asked any questions, allowing Raven to dart away without another word. When those things were done, Raven climbed out of the town and collected her belongings.

The sun was sinking, falling slowly down upon the trees across the river. Phendaril's group would make their way to the ship around the far side of town and through the water. At least, that's how she would get there. She expected to be afraid, but she wasn't. Her heart didn't race the way it used to before a challenging hunt. She was calm, cold, and empty. The tears were gone now, and her feelings drained out with them, leaving her too emotionally exhausted to care. That was good, though. She had nothing to distract her from the task at hand.

Then she saw them. A line of nine elves being led to the square where the gallows waited. At least three looked like they had been considerably roughed up during their stay. The one in the front, the ship's captain, she suspected, required guiding because his eyes were swollen almost shut. He would be a problem during their flight to the river. The one behind him had been roughed up almost as badly, though she could at least see past her injuries enough to walk independently. The other, fifth in the line, was limping slightly. Another risk to their escape.

Raven dropped to the lower branch and moved further along it, closer to the fence. There were four guards with the line of prisoners. Another three stood around the gallows, and a fourth man watched from one side with a distinct air of authority. She suspected he was the constable.

The guards on the nearest watchtower faced inward, watching the elves being marched out now when they most needed to be paying attention to the fence itself. Raven seized the opportunity, sprinting lightly down the branch and leaping from the end. Her jump took her over the fence and onto the roof of the nearest building. She landed light and crouched low, jumping quickly off one side into the shadow of the structure. From there, she snuck along the wall and climbed onto the low roof of a woodshed tucked against a two-story house. The overhang of the main roof cast the shed in deep shadow. She had a good vantage of the proceedings from there and plenty of concealment with dusk moving in.

She spotted Marek without difficulty. He stood cloaked at the edge of the gathering crowd. While she watched, he started making his way toward the prisoners being walked up. Some of the overwhelmingly human audience shouted racial slurs at the captive elves. The few elves looking on started to back out of the crowd and disappear down the side streets. Raven didn't blame them. This wasn't a safe place for them right now.

Marek got close enough to the prisoners to say something to a few of them. Then one of the guards came up, asking him to step away. Rather than do so, Marek shoved the man, drawing the attention of the other guards. Raven caught a glint of steel in the hands of one of the elves. Marek had managed to slip one of them a dagger.

From that moment, things moved quickly. One of the other guards noticed that same glint of steel and started drawing his sword, striding swiftly toward the prisoners. Raven sighted and let her arrow fly. The guard twisted, grabbing at the shaft suddenly protruding from his upper arm. The crowd panicked, onlookers now crying out and scurrying to get away as some of the other guards drew their weapons.

The elves pulled together for what seemed like mere seconds, then they were running. The guard in the best position to stop them went down with another of Raven's arrows in his thigh. Marek decked the guard he was grappling with across the temple. Then he too bolted.

Raven tossed her bow over her back and leapt up to the rooftop. She made her way from rooftop to rooftop along the line of buildings closer to the water. She could see the elves and Marek running below. The injured female and the male with the limp were making good speed despite their limitations. The captain was struggling, though one of the others was trying to guide him. Both had fallen to the back. Marek sprinted past, not giving them a second glance.

Raven found a quick way down when she got closer to the docks, jumping to the roof of what she suspected was another woodshed. At the end of the dock, the galley was casting off. The name painted near the bow read Syrasenne, the elven word for reclamation. It struck her as rather apropos. The first escapees were almost close enough to jump to the ship. Marek was a few strides ahead of her when she hit the ground, gaining on the elves in front of him. He was enhanced. Like her, he would be able to run faster.

Raven slowed and turned to see where the two in the back were. They were a fair distance behind her, the captain stumbling despite his companion's efforts. Then the elf helping him pitched forward, hitting the ground face first, an arrow in his back.

The captain cast about with his hands, trying to find help. Raven hesitated. Someone grabbed her arm and started pulling her along.

"Run!"

The captain pitched forward, also with an arrow in

his back. Raven did run then. Marek released her arm when she started moving. Ahead of them, four of the elves had made it onto the ship. It was out of jumping range now, so the other three dove from the end of the dock, swimming for it. Raven ran harder, keeping up with Marek, her feet pounding on the rough wood. They were almost to the end.

Then pain exploded through the back of her thigh, and her leg buckled. She tumbled, her shoulder striking the side of the dock. Then she was in the water. Another arrow burst into the water beside her head. She tried to kick to get back to the surface, but her leg didn't want to work for her. Someone else dove in next to her and grabbed under her arms. The sudden rough embrace squeezed her chest, and the air was pressed from her lungs. Her body reflexively gasped for air, drawing in water.

Hands dragged at her. She was above the water now. There was another blast of pain as her shin hit something hard. Then she was on her hands and knees, throwing up river water on the ship's deck while pain streaked through the back of her leg. She finally sucked in a breath and couldn't stop coughing for several seconds. When the violent coughing fit finally ended, she sagged over onto her side.

Someone started to move her pack and her bow out of the way. Still trying to catch her breath, she grabbed for her things and glared up at whoever was touching them. Marek backed up quickly. Phendaril glanced down at her, and his eyes widened. Then he turned away, his attention engaged in exchanging fire with some archers on the docks. Raven closed her eyes. Her chest constricting so hard it was almost like being underwater again. However they would feel about what she was, it was too late to hide it from them now.

Someone knelt behind her and placed a hand on her

shoulder. She glanced up to see one of the elven males who had arrived with Phendaril.

"This is going to hurt."

She simply nodded. Then she cried out when he yanked the arrow out of her leg. For a few seconds, she thought she might vomit again, but she managed to hold it back until her gut calmed. The pain was worse than any of the many injuries she'd sustained training or hunting with Jaecar. The elf tied something around the wound. Marek had disappeared from her line of sight, but Phendaril returned, lowering his bow. He took a step closer, looking down at her with narrowed eyes.

"Take her below with the other three and have Synal care for that wound."

"You saw that she's–"

Phendaril cut him off. "We'll deal with it later."

The elf nodded and moved to lift her. Raven was in considerable pain, but she was aware enough to recognize she wasn't among friends here. She twisted in his arms to grab her pack and her bow. He managed to lift her then, giving her an exasperated look.

"I'd have brought your things down."

The position he held her in pulled at the wound, and she answered through gritted teeth. "Before or after you dug through them?"

He didn't try to deny it.

She yearned to pull out Jaecar's documents and see if the treated case had kept them safe in the water. With the elves and Marek there, it would have to wait.

He took her below deck to a hold crowded with cargo. The two roughed-up prisoners were there, along with a third whose arm had been grazed by an arrow. A fourth, a female she suspected was Synal, was tending the injury. Her long flaxen hair was worked into a braid wound on the back of her head to keep it contained. She glanced over at them, giving a slight start when she met

Raven's eyes.

"She took an arrow to the back of the leg," the elf holding her explained.

"Put her there," Synal gestured to a spot slightly away from the other three.

"She's–"

Synal cut him off. "I have eyes, Leral. Put her down."

He did as she ordered, setting Raven down a little more abruptly than necessary before heading back up the stairs. She watched Synal finish cleaning and bandaging the arm wound. The elven healer worked with her jaw clenched. Her eyes were moist, tears on the verge of spilling over. The two whose injuries occurred in the prison were both leaned back against the crates, their eyes closed. Both had clear tracks of tears down their dirty cheeks.

When she was done, Synal turned to Raven, who felt faint before the continuing onslaught of pain in her leg. "We'll need to get your pants off and roll you over where I can take a better look at the wound. I can use your cloak to keep you covered." She reached for a flask. "This will help with the pain."

She held the flask out to Raven, who accepted it with considerable skepticism.

"Go on," Synal encouraged as she turned to gather the medical supplies and bring them closer.

Raven took a swig of the substance, bracing for something terrible. To her surprise, it had a hint of lavender, the faint earthy taste of mushroom, and a slight burn of alcohol. Overall, it wasn't that bad. She handed it back, and Synal nodded approval.

Raven tried hard not to think of the other three elves in the hold as she and Synal painfully worked her pants off. She turned on her side. Warm blood ran across the back of her leg when Synal began to inspect the wound, the coppery scent cutting through the smell of the escaped prisoners. She ground her teeth and clenched her fists, determined to bear the pain in silence.

"It's a deep wound, but you're lucky. Being elven and Silverblood, you should heal very quickly. That tincture should be starting to help with the pain, so I'll get this cleaned up and properly bandaged. Then you can get some rest."

"I know some of you didn't reach the ship," Raven said, trying not to focus on the pain, "I'm sorry. I wish we could have–"

"Hush." The tightness in Synal's voice said she was struggling with tears. "We were all heading for our ends back there. If the two of you hadn't been willing to help, I'm not sure any of us would be here right now."

Raven said nothing. She had assumed Phendaril would have found another way to save them. With only himself and three other elves to do so, maybe he wouldn't have.

As Synal worked, the pain became less severe. A sense of calm stole over Raven, attesting to the strength of the tincture. It was also making her exceptionally sleepy. When the elven healer finished and secured the bandage, Raven mumbled a slurred thank you.

"You're still awake?" Synal sounded a little surprised. "You must have quite the constitution to fight that tincture. I've never worked on your kind before, though. Maybe that's expected."

A burst of panic pushed back against the lull of the drug. Raven reached for her pack and bow, drawing them closer to her.

Synal clucked softly at her. "You saved my life and that of many of my companions. I won't allow a soul to touch your things while you rest. Besides, it will take a couple of days to get to Amberwood going against the current. You'll have to sleep eventually. I'll get someone to help me move you to a bed."

Raven was distantly aware of her leaving. She partially woke when someone picked her up and took her back in the hold to lay her on a rough cot. Her eyes wouldn't stay open.

"If you touch her things, I'll remove your fingers one at a time," Synal warned someone, and her tone made Raven believe she meant every word.

Though she tried hard to open her eyes then, the tincture was in control. It drew her weary heart and exhausted body down into a deep slumber.

CHAPTER THIRTEEN

Raven's father took her small bow and smiled down at her. "You did well today."

She kicked at a stick in her path. "I didn't get anything, and I scared away the doe you were going to shoot."

He shifted the bow to his other hand, holding it along with his. "You're only eight, Raven, don't be so hard on yourself. You tracked that deer better than I could at twice your age. This bow and hunting are both new to you. By this time next year, you'll be bringing home all of our meals, and I can sit before the fire with my feet up on these cold winter mornings."

Though she tried to hang on to her discontent, his words teased a smile out of her. "I'm still going to expect you to help," she declared.

His crooked grin was full of fond teasing. "We'll see."

The small paddock alongside the house came into view through the trees with its lean-to-style shelter that stood open on three sides for the two milking goats they kept. Beyond that, like the paddock and lean-to, the house was so covered with living mosses and other greenery her mother somehow kept alive that it was typically hard to pick out of the surrounding forest. This time of year, the woodpile stacked up next to the house made it a little easier to see that someone lived here.

The goats were shifting about, more active than usual.

They moved back and forth a few times, then stopped, peering into the thick woods on the east side of the house. Her father placed a hand on her shoulder and slowed his walk, dragging her pace down as well. She glanced up at him, unease prickling her skin at the way he stared into those woods, eyes searching for anything amiss.

There was a hiss and thwack as a crossbow bolt struck his left shoulder. He cried out, sinking halfway to one knee. The bows dropped from his other hand as he grabbed for the wounded shoulder. A man stepped out of the woods behind them and struck him across the head. The blow knocked him over on his hands and knees. Then the injured arm gave out, and he toppled to the ground. Two more men stepped out of the trees nearer the house.

The man who had struck her father glared down at Raven. His dark eyes bored into her from under thick, angry brows. "Half-breed mongrel," he snarled.

"Run!" Her father shouted.

The man grabbed a fistful of her shirt and started to lift her. Her father drew the dagger he carried at his belt and swiped out. The man jumped back in time to avoid the attack, still holding Raven. He swore and kicked her father in the ribs hard enough that he curled in on himself, groaning, his eyes glazing over with pain. Raven grabbed the man's wrist and pulled herself close enough to bite him, tasting his blood in her mouth. With a shout, he threw her down. She jumped to her feet and ran.

She ran as hard and fast as she could, following landmarks that would take her to Jaecar's keep. She was only eight, though. Her legs weren't long enough to carry her as far and fast as she needed them to, and the keep was a fair distance away through dense woods, but it was the only place she could go for help. When she got to the keep, she stumbled over the rubble of the collapsed courtyard wall, gasping for breath. She didn't bother knocking on the keep door. Instead, she burst in, surprising Jaecar, who was cutting up some meat for a meal. Tears were pouring down her cheeks, and she could barely speak through her desperate gasping. She had to, though. She had to find her voice. This time, she would save them.

"Men," was all she could manage to say.

It was enough. Jaecar threw down his cutting knife and stormed toward her. The towering warrior lifted her in one arm and grabbed his sword with the other hand as he rushed through the door. His long strides were much more efficient than hers had been, consuming the ground as he ran them back toward the house. Still, it wasn't close, and it took time. Too much time, considering how long it took her to reach him, struggling through the woods on short legs.

When they were close to the house, cruel laughter reached their ears along with muffled screams. The stench of something burning wafted through the trees. Jaecar set Raven down. He placed a hand on her chest and met her eyes.

"Wait here," he whispered.

He didn't wait for a response, turning to start a careful approach. Raven waited a moment. She heard the familiar sound of an arrow striking flesh and a muffled feminine scream. Part of her wanted nothing more than to run away, but she couldn't. Tears poured down her cheeks again and her trembling legs, still weary from her long run, threatened not to hold her up as she followed Jaecar.

For a moment, the scene in the paddock wasn't real. It was something from a nightmare. A nightmare she'd had a thousand times. Something she could wake up from, and they would all be fine.

Oddly, she noticed the goats first. Each laying dead in the paddock with their throats cut, blood soaking the ground around them. Then the man with the angry brows stood at the edge of the paddock leveling a bow, her father's bow, and let an arrow fly. Her gaze followed the arrow *until it sank into the thigh of the elven female bound to one of the front two posts of the lean-to. The elf screamed, the sound muffled by the gag tied in her mouth. Two more arrows stuck out of her other thigh, blood soaking all the way down the leg of her pants, and another stuck out of her shoulder in about the same spot the crossbow bolt had struck Raven's father. The female sagged against her bonds, unable to hold herself up anymore.*

The female. Her mother.

And her father? Tied to the post closer to the house was another familiar figure. Two more strange men were throwing sticks and chunks of wood from their woodpile into the fire that burned at his feet and up his legs and torso. His clothes were all on fire, and the flame was licking up toward his hair. He writhed against his bonds, his screams muffled by a gag in his mouth.

Raven wanted to scream, but she couldn't breathe.

Then Jaecar surged out. Moving like a deadly wildcat, he sprang over the paddock fence and brought his sword around into the thigh of the man wielding her father's bow. As the man fell, his look of surprise twisted something black in Raven's gut. Hatred boiled up in her, followed by a sick satisfaction when Jaecar sidestepped and drove his blade through the back of the falling man.

The other two turned around at their companion's choking cry. Both had set their weapons aside to tend the fire. Now they scrambled to get clear of Jaecar's fury.

Raven didn't watch to see what happened. She ran to her mother and started working desperately at the knots that bound her. She was sobbing hard enough now she could barely see what she was doing and couldn't catch her breath.

Then Jaecar was there, cutting through the ropes with a dagger. He lowered her mother to the ground and pulled the gag out of her mouth.

Her voice was weak when she spoke. "Arek?"

Jaecar said nothing. He glanced to one side. Raven

followed his glance and saw her father lying on the ground. His clothes were burned off, along with much of his skin. A low wheezing sound came from him. In the time it had taken Jaecar to kill the other two men and put out the fire, it had burned away his hair. The skin of his face was so burned she could hardly recognize him.

A sob escaped her mother. She reached for Raven. Blood ran from her wounds. So much blood. Raven grabbed her hand and held it, terrified by the fact that her mother's grip was weaker than her own.

"I'm sorry. We can't keep you safe anymore, my little Raven," her mother murmured. Then something changed in her expression. "Are they dead?" she asked, her voice weaker than it had been mere seconds ago.

Raven nodded, unable to find her voice.

"Dead or dying," Jaecar confirmed.

Behind Raven, she could hear her father's wheezing breaths coming slower and weaker. The stink of charred flesh and the thick, cloying stench of blood closed around her, suffocating her. Someone else nearby was groaning. She hoped they were suffering.

"So many spirits to choose from." Her mother managed a faint smile, then began speaking under her breath in a language Raven didn't recognize.

Confusion rattled her, and though it didn't seem possible, Raven began to cry harder. Behind her, she no longer heard her father breathing. Jaecar was silent. The only sounds were those of her mother's strange words contrasted by the appallingly normal sounds of birdsong and a breeze whispering through the foliage.

As Raven watched, her mother's eyes turned black, then silver spread out from the pupils until her irises shone with a metallic gleam. When they were entirely silver, the chanting stopped. Her eyes closed, and the last breath gasped from her lungs. Her hand fell limp and heavy in Raven's grip.

Then there was pain, and Raven screamed.

•

Raven struggled up from her tormented sleep. Someone was shaking her arm. The ground beneath her was unsteady. The subtle shifting sent a wave of nausea through her. Pain throbbed in the back of her leg, bringing up the memories of running from the town and being shot. They hadn't let her drown but had they known what she was at the time, they might have. They did know now, didn't they? At least they hadn't thrown her overboard in her sleep.

"You were having a nightmare," a woman's voice said.

Not a nightmare, a memory worse than any nightmare. She opened her eyes to see an elven female sitting on a cot across from her in the cramped hold. Bruises and cuts covered her face. One of the three elves who had been roughed up by the town guards in captivity. She tilted her head at Raven, narrowing her eyes a little.

"They said you were a Silverblood, but I didn't quite believe it until this moment, looking into your eyes. I saw your hair and nails while you were sleeping, but I could have blamed that on poor lighting down here. Your eyes, though..." She shook her head then, and a slight flush colored the little skin that wasn't darkened with bruising, almost as if she just realized she was speaking out loud. "Apologies. You and the other Silverblood helped save us. You've earned your place on this galley. I'm Narene."

Raven pushed herself upright. "Raven."

"Raven." Narene smiled to herself. "Not a typical elven name, but I suppose it suits you."

She glanced away, hiding the tears that stung her eyes as she recalled how similarly Eamon had reacted to her name.

There were footsteps above them, then two pairs of feet in different styles of boots started down the stairs. Phendaril and Marek entered the hold, both coming to a stop at the foot of the cots where there was a little more room to stand. Raven was still trying to shake off the ill feeling from her dream. She hadn't relived that day so vividly in her dreams in some time. It brought back the feelings of vulnerability and helplessness she had felt as a child. She hated it.

Marek was staring intently at her, and she fought the urge to put on her cloak. It was too late to hide. She glanced to the side where her things were tucked along the edge of the cot against the ship's hull. As far as she could tell, Synal had kept her word.

"Narene," Phendaril inclined his head to the elven female, "if you're well enough, could you take over command of the ship?"

"Of course." Narene gave him a nod before getting up from the cot and slipping out between the two. Something that might have been pity showed in the quick glance she cast back at Raven before disappearing up the stairs.

Phendaril stayed where he was, leaning against the hull in the shadows while Marek walked closer. He stopped, staring down at her in the shifting lantern light. Raven made herself meet his eyes, trying to ignore how desperately she wanted to crawl under the blanket or her cloak. The average person she would assume she could take in a fight. These two were different. She had seen both of them fight. Phendaril was elven, blessed with a speed and agility that exceeded most humans, and he had shown that he could handle a blade. Marek had the enhanced abilities of a Silverblood, and she didn't doubt he had combat experience and training.

"More than one person died to make you," Marek stated, his tone flat and cold, almost angry.

Raven focused on her breathing. There was grain in some of these crates. She could smell it and many other things she couldn't quite identify by scent. Supplies for Amberwood.

What was Amberwood? Where was Amberwood? Would she make it that far?

She narrowed her eyes at him. "I want my dagger back."

Phendaril, who had been using a knife to clean his nails, glanced over at them, curiosity clear in his gaze.

"It *was* you," Marek said. "I thought there was something familiar about you back in the woods. The way you hid so comfortably in that tree, the sound of your breathing."

He sat on the other cot, and she slid back closer to the hull, placing her hand next to the hilt of her sword. A quick glance at Phendaril, who narrowed his eyes, told her the elf had noticed the weapon there even if Marek had not. Marek drew her dagger from his belt and held it out in front of him, not offering it to her but merely showing it. Phendaril took a few steps closer, a new intensity in his gaze when he peered down at the weapon.

"As I recall, you left it behind," Marek said, his frosty look daring her to argue with him.

"In the side of the beast you tricked me into fighting," she countered, accepting his dare. If she was going to die at their hands for what she was, she refused to do it cowering.

"I recognize that work." Phendaril gave her a suspicious look. "This blade must have been expensive."

"It was a gift." She drew out the sword. "Part of a matched set."

Phendaril held his hands out, palms up, a reverence in his gaze she knew did not extend to her as the weapon's owner. He at least had the decency to meet her eyes and ask. "May I?"

A vehement no sat silent upon her lips.

Phendaril's people, at least Synal and Narene, had been nice enough to her. They seemed to feel they owed her something. Maybe she could leverage that if she built more goodwill with them. She nodded and relinquished the weapon to him, her gut clenching as it left her hands. The last thing Jaecar had given her, now in the hands of someone who could quickly turn out to be her enemy.

He examined the weapon closely, running a finger over the engravings in the upper part of the blade and inspecting every aspect of the hilt. He offered it back to her as respectfully as she had handed it to him. The respect was for the weapon. Of that, she had no doubt, but she could appreciate that he treated it so. Then he glanced down at the dagger in Marek's hands.

"I know the elven swordsmith who made these. It would be a shame to separate such a perfectly matched set."

Marek frowned. "Her existence is a crime against Brotherhood law."

Something flashed in Phendaril's eyes that made Raven inch back a little. "Her existence also betrays a lie told by your Brotherhood. Several lies, in fact. She may be in the wrong here, but I'm not convinced she's the only one who is. You both helped free my companions, so I suggest we call a truce as long as you are on our ship. We can deal with these things when we reach Amberwood."

The two stared at one another. For several seconds, Raven was convinced they would cross blades right there in the cramped hold of the galley. Then Marek broke eye contact and handed her the dagger. She took it quickly, not willing to chance him changing his mind. Phendaril gave a slight nod, and she was briefly inclined to thank him, but something in his eyes convinced her to keep her gratitude to herself.

"Some of my crew could use a bit of rest." He looked down at her, his gaze settling on the dagger and sword for a few seconds. "If you think you can handle it, I'll have someone come down and help you up to the main deck so they can use the cots for a while."

Raven's stomach turned. Both he and Marek were more than capable of assisting her up top. That neither of them seemed willing to do so told her a great deal about what they thought of her. She didn't look at him when she answered, swallowing back the urge to spit at him.

"I can manage."

When someone came to help her up top, she took her things with her and found a quiet spot near the deck railing to sit and watch the river go by.

The journey up the river took only two days, though it felt like more, trapped on the galley with a crew of strangers. Narene told her they could cover the same distance in about half the time, going the other direction. Though it looked calm, the current was strong enough to make traveling against it tedious, especially in spring when snowmelt made the river stronger and faster. After the encounter in the hold, Raven avoided speaking to anyone on the galley more than necessary. Synal insisted that she get plenty of rest to heal her wounds. She took advantage of those orders as much as she could, and the injury did start to close as quickly as the elven healer said it would.

Late afternoon of the second day, they pulled up to a dock that had recently been rebuilt, judging by the freshness of the wood.

Synal walked up next to her and said softly, "Welcome to Amberwood."

Karsima stood at the entrance to her hut and watched the ship being secured at the dock. There were strangers on board. Two different cloaked figures, one masculine and one feminine in build. The man wore the colors of the Brotherhood. The woman appeared to be limping, though she jerked away from Jael when he reached out to offer help coming down the plank. Phendaril stood on the dock with his arms crossed, watching them both like a jailer might watch prisoners he expected to have problems with. Narene followed the two down. Her face looked bruised and slightly misshapen from this distance.

"Jenner, send Phendaril up here. Make sure he brings the captain, the first mate, and the two strangers. I want a report on how things went in Manderly, and I would rather like to know who the strays are that my abused-looking crew brought home with them."

"Yes, milady." He started walking toward the docks.

Karsima turned back into the hut and went about making sure it looked more like a council chamber and a little less like a bedroom. She threw scattered clothes behind a privacy partition that hid her bed mostly from view. An addition made yesterday morning. Timely, it seemed. As a finishing touch, she lit a few more candles and pulled the curtains back from the windows. The fading late afternoon light would help her get a better look at the strangers and at Narene's injuries.

Several minutes later, Jenner ducked back in. "They're here, milady."

She gave him a nod as she moved to her comfortable spot behind the map table. Standing behind an array of spread-out maps made her feel more official. "Thank you, Jenner. They can come in."

He opened the curtain over the doorway and stepped back to allow them in. A wide variety of expletives rushed to her lips when Narene walked in at the head of the group, though she let them die there unspoken. The elven woman's face was much worse up close. She had taken a considerable beating at someone's hands. Not the kind of beating one got in a brawl, either. It was more of the sort one got when they couldn't fight back.

Anger surged in Karsima, but she tamped it down. She had a responsibility to keep a level head. The man who followed Narene in drew his hood back as he entered. When she met those silver eyes, a chill swept through her, but she made herself nod a calm and respectful greeting. He moved to stand on the far side of Narene, angling his stance to watch the cloaked female as she limped inside. She kept her gaze lowered, and her hood pulled too far forward for Karsima to see anything of her features.

When Phendaril walked in next, her heart sank. She met his eyes. "Captain Kovel?"

Phendaril shook his head. "The constable took our presence in the woods as proof of their guilt. He sent his men after us and was going to have the crew hung. The Silverbloods helped us free them and take the ship, but we lost Kovel and two others."

She would ask later who the two others were. She didn't have the heart to talk about it now. Besides, something else he had said caught her attention. He had said "Silverbloods," suggesting that more than one of them was involved in the rescue. She looked to the man, who inclined his head slightly.

"Silverblood Adept Marek, milady," he offered before she could ask, his attention still more on the cloaked figure than on her.

Karsima turned to the female. "And you are?"

She thought she noticed a faint tremble in those pale hands as the female reached up to draw back her hood. The reason why was immediately apparent. She had the same silver irises as Marek. Her long black hair also had a silver sheen, as did her fingernails. She was a Silverblood like Marek, only for her, that fact put her in considerable danger. According to the Brotherhood, her existence wasn't just forbidden; it was impossible. No wonder Marek couldn't keep his eyes off her.

"You're a Silverblood?" Karsima asked, needing to hear her confirm it no matter how obvious it was.

The female nodded. "Raven." She glanced at Marek and quickly added, "milady."

"And an elven woman," Karsima added, not asking so much as observing the peculiarity of the combination.

"Half-elven." Phendaril's harsh correction drew everyone's attention to him.

"How can you tell?" Marek asked.

The hint of fascination in Marek's tone told Karsima he didn't know much about this anomalous female in the hut with them, but he wanted to learn more. It made her worry for Raven. That was a peculiar thing unto itself. The half-elf was a stranger, but the tremble in her hands, the pallor of her skin, and the slight backward lean to her posture made it clear she wanted nothing more than to bolt back out the door. She was plainly terrified. Something in those strangely colored eyes spoke of a deep pain in her that had naught to do with physical injuries. It was almost impossible not to pity her.

Phendaril met Raven's eyes as he answered Marek's question, his unforgiving gaze honed in steel. "Her features are too beautiful to be human and too soft to be elven."

If she listened only to the words, it almost sounded like a compliment, but she could tell by his tone that he didn't mean it that way. His callousness surprised her. He was usually more sympathetic to half-breeds, who were often the product of rape. Especially given that he had lost someone dear to him because of such a crime. Then again, this lack of compassion she saw in him might have something to do with the death required to make someone a Silverblood. However this female became remade, someone else had to die to make it happen.

Raven leaned away from Phendaril and lowered her gaze. The tremble in her hands was more apparent now. She wasn't Karsima's responsibility. In fact, she was a liability to herself and anyone around her, especially now that the Brotherhood knew she existed. Or at least one of them did, which meant the rest would soon enough. Still, as long as she was in Amberwood, Karsima couldn't ignore her need.

"Captain Narene." The elven first mate quickly met her eyes, lifting her head slightly at the new title. Karsima struggled not to flinch when facing that badly bruised countenance again. "Go have your injuries seen to. We'll discuss your ship and crew later. Though you may wish to name your second and put them in charge of unloading."

"Yes, milady." She offered an abbreviated bow before leaving the hut.

Karsima watched her leave. Milady was spreading like a plague now. With Marek there, she was almost glad of it. He might be a little more manageable if he viewed her as an authority figure. "Adept Marek, if you aren't in a hurry to move on, I have several uses for someone of your skills. With compensation, of course." Not that she wanted to keep his kind around, but she did have a beast-infested land to clean up, and Silverbloods were renowned for their fighting skills. That was why they were often hired for such jobs, despite their distasteful origins.

He responded with a nod. "I'm open to discussing it."

"Good." She glanced at Phendaril, still mystified by the irritable tension overshadowing her friend's features. "Phendaril, don't go far. I want a full accounting of what happened in Manderly, but first, I would like a few minutes alone with Raven."

No one moved. Karsima cast a firm look at Marek, then a slightly more scathing one at Phendaril. Considering they had discussed the importance of him acknowledging her authority publicly, there was little excuse for him defying it now.

"By alone, I meant just the two of us." The clarification should not have been necessary, but she was willing to say it in as many ways as she had to in order to drive her point home.

This time, Phendaril walked as far as the door, but he stopped next to it, his unyielding gaze focused on Marek now. The adept turned his full attention to Karsima for the first time since entering the building. The Brotherhood had a certain autonomy, and a degree of authority was granted to its members. In Habarin especially, their laws were integrated into the kingdom's laws, and those who violated them were handed over to the Brotherhood for punishment. In Andioch, they had less authority but were still given free rein to deal with those who violated their laws. Here, in the swath of neutral land between the two kingdoms, those things shouldn't matter as much. Still, if he chose to call upon the status of his title and affiliation, she wasn't sure they would get far fighting him on it.

Raven looked like a fox caught between two wolves with the two males standing to either side of her. Karsima didn't doubt that she could use the sword and bow she carried. However, she was still one female, and whatever enhancements the magic gave her wouldn't free her from the misery in her eyes. She needed an ally.

Tempering back her own fierce pride, Karsima met Marek's eyes. "Please, Adept Marek, if you wouldn't mind." She gestured toward the door.

For a second, she thought he would continue to ignore her or offer up an argument, but he finally answered with a nod and walked out. Phendaril followed behind him, leaving her alone in the hut with this theoretically impossible creature.

Karsima moved a rock on her desk that weighed down some of the maps sketched by her scouts. Phendaril's scouts, she supposed, since he was the one she'd put in charge of all of that. She pretended interest in them, though she was much more intrigued by the soft exhalation from Raven and the way the tension in her shoulders eased a fraction. She was still far from relaxed, but the absence of the two males appeared to lift a significant burden off her, as Karsima suspected it would. Raven shifted her stance, wincing when her injured leg took more of her weight for a second.

"I have trouble believing you did this to yourself."

Raven looked puzzled for a moment, then she said, "I took an arrow in the leg while running to the galley."

Karsima struggled to keep from chuckling at that. "Not the injury."

There was a moment more of confusion, then Raven flushed brightly. "No. I didn't choose to become a Silverblood."

"I expected as much. You helped rescue my ship and my friends even though we're all strangers to you. How did you become involved in this?"

"A..." She paused, looking like she couldn't figure out the right word. Just as Karsima considered trying to prompt her, Raven decided and continued. "A friend agreed to help Phendaril." Her voice cracked a little on the word friend.

The young female was fond of short, unrevealing answers. "Did this friend stay behind?"

Moisture rose in Raven's eyes, and Karsima's chest tightened in sympathy. The three they had lost obviously weren't the only losses.

"He died when the guards attacked." Her voice cracked again, raw with emotion and the war she was waging trying to control it.

"Where are you planning to go from here?"

Raven's hard swallow and the weighted silence confirmed what Karsima suspected. This young female was alone. Whether she had family somewhere or not, she didn't feel like she had anyone she could go to. It wasn't Karsima's problem. Raven was an unauthorized Silverblood, making her a risk to keep around. Because of Marek, the Brotherhood would know of her existence before long. Karsima could not do much to stop that. Still, she couldn't turn her back on someone obviously lost and in pain.

"I could offer you work here if you're interested."

Raven looked at her then, a flicker of something shining in those silver eyes. Hope perhaps, if she wasn't too deep in her sorrow to feel such a thing.

Encouraged, Karsima continued. "We're trying to reclaim this land. We could use fighters and workers. If you stay, I'll put you to work helping rebuild the town and clean out our infestation of unpleasant creatures, assuming you can use that bow and blade."

"I can," Raven answered. "What about Marek?"

There was a lot of meaning behind that inquiry.

Unfortunately, she couldn't give the young half-elf the answer she wanted. "I'll see what I can do about him, but ultimately he's not my subject to command. I assume, given your injury, that you met Synal?"

Raven nodded.

"You should be able to find her in the big building across from here. That's our temporary healer's building. It has some rooms in the back that we set up as living quarters. She can find you a spot with them for now. Rest that leg. I'll have work for you soon."

Raven nodded again and turned toward the door, then hesitated, glancing back. "Thank you, milady."

Karsima answered with a nod of her own and watched her leave. She got less than a minute of peace before Phendaril swept back through the curtain. She had expected as much. He would have been watching for Raven's departure. He strode toward the map table like he meant to plow through it.

"I don't recall asking for you to return yet," Karsima stated bluntly, her irritation rising in response to the tension coming from him.

"What are you doing?"

"Helping someone in need. In this case, I'm also helping our cause in the process." Karsima met his dark glower. "What are you doing?"

"She's a Silverblood. You saw the hair and the nails, not to mention the intensity of the silver in her eyes. More than one person died to make her what she is."

"What about her bothers you so much? Yes, she is a Silverblood, and it's painfully clear she didn't make herself that way. You should have been able to see that on your own if you weren't busy being so unusually obtuse." She barreled past his scowl. "Given how young she is, I would venture that she hasn't been this way for long. Her life can't be easy. Despite that and the loss of her friend, she chose to help us. I intend to repay that as best I can before Marek hauls her off to the Brotherhood to be executed."

Phendaril stared at her for a few seconds in silence. His expression and the rigidness in his posture relaxed a fraction. He didn't have the decency to look apologetic or even properly chastised, which caused an itch of irritation to form in the tightening space between her shoulder blades. She did her best to ignore it.

He glanced toward the door as if he could still see the young half-elven woman through it. "If it makes you feel better, Marek appears inclined to entertain whatever offer of work you mean to give him."

"Good," she snapped, recognizing the irony of the fact that she was now the one in the worse mood. "In a few days, with the help of two Silverbloods, we should be able to get back into the upper residential quarter of the old town. Based on your last few scouting missions, it sounds like the buildings there are intact enough that we can probably start using several of them while we rebuild."

"Any new threats reported in the area?"

"No. Nothing new. As though fell rats the size of large dogs and an ill-tempered dire bear holed up in the old tavern aren't enough." She found herself gazing at the door. "What was he to her, the man who died in the guard attack?"

"He was elven. His name was Eamon," Phendaril offered, his voice taking on a tone of respect and remorse now. "I don't know. More than just a friend, I think."

She smiled gently at the return of the friend she had known most of her life. She started over to where she kept a few bottles of mead and a couple of mugs to take the pressure off those more sensitive conversations. "Sit down and have a drink with me. Tell me what happened in Manderly."

Over the next couple of days, Raven spent much of her time hiding in the healer's quarters. The first moment she had any privacy, she finally pulled out the case. She was relieved to find Jaecar's documents undamaged by her fall in the river. She tucked her things away after that and snuck out to wander into the woods around the camp several times when she knew Marek was busy. Her leg was recovering quickly, and the walks were good for it. No one among the others bothered her, though many of them did give her wary glances. Word of her unusual nature had already permeated the camp.

Synal was perceptive and quickly became an ally. She would drop little side comments to let Raven know when Marek was occupied with other things, such as meeting with Karsima, to help her slip out for walks. The adept did come asking about her a couple of times, but Synal and the other healers were masters at concocting reasons for her to be unavailable.

The camp was big and smelled perpetually of campfires and cooking food. It almost seemed like as many people as there had been in all Manderly. Although, she had never seen all the residents of the river town out at one time. There were only a few usable buildings here, so most of the populace was out in the open more often than not. There were children as well, though not many. The most remarkable thing was that the elves and humans worked peacefully together on the myriad tasks before them with no apparent disparity in treatment.

Those tasks covered everything from caring for the small collection of livestock to mending clothes or armor, sorting through recently arrived supplies, and walking circuits around the perimeters to watch hostile beasts. Everyone appeared to have something to do except her, though Karsima's words suggested that would change soon. Raven hadn't considered asking if she would be paid for her services. Marek undoubtedly would be. Jaecar always told her the Brotherhood warriors were little more than fancy mercenaries. She held those words close. It made him seem a tiny bit less intimidating.

On the morning of the third day, she woke to a summons from Karsima. Jenner stated expressly that the town constable wanted her to have a good meal before coming. Since they always had injuries to care for, the healers were brought food at regular intervals. At Synal's encouragement, Raven took advantage of the morning delivery, eating a little faster than usual. The summons meant, she hoped, that she would finally have something worthwhile to do. A job would allow her to make use of her time and get a break from the suspicious glances and unspoken questions.

"That leg could use a little more rest. Don't let Karsima send you on some crazy hunt where you'll hurt yourself," Synal warned as Raven headed for the door with her sword and bow.

Raven nodded and gave a quick wave before hurrying out.

Synal seemed kind and understanding. Like Eamon. It was a good reason to avoid getting to know her too well. She didn't think her heart could take that pain again. Eamon had not been in her life long, but he had become, in those few days, her first friend and her first kiss. At least she didn't have to worry about losing those things again. They were already gone. However, there were plenty of other things she could lose if she let herself have them.

Her leg still hurt some when she pushed it, but it was healed enough she wasn't going to let it stop her from doing something if Karsima had a job for her. She needed this. She needed someone to tell her to go hunt dinner or check the noises near the north wall. The things Jaecar had asked her to do almost daily kept her from despising her isolation any more than she did. On the days he didn't have her completing tasks, he drilled her on her skills or practiced with her.

Outside, she spotted Marek standing near a rough-made open shed that served as a makeshift armory for the camp. He noticed her at the same time and inclined his head slightly as if they were on civil terms. As though he didn't believe her to be a freak that shouldn't exist. She declined to respond, sweeping her gaze past him to spot Phendaril a little farther to the right, smirking at their one-sided exchange. Raven's attention caught upon him for several seconds, observing how the morning sunlight brought out the deep red tones in his long dark hair. She had never seen hair that color. Then again, the number of humans and elves she had seen in the flesh over the last week had increased dramatically from the previous twenty-two years. As a result, there were many things she was seeing now for the first time.

Phendaril raised an eyebrow at her extended look, and she flushed as she glanced away, focusing on Karsima's hut ahead. Jenner opened the curtain to let her in when she approached, refusing to meet her eyes as usual. As much as she hated that, at least she no longer needed to hide within her cloak. They knew what she was here.

Karsima stood in her usual spot behind the desk. Raven wondered if the woman took that position any time she knew someone was coming or if she simply never left the spot. She stopped inside the door, unsure what was expected of her now. Karsima was obviously the leader here. What was the proper etiquette?

"Please, Raven, I'd like to show you something." Karsima motioned her closer, then took a brief moment to bind her thick waves of dark blond hair into a knot on the back of her head.

Raven approached the big table. There were dozens of rough, hand-drawn maps strewn across it. Some of the maps had sketches of various creatures on them. Wolves, bears, and something that looked like a dragon. Others, less artistically inclined, had merely labeled different areas giant wasps, harpies, and so on.

"These are maps of the area our scouts have been putting together as they explore. We're trying to catalog all the hazards and where they're located."

The maps became instantly more interesting. "Why?"

Karsima looked up at her. She brushed an escaped tendril of wavy hair out of her face. Raven met her gaze, envying those beautifully simple blue eyes. Then she realized Karsima was gazing back into her eyes, equally captivated. Raven dropped her attention to the map, catching the other woman's faint smile from the corner of her eye.

"A number of us lived here when we were younger. We grew up in these woods. It was a wonderful community until a couple of lords asserted that they each held a deed to Amberwood and decided to quarrel over who owned the territory. The former Lord Darrenton believed his claim was the legitimate one. Lord Bannerly argued that his was. Obviously, both couldn't be. They could have gone before the kings and had it resolved that way, but they chose a more destructive route.

"Bannerly sent his army up from Chadhurst to occupy the town. When Darrenton found out, he sent his army down from Pellanth to lay siege. The battle quickly turned bloody, and the people who lived here suffered for it. They began to lose their livelihoods and their lives in many cases. By the time Lord Darrenton's men managed to edge their way to victory, large sections of the town had been razed. The carnage lured in enough deadly predators that hunting and farming the surrounding land became too dangerous. Most of those who hadn't died or fled during the fighting left soon after.

"Darrenton made Bannerly renounce his claim to the land. However, the town was so devastated by the time it was over that neither wanted it anymore. Darrenton gave the deed to his eldest and least favored son. That son died in a battle sometime later, I believe. The deed was lost, and the land forgotten." She offered Raven a conspiratorial wink. "At least, it was forgotten by them.

"I was nine when my family fled the fighting. Now, almost twenty years later, I've managed to gather enough of those former inhabitants and some newly interested, adventure-minded folk to try to make something of this place again."

"You gathered everyone here?" Raven was impressed.

"Phendaril helped me track some of those we knew growing up. Everyone we found who was willing to join us reached out to others they knew. Things have a way of growing like that." A distinct hint of pride showed in her smile now.

Raven tensed and glanced toward the door at the sound of footsteps outside. She heard Phendaril's low voice asking if Karsima was still talking to "the half-elf." His tone made it clear that it wasn't a compliment, though it was a little less derisive than the tone he used to say

Silverblood. At least she wasn't alone at the bottom of his regard, though Marek didn't have the misfortune of being a half-breed too.

"Is Phendaril growing impatient?"

The question surprised Raven, and she met the woman's eyes again.

"I know elves and Silverbloods both have exceptional hearing. I can only imagine yours is a little better than either. Besides, Phendaril is itching to get away from the camp, and he's the only one likely to try to interrupt us." She glanced toward the doorway then, her tanned brow furrowing slightly. "With the possible exception of Marek, who doesn't appear to have much concern for etiquette himself."

It dawned on Raven then what this probably meant, and her gut flopped itself into several knots around the remains of her breakfast. "You're sending me out with him?"

"If by him you mean Phendaril, then yes. If by him you mean Marek, well, then also yes." She looked at Raven and chuckled lightly. "Don't panic. There will be others with you, and Phendaril is under strict orders to ensure he and Marek treat you with respect. You're part of the unit today."

Part of the unit? A giddy sensation rose in Raven's gut, threatening to make her smile. She smashed it down with the memory of Eamon lying dead by the waterfall pool. That tactic was a bit too successful, and she had to blink back tears. "What's our job?"

Karsima pressed her lips together for a second, her troubled gaze trying to dig past Raven's careful mask of neutrality. She shook her head slightly and pointed to the center of the map on the top of the pile.

"This is the upper residential area of the old town. The buildings here were built well. Many of them are in good enough shape to use as temporary headquarters and residences while we rebuild. The problem is that the area is infested with fell rats. Big ones. And a dire bear has converted the tavern into his den. If I remember the place right, he has good taste, but we need to get them all out if we're going to move in.

"Phendaril thinks the fell rats can be weeded out significantly from the rooftops. You'll be going with several of our best archers. According to what he told me, you're impressive with a bow. Considering his skill, I'll take that as quite the recommendation." Karsima paused then, and Raven looked up to see a hint of tears in the other woman's eyes. "He told me you took down two guards that were coming up behind him. Thank you for that. I couldn't do this without Phendaril here. He may come across as an ass sometimes, but he is the rock that I lean on."

Raven shifted and turned her attention to the map once more, suspecting that it was unwise to agree too strongly with the ass part of that sentiment. "Are the rooftops safe?"

Karsima allowed her to put them back on track. "Yes. Not all of them, but Phendaril and his scouts have done a fair bit of cautious investigating. They can get the group up on the rooftops. You should be able to take down many of the rats from above. The rest will have to be cleaned out in a sweep from the ground. The bear is a different problem. No arrow is going to take that beast down. I'm trusting the unit to figure that out. My first request is that you all come back alive. My second, if you can do so without failing the first, is to make it possible for us to move into the old town. Do you have any questions?"

"No, milady." A new lightness filled Raven as she spoke the words. Going anywhere with Phendaril and Marek made her uneasy, but this was a job. It was a task to focus on that was solidly within her skill set. This would give her something to think about other than the plans she and Jaecar never got to see through or the possibilities she had missed out on with Eamon.

"Go on then, and good luck." Karsima gestured toward the door with a slight jerk of her head.

The moment Raven stepped through the curtain, Phendaril stood up from where he'd been reclined against the wall alongside the door. He gave her a quick appraising look. "Are you ready?"

She offered him a curt nod.

"Your bow, it's a little long for you."

She fell into step with him as he started to walk toward where Marek and several others waited. Most were elven, though there was one human aside from Marek and one female other than Raven.

"It's fine. I've been using this bow for years. I would think you could appreciate my skill with it if anyone could." She wasn't about to tell him it had been her father's bow. The one he carried the last day of his life when they had gone hunting together. The same bow that had been used to shoot her mother. If she used this bow until the day she died, maybe she could eliminate that stain from its history.

She expected a glare or at least some kind of argument, but the sidelong glance she got held something more akin to approval. His words, however, were not as appreciative.

"Just make sure that wasn't a fortunate accident."

Raven scowled. "Unfortunate would be more like it."

His laugh caught her by surprise. She might have questioned it, but they were joining up with the others now. Marek approached her, a hint of something predatory in his stare, though he simply stood silent next to her when Phendaril turned to look at them all. The elven leader's regard lingered a moment longer on the two of them, but he swept in all of them with his gaze once he started to speak.

"This is a task many of us have been eager to take on. It will mean a chance to get a real foothold in the area and start rebuilding the town. The fell rats there are some of the biggest I've seen, but they're going to be easy next to that old beast living in the tavern. It shouldn't take us more than an hour to get there if we keep up a good pace." His gaze locked on her then. "Is your leg up to this, Raven?"

Her cheeks warmed at being singled out. She met his eyes only because it made it easier to ignore the others looking at her.

"I'll be fine."

"I suppose you are a Silverblood." A touch of venom laced his tone when he spoke the title, and Marek stiffened slightly beside her.

Phendaril let her gaze go then and focused his attention on a couple of the others. "We'll be going up on the rooftops when we get there. Some of those rooftops haven't aged well. I need you to follow my directions when we're up top. I don't want to lose anyone to an easily avoidable accident. If you have any issue with following me, I suggest you stay here." Now his gaze flickered to Marek.

When the adept offered no response, Phendaril gave a slight nod and turned away. "Let's get going then."

CHAPTER SIXTEEN

The jog they maintained for most of the trip was more painful than Raven expected it to be. She refused to complain. This was her chance to prove that she was valuable. She wasn't sure why it was so important to her to do so. She owed them nothing. They didn't owe her anything either. They had risked themselves to pull her from the water when she took the arrow in her leg and tended the wound. She didn't know who made the call to save her then or who was involved in the rescue. Still, since she suffered that injury rescuing their crew and protected Phendaril in the woods, she didn't owe them a thing at this point.

She wasn't sure if her goal was to try to convince them to let her stay. A few, mostly Narene, Synal, and Karsima, had been nice enough to her. Some were not as kind, primarily Marek and Phendaril. The rest seemed inclined to simply avoid or ignore her. That could change over time. It might be possible to carve out a place for herself here, given how much help they needed. Although, that would require convincing Marek not to drag her off to the Brotherhood to be punished for her involuntary crime.

She glanced over at the Silverblood warrior. As if aware of her attention, the rugged adept looked at her and offered an enigmatic smile. Raven focused forward again, her gaze coming to rest on Phendaril's back. It was hard not to notice the elegant elven bow he carried or the lean, muscular build designed for speed and agility. Her face warmed, and she turned her attention to keeping her strides even to hide the pain each step caused her.

Maybe it wasn't them she was trying to convince. Maybe she needed to prove to herself that she deserved a place in their world. What would it take for her to believe that?

For a time, the land they traversed appeared to be old farmland once carved out of the forest, now gradually being reclaimed. Barns and houses, many collapsed or collapsing, were overrun with vegetation. Several had trees growing up through them. The trees here were primarily young, with a few old giants interspersed among them that must have been spared in the initial clearing.

The young forest smelled vibrant and healthy. Not the same as the forest she had grown up in, but similar enough that the scents and sounds surrounding them comforted her. It made the strangers around her a little easier to accept. This beautiful forest was welcoming. Enough so that it occurred to her, if things went poorly, she might be able to simply lose herself in these woods and survive here on her own. Jaecar, and her parents before him, taught her how to live off what the wilderness had to offer.

The forest floor picked up a gradual upward slope, and the trees opened some. Ahead of them, the trees became scarcer and the remains of buildings more pervasive. Far beyond the crumpled bones of the homes at the bottom of the hill, she could see partially collapsed remains of a big manor house. Closer and up a slightly steeper hill to their right, a large cluster of buildings, many two stories, appeared more intact. Nature had reclaimed much of the roadway and was attempting to retake the land under and around the buildings on the outskirts of the old town. Farther in, the roads were cobbled and the foundations more substantial. The forest was still locked in battle with that part of town.

They didn't follow the main road. Phendaril signaled them to slow and took them up a side road that wound around the hillside and up to the edge of the upper residential area. They hadn't reached the first of the larger buildings when he stopped them and drew his bow. A rat, easily as big as a goat, lay twitching in its sleep in the street, stretched out in the warming sunshine of mid-morning. The arrow struck true and deep, with the impressive power behind the shot. The rat jerked when the arrow hit, then didn't move again.

Phendaril turned to them, speaking in a low voice. "That building," he pointed to a two-story structure a couple of houses in, "is our first goal. We'll go up over there." He pointed to a spot where a collapsed lean-to created a ramp up to the roof of a shed.

From there, Raven could see where it would take them up a series of levels to the roof of the building he had indicated. Of course, the route she plotted with her eyes assumed that the footing was stable. They would have to rely on him and any others who had been here before for that.

"The footing up to that point is variable. We'll go up single-file. Talis and Veylin helped me scout this area. Two of you will go behind me, then Veylin. Two more, then Talis. Adept Marek, you can bring up the back. I expect you can handle anything that might be inclined to come up behind us."

Marek gave a quick nod.

Phendaril lined them out the way he wanted them, putting Raven third from the back with Talis between her and Marek.

"Follow exactly in each other's footsteps. If any one of you diverges, you could fall through. You don't want to be trapped in one of these buildings with a pack of panicked fell rats." He looked at each of them, waiting on a nod of confirmation before turning to the next in line. Then he gestured for them to stay in place while he retrieved his arrow. When he was back, he motioned them to follow and led them around to the collapsed lean-to.

Raven glanced a few times down the road into town. It wasn't hard to spot more fell rats. Dozens slept out in the bumpy streets where the cobbles were being lifted by the relentless persistence of nature growing up through them. One rat jerked awake, and its disturbed neighbor snapped at it. The two tussled briefly until a much larger rat snarled at them, and they quieted down, each finding a different spot to rest. Through it all, none of the beasts noticed the group of elves and humans creeping low and quiet in a careful line up onto the rooftops.

Once they were up on their target roof, Phendaril motioned them forward to where they had a good view of the square below. From this vantage, she could see that the rats had brought in piles of old hay, dead grass, branches, and leaves to create nests throughout the streets. There were eight of the creatures sprawled around the well in the middle of the square. The stink of them wafted up to the rooftop, making her stomach tighten with revulsion.

It was curious that they didn't appear to be nesting in the buildings. Of course, it was also possible that the buildings were already too full, driving the rest into the streets, though she hoped that wasn't the case. One building at the top of the square had no rats near it. That structure, with a massive hole where the door had been, had to be the tavern the dire bear had made into his den.

She glanced at the buildings up the street, and a movement caught her eye. Two rats had nested on top of a partially collapsed roof about four houses in from where they were. They were almost invisible, half-covered in dead grass, until one of them moved. The other followed suit. Both lifted their noses up in the air, sniffing. Given the direction of the light breeze, she suspected she knew what they were smelling.

She waved a hand, catching Phendaril's attention, then pointed toward the two stirring creatures. He saw them instantly and turned back to her. After a second of hesitation, he gestured to himself and pointed to the one on the right. She nodded. They both drew their bows and nocked arrows. She aimed at the rat on the left, which was starting to stand now. She took a breath, tuning every sense to Phendaril, listening and feeling for the moment he would let his arrow fly. At the slightest change in his breathing, she let her arrow go. The two struck their targets at almost precisely the same moment, dropping both rats instantly and with barely a sound.

Phendaril looked over at her, holding her gaze for several seconds, his expression unreadable. Then he moved closer to the center of the roof and beckoned for them to join him. They all crouched around him.

"The bear tends to come out toward dusk. It's a heavy sleeper. If we move fast, we can probably clear out most of these bastards without waking it. If we target the ones toward the center, the others will run for the shelter of the nearby buildings. If we target the ones closer to the buildings, however, the rest will be more likely to panic and move toward the middle." His gaze shifted to Raven again, flickering briefly to the bow that rose over her shoulder now.

"We'll spread out around the rooftops here," Phendaril resumed after a few seconds of contemplative silence. "We take them down as quickly and quietly as possible, working from the outside in. If the panic of the rats doesn't wake the bear, the smell of blood will eventually. If it comes out, don't shoot at it. An arrow will only enrage it. It can't reach us up here. We keep weeding out the rats. When we've killed or driven off the rats, I want two of you – Talis, you and... Raven – to stay up top. Use your arrows sparingly and only if you get a shot that will do some damage. The eyes or nose, for example. The rest of you will go down with me to deal with the bear on the ground."

"Do we have to kill it?" It was Talis who asked, his thoughtful gaze on the tavern. "We could just drive it away."

"We'd run the risk of driving an enraged dire bear toward the camp," Marek answered. His attention was on the rats, perhaps counting their numbers and considering targets.

"Adept Marek isn't wrong. Besides, we have over 100 people to feed now. It won't go to waste." Phendaril waited for a nod of understanding from Talis before continuing. "We need to surround it. We can harry it like a pack of wolves. Dodge in for a strike and back out. Frustrate it into leaving an opening. We have to pay attention to each other. If one of us is getting into trouble, we need to draw it off them." The look he gave Marek then wasn't one of confidence.

"I'll do my part," Marek stated, his flat tone telling them what he thought of Phendaril's lack of trust.

Phendaril proceeded to break them out into three groups. He sent Raven with Veylin and another elf. They would go to the roof of the building across from the tavern. Marek and the other man would go with Talis to a building across from the one they were on. The remaining elf would stay with him on this building. He assigned them each groups of rats to concentrate on initially, ensuring the first beasts taken down were in front of as many doorways as possible to keep others from fleeing inside.

The six archers heading to other buildings made their way back to the edge of the residential area and then split into two groups led by Talis and Veylin. Veylin led Raven's group cautiously down one of the streets, far enough to get to a ladder that appeared to have been intentionally set beside one of the buildings. They scaled it one at a time, then followed her across a beam that was all that remained of the roof of that building. It wasn't that much different than balancing along tree branches. Although a glimpse of the broken-down rubble below told Raven the landing would be a bit more painful. There were also a couple of rats in the shadows of the interior. Though they were so motionless, she wasn't sure they were alive. It did confirm that they went inside at times, which meant there would be more of them to deal with when they were done outside.

Once they were on the building Phendaril had indicated, Veylin turned to her. "You're staying up here, so you get first pick of spots. Make sure you have a good view of the whole square. The bear might move around a lot. Check your steps and pick a strong spot. We don't want you falling through the roof when we need you most."

Raven nodded and started toward a round-topped dormer. The area where the dormer and the main roof came together would have more reinforcement. It also appeared to provide a good vantage point for the entire square. The other two chose positions closer to their route down. When everyone was in place, she looked over at Veylin. With a series of gestures, the elven woman assigned them each a portion of their group of rats to focus on.

When the last group with Talis was in position, they all readied their bows and turned to watch Phendaril for his signal. Marek had taken a spot on a lower level of the building he was on since his crossbow would have less range than the longbows the rest of them were using. He could also jump down from that perch, putting him on the ground faster when the time came. Maybe she would get lucky, and the bear would eat him.

Raven smiled to herself and waited for Phendaril's signal. She would need to conserve arrows and make her shots count if she was to have ammunition left to use on the bear. Her first picked target was sleeping on the front steps of one building, its body across the doorway. The fell rat's whiskers twitched in its sleep and its legs, much longer for its size than those of the comparably diminutive relatives she was familiar with, moved now and then as if it were running.

Phendaril aimed his bow and gave a slight nod. Eight rats were struck down, making little if any noise. A few of the others near them started to stir. Raven loosed her next arrow quickly, targeting one of those. In the next volley, someone's arrow didn't kill the target, and the rat began shrieking and thrashing. A surge of activity rippled out from that point as the rats started to wake. The team kept firing, taking them down as fast as possible while the groggy beasts scrambled to escape.

As expected, most of the rats were repelled by dead lying closer to the buildings and surged toward the center. A couple went up onto the well and fell through the rotting wood covering it. The other beasts dropped quickly. Five volleys of arrows left far more dead and dying than alive, and the remaining few made a break for the street leading out of town. They quickly moved out of Raven's line of sight. She left it to the others to decide if they would let them go or give chase. Something else had her attention now.

A deep huffing came from the entrance of the tavern. Veylin and the other elf started making their careful way back over the buildings toward where the ladder waited. Phendaril and the elf who stayed with him were also heading down, as was the human scout with Talis. Marek jumped off the lower roof and landed on his feet in the middle of several rat corpses.

The bear ventured half out into the light, and Raven sucked in a sharp breath of surprise. It was three to four times the size of the bears she had encountered back home. Its bulk filled the massive hole around what had once been the door to the tavern. Its scarred, grizzled muzzle spoke of many brutal fights over a long lifetime. Drool ran from its lips as it sniffed air that was now thick with the metallic tang of blood. It took a few more steps out into the open and let out a roar of challenge that made the rooftop she was on tremble.

Marek didn't move a muscle, but the dire bear hadn't survived this long through luck. It sniffed the air a few more times, and its big head swiveled toward the adept. Raven started to aim her bow. The instant she released the string, aiming for an eye, the beast surged into a run, and the arrow hit its flank. It let out an angry roar. With Marek as the only visible threat, it kept to its course. Faced with a few thousand pounds of enraged bear, the adept turned and bolted through a doorway behind him. The beast lunged after him. It slammed into the door frame, unable to get its bulk through. The impact rocked the building, and the roof collapsed with Talis still on it. Talis disappeared in a cloud of dust and debris.

The bear began swiping at the doorway, ripping through the wood framing. Then two more arrows struck its backside. It spun to face Phendaril and the other elf who had entered the square. It started to charge them, forgetting Marek now that he was out of sight. Veylin and her companion entered the square. They shot arrows into the thick flank, pulling the beast's attention to them. Marek emerged from the building, shaking the dust out of his hair and drawing his heavy sword. A line of blood ran from a cut on one cheek. The other human who had been in his group came running up the street to join the battle.

The bear swung out, narrowly missing the other elf from Raven's group. It was much faster than she would have expected for a creature of that size. Phendaril leapt in, getting its attention with a quick jab to that flank before bounding back out of reach. Someone on the other side mirrored the attack a few seconds later, drawing it that way again.

Raven sighted along her arrow. Jaecar's voice spoke in her head, low and soft so as not to startle her prey.

"A good shot will always come from a place of calm. You must be able to pull away from fear or excitement and focus solely on the physical action."

She drew a breath and exhaled. Below her, Veylin jumped in to harry the bear. On her leap back out, she slipped in the blood of one of the rats and went down. The animal turned on her, and Raven let the arrow fly. It drove deep into the beast's right eye. The bear reared back, roaring and reaching for its face with massive front paws. Marek, who had been ready to step in to harry the beast, lunged under the upright animal, slashing his long blade deep into its belly. The bear stumbled to the side. As its feet hit the ground, Phendaril rushed in, clutching a handful of fur, and swung up, landing on its shoulders like he meant to ride it. He wrapped his arms around its neck, reaching under its throat, and cut deep with his blade. The bear thrashed once, violently enough to send Phendaril flying, though he managed to land in a roll and come quickly up to his feet. Then it staggered a few times and slumped to the ground. The others retreated from the fast-spreading pool of blood.

They all stared at it for a few stunned seconds, then Phendaril and the remaining scouts sprinted toward the building that Talis had been on top of. Raven started to make her way down. By the time she reached the square, Phendaril and one of the other elves were carrying Talis out of the building. Talis was covered in dust. His clothes were torn and bloody in several places, one arm bent where there were no joints, the jagged end of a bone sticking out through the skin.

Phendaril paused, digging through the pack they had pulled off the injured elf to glance up at an elven man with long black hair. "Jael, run back and get Synal. Go as fast as you can."

Jael nodded and broke into a sprint back the way they had come.

"You didn't bring a healer on a mission like this?" Marek asked.

Phendaril glared daggers up at him. For a few seconds, Raven wondered if she might be put in the awkward position of needing to save the adept's life.

"I did bring a healer. I left him on the rooftop so he wouldn't be in danger. It wouldn't have been a problem if some ass hadn't drawn the bear into the building."

She suspected Marek's answering sneer might have gotten him killed if Phendaril hadn't already turned his attention to her.

"Do you have any experience with healing?" he asked.

Raven shook her head. "Minor injuries. Nothing like that." She glanced at the wound and quickly away, her whole body twinging with a sympathetic pang.

He turned to the other human. "Darus, see what you can do for some of the less severe injuries. Veylin, help me stabilize this arm and slow the bleeding so we can keep him alive until Synal gets here. The rest of you can start sweeping the buildings around the square for any remaining rats. Be careful, though," he added with a pointed look at Marek, "we don't have a healer right now."

Raven hurried away, eager to do anything that didn't involve standing around listening to Talis's pained groans or looking at parts of him that were supposed to be on the inside. Her relief at getting away didn't last long. Before she reached the first house, Marek appeared beside her. She quickly glared at him, not trying to hide her irritation at his arrival.

He chose to ignore it. "Leral agreed that it made more sense for one of us to stay outside and begin collecting arrows while the other two go together for safety. Less risk of someone else getting hurt that way."

Now she knew the last elf's name at least. "I presume you selflessly volunteered to be the one to kill rats with me?"

She caught his shrug out of the corner of her eye. "We are Silverbloods. We're uniquely suited to this kind of work," he answered with a pleased grin. "That was quite a remarkable shot. You've had training."

She stopped before the first building and made herself face him, struggling to quell the jitters in her gut that were worse now than when she was trying to shoot a raging dire bear in the eye. "What do you want with me?"

She didn't believe the benign smile he offered her.

"I want to know who made you and why?"

"My parents, because they were feeling amorous," she answered sharply.

He chuckled, but there was a matching sharpness in his gaze now. "You know that isn't what I meant."

She drew her sword and entered the building. The dark space smelled musty, more like a cave than a human dwelling.

Marek entered behind her, his crossbow out and loaded. "Elves and women can't survive being remade by the magic. Everyone knows that. How did you survive?"

She answered in a lower voice, hoping he would take the hint and be quieter. "Given the evidence before you, maybe you should be asking your Brotherhood why they lied to you instead of pestering me about it. I didn't ask for this any more than I asked to be born a half-elf."

"If it was done against your will, why are you so reluctant to tell me who did it?"

A soft shifting sound in the next room caught her attention. Ignoring him, she crept toward the opening, stepping around the remains of an old cabinet. She brought her sword in close and moved through the doorway at an angle. The next room was darker. The floor from the level above had collapsed, and some boards blocked the light from the window. As soon as she crossed the threshold, a rat leapt at her from atop an old dresser. Raven stepped aside and then forward, bringing her blade up to lay open its side from just under its near front leg to its hip. The rat hit the ground with a thud.

"Well done. Who trained you?"

She jumped when Marek's crossbow fired next to her head, the bolt vanishing into a dark shadow in one corner that had started to move. Taking a deep breath to try to calm her nerves, she made herself face him again.

"I would feel much better about this if you would stop talking."

To her surprise, he did. Sweeping the buildings in and around the square took several hours. A little less than two hours after they started, Synal and another healer arrived on horseback. An hour later, they came out of the last large structure to find about 15 more elves and humans out doing cleanup around the square. Two ox-drawn carts were being loaded with rat corpses. She spotted Phendaril a few times, alternating between overseeing the dressing of the bear's carcass and helping drag rat bodies out of some of the first buildings they had swept.

Raven leaned back against the door frame of the last building, exhaustion dragging at her limbs. Her leg throbbed, complaining bitterly about the hours of use. Marek holstered his crossbow, then leaned one shoulder against the opposite side of the door frame, facing her.

"I'm impressed."

She offered him a weary glower.

"I'm serious. You handle your blade as well as or better than many of the Silverblood warriors I trained with. And your archery..." He offered a genuine smile then, a surprisingly attractive expression on his rugged features, and nodded to something off to her left. "I think several of us admire your skill with that bow."

Raven looked in the direction he had nodded to see Veylin walking up. She held out a water skin to Raven. Suddenly water sounded like the most fantastic thing in the world. She accepted the offered skin, though her arm was almost too leaden with exhaustion to hold it up. After a long drink, she handed it back to Veylin. The elven woman gave it to Marek then and proceeded to beam at Raven.

"I didn't get a chance to thank you earlier for that timely shot. I wouldn't be feeling so spry right now if not for you."

Raven shrugged, glancing uncomfortably away only to spot Phendaril walking toward them. Killing reeking fell rats was preferable to the social time that appeared to be developing.

Veylin's face colored a bit then. "I don't usually fall on my ass in the middle of a fight."

Raven hesitated. There seemed to be a hanging expectation that she would say something now, but she had no idea what it should be. Was she supposed to make light of the moment? Use it as a teaching opportunity like Jaecar would?

"It could have happened to any of us," Marek offered

into her silence.

Raven's cheeks grew warm. Of course, he would know. He had probably spent his entire life interacting with strangers. That didn't make her feel better about it.

"Thank you... for the water," Raven added the last bit when the elven woman looked confused.

"Oh. Of course." She turned away. "I better get back to helping with cleanup."

"You've worked hard enough, Veylin," Phendaril stated, now close enough to hear what they were saying. He stopped next to her. "Take a break."

"If you insist, milord," she offered him a playful bow.

The faintest hint of a smile tugged at the corners of his mouth. When Veylin walked away, he turned to them. "You two did an impressive amount of work."

Glancing at Raven's sword, he drew a cloth from one pocket and held out a hand. She offered it to him, trying to hide how much effort lifting it required at that moment. He took the weapon, wiped the blade clean, and gave it back to her.

Synal walked up to join them, giving Phendaril a cross look. "What are you thinking?" she demanded, gesturing toward Raven's leg. "You know she's injured. You were there when it happened."

Marek's smile was one of cruel amusement now as he watched the healer reprimand Phendaril. Raven gave him a scowl, and he schooled his expression to something more benign.

"I'm fine," Raven defended.

Phendaril didn't appear bothered by her anger. "How's Talis?"

Synal's jaw tightened at his inquiry. "He's stable. If nothing gets infected, he should live."

The way she deliberately didn't look at Marek told Raven someone had recounted the incident and his role in it to her at some point. The adept had gone down to the ground too soon. The fact that he hadn't needed to go around like the others was no excuse for deviating from the plan. Then again, he was probably used to working alone, given that was how the Silverbloods often did things. The mistake could have been an honest one. Did that matter if it almost got someone killed?

Synal turned her attention to Raven. "Why don't you come with me, and I'll decide if you're doing fine?"

Raven looked to Phendaril. As soon as she did it, she realized she was asking him for permission because she had always had someone there to ask. He was the figure of authority she had chosen in Jaecar's absence. A sounder choice than Marek, who she didn't trust given that the Brotherhood were the ones who made her existence a crime. Still, there was a certain awkwardness to the fact that she was supposed to be an adult, and her instinct had been to get his approval before leaving with Synal.

She didn't give Phendaril time to voice whatever thoughts lurked behind his pinched brows or make a decision regarding her going with the healer, if he even intended to do so. Instead, she ducked past him after Synal, who had turned and was walking toward where a sedated Talis was being secured on the stretcher they would use to take him back to the main camp.

Karsima sat reclined back with her feet on the map table when Phendaril finally answered her summons. She hadn't honestly expected him any sooner. He would have seen to it that Talis was settled in with the healers and that his team had eaten before he came. Would that team include the two Silverbloods tonight, or would he leave them to their own resources? She didn't know, though she was curious to find out. What she did know was that he wouldn't take the time to feed himself before coming to see her, which was why she had asked Jenner to bring enough food for two to her quarters.

Phendaril stopped in the doorway, a lock of dark auburn hair falling across his shadowed eyes as he tilted his head and smirked at her. He looked a little tired but not as unhappy as she thought he might, considering one of his people had been seriously injured. That meant things must have gone well enough otherwise.

"Not standing on ceremony tonight?" He asked, walking up to the table.

She lifted her mug to him. "Not standing at all, my friend. I'm sure you've had enough of that today." She gestured to the chair she had placed across the table from her, then to the waiting food and drink. "Join me."

His weary smile told her she had guessed correctly

about his lack of nourishment and made the right choice. He removed his weapons and settled into the chair. The food was getting cold, but that didn't stop him from digging in.

"I've gotten several accountings of the events in the old town today from those who heard about them and from Jael. I'd be interested in a few more details from you."

He swallowed the bite he had taken, washed it down with some mead, then gazed across the table at her. "I can assure you that you will have your own private quarters in town by the time Alayne returns. Anything else you wanted to know?"

Karsima smiled at that. Private quarters. Someplace she and Alayne could have a proper reunion after months apart. "You do know the way to a woman's heart."

He chuckled and took another bite of bread.

"How did our new arrivals fare today?"

He swallowed some more mead, his expression sobering. "If you've received several accountings, then you already know how they fared."

She gave him a long-suffering look. He was being deliberately evasive, and she wanted to be sure he knew she was aware of it. "You know what I'm asking for. I want your insight. I know what happened at face value, but I want more than that."

He sat back and took a deep breath before speaking. "Marek is as skilled and strong in combat as you'd expect a Silverblood adept to be. He isn't one for following orders, however, unless it serves his needs to do so. He didn't wait for the rest of us when he should have. He was instrumental in helping finish off the bear, but his lone mercenary attitude almost got Talis killed today."

Karsima nodded, trying to cling to neutrality. She was gathering information, not placing judgment. Not yet. A refreshing evening breeze rippled the curtain over the door, the cool air helping to keep her anger at the injured healer in check.

"I understand he also helped sweep the buildings."

"Yes." Phendaril's scowl told her that effort hadn't helped redeem the adept. "I assigned the two Silverbloods and Leral to the task. Marek decided himself that Leral should start cleanup in the square, and he and Raven should be the ones to clear the buildings together. I'm not sure he would have been so amenable to the task had he not seen an opportunity to learn more about her."

Interesting. "Do you think he accomplished that?"

Phendaril gave a sharp shake of his head, some frustration creeping to the fore. "I don't know. It was a substantial undertaking that took several hours. She didn't appear any more enthusiastic about his company when they were done than she did before they started. Still, I can't claim any special insight into what occurred in between. She's about as forthcoming as a stone."

There it was. That edge of anger that was distinctly connected to the subject of the half-elven female. It wasn't like him. "And Raven?"

His gaze turned inward, reflecting on the events of the day. "She's resistant to being part of the group. Not in the same way Marek is. I don't think she knows how to be. She doesn't trust any of us. At the same time, when we were up on the rooftops, it became fairly evident that she knows how to work together with someone when it matters."

"Perhaps she hunted a lot with the male who died in Manderly. Eamon," Karsima suggested.

Phendaril shrugged. He was silent for several seconds, and she was intrigued to see some of the tightness in his jaw relaxing away as he thought back on the events from earlier. "When we first got up to the rooftops, she pointed out a couple of rats that were a possible threat to our position. I signaled for her to help me take them down.

She followed my cues perfectly. She even fired almost the same instant I did, even though I didn't signal that. It was a little unnerving how exact her timing was. And that shot she fired into the bear's eye I would have called impossible had I not seen it myself. It may have saved Veylin's life."

"She's got good instincts and the ability to work as part of a team." Karsima tapped her fingers on the table, pondering, while Phendaril took advantage of the lull to finish his meal. "We're going to need all the help we can get for several days to make a few houses in that part of the town livable. After that, if she's still here, send her out with some of the scouting and hunting groups."

"And Marek?"

Karsima tapped out part of a drinking tune with her fingernails, gazing at the pile of sketched maps showing myriad dangers in the area. "He'll want to keep an eye on her. There's no harm in letting him go along if it's a trip you're on. Otherwise, find him some solo work that won't require anyone else to put their life in his hands."

There was a slight disgusted emphasis to the usual hint of sneer his scar gave him. "How much are we paying him?"

"He's kept his rates remarkably reasonable. I think he's curious about what we're doing, and I get the feeling he wants to study her. The minute he takes her back to the Brotherhood, they'll take her out of his hands. I don't think he wants that yet, so he's using the excuse of helping us to keep her to himself right now."

Phendaril pushed his emptied trencher to the side and put his feet on the table, mirroring her position. He pulled out the band that held his long hair back, letting it fall forward onto his shoulders, and closed his eyes for a moment. The rest of the tension eased from his features as he drew in a deep breath and let it out again. Even with the scar, he was unfairly handsome. Lashes thick and long enough to make any woman jealous framed his dark, slightly angled eyes. The image of elven perfection. Strong, fierce, and elegant. She might not be interested on an intimate level, but she couldn't help noticing.

Karsima smiled softly to herself. "Remember when we spent the summer hunting for dryads out by Amberwood spring?"

He let out a soft laugh and opened his eyes. "We were, what, about seven? It went well enough until we found one. I don't think I've seen you run that fast since."

Karsima dipped her fingertips in her mead and flicked them at him. "I seem to recall you running at least as fast."

An edge of playful threat showed in his answering grin.

She let the warm affection spreading through her chest come into her smile. "I do seem to recall that you stayed a little behind me so you could protect me with your life if she tried to take me."

A nostalgic smile took the sorrow and pain from his features for a moment. In that instant, she could see the child he had been in him still. Oh, how she missed those carefree days before the lords brought their petty war to Amberwood. Before they were separated by their fleeing families. His life had not been as easy as hers in the years before they found one another again.

Then the expression faded, and that deep sorrowful darkness stole over his features again. He took a long drink of the mead.

"You should consider a wash, Phen. You smell like dead rats."

He swallowed the rest of his drink, then stood up and offered a slight jesting bow. "Yes, milady." He picked up his weapons and started for the exit.

"And Phen."

He stopped and turned back to her. A slight sway in his movement told her he wouldn't be awake much longer.

"Did you tell Raven she did well today?"

He frowned. "She's an adult. I don't think she needs me holding her hand and singing her praises to know she did well."

"That's where I think you're wrong about her," she countered, wincing inwardly at the sharp edge in her own voice. Then again, maybe he needed that to see what he was missing. "She's young, and she lost someone important to her because of us. I'm not sure she had anyone else. Now she's here, fighting for *our* cause while surrounded by strangers, one of whom believes she should die just for what she is."

"Send Marek on his way then," Phendaril answered, skipping past the subject of his own accountability in the young woman's current predicament.

If only it were that easy. "You know he'll take her with him."

Phendaril bowed his head and rubbed his temples with the thumb and forefinger of one hand. He felt it, too, the weight of the task they had taken on here. Raven was another potential source of problems piled on top of that monstrous undertaking. She saw how hard he tried to balance the burden of it all on his scouts and hunters, so they didn't burn out. He never did the same for himself.

"Get some rest," she prompted.

He didn't move immediately. Instead, he stared for a long moment at the doorway, then he said, "If you think it's the right call, maybe we don't let him take her."

After dropping that heavy comment on her, he left the hut. Karsima wanted to hate him for those words, though she had been thinking it, and she didn't doubt that he knew that before he said it. One didn't defy the

Brotherhood. They were powerful. Their rules were generally respected by the authorities in the kingdom of Andioch and held up as equal to law in Habarin. The Brotherhood held sway over many of the lords in the larger cities. As far as she knew, they might even have influence over the king himself in Habarin.

She couldn't forget seeing Raven that first night there. A beautiful young thing. Terrified and broken, yet still trying hard to hold the pieces of herself together. Silverblood or not, she was still just a half-elven female alone in a world with no tolerance for weakness. Physically, Raven couldn't be called weak, but she was vulnerable in other ways. How much risk to everyone else was protecting one half-elven woman worth?

CHAPTER NINETEEN

When they returned to camp that night, Raven slept as soundly as she ever had after a hard day of training with Jaecar. Exhaustion left her free of nightmares or the memories that masqueraded as such. She didn't have to fall asleep fighting back tears while thinking about her parents, Jaecar, or Eamon. She simply succumbed to fatigue, the throbbing in her leg numbed by one of Synal's tinctures.

Morning arrived with a flurry of activity. According to Synal, a significant portion of the camp was getting organized to head into the old town's newly cleared upper residential area to start preparing it for occupation. A couple of the other healers were preparing to go, though she wouldn't. Talis couldn't be moved, and there wasn't a building set up for the healers in the old town yet anyhow. Raven would likely be invited along to help, at least according to Synal.

Raven gathered her things, including her pack, and left the building. She had never built anything like this before, though she had helped Jaecar with repairs on the keep often enough. The work up in the old town was sure to be exhausting. She liked what being exhausted did to her, and learning a few new skills might prove worthwhile.

She hadn't gotten more than a few yards from the

building when Marek wandered up from whatever rock he had been lurking under. His hair was damp, and his clothes were cleaned of the grime that had coated them after yesterday's work.

He looked her up and down and chuckled. "You look as lovely as one of those rats we cut down. And you smell just as nice."

The fact that her face heated in response to his comments only made her ire greater. "And you could pass for a drowned one."

He laughed, unruffled by her defensive temper. "There are some makeshift bathhouses of sorts behind the medical building. You should have time to clean up before we head out. I can show you the way if you like."

A strong urge to defy him outright surged in her, but she could smell the rats on her now that he had mentioned it. To refuse the idea of a bath merely to avoid giving him even the tiniest sense of victory would be self-defeating. Besides, she had spotted Veylin up the hill talking to Phendaril. Both look as if they had bathed. She didn't want to be the only one who hadn't.

"I can find my own way." She turned and started around the building in the direction he had come from.

As he'd told her, a line of four small, rough-built structures stood behind the healer's building. A couple of the camp's residents, one man and one woman, were standing outside them. As she approached, the man was knocking on the door of a tiny bathhouse.

"You've been in there long enough. Dry off and come out."

Raven didn't catch the muffled response from within because the woman was now approaching her. When their eyes met, the woman cut her gaze quickly away and stopped, letting Raven finish closing the distance.

She offered a vague nod in Raven's general direction. "Are you going up to the old town?"

"I am," Raven answered, not sure if she needed to add anything to that.

"The bath on the far right has fresh water for you." The woman pointed to the indicated building as if Raven might not know which one was on the right. "If you want the clothes washed, we can take 'em down to the creek, but they won't be dry before you leave. If you have something else to wear, we can hold on to them for you or send them up to old town later."

Raven nodded and hurried away, closing herself in the dim little building lit by one fading candle.

Thanks to Eamon, she did have a change of clothes in the pack she was carrying. She made quick work of a bath, hyper-aware that she was naked within the small structure amidst a camp full of strangers. The water in the tiny wooden tub was also rather cold, which helped motivate her to move quickly. Despite the uncomfortable aspects of the experience, she emerged from the bath refreshed, her confidence boosted by the fact that she was no longer the odd rat out.

She left her soiled clothes with the woman and started toward where many elves and humans were gathered around several ox-carts full of supplies. The group heading to the old town was large but still smaller than the group staying, which only added to its appeal. Phendaril was there, as well as Marek, Jael, Darus, and Leral. Veylin came walking up from another part of the camp. When she spotted Raven, she adjusted her course to intercept. Raven fought the urge to change her direction, knowing the evasion would be a little too obvious here with so many people watching.

"Coming up to work with us?" Veylin offered a friendly smile as she fell into step.

Raven realized then that no one had invited her to join the work party the way Karsima had asked her to join the unit yesterday. Synal had suggested they would.

Perhaps the fact that they hadn't meant she shouldn't be assuming her welcome.

She slowed her stride. "If it's all right."

Veylin's smile broadened. After the incident with the bear, she no longer appeared to see Raven's differences. Or maybe she simply didn't care about them anymore. "Of course it is, if you can still lift your arms after killing all those rats yesterday."

The admiration in the elven woman's tone and that warm smile tugged at something in Raven, making her want to smile in return. Instead, she turned her attention to the waiting group, remembering the harsh tone Phendaril had used when he pointed out that she was half-elven, and the way Marek had called her existence a crime on the ship. Both men were watching her. Thinking of those things accomplished her goal.

"I'm sure I'll be fine," she answered, the urge to smile gone.

"I've no doubt," Veylin countered, her enthusiasm untouched by Raven's subdued response. She pulled her long brunette hair back over her pointed ears and began braiding it.

Marek started taking a step toward them when they joined the group, but Phendaril was faster. He strode over to intercept them and nodded a greeting to Veylin before giving Raven an appraising look. Whether he approved of her appearance or what he hoped to find in his brief assessment, she couldn't tell, and she tried hard not to care.

"The carts are full of supplies, but if you need to give your leg a break, you can ride one of the horses," he offered.

Her gut dropped to her feet.

Phendaril's brow furrowed as if he had seen it happen.

"Thank you," she managed, amazed that her voice

didn't shake, "but I think the walking is good for it." She forced herself not to glance at any of the horses, knowing her fear would show through.

"All right." He turned to the group and lifted his hand. With a quick gesture, he started them moving. Then, to her unpleasant surprise, he glanced back at her. "Walk with me a moment."

She wasn't sure if it was intended as an order or request. It was hard to tell with him. Could she refuse? She glanced up at the group and spotted Marek watching them as the carts began to move past him. Veylin was already leaving them behind, seeming to take Phendaril's words as a dismissal. If she refused to walk with him, Marek would almost certainly fill in the vacant space. She wasn't sure yet whose company she dreaded most, but Marek had already placed several questions to her that she didn't want to answer. Avoiding him was worth giving Phendaril a chance.

She nodded to him.

He started walking, moving off to one side of the rest of the group. The opposite side from Marek, which she suspected was not an accident. He didn't say anything as they made their way out of the camp proper. His silence lasted long enough that Raven began to wonder if there might be some other purpose to the request or if he simply wanted to walk with her. Once they passed the edge of the camp, and he had subtly steered them further away from the group, he glanced over at her.

"You can't ride, can you?"

Her cheeks lit on fire. This was one situation where honesty seemed the safest approach. Someone else might try to put her on a horse if she suggested anything other than the truth. "I've never even touched a horse," she admitted.

He didn't speak for a time after that. His prolonged silence kept the burn in her cheeks and made her long to run off into the trees. Something told her that hadn't been the reason he wanted to talk with her, though. At least not the only reason. Niggling curiosity was enough to keep her from bolting. For now.

"I love these woods," he said finally.

She would stake all her coin that this also wasn't what he wanted to talk to her about. When she made herself look over at him, his attention was up, peering into the branches above them where a few forest birds and other critters flitted along, observing their passage. Below those branches, emerald grasses grew up in places where the land had once been tilled as farmland. It wasn't a natural combination, but it was lovely and easy to move through.

"It is magnificent," she offered.

It wasn't a lie. This forest was arguably more beautiful in some ways than the one she had grown up in, though she missed those rolling wooded hills.

The faint start of a smile touched his lips. He glanced over at her, and she faced quickly forward. He looked ahead as well. After a little more time passed, she dared another glance and caught him scanning the group, his discerning gaze searching for any issues he might need to address. Always on duty.

"By the end of the week," he began, his change in tone telling her this, finally, was the reason they were walking together, "once we have a good start on rebuilding, I'm going to begin sending more scouting and hunting parties out. If you think you'll be around that long, I'd like to send you out with some of them."

She almost looked for Marek in the group, but she didn't want him to catch her doing it, so she kept her gaze ahead. The adept might have some ideas about how long she would be staying here. Not that she intended to go with him if he decided to take her to the Brotherhood. She could quickly become lost in these woods.

"I'd be willing," she answered cautiously.

"Good. This evening, I'll introduce you to Helar. He's the elf driving the lead cart. He's a skilled leatherworker. If you're going to go out with my units, I want you to be a little better protected."

She thought about the coin she had hidden away. How much did leather armor cost? Would the contents of that pouch be enough? "I'm not sure I can afford it."

There was that faint almost-smile again.

"Don't worry. After yesterday, I'm confident t hat you'll earn it quickly enough." He started to turn as if he meant to return to the group. "I'll let you be for now."

"I..." Her gaze jumped to the others, picking out Marek, who was watching them again. She looked away from him, anxiety quickening her pulse. If Phendaril left, the adept would come over, of that she had no doubt. Still, she couldn't bring herself to ask the elven leader to stay, especially given how his disdainful tone from her first night in Amberwood kept playing back in her mind.

Next to her, Phendaril drew in a breath and exhaled softly as though focusing on a difficult shot. He settled back in beside her. "What do you know of the trees around here?" he prompted.

Somehow, he had recognized her fear and responded to it with the unspoken offer of his continued company. A mixture of gratitude and guilt swept through her. Guilt for the burden she presented and gratitude, not only for the fact that he would stay, but also because he didn't use this as an excuse to ask her about herself. To show her appreciation, she forced herself to engage, asking him about the different trees and plants in the forest here, of which he turned out to have boundless knowledge.

What he knew of the edible plants around Amberwood was of particular interest, given that she might have to flee at some point. They fell behind a few times when he knelt in the dirt to show her distinct markings that indicated which of two similar-looking plants was safe to eat or what portion of a specific flower was most poisonous. By the time they were within view of the old town's upper residential area, he had collected a bundle of plants he thought the healers would find helpful. Raven had gathered a great deal of knowledge about the local plants and quiet respect for this less abrasive side of the elven leader.

CHAPTER TWENTY

Once they were in the old town, the job of coordinating efforts appeared to fall to Phendaril. He took his leave of her and started putting people to work. There were still some rat carcasses to remove. Primarily those she and Marek had dispatched inside the buildings toward the end of the previous day. Nests and other less pleasant deposits had to be cleaned out as well. The bear had been dressed and cut into pieces, most of which were transported back to the main camp. A fair amount had also been left here in a hastily constructed container for use in meals.

Once the streets were cleaned and the buildings cleared of dead rats, they would start hauling other debris out of the structures and inspecting to see which ones were still in good enough shape to be used and which had to be rebuilt. Phendaril specifically assigned Marek and Jael as one team and Raven and Veylin as another to start clearing buildings on the northeast side of the square. Somehow, when Raven entered the first building in her assigned area, Marek, not Veylin, joined her.

"How did you convince Jael and Veylin to switch?" She let her displeasure show through in her tone to hide her fear of him.

"We worked well together yesterday. I thought it

would be a shame to break up such an effective team." He walked over to the lone rat corpse lying not far from the doorway.

"We only worked well together because you were amenable to keeping your mouth shut," she snapped.

He chuckled and grabbed the dead beast by its legs, hefting it with little apparent effort. Anyone else, at least anyone not a Silverblood, would have struggled with the creature's weight. She stepped back to let him pass so he could toss the beast out through the door.

"You don't like me, do you?" he asked as he stepped back in.

She tilted her head and narrowed her eyes at him. "Something about having my existence declared a crime didn't sit well with me."

He gave a nod and started to pull at a tall broken cabinet that seemed to be fastened to the wall somehow. After several seconds, he paused to look at her. "I can understand that, but I was a little surprised to find out the woman I trusted with my life couldn't possibly exist according to the Brotherhood."

She fought the urge to ball her hands into fists. What did he hope to accomplish by talking to her? And why was he nicer to her now? It made her skin crawl. "Your Brotherhood is wrong?"

"Obviously." He hauled on the cabinet again. It creaked and cracked but held firm. He stepped back to look at her, gesturing to the stubborn furniture with one hand. "Could I trouble you?"

Raven heaved a deep breath and walked over. Together, they yanked the cabinet free and moved the awkward structure out to the street. Everything pulled out into the street would be dug through to see what materials were reusable and what was unsalvageable trash. Despite her apprehension, they quickly fell back into the silent focus of the previous day, hauling out everything that wasn't part of the structure.

In the fifth house they worked on, they found a spear embedded deep in the wall opposite the door and a helmet with a substantial dent in it underneath a broken dining table. Any human remains that might have accompanied these relics from the last battles here had long ago been dragged off by scavengers.

Raven found a tightly sealed chest in the back corner of one room. When she managed to pry it open, a collection of well-preserved books greeted her. She knelt next to it and pulled the first one out carefully, opening it somewhere near the middle. Even her enhanced vision couldn't make out the words with the scant light coming from outside, but she could see that there were words.

She smiled.

Marek stepped into the doorway and leaned against the frame. "You read?"

She frowned, trying not to be offended by the surprise in his voice, and said nothing.

"I just have one question."

Raven closed the book and looked up at him. "I find that hard to believe."

He grinned. "Who made you?"

She briefly considered playing stupid and forcing him to clarify the question. It would only delay him for a few seconds, though. "Let me ask you a question. If you were me, would you answer your questions?"

He wasn't willing to be sidetracked this time. "Who are you protecting?"

She was protecting her dead mother, which didn't make much sense when she applied any logic to the situation. Still, something about telling him felt like a violation of those few memories she had of her mother. She remembered a beautiful elven woman overflowing with smiles and happiness that she shared liberally with her husband and daughter. Those memories were always chased away by that last image of her mother's eyes changing as she died, strange words spilling from between her lips. Part of her resented the woman who had done this to her. It was hard to reconcile that woman with the loving, happy mother she remembered from the rest of her early childhood. Admitting that her mother did this to her might break the flimsy barrier that separated the two in her mind.

She put the book away, closed the chest, then stood to face him. "If I gave you their name, would the Brotherhood let me be?"

It didn't surprise her that he couldn't meet her eyes suddenly. He stood up straighter. A hint of something that almost seemed like distress clouded his features. "I doubt it."

"Because I expose their lies?" Anger flashed in his eyes at her words. She couldn't back down now, though. It would be like showing weakness in front of a hungry predator. Any hint of fear would invite it to attack. "The fact that I live and breathe is a crime to them, but I didn't ask for this. I just want to survive. Why is that so much to ask?"

"Raven." He brought one hand up and took a step toward her. When she stepped back the same distance, he didn't advance any farther. "I'm not sure what to tell you. There are laws. There are rules about how this works."

"Rules that have already been broken," she countered.

Even in the poor lighting, she could see the distinct distress that furrowed his brow, just as she knew he would be able to see the unshed tears that welled in her eyes. His hand sank to his side. She slid the chest of books out from the wall.

"Help me take this outside."

He silently joined her, taking hold of the other side and helping her lift it. Books always weighed a lot.

Jaecar once told her it was because of all the knowledge they carried. That memory almost set the tears free. She swallowed hard and gave a nod to let Marek know he could start backing out into the main room. They moved through that room, which they had already cleared of obstacles, and made for the front door. The sunlight beyond was starting to change, taking on an orange cast as the sun sank toward the horizon.

As Marek backed into the street with his half of her find, she spotted Phendaril approaching. The look the elf gave Marek's back could have withered acres of crops all at once.

"Here's good," she said, not caring where "here" was.

They set the chest down in the street. Marek, perhaps catching something in her expression or hearing Phendaril's footsteps, turned to face the approaching elf.

Phendaril stopped and glanced over them. His icy gaze came to rest on Marek. "I understand you took it upon yourself, again, to alter my orders."

Marek stood straight, a hint of challenge in his rigid, forward posture. "Raven and I are uniquely suited to work together."

"If you can't follow my orders on something this simple, how am I supposed to trust you when it matters?"

Marek's smile was barbed with malice. "I suppose you could cancel my contract if you think it will be a problem."

Raven's gut did a flip. If they canceled the contract, Marek would leave, and he would not allow her to stay here in peace. She was sure of that, even if he had seemed a little more sympathetic to her position today. As the two men stood there, measuring one another up in silent challenge, it occurred to her that was precisely what Marek was threatening. He didn't say as much, but he was using his power over her life to get his way, and

Phendaril knew it. There was no reason it should, but the threat held sway with the elf, driving back whatever harsh words rested on the tip of his tongue. Phendaril's expression told her he didn't like swallowing those words, but he did so. She wasn't sure how to feel about that.

"There's food prepared over near the tavern. Get something to eat," Phendaril said, breaking the stalemate.

Marek didn't answer. He didn't look at Raven either before stalking off in the direction of the indicated building, but she caught his faint smirk as he turned away. She stared after him for a few seconds, clasping her hands so Phendaril wouldn't see them shaking.

"What's in here?"

She looked at Phendaril. It took a couple of seconds to recall what she had been doing a few minutes ago. Then she remembered the books, her excitement at the find returning, if a little more subdued this time. She crouched next to the chest and opened it, lifting out one of the treasures within and holding it up for him to see.

"Books." She stood then, opening the volume carefully, a smile finding its way onto her lips as her gaze danced across the words on the page. "This one's a history of Pellanth. It's still in fine condition. The chest was sealed well enough that they're still readable."

"You read?"

Something in his voice caught her attention. It wasn't surprise, but more like appreciation. She looked at him, a little startled to find that he had come close enough to peer over her shoulder at the book. She sucked in a quick breath, and he took a hasty step back. She gave herself a few seconds, waiting to speak until she was sure her voice wouldn't tremble.

"I love to read."

"You read, shoot a bow, and wield a sword, but you've never touched a horse."

She shifted away and turned to glance at him. He had the unsettling look of someone who had solved some part of a puzzle, and she didn't like that. Then he smiled at her. A hint of softness came through in the expression that hadn't been there before. It was far more alarming than his usual steely regard.

"We'll find a safe place for the books where you can peruse them at your leisure. I'm sure Karsima won't mind sharing them. For now, however, you should get something to eat. Then I'll introduce you to Helar."

Raven put the book away. Before closing the lid, she ran her fingers lightly down the row of spines. She was famished, yet she longed to know what else was in those pages.

Her stomach growled, and she hastily shut the lid, hoping the thud of the heavy top making contact would mask the sound. Phendaril's expression offered no insight as to whether he'd heard the grumble in her gut, so she hurried toward the tavern before it could do anything else embarrassing.

The square was now clean of nesting materials and corpses. Piles of stuff that had been pulled out of the surrounding buildings lined the parameter. Several people were still hard at work sorting through those piles. Perhaps they had already eaten or simply weren't that hungry yet. She heard Phendaril's voice and glanced around to see him off now talking to a couple of human men she hadn't met. They were pointing at some of the buildings. Turning her attention to them, she discovered that they were discussing what buildings were usable and which would need immediate repairs. Not something of interest, given that she didn't expect to stay that long.

Near the tavern, tables and chairs had been set out, moved from inside the building, and repaired as needed to give the weary workers a place to rest while they ate. She envied the sense of community here, even as that cluster of so many individuals gathered in one place made her want to run for the trees. The food was being prepared alongside the tavern. The bear that once resided there provided meat for their meal.

Most of those gathered ignored her. Those who did glance her way did so with more curiosity than concern now. It made the walk up to get a bowl full of the stew and whatever potent-smelling drink they were sharing a little more uncomfortable than she liked. If she wanted to eat, she had to deal with it. She was too weary for hunting and cooking her own meal this evening. Everyone in the group that was serving the food avoided meeting her eyes. Did Marek get the same reaction, or was it different for him since being a male Silverblood warrior made him an accepted part of society?

She turned around, her gaze skimming over the crowded tables. Then she looked past them, closer to the center of the square, where three different campfires were slowly gaining momentum. A few humans and elves gathered around each fire, but there was still plenty of room for more without the crowding. The rightmost campfire had three individuals around it. She angled her course toward it.

By the time night had fallen and Raven had finished eating. People began to gather around the fires in greater numbers. She moved away, slipping off into the shadows, deliberately avoiding Phendaril, who she worried might come to introduce her to Helar. She wasn't ready for someone else new, not yet. A short distance outside the residential area, she found a tree she had spotted earlier and climbed up into it. She secured herself to the fattest branch on the town side and watched the light of the fires gradually weaken. Before they had died down completely, she was sound asleep.

CHAPTER TWENTY ONE

Karsima rode into the upper residential area early the next morning. She brought twenty fresh workers from the lower camp to help with rebuilding efforts. She wasn't surprised to see that everyone was hard at work when they arrived. Many of these people were here because they grew up in the original town of Amberwood, like Phendaril and her, and wanted to rebuild. Most of the rest came along with someone from that first group looking for a better life than they had before, and they were willing to work to make it happen. They were all here, whatever their motivation, to build a new home from the ground up.

Most of them were, anyhow. One notable exception was Marek, who she spotted outside the edge of town helping a group empty one of the ox carts of junk lumber that couldn't be reused. Once the cart was unloaded, it would be used to haul in a load of timber being cut over by the edge of the tree line. It was a relief to see him there and not off shadowing Raven, but the fact that he was working as hard as he was bothered her. It suggested that he was still too fascinated with Raven to cart her off to the Brotherhood, which might seem like a good thing. Still, his continuing presence also meant he was unlikely to consider forgetting she existed when he finally left. It had been too much to hope that he would lose interest in her and let her alone.

Everyone who noticed Karsima riding in with Jenner close behind acknowledged her with calls of greeting or nods of varying enthusiasm. Raven, her hair pulled back in a long braid, was working at the entrance to the square, standing outside one of the buildings. Veylin enthusiastically explained to her the fine art of sorting the piles into usable and not usable materials. The elven scout waved at Karsima with the same enthusiasm. Raven offered a nod that appeared respectful enough, though her gaze was wary. The young female had significant trust issues, but that shouldn't come as a surprise. In her situation, unsanctioned as she was, anyone might choose to turn her into the Brotherhood on a whim.

Phendaril was walking over from where he and Jael were working on preparations to replace the damaged portion of a wattle and daub half-timbered wall on one house. His course was set to intercept Karsima. He had cast off his jacket and had his shirt sleeves rolled up to keep cool, though it had the added effect of showing off the lean musculature of his arms. The black strip of cloth tied around his head to keep sweat out of his eyes, combined with the scar, made him look like some kind of dashing and dangerous rogue.

She dismounted and turned an amused grin on him. "It's a good look. If I weren't already in love with someone..." She trailed off with a teasing wink.

"Don't tease, or I'll give your future quarters to someone else," he countered.

The faint sparkle of humor in his eyes and the smile tugging at the corners of his mouth told her what she needed to know about his mood. "I believe I get to pick my own quarters. Part of the privilege you voted to give me." She glanced around the square, noting how earnestly everyone appeared to be working and how much better things already looked. "I'm impressed. I didn't expect it to progress this quickly."

"Now that you brought me some fresh victims, it should go even faster." He glanced around at the group that had followed her into town, many of whom were busy finding places to make themselves useful.

"Did you introduce Raven to Helar?"

Phendaril followed her gaze to where the young Silverblood half-elf was now digging industriously into the pile of debris with Veylin. The latter appeared to be chatting merrily away at her. For her part, Raven looked content to let Veylin ramble on, offering a slight nod now and then to show she was still listening, or at least give that impression. Karsima was surprised to see her interacting at all.

Phendaril's brow furrowed, and the muscles in his jaw tightened. "No. I was going to after we ate last night, but she disappeared. I half didn't expect to see her again this morning, but she came wandering in with the sun from somewhere outside town. I think she slept in the forest." He gave a slight shake of his head. "If I hadn't run into her in Manderly, I'd say she was more isolated than even you suspected before coming here, but it doesn't quite add up yet." He met her eyes then. "She's never touched a horse before. How is that possible if she's been out in the world at all? And yet she can read, hunt, and fight."

"All things that can be learned quite effectively without leaving the comfort of one's own home depending on who you know."

"True," Phendaril agreed.

"Do you think she lived in Manderly?"

Veylin tossed part of an old cabinet on the trash pile, turning away as soon as she let go. The heavy piece hit the pile hard, sending a smaller fragment of wood flying toward the back of a man walking past. Karsima tensed, but she didn't have a chance to even shout a warning. With an agile little bound, Raven snatched the projectile out of the air, tossed it back into the pile, and calmly returned to her work.

Phendaril breathed a soft laugh and shook his head again.

Karsima took a deep breath, letting the brief tension fade some. Socially, Raven might have some issues, but she was proving to be quite handy to have around. "I expect you to get her over to Helar so he can adjust the armor measurements for her before the end of the day. Right now, however, it looks like Jael could use some help bracing the rest of that wall."

He glanced over at the elven scout struggling to get a heavy post into position. He arched one brow at her. "Care to assist?"

"Maybe later. I have a few people I want to talk to first."

Phendaril cast a wink over his shoulder at her as he started walking away. "Of course, you do."

She gave him a mock glower, then, as soon as he was out of earshot, turned to Jenner, who stood waiting patiently behind her. "Bring Raven over if you would."

He gave a slight bow, another deferential behavior he'd recently adopted that was spreading like a plague. "Yes, milady."

Sudden tension showed in Raven's rigid posture when Jenner approached her, but she nodded and followed him back over. The slight hitch in her walk was less noticeable than it had been yesterday morning. Her leg was healing quickly despite how much time she'd been spending on her feet.

"Raven, milady," Jenner introduced unnecessarily before stepping off to one side.

She was starting to suspect that his exploration of how to be a good assistant would eventually require more dramatic intervention. Now wasn't the time to address it, however.

"Milady," Raven echoed tentatively, making it sound almost more like a question.

"Your leg appears to be improving. How are you holding up with all the work?"

Raven shrugged. "I like being busy."

Of course, she did. It gave her less time to think about things she wished to forget, which Karsima suspected there were a large number of, and less need to be overly social. "I had asked Helar to start preparing a set of armor for you before you all left yesterday. You're built a lot like Veylin, so he's using her measurements right now, but I would like it if you could visit with him before the day is out. I would hate for him to have to rework it too much."

Raven shifted a half-step back, her eyes narrowing with suspicion. "Phendaril didn't ask me if I planned to stay until after we left camp yesterday."

Karsima waved the comment off. "Helar's always got some pieces premade. It's not that big an undertaking to put together a full set and make some adjustments. And someone would make use of the armor if you didn't. It was a reasonable gamble." She glanced around. Her attention caught upon Phendaril, who appeared to be correcting Jael's method of positioning the post. "That's all I wanted to talk to you about. I'm glad you're recovering well."

Raven nodded and turned a little as if expecting to be dismissed back to her work.

"Would you be kind enough to take Jael's place over there and tell him I'd like to talk to him?"

Raven followed her gaze, spotting the two elves. Her jaw tightened. The sun glinted off the silvery sheen of her neatly braided black hair. One of several not-so-subtle reminders that she was different from the others here. For a second, she didn't move, and Karsima wondered if she might refuse the request. Then she gave the faintest nod, meant in answer to whatever thoughts were going on in her own head, Karsima suspected. She didn't say anything before walking over to where the two males were working.

When Raven got close enough to speak to them, Karsima could see her hands trembling. She clasped them together to hide the shaking as the males noticed her and turned to face her. Jael nodded to whatever she said and passed her the post he was positioning.

Karsima ignored Jael's approach, watching intently as Raven shifted the post into place. Phendaril started to speak but stopped mid-sentence, his mouth slightly open. He cocked his head, looking at how she had set the post. Then he looked at her, his expression edging toward appreciation, and nodded. If only Raven knew that such an expression from him was like a shower of praise from most anyone else, she might feel a lot better about the work she was doing.

Jael stopped next to Karsima, his gaze following hers back to the building and the pair working in front of it. "You needed me?"

She offered an apologetic smile. "Not really. I just wanted to see how the Town Marshall and our newest recruit were getting along."

Jael used one arm to press the other across his chest, stretching his shoulder. "Does he know you've given him a title, milady?"

A soft laugh escaped her. "Absolutely not, and I would ask you not to share it with him yet. I suspect I'll need a long evening with Alayne's backing and a boatload of elven wine to get this one past him."

Jael chuckled, switching arms as he moved to stand beside her and watch them work. "And are you happy with what you see?"

Karsima observed in silence as Raven held the post,

and Phendaril secured it in place. When they were done with that one, they moved to the last brace, each taking up their positions without saying a word to one another. It took a mere minute or two for them to get that brace secured, then they moved to the part of the wall that needed the repairs. Raven picked up a heavy hammer meant for bashing out the portions to be replaced and offered it to Phendaril. He started to reach for it, then he grinned and took a step back, gesturing to the broken wall. Raven responded with the shadow of the same grin and stepped up to the wall. She hefted the hammer with relative ease, her magic-enhanced nature showing through in her strength. The section she struck broke inward at the first powerful strike. Phendaril nodded his approval again.

That they worked together so efficiently, despite Raven's apprehension around others and their lack of familiarity, was a bit of a surprise. The synergy to their unspoken coordination intrigued her. She also found it somewhat concerning. Maybe she had overlooked something there that might explain why Phendaril was so harsh with Raven at first. It wasn't that she would be surprised to find him attracted to the half-elf. Raven was beautiful and not in an ordinary way. Unfortunately, her situation would lead to nothing less than heartbreak for anyone foolish enough to take an interest. Usually, she would say Phendaril wasn't that kind of fool, but watching the two work together made her wonder.

The one thing she did know was that her friend wouldn't hold up well to emotional pain of that magnitude. Not again.

"Is everything all right?" Jael asked.

Realizing she hadn't responded to his question, she dredged up a faltering smile. "They seem to be working well together," she answered lamely. She glanced around and spotted Veylin struggling with an old cabinet. "I think Veylin could use some help if you'd be willing."

Jael nodded, hesitating a moment to try to catch her eyes, but she looked away. After a few seconds, he shrugged and trotted over to help Veylin, leaving Karsima to her new worries.

After a surprisingly pleasant day working with Phendaril, it was a little easier than expected for Raven to get through the process of letting Helar take her measurements that evening. The muscular elf mostly muttered to himself as he made marks on the armor pieces, then he grumbled something that sounded like a thank you and shooed her away. She ate quickly after that and disappeared into the woods to let her mind and body recover from the day without having to engage anyone else.

The next several days blurred together, each spent laboring to make the upper residential area livable. By the fifth day in town, several buildings were in good enough shape that people were starting to move into them. They had little in the way of furnishings, but that could be dealt with over time. Karsima took one of the larger homes. She invited a few others, including her constant assistant, Jenner, to set up their sleeping rolls in some of the side rooms downstairs for the time being. Raven overheard her offering a spot to Phendaril that he politely declined, saying it wasn't close enough to the forest. He took up residence in a smaller house nearer to the edge of town, letting Jael and another of the scouts stay with him for a couple of days until other options became available.

Raven was offered a room in the building across from the tavern that they transformed into the new healer's building. The same structure that she had shot the bear from the roof of. There was a kind of poetry to that, so she accepted, trying to pretend it didn't please her to see Synal move in as well after they brought Talis up from the lower camp. Talis appeared to be doing better. He was walking around more, enough so that Synal spent a fair amount of her time reprimanding him for not getting enough rest. The way she lovingly administered to him while he made sure to defy her orders only as much as necessary to keep her checking in regularly told Raven their relationship went deeper than simple friendship or had the potential to.

She thought Jaecar would have appreciated that the healer's building and the tavern were the first two establishments brought to a usable state. They started serving meals from inside the tavern by evening on the fifth day. Many workers were now able to eat at tables within the building. However, with their numbers, most still had to dine at tables out front or campfires placed throughout the square.

On the sixth day, Raven joined the same group that she had gone with to clear out the rats and the bear in reconstructing part of the upper floor of one of the houses. Only Talis was missing. Veylin managed to keep up an almost constant run of banter with whoever was willing to engage. Surprisingly, Darus, the one human scout in the group, rivaled her ability to keep up an unending stream of chatter. Between them, it wasn't necessary, or at times, possible, for anyone else to talk. It was welcome, in a way, because it kept Marek from asking her personal questions and negated the need for her to hold up a conversation.

They stopped briefly at lunch to eat, everyone too hungry by then for much chatter. It was midafternoon when she paused for another quick break, going to gaze out the window while she rested her arms. She set the hammer she'd been using on the sill. Down in the square, a couple of men were carrying the chest of books she hadn't yet had a chance to look through to Karsima's residence. She watched it vanish into that big house with a sinking sensation in her middle. She wasn't going in there to ask for the books. Not with so many people always wandering in and out. Not with Karsima's discerning blue eyes always watching her.

"Is everything all right?" Phendaril stopped a couple of feet back from her, glancing out the window curiously.

She nodded, quietly noticing that his presence didn't make her as uncomfortable as it had a few days ago. During those days, they had worked together several times. She always fell into an easy rhythm with him, much like she had been able to do with Jaecar.

She watched him for a few seconds as he gazed out the window, his dark eyes thoughtful, his profile pleasant, though in a different way than Eamon's had been. He had a little more definition and hardness to his features, but that fierce strength spoke to something in her in a manner she wasn't at all accustomed to. Then he turned to her, and she realized that he still made her uncomfortable, but no longer in a fearful way. It was in the way she wanted him to look at her. The way she yearned to have his approval. Her pulse raced a little when he shifted a half-step closer. It hadn't done that before, or she had simply been too wound up with anxiety to notice.

He angled his head slightly then, his eyes narrowing with puzzlement as though not sure what to make of her regard. What was she supposed to say if he questioned her look? What did other people say at such times?

"Anyone have a hammer I can borrow?" Marek strode up to them, his icy gaze cutting into Phendaril.

Raven picked up her hammer from the sill and held it out to him, hoping her silent response would discourage him from lingering. Marek smiled at her, the ice from a second ago melting from his silver eyes. When he took the hammer, he grabbed it well up the handle, his fingertips brushing her wrist. Raven jerked back, her breath catching in her throat. The sensation of being touched by a stranger was still unsettling, almost more so after her brief time with Eamon. Being touched by Marek, in particular, was markedly worse, especially given the odd heat that followed behind that contact, lingering on her skin like a light burn.

Phendaril glared daggers into Marek, but the adept simply turned and walked away as though he hadn't noticed. When Marek was gone, Phendaril looked at her again, his expression guarded now. "I think Veylin could use help with that stair railing."

Raven merely nodded. She rubbed at her wrist as she walked away, trying to get rid of the lingering trails of heat where Marek's fingers had touched. Veylin grinned at her when she walked up, the welcome in her eyes helping ease a little of Raven's discomfort.

"Is it hard being the object of two male's affections at the same time?" she asked in a low voice, her tone playful.

Raven glanced up at where Phendaril was now working on one of the door frames, trying not to let herself notice the shape of his hands and the sheen of sweat over his muscular arms. For a few seconds, she had trouble evening out her breathing.

She shifted her gaze to Marek, who was setting down the hammer she had given him beside another exactly like it. He knelt to help Jael position a board to repair part of the floor. He, too, was strong and handsome, and he still made her want to run to the forest and never come out.

"I don't think affection is what I'm the object of," she muttered. Maybe it was time to leave this place.

Veylin only shrugged.

Raven took hold of part of the railing, helping Veylin line it up where it needed to be so she could start nailing it into place.

If she left now, it would be with no more information than she had arrived with as far as the documents she carried were concerned. It was hard to want to trust anyone with them, though several people here had been welcoming enough to her. Veylin, in particular, treated her almost like a friend.

"Veylin?"

The elven female paused, giving Raven her full attention in a way that reminded her of Jaecar. It was likely only because she was unaccustomed to Raven starting a conversation. Still, it was nice in a nostalgic way.

"What is it?"

"Can you read?"

Veylin glanced away, her smile fading a fraction. "Only elven, and not very well at that." She brightened again quickly. "Karsima can read several languages, though. She studied at the university in Chadhurst. I believe she taught Phendaril too."

Raven's thoughts veered wildly off subject. She caught herself looking over at Phendaril again. "They're close?"

"Phendaril and Karsima? Very close. They were childhood friends here in Amberwood. During the siege, their families left at different times, and they were separated for several years. Then, as I understand it, Phendaril tracked her down at the university. They stayed in Chadhurst for a long time while Karsima finished her schooling. During those years, Phendaril made several trips to Amberwood to see what was happening here. By the time she was done with her degree, they'd managed to track down a fair number of former Amberwood residents, myself included, and put together a plan to reclaim the area."

She should have expected that. The two often consulted that she had seen, though she'd assumed, perhaps ignorantly, that it was a more professional relationship. He managed the scouts while Karsima oversaw the rest. They did seem to have a strong rapport, which made sense if they had known one another that long. Maybe his frequent visits to her home weren't just business. Although, if Phendaril and Karsima were more than friends, why would Veylin suggest that he was interested in her?

Not that it mattered. She gave herself a mental shake and turned her attention back to the female beside her.

"Anyhow," Veylin was saying, "if you need someone who can read well, I'd try one of those two."

The mere thought made her nauseous. "What about Synal?"

"Oh," Veylin straightened, looking almost surprised, "that's a good idea. I'd bet she can read as many languages as Karsima. She studied medicine in the elven hospital in Pellanth."

"Raven!"

She startled, almost losing her grip on the railing. In the doorway below, the leatherworker, Helar, stood squinting up at them. The daylight coming in the door around him was starting to change with the onset of late afternoon.

"One minute," Veylin called down when Raven didn't answer.

Raven gave herself a mental kick for failing to respond appropriately yet again.

Veylin grinned excitedly up at her. "Your armor must be ready. Let me get this tacked in place, then you can go."

As Veylin hastily finished pounding in several nails, Phendaril walked up behind Raven, placing a hand on the railing alongside her. "Why don't you go with her, Lin. I'm sure she'd rather not have some strange man helping her try on her armor."

Raven glanced up at him, gratitude swelling in her. She hadn't considered that someone might have to help her try it on. Though it made sense, given that she had never worn armor like this.

"Certainly. Beats pounding nails by a long shot." Veylin tossed the hammer in Phendaril's direction and spun to head down the stairs.

He met Raven's gaze as he snatched the hammer out of the air, the barest hint of a smile touching his lips. "You're welcome. Now go." He gestured toward the door with the business end of the tool.

Raven didn't wait. She didn't want to find out how fast her pulse could go if she stayed standing there that close to him. She could thank him for his foresight another time.

•

Helar was remarkably skilled. The armor, its final finish a hint shy of black, fit beautifully with a few minor last-minute adjustments. It was far more comfortable than Raven expected it to be. Veylin spoke through most of the process, primarily gushing about Helar's skills and how much she loved the armor he had made her. It was remarkably elegant and had some of the same markings as her sword and dagger etched into it. Since she didn't believe he had ever seen the weapons unsheathed, she had to assume someone else told Helar what was on them, making Phendaril the most likely suspect.

She stepped out of the building they had used for fitting into the fading light of evening with an armful of armor. The excitement that came with this new acquisition made her uneasy. She tempered it by telling herself they would probably make her return it all when she left. She spotted Phendaril directing two men carrying the chest of books back out of Karsima's house. He pointed at the healer's building, then turned to talk to someone else. She stopped and watched as they carried the chest inside. A strange sensation blossomed in her chest, and she wanted, for the first time in her life, to walk up and throw her arms around someone she hadn't grown up with.

She walked as fast as she could over to the healer's building and ducked inside. The men not only brought the chest into the building, they set it against the wall inside her room. Tears welled in her eyes, and she ducked into an empty room to wait until they left. Then she hurried over, set her armor on the bed, and opened the chest. All the books were still there, though someone had taken them out and cleaned them off.

Raven sat and began perusing the collection. There were several volumes on the history of some of the larger cities in the region, a guide to the local wildlife, a book on regional plants, and a massive tome of alchemy. There were also a few books of fanciful tales that she sat and flipped through for a short time. The last book she pulled out was written in a language she couldn't read, but the characters looked familiar.

Excitement burned away the day's exhaustion as she pulled out Jaecar's documents and matched the characters up. Whatever the writing was, they were definitely the same. That meant she could ask someone about the book instead of showing them the documents first. If they couldn't read the book, she didn't need to risk letting them see the real reason for her inquiry.

"You'd best get something to eat before they eat it all," Synal called from the main room.

Raven glanced up, becoming aware of the aromas of cooking that wafted through the open doorway. She tucked her things away and closed the chest, then headed out to appease the grumble in her stomach. Most of the workers had claimed their meals and were eating. There was still plenty, though. She collected food and drink and wandered out of the tavern toward one of the fires.

Most of them were well-occupied by now, though the one closest to the town entrance had only Jenner and Karsima there. A trencher and mug rested next to one currently unoccupied seat, which meant an unknown third would likely be returning soon. Still, three was manageable, even if one was Karsima. She walked up and stopped next to an empty chair made from thick branches some workers had gathered from the trees they cut down.

"Is this taken?"

Karsima inclined her head toward the chair. "No. Please, join us."

The welcome made her want to go sit somewhere else, but walking away now would undoubtedly come across as rude. She sat and started eating. She had been there no more than a minute when Marek strode up and claimed another empty spot without bothering to ask if it was available. Then Phendaril came out of one of the other buildings and sat where the abandoned trencher had been waiting.

Raven made herself keep eating, fighting the urge to flee. The others appeared focused on their food as well. When she was done, she set down the trencher and debated how soon after finishing her meal was too soon to get up and leave.

"Raven," Karsima started, bringing everyone's attention to bear on Raven all at once, "where are you from?"

She swallowed, hoping that staring into the flickering firelight would make it hard for them to tell how close she was to throwing up her freshly consumed meal. "South."

"Chadhurst, Manderly, Lathwood, Andel..."

Raven started to look up then caught herself, but it was too late.

"Andel." Karsima sounded pleased. "That's where they have that statue of... oh, who is it?"

No one said anything. They simply watched her. Raven thought this might be the right moment to run. The chest of books and the armor in her room gave her pause, though. "I lived near there. I never really went into town."

"Thadner Malcus," Marek offered then. "I believe they tore down the statue of the town's elven founder to put it up."

Was he offering up information he had only just recalled, or had he deliberately held back that answer long enough to make her feel like she had to reveal something of herself? She suspected the latter. Not only that, but she also got the sense that he wasn't the only one of them who had known the answer. Yet, they had all waited, letting her suffer before their expectant gazes.

"Excuse me." She got up and left the fire without giving anyone time to respond.

She took her trencher and mug back to the tavern, then slipped through the shadows and down the side street, heading out of town. She hadn't slept out in the woods for several nights since she now had a room separate from others. Tonight it seemed like a viable option to get her away from everyone else.

She didn't get much past the last house when she caught the sound of someone following. Placing a hand on her dagger, she spun around. Phendaril held his hands up but continued walking toward her.

"We're not your enemies, you know," he said softly.

She took her hand away from the dagger. "I'm not so sure."

"Karsima wasn't trying to upset you. It's her job to watch out for the people here. Part of that is knowing who they are."

"And she's in charge, so the rest of you just followed her lead?"

He stopped a few feet away from her. Did his elven eyes see as well as her Silverblood eyes in the dark? Could he see her torment? Could he see how bad she wanted to be just one of the people here? Did he have any idea how much wanting that terrified her? It would never last. Not as long as her very nature could create such conflict, and that would never change.

"What do you want?" Her voice trembled when she asked.

He started to take a step closer before uncertainty flickered across his features, and he settled back where he was. He was responsive to her reactions, and she wasn't sure whether that was a reason to like him or be that much warier of him.

"I wanted to make sure you were all right."

"I'm fine," she lied.

"I also wanted to ask if you would join my hunting party tomorrow. The wyvern south of here hasn't been spotted for several days. It's a good chance to clear out the harpy's nesting there. We'll be heading out at dawn tomorrow. I'd like to have an archer of your skill in the party."

Leaving town meant fewer people around. "Is Marek going?"

He shook his head, the hint of a smile tugging at the corners of his mouth. "Not this time."

"Then yes, I'll come."

"Thank you." He stood watching her for a few seconds. "Are you sure you're all right?"

"I just need a few minutes." She managed to keep her voice steadier this time.

"I'll let you be then." He turned and started walking back.

She wanted to say more to him, but that meant inviting his attention. Her pulse began to race, and she struggled to find her voice. He had gone a fair distance when she finally pushed past the fear. "Phendaril."

Despite how softly she'd said his name, he stopped and looked back.

"Thank you... for the books."

The flash of genuine smile he gave her before turning away again made her breath catch in her throat. "Good night, Raven."

•

Karsima watched Phendaril disappear down the street. She had no doubt about where he was going, and it pleased her that he was taking a more active interest in Raven. The young woman needed someone to show they cared enough to at least check into her well-being. She only hoped that encouraging him to do so didn't wind up being a mistake in the end.

She caught Marek's glower as she turned back to the fire.

"You'll drive her off if you pull too many stunts like that," he warned.

"I saw how quickly *you* came to her aid," she countered, arching a brow at him. "You want to know her story as much, if not more than the rest of us." Jenner stood and collected her mug and trencher along with his own, starting off toward the tavern with them as she spoke. There was little point in telling him he didn't need to wait on her. He'd made it clear he wasn't going to listen. "Thank you, Jenner."

A soft, "milady" drifted back to her.

Marek waited for Jenner to get out of earshot before speaking. "Until this evening, I was under the impression you and your elven pets were trying to protect her from me."

Karsima knew he was baiting her. It was hard not to let her resulting anger show, but she kept her voice even. "There are no racial divisions here, and I would ask you not to try to create any." She glanced over at him, noting his smirk with another flare of irritation. "As for Raven, she's stronger than you think she is."

"It doesn't matter how strong *we* think she is." Marek leaned back in his chair, resting one ankle on the opposite knee. "What matters is how strong *she* believes she is. Whoever was protecting her and keeping her hidden is obviously gone. They prepared her to take care of herself as long as she was alone but not around others. I'm afraid this environment might break her."

Karsima hid her own doubts behind a cynical laugh. "Or maybe this is exactly what she needs. A community willing to overlook differences and work together. Regardless, she's going out on a hunt tomorrow. That will give her a break from all this company."

He cocked one brow at her, expertly mimicking her earlier expression. "You don't want my skills on this hunt?"

"Not this one. I need you elsewhere. There is an old mine entrance about a half a day's walk to the east of town. The mine's infested with corpse eaters. One tunnel in the crypt on the edge of town collapsed into a mine tunnel that apparently ran alongside it, and they infiltrated the crypt. We drove them out with smoke and collapsed the mine tunnel to block their return, but one of our scouts heard digging back in there yesterday. I suspect we won't keep them out of the crypts as long as they're nested in the mines. I'd like you to look at the mine and crypt maps tomorrow and put together a party to go clear the bastards out."

He was eyeing her thoughtfully now, his fingers crossed in front of him. "I can put together my own hunting party. Anyone I choose?"

Karsima knew what he was asking. She stood up, glancing in the direction Phendaril had disappeared. It was a risk, but this situation would come to a head one way or another. "Yes."

CHAPTER TWENTY THREE

Knowing she was going out with a hunting party at dawn convinced Raven to come back and sleep in her room after Phendaril left her. Before she went to sleep, she hid Jaecar's documents under the makeshift cot. Early the following day, she fastened the final buckle of her armor into place the way Veylin had shown her and grabbed her weapons. Then she slung her pack over one shoulder and opened the door to her room.

Synal was awake already, tidying an array of tinctures and salves on a nearby shelf. When Raven emerged, she hurried over, grabbed a small sack off the nearest empty bed, and held it out to her. "I know Phen can push a fast pace. You'll need nourishment, so I packed a couple things for you. There's also bandages, a dram of my numbing tincture, and a bit of wound salve in there... just in case."

It was odd, but Synal offering up this collection of items she had gathered unbidden for her made Raven's throat hurt and her eyes sting with the threat of tears. Only the press of arriving dawn allowed her to push that swell of emotion away.

"I..." She trailed off when Synal held up a hand.

"You can thank me by being careful. I'm counting on your remarkable archery skills to help ensure that everyone makes it back alive and without any serious injuries. Besides, Phendaril's been less distant lately. I think the two of you working together more might be good for him... and for you."

Raven wanted to ask what the healer meant by that, but she couldn't bring herself to form the words. Instead, she took the bag and offered a nod. She stuffed it into her own pack on the way out the door.

Phendaril, Jael, and Darus were waiting by the well in the center of the square. Minutes after Raven went to stand with them, Leral, Veylin, and another young human man Phendaril greeted as Sameth, joined them. A few minutes later, one of the healers Raven had heard addressed as Ellandra rounded out the small company.

That gave them eight again. The exact number they had when they first cleared out this section of town. Sameth took Marek's place, which was fine with Raven. Ellandra stepped into Talis's place as healer, though she wasn't equipped for fighting. Her only weapon was a hunting dagger at her belt. That meant they had one less archer this time.

Phendaril nodded a greeting to the healer. "Remember, if we run into trouble, you need to stay back out of the fighting until it's over. We don't need another injured healer."

Ellandra met his gaze steadily. "If we run into trouble, you'll have to drag me out of hiding afterward. I promise there won't be any misplaced heroics coming from this healer."

Phendaril offered an appreciative smile. As reserved as the expression was, it still brought out a hint of something beautiful in his well-defined features. He caught Raven's gaze as he turned around, and her cheeks warmed, giving him more insight into her private thoughts than he might have had otherwise. His smile transformed, warming into something more intimate. She glanced away, pretending that her sword belt needed adjusting. His soft chuckle caught her attention, but when she snapped her gaze back to him, he was walking past the others to take the lead as though nothing at all had occurred between them. Perhaps it hadn't.

They kept a brisk pace, heading south of the remains of Amberwood and a little east. The trek started as a gradual incline toward the southern edge of the old town where the partially collapsed manor stood, its crumbled remnants taking her back to the keep she grew up in. A twist of longing in her chest drove her further off to the side of the group. No one, not even Veylin, tried to drag her back in. They were quieter than usual today, focused on the coming encounter or wary of other beasts that might be lurking along the route.

It suited Raven. Her conversation skills were significantly lacking.

Ellandra appeared less comfortable with the pace they kept, though she never complained. Phendaril gave them a few breaks. She assumed that was because they had farther to go this time than when they cleared the rats. Or maybe he was simply being considerate of Ellandra's discomfort.

The route got steeper as they went, and the woods thinned. The sun that peered down was warm, bringing out the smells of the trees and undergrowth. An occasional bright white cloud passing over kept it from becoming unpleasant as shade from the trees grew scarce. The grasses that grew up here weren't green and vibrant like lower down. Here they made a golden blanket along the steeper hillsides. They had a dry scent, evocative of clean straw baking in the sun. Not far in the distance, rocky outcrops jutted up from the rolling hillsides. There wasn't much cover there, which meant they would have difficulty sneaking up on their quarry.

Raven watched the more prominent outcrops and quickly spotted a large bird rising from somewhere within them. The creature's size told her it was one of the harpies they were searching for, but she glanced at Phendaril for confirmation. Somehow, he happened to be looking at her at the same time and nodded. She faced forward again. Was it a coincidence, or had he been looking at her more than in that moment, watching as she discovered this new landscape? If so, what was he hoping to learn from his observations?

He moved over beside her then. "Have you ever encountered a harpy?"

She nodded. "There were some west of my home, but they were far enough away not to be a real problem. I had one steal a kill once. It was an ugly beast, though watching it fly was beautiful."

He gave her a curious sideways glance before raising his voice so the others could hear. "We have harpies nearby, and something bigger has been seen flying out here from a distance. At least two of us should have bows ready from this point forward. There is a bit of difficult terrain ahead that might require having your hands free. We can alternate who has their weapons out if needed in those areas. For now, Raven and I will take point."

Doing her best to ignore the swell of pride at being selected, she drew her bow and nocked an arrow, taking a position at the front with Phendaril. After hiking a while longer, they neared the outcrops. The terrain became more challenging, with dangerous crevices splitting the ground in places and abrupt elevation changes as they navigated rocky ravines. At those points, they alternated who kept armed watch until everyone was safely through.

After a second rugged ravine, they came up within sight of three harpy nests built on top of some of the higher stone outcrops. Raven, who had led the way through the ravine this time and now had her bow out and armed, spotted a large, feathered creature resting in one of the nests. Likely a female almost ready to lay her eggs, given the time of year. Harpies had one or two viable eggs in a clutch. The eggs and the hatchlings were attractive prey for several species of opportunistic hunters and scavengers.

Phendaril strode up next to her.

"Do we have to kill them?" she asked softly, gazing up at the occupied nest.

"Unfortunately, they're close enough to threaten the livestock once we move the rest of the lower camp up to town. Their nests also attract troublesome creatures like fell rats and wyverns. We don't want more of those this close to town. However," he grinned and reached into his pack, drawing out a treated skin. When he pulled the cork, she instantly recoiled from the stink.

"What *is* that?" She took a few more steps back from him, fighting the urge to pinch her nostrils shut.

"This is a pheromone from the fell rats." He replaced the cap. "I've got junk arrows with cloth wrapped around the tips in my quiver. We'll soak the cloth with this and shoot a couple into each of the nests. The harpies will never use those nests again once they stink of fell rats. Veylin and Sameth will stand by with real arrows in case we get attacked while the rest of us are shooting this into the nests."

The idea made her inappropriately happy. Why it should matter that they had devised a plan to drive the beasts off rather than kill them was beyond her. They were only harpies. Yet, knowing that reclaiming Amberwood didn't mean simply slaughtering any creature that posed a threat was reassuring somehow.

Ducking her head to hide her pleased smile, she walked a little farther in, around a jut of rock to where she could get a better view of the land ahead. A bowl-shaped depression opened before her, with a significant fault splitting it down the middle. She spotted two more harpy nests in the rocks on the far side of the depression. She glanced back at Phendaril, gesturing ahead when he looked her way. He gave a nod. Raven led the way past the jut of rock and into the depression, finding a position where they could place Ellandra in the center of the ring of archers. From there, they could start making the nests inhospitable to their feathered occupants.

When they were in position, Phendaril passed junk arrows around to those who would be shooting them. He poured the pheromones on them before handing them off. Raven's stomach clenched at the stink as she accepted two of the rank projectiles. When all the shooters had arrows, Phendaril assigned them nests with a quick series of gestures. They took aim, holding for his soft command. When it came, everyone released, and the gentle whoosh of arrows cutting through the air was followed by a series of thwacks when they drove home into the nests.

Phendaril's arrow sank deep into the base of the occupied nest. The harpy there lurched up, its humanoid figure covered in dark feathers, and emitted a harsh shriek of rage. The face was somewhat human, only with far more severe angles to the feathered cheeks, jaw, and forehead. Relatable outrage was apparent in its expression despite those sharp features.

The shriek brought two, three, and then four more harpies out from within the rocky outcrops. The beasts attacked in groups, so it was no surprise when all four came swooping toward them. Raven lifted and aimed her bow in one smooth motion, aware of Phendaril doing the same beside her. Their arrows flew together, hers cutting close to the shoulder of one beast, his grazing the leg of the next one over. They were warning shots meant to drive the creatures off. Those two recoiled and hovered, reconsidering their attack. The two behind them followed their lead, pausing in the air.

Sameth let an arrow fly, tearing a few feathers from one's wing. That was enough. The four creatures let out several painfully high-pitched cries of rage before veering off in a different direction. As they flew, three more harpies rose from the rocky landscape to join them. The one whose nest Phendaril had struck let out a last shriek at them, close enough that Raven could see spittle spray from its beak-like mouth.

As the threat passed, she began to reach for a junk arrow to shoot into another nest when a different sound caught her attention. Behind them, from somewhere in the fault, she heard a low throaty growl that was barely audible even with her enhanced hearing. She turned toward the opening in the center of the depression. A few more arrows flew behind her, hitting other nests.

Something moved in the dark shadows of the fault.

"Watch out!" She shouted.

No one had time to react to her warning before the wyvern surged out of the opening. It lunged up into the air, then twisted and dove at them, magnificent green wings that gradually changed to brown at the edges casting a broad shadow over them. Everyone in the party dove to the ground on either side to avoid getting struck. The wyvern angled up once it was past them and swept toward the forest, disappearing from sight.

Raven stood.

Phendaril got to his feet, gazing at the fault the creature had come out of. "Not the most practical roost."

"It's a forest wyvern, not a dragon," Ellandra stated from where she was still sitting on the ground, brushing the dirt from her hands. Her voice shook. "Their smaller size lets them be more creative with their roosting options."

The others were standing. A couple took time to

brush off their pants, though most of the scouts didn't appear to notice the dirt.

Phendaril stepped over and offered Ellandra a hand up. "I didn't know you had an interest in beasts."

The fondness in the shaky smile she cast up at him made something curdle unpleasantly in Raven's gut. She forced herself to look away, scanning the sky for the wyvern or more harpies. Why should she care if the healer had feelings for him?

"Just a hobby," Ellandra replied. "At least it wasn't too interested in us."

Phendaril glanced around, also searching the sky. "I suspect the shrieking woke it. It may not have realized we were even here before it came out. Come on," his gaze swept them all in, "let's finish up and head back."

They spent the next hour working their way through the outcrops. They shot reeking arrows into the nests they found or poured the pheromone concoction in directly when they could reach. The few more harpies they encountered were easy to drive off with warning shots. When they eventually turned back toward town, Raven lingered toward the back, watching Phendaril. She wanted to talk to him, but they were back in the cover of the trees before he wandered away from the group enough for her to feel comfortable approaching.

"Phendaril." He glanced at her, a glimmer of pleased surprise in his welcoming smile that almost drove her off again. If not for the fact that retreating would prompt more questions, she might have done so. Now that she had his attention, there seemed nothing for it but to forge ahead. Besides, she would never learn to deal with others if she continued to keep them at a distance. "Will you leave the nests there?"

He nodded, twirling a stick he had picked up around and between the fingers of one hand in an elegant little dance that he appeared to be paying no attention to.

"It's prime nesting ground. If we knock the nests down or burn them, more harpies will move in and rebuild. If we leave them here and douse them with fell rat pheromones a few times a year, they'll avoid the area."

"What about the wyvern?"

"From what our scouts have seen, it's been scavenging off the harpies a great deal. I suspect it's young, looking for a territory of its own. It may move on without the harpies to provide easy meals. Or it may stick around, in which case we'll probably have to do something about it. We'll give it a week and see what happens."

She nodded and let herself drift away from him, not sure where to go from there with the conversation. Phendaril didn't try to stop her. His attention turned to Ellandra, who lagged a little.

"Let's take a short break. We could all use a few minutes rest."

Ellandra cast a look of the profound appreciation at him that brought back that strange curdling sensation in Raven's gut. She wandered into the trees to a point where she could see Phendaril's expression as he walked over to talk to the elven healer. Ellandra had picked out a log to sit on next to a close circle of trees that cast a deep cooling shade over the area.

Phendaril leaned against a tree next to the log. His smile struck Raven as at least as friendly as the one he'd given her a moment ago. "How long have you had an interest in beasts?"

Raven jumped up into the branches of the nearest tree, trying not to hear Ellandra's response. Once up to the lowest sturdy branch, she strode out along it and hopped over to a similar branch on the next tree.

"Impressive balance," Veylin called.

Raven's cheeks warmed, but she kept her attention on her foot placement. Her gaze moved along to another branch, and she jumped over, landing lightly on it. She planned out her route several steps ahead and began to follow it, continuously searching for the next viable landing spot. Then something shifted in the shadows a couple yards back from where Ellandra was sitting. Raven narrowed her eyes, peering into the shade, and caught the glint of the wyvern's eyes in the darkness.

She broke into a sprint along the branch, drawing her bow and nocking an arrow as she leapt to another. The wyvern surged out from where it was hiding among the deeper shadows, its dark brown and green scales offering perfect camouflage. Phendaril spun toward the sound of movement, reaching for his bow with one hand while grabbing Ellandra to yank her out of the way with the other. The healer stumbled, falling to the ground still within reach of the wyvern's lunge.

Raven leapt toward the creature, releasing an arrow as she dropped through the air. She hit the ground hard a few feet from Ellandra, landing between her and the wyvern and curling into a roll to reduce the impact. Her arrow struck the beast inside one nostril where the flesh was soft and sensitive, giving easily before the sharp point. It had the desired result. The wyvern lost interest in Ellandra. It twisted to the side and came for Raven instead.

Though she'd managed the roll, the landing was hard enough to leave her dazed and jar her bow out of her hands. She spotted the weapon lying a few feet past her leg and sprang for it, but the beast was faster. It lunged into her path and grabbed the bow in its teeth. Something broke in her chest when the bow snapped into pieces in those powerful jaws. More arrows flew from farther back, hitting the wyvern's impervious scaled hide. It shook its head, casting the shattered pieces of the bow aside, and charged Raven again.

She couldn't move. Her gaze followed the remains of the bow as the fragments hit the ground. A weight like iron landed in the pit of her stomach. Her father's bow was destroyed.

The wyvern's jaws opened as it lunged for her, then an arrow flew from its mouth, coming up through the soft flesh under its throat. The beast screamed, blood spraying from the wound. It wheeled and charged through the trees until it reached a spot with enough clearance to spread its wings, then surged skyward.

Raven knelt there, the remains of her father's bow filling her vision. The wyvern might as well have crawled inside her and started tearing her apart from within.

Ellandra bent down next to her, her voice trembling. "Are you hurt?"

Raven shook her head.

"You just saved my life," Ellandra breathed. "That was amazing."

Raven didn't answer.

"We should move on. It could come back," Phendaril prompted. He came to stand beside Ellandra. "Are you sure you're all right, Raven?"

She made herself get up, ignoring the hand he offered. She didn't look at any of them. She couldn't. "I'll catch up."

"I'd rather not leave anyone alone out here," he countered.

"I'll catch up."

Ellandra started to walk away. Phendaril stood there for several seconds longer as if he might argue with her. Then he too turned away, the rest following him. Raven stood listening to the sounds of their footsteps through the undergrowth. They made surprisingly little noise as they went. One set of footsteps, marginally louder than the others, was probably Ellandra since she was the only non-scout in the group.

When she could no longer hear them, Raven sank

to her knees next to the shattered bow. She curled over it, sobs tearing free. The bow her father carried on their last hunt together. The bow she had reclaimed after that bastard used it to shoot arrows into her bound mother. The bow she had used on every hunt, alone or with Jaecar, since she was big enough to wield it. Losing it was like losing each of them again, even Eamon, who had so admired her skill with it. All of them lost to her, and now it was gone too.

Swallowing pain into the hollow in her gut, she wiped at her damp cheeks. After a few minutes more, she stood and headed into the trees in the direction the others had gone, making no effort to catch up.

CHAPTER TWENTY FOUR

Raven wandered into town as dark was falling. Phendaril, who she had spotted watching the road from one of the rooftops, came down soon after she walked in, though he didn't approach her. Dinner was being served, so she claimed her meal and disappeared into her room to eat.

When she woke in the morning, her trencher and mug lay discarded on the floor next to the bed. A reminder that a whole community waited outside her door. It took considerable effort to make herself get up and carry the items back down to the tavern. From there, she found a group with no one she knew in it that was hard at work rebuilding the floor of one of the buildings and offered to help. She threw herself into the process, evading their occasional attempts to engage her in conversation.

They stopped in the early afternoon for a break and refreshment. Raven didn't join them. She found a quiet corner away from the activity to snack on leftover dried meat and other morsels that remained from the previous day's excursion.

When she wandered back out into the square to return to work a short time later, Karsima ambushed her.

"I understand I have you to thank for the fact that Ellandra's still with us?"

Raven shrugged, casting one wistful glance toward the building she had been working on. "I was just in the best position to do something."

"Whether or not that's true, that's the third time you've saved one of our lives. I understand you need a new bow if you're going to join any more hunts."

Raven said nothing. She couldn't bring herself to answer in the affirmative, but denying it meant refusing the chance to go hunting or scouting. That was the work she preferred, away from the crowds, out in the woods.

"Come with me," Karsima started walking. "They've set up a temporary armory on the side street there. You can test some bows on the targets and see if anything suits you."

Raven followed. What else was she supposed to do?

The temporary armory was in a building that looked like it might have been a shop of some kind. When they passed, a glimpse through the open doorway revealed a multitude of weapons and various pieces of armor set out on racks and tables within. The open grassy stretch alongside the building, which she assumed had once served another purpose, now had archery targets set up at the back. A variety of bows were arranged against the wall of the building.

She followed Karsima to the row of bows. The town leader stopped there and faced her, offering a smile that was so full of encouragement Raven found herself despising the woman for it. Tall, well-built, and beautiful, with those dark golden locks and striking blue eyes. Karsima and Phendaril had known one another since childhood. What would it be like to have someone in her life who had stood beside her for that long?

Karsima taught him how to read.

Raven cast a look of pure loathing at the bows but did as expected and picked one up, more concerned with the draw weight than the length. Her father's bow had been a little too long for her, but she had adapted her style to it.

"Whatever bow suits you most is yours."

Karsima was trying to be helpful, Raven supposed, lifting her lip in a silent snarl of directionless rage while aiming at the target. She let the arrow fly. It struck solidly in the center of the target. It was a good size and draw weight, but she hated the bow. She hated the way it felt, the way it looked, even the way it smelled. Hating it kept her from crying as she put it down and tried another. It would be the same with all of them. She should just take one and be done with it.

She shot the following two bows, grouping the arrows neatly in the center of the target. Several of the folks nearby had stopped whatever they were doing to watch. She heard appreciative comments on her aim, followed by more about how she had saved Ellandra from the wyvern. Someone else mentioned Veylin and the dire bear and the rescue of the elves down in Manderly. The admiration in their tones caught her by surprise. She hadn't realized she was developing a reputation among the citizens of Amberwood, but, judging by those remarks, they held her in esteem, mainly from a distance.

She shot another arrow into the grouping and set the bow down. She resented that bow too. There was little chance she wouldn't hate them all. If she took one, maybe Karsima would let her go back to building the floor.

"Take this one."

Raven turned at the sound of Phendaril's voice. He stood behind her, holding an elegant bow carved out of pale amber wood with grains of deep red running through it. Its graceful lines curved like water sweeping around a perfectly formed stone. Even at a glance, she could see that the craftsmanship was flawless.

She met his eyes, seeing conflict in them, and shook her head. "I can't take this."

He lowered his voice so the entire audience wouldn't hear, though a few, like Karsima, were still close enough. "I saw in your face what you lost when you lost that bow. You've done a great deal for the community here." His gaze shifted to the bow in his hand. "My father made this bow out of amberwood from these forests. It belonged to an extraordinary archer. She was killed when her party was surprised by a beast the same way we were surprised by that wyvern yesterday." He looked into her silver eyes again. Her curse. "The difference is that you were fast enough to make sure no one died. Honor her memory and me by using her bow."

"You fired the shot that drove the wyvern away." She didn't need him to confirm it. Until that moment, she hadn't considered that someone else had saved her when the impact from her jump and the loss of her father's bow left her reeling. Now that she said it, she could see in his eyes that it was the truth.

"Take it, please." His voice sank lower still, meant for her alone this time.

Raven took the bow. The weight and length were perfect when she drew back the string and fired. The arrow forced its way deep into the center of the tight cluster she had made in the middle of the target. She turned, determined to thank him. Not just for the bow but for his help with the wyvern as well. He was already gone. Karsima was staring back toward the square. Raven followed her gaze, spotting Phendaril as he headed for the tavern.

Karsima turned back to her. "I guess you found your bow." She gave the weapon a pained look before striding away, saying something under her breath about work she had to do.

Raven returned to her work after storing the bow

in her room. That evening, she joined the group she had worked the day with around one of the fires to eat. It took her a while, casually scanning the area, to spot Phendaril. He wasn't among the visible groups, not even with Karsima, who sat conversing with Marek, Jael, and Veylin. She eventually spotted him, nearly invisible in the darkness, sitting upon the rooftop she had shot the bear from.

Sucking up her courage, Raven dropped off her trencher at the tavern and collected two new mugs of mead. It was awkward climbing up onto the roof with them, but when she got close to the top, a hand came down to take one and then the other from her. She followed Phendaril back to where he had been sitting overlooking the square and sank down cross-legged beside him. For a few minutes, neither of them spoke. It was hard to start a conversation under normal circumstances. Doubly so when the person she wanted to talk to made her pulse race like she was under attack.

"It was my father's bow," she finally said, unable to stop the tremble in her voice.

"I'm sorry. Is he..."

She nodded quickly, so he didn't have to finish the question. "Tell me about her, the one whose bow you gave to me today."

Phendaril drank from the mead she had brought him. She took a sip of her own. Now that she was becoming accustomed to the drink, she could probably get away with a few sips from a second mug.

Below them, the elves and humans who made up the populace of Amberwood were laughing and conversing in good-natured exhaustion after another day of hard work. More from the lower camp had come up. She didn't think they were all there yet, though it was getting closer by the day as more buildings became usable. Sometimes she liked hearing their laughter. The comfortable, happy sound could be uplifting. Other times it made her feel more alone.

This evening, a twist of black resentment had begun coiling in her chest. That part of her hated that this was their normal life and that it came so effortlessly to them. Since joining Phendaril on the roof, however, that blackness had retreated.

"Her name was Celaena. She was the best archer in Amberwood when I was a child. She also happened to be my aunt. She coordinated the scouts and the hunting parties for the town, much the way I do now, I suppose. When the two lords went to war over Amberwood, our house got destroyed in a barrage from Darrenton's prized collection of catapults and ballistae. My younger brother and my father were killed in the incident. My mother convinced Laena to leave town with us after that.

"Thanks to her, we never wanted for food or coin. She caught enough to keep us fed and sold whatever meat and hides we didn't need. Eventually, we settled outside of Lathwood. She went to work for the constable doing the same kind of work she had done in Amberwood. She started taking me out on hunts with her there. Taught me everything she knew about archery and the creatures and plants of the forest." His soft smile held remembered affection. "It was there that she died trying to save another scout from an enraged dire bear. An old temperamental beast much like the one we faced here."

"What did you and your mother do then?"

He leaned back a little and drew in a deep breath. His gaze sank to the contents of his mug. "My mother died about a year before that. When Laena died, nothing remained to keep me in Lathwood. I decided to try to track down an old friend."

"Karsima?"

His glance was full of curiosity, wondering perhaps how she had made the connection, but he only nodded and took a long drink from his mug before continuing. "Yes. We were practically inseparable as children. We swore to find one another again when my family left Amberwood. I tracked her down in Chadhurst. She always said she would get a real education when she got older, so I looked at the university there, and that was where I found her. While she finished her degree, I learned what I could about the situation in Amberwood, and we made plans to reclaim it."

Raven nodded and took another drink. Then she clutched the mug in front of her to hide the shake in her hands. Maybe a day would come when talking to someone like this wouldn't make her so nervous. "You make it sound so easy, moving around the world, interacting with it."

Phendaril chuckled and shifted, so he was turned toward her a little more. "I don't know if it's really that easy or if you just get used to doing it. You grew up rather secluded, I gather."

Her throat tightened. She forced her voice past the constriction. "I grew up with my parents in the woods until they died. Then I lived with an old warrior who trained me to fight, hunt, and read, but not to ride," she added, taking comfort from the light laugh it earned her. "I..." She swallowed hard, struggling the keep her voice steady.

"You don't have to talk about it," Phendaril said softly.

The kindness and sincerity in his tone made her more determined to offer him something in return. "I had never spoken to a stranger in my life before I approached Eamon a few days prior to your arrival in Manderly."

The prolonged silence that met that revelation made her stomach do flips. What would he think of her now?

A broken little half-elven Silverblood female. Wrong in every way and completely lacking any experience in the world outside her hidden refuge.

He took another drink of his nearly empty mead and stared down at the fires below. A lock of that dark auburn hair slipped over his fine, pointed ear, obscuring her view of his face. She was a little shocked by the sudden urge to reach over and brush it back so she could better admire the defined line of his jaw. Even the scar down the side of his nose had become something she appreciated when she looked at him. It had a story to tell that she yearned to know but still didn't dare to ask about.

She downed a swallow of mead and wiped her lips. Drawing on the dwindling reserves of her courage, she glanced over at him. "You must think me rather pathetic."

He met her eyes, a spark of unexpected enthusiasm in his sudden bright smile. "On the contrary, I think you're rather remarkable. Look at everything you've done in that time. And you've become something of a hero to many individuals here. Ellandra can't stop talking about how you dove down between her and the wyvern." He made a dramatic diving gesture with one hand "The story of the fight with the dire bear is still the most popular tale in the tavern in the evening. Even Synal boasts about how you took an arrow in the leg helping save the crew down in Manderly."

His smile changed then, the enthusiasm fading in the wake of something more profound and substantially more disconcerting. "Knowing how new all this is to you, I would say that the way you've helped rebuild this place, working all day amidst so many strangers, is at least as heroic as those other things."

Nothing in his tone or expression suggested he was deceiving her in any way. She wanted to bask before the warmth of his admiring gaze forever, but she couldn't. "You weren't so excited about me when we first met."

The smile faded, and she instantly missed it.

"I was wrong." He didn't look away, so she did. "I don't like Silverbloods. Most of us don't. They may be exceptional at many things, but they become that way by sacrificing another life. Anyone who would choose that for their own selfish gain can't be trusted–"

"I..." He held up a hand, and she trailed off.

"I recognize now that you didn't *choose* this. I'd love to understand that better, but I won't press you on it. I have also known many half-elves in my time. Most of them were the product of rape. I let my hatred for the men who would do such things and my dislike for Silverbloods color my reaction to you. You didn't deserve it."

Raven could hear the words in her head as if he had just spoken them. Somehow, they still stung. "You said..." She trailed off again when he leaned closer, staring into her eyes.

"I said your features were too beautiful to be human and too soft to be elven."

The warm tone and the admiration in his gaze stole her breath for a second. "You didn't say it quite like that," she murmured.

He exhaled a small laugh. "No, I most certainly didn't."

For a few seconds, she sank into the depths of those eyes. Then a flash of panic burned through her. She leaned away and stood.

"I could use a little rest." She picked up her mug and his empty one. "Thank you," she offered as she headed for the way down.

"Good night, Raven," he called after her.

She climbed down to the broken cobble street and instantly went alert, peering into the shadows. It took mere seconds to pick Marek's gleaming silver eyes out of the darkness. As soon as she spotted him, he came toward her.

"That's why I need you."

She tensed. "What do you mean?"

"Like me, you can see in the dark better than even the elves." He gestured in the direction of the square and fell in alongside her when she started walking that way. "Karsima's charged me with clearing the corpse eaters out of a mine east of here. The tunnels run up next to the crypt tunnels, and she's concerned about them breaking through again. My party is heading out in the morning, and I hoped you would join us."

She glanced over at him, trying to be at ease with the friendly-looking smile he offered.

When she didn't speak, he continued. "Karsima said I could select my party, but I know this job has unique challenges. I don't want to be responsible for someone else getting hurt. I'm taking a couple of others with me, but only for support if there's trouble along the route. I plan to enter the mine alone unless you're willing to come. Together, you and I could take care of this problem. You must know I'm right."

She drew in a breath, clinging to the courage that had sustained her through the rest of the evening. "I'm not sure I trust you, Adept Marek."

"Just Marek," he countered. "Give me this chance."

She stopped and turned to face him. He did the same. Something about those silver eyes made them hard to read. Were hers that way too? Did others have as much trouble reading her eyes? If so, it would explain more of the mistrust toward Silverbloods.

Somehow, Marek had found time to keep the stubble of his beard neatly trimmed and shaped. The smile he offered was unexpectedly open and pleasant. It made her want to trust him, though she couldn't quite bring herself to do so. Still, he hadn't tried to drag her off to the Brotherhood, and he had been giving her space lately. Maybe?

"Just a day trip? Out and back?"

"I'm guessing so, though it is a couple of hours out, according to Karsima. If the infestation is significant, we could be stuck there overnight."

At least he didn't appear to be trying to hide anything. Would she recognize it if he were? "All right. Where are we meeting?"

"The well. No later than dawn. I want to try to get out and back in one day if possible."

She nodded. "I'll be there."

CHAPTER TWENTY FIVE

It was nearing noon when Phendaril tracked Karsima down. She had just finished a meeting on the edge of town to discuss the management of crops now that they were almost ready to move the rest of the lower camp up. The gardens they planted at the lower camp would be transplanted, and larger fields prepared. There would be a lot more mouths to feed when Alayne arrived with the Stonebreakers.

She had asked Phendaril the night before to reach out to his scouts about the best areas to hunt sustainably. After so many years as his friend, it wasn't hard to predict that he would venture out before sunup to try to catch the ones on patrol before they left their evening camps. That meant he was away when Marek's party ventured out that morning. Now she braced herself to face the storm.

His smile as he approached was unusually relaxed. Karsima strode over to meet him, deliberately trying to keep their encounter away from curious onlookers.

"How did it go?"

"I have a whole set of rough sketches I left in your office showing where the local herds are and their numbers. I also got a detailed rundown on what predators are using which herds for sustenance. I think we should be able to manage well enough until we get our livestock built up." He glanced back toward town. "Have you seen

Raven this morning?"

That came up faster than she had hoped. "You two talked last night?"

"Yes. She even volunteered a little information about her past. I think she's starting to become more comfortable."

Raven might be becoming more comfortable, but the glimmer of pleasure in his eyes made Karsima distinctly uncomfortable. "Phen." She waited until he looked at her, his smile faltering before whatever he saw in her expression. "Help her. Don't fall in love with her."

His eyes narrowed. "I can handle myself," he snapped.

"You gave her Laena's bow?"

He glanced away, the muscles in his jaw jumping as he clenched his teeth. He took a deep breath and let it out before speaking again. "The bow Raven lost belonged to her dead father. Laena's bow was serving no purpose. In her hands, it will have a purpose again." He cast another meaningful glance toward town. "Do you know where she is?"

"I do. Marek took her with him to clear out the corpse eaters in the mine." It was like watching a storm cloud roll in, complete with the lightning flashing in his eyes. Karsima braced herself for the thunder.

"I thought you told me not to let her go out with him unless I was there. Now you're sending them out together on a dangerous excursion that could take a couple of days?" He pointed fiercely in the direction of the mines. "He'll get her killed or, more likely, kill her himself."

"Don't shout, Phen." She gave him a withering look that appeared to have no impact. "Raven's proven she can take care of herself. The biggest threat to her right now is if he decides to tell the Brotherhood she's here. I can only see one possible way to prevent that, and that's by convincing him he doesn't want to tell them about her. Raven's won you and more than half the population of Amberwood over in the short time she's been here. She's her own best defense when it comes to Marek. If she can't convince him she's worth letting live, then there's nothing we can say to do so."

"We could kill him."

Karsima glanced around to see if anyone was in earshot. "Blast it, Phen. We're not murderers. Besides, killing a Silverblood adept would put us at war with the Brotherhood. That's not a war we can win."

The cold anger in his eyes chilled her. It was that cold again that had taken root in him sometime after they were separated as children. The things that happened in their years apart created a dark place in him that she simply couldn't reach. She didn't doubt that part of him was perfectly willing to murder a Silverblood warrior to protect this strange half-elven female he had taken a fancy to.

He stalked a few feet away. Karsima drew in a calming breath and followed him.

"You need to give her a chance to take care of herself. You know she's more than capable of handling herself physically–"

He whirled around on her. "Against another Silverblood?"

Her anger surged in response to the fact that he had managed to startle her. She made herself breathe again. Slow and steady. "You can't hide her from the beast that already knows where she is. I think she can win him over. Give her a chance."

"I'm going after them," he stated.

It was apparently time to try a different approach. "No, you're not. Do you really want to show her that you have that little faith in her?"

He turned to stare in the direction Marek and his group would have gone. The hand he ran roughly through his hair trembled with barely controlled anger.

"I need your help here. Alayne and the Stonebreakers will be here any day now. This place isn't quite ready for that sudden surge in population."

"The Stonebreakers are accustomed to sleeping under the sky," Phendaril countered.

"Phen, please."

She watched him pace back and forth a few times. Stopping to stare off in the directions of the mines at the end of each lap. Then he turned a little, his gaze moving to the town that was being gradually reborn. The town they had come here together to rebuild.

"All right," he conceded, "but if this goes badly, I will remember the part you played in it." He stalked away without a backward glance.

Phendaril didn't speak to her again that afternoon. By early evening, it no longer mattered. Five riders rode into the old town with a long line of Stonebreaker warriors, workers, and their families marching behind. The conglomeration of leather and metal armor the Stonebreakers wore made them look bigger than they were, and they tended to be built big anyhow. As many dark-skinned women as men were armed and armored, which struck Karsima as admirable. A trait that was generally more common among elves than humans. The Stonebreakers were typically solitary people, but if Alayne had convinced this clan to help rebuild Amberwood, she wasn't going to question it.

It was the rider leading the group that most concerned Karsima. Alayne's fiery red hair was tamed down into a long braid flung over one shoulder, and her skin had been kissed by the sun to a soft, warm tan. She was the most glorious creature Karsima had ever seen, riding at the lead on her a fine sorrel mare whose coat almost matched her hair.

As soon as Alayne spotted her, a grin curved her

lips. She kicked the horse to a canter, skidding to a stop in front of Karsima. Then she leapt out of the saddle and threw her arms around her. Karsima returned the embrace, bursting with a joy so powerful she thought she could probably fly at that moment.

"It's been too blasted long," Alayne declared, then she kissed her hard.

When she drew away, Karsima was breathless. She couldn't tear her gaze away from the passion in those vivid green eyes. "Jenner," she called, hoping the man still stood in earshot, "can you help them settle in like we discussed. I need to get a full accounting of people and resources they've brought from Alayne."

"Yes, milady."

Alayne didn't break eye contact either as she called out, "Garnath, this gentleman," she gestured in the general direction of Jenner's voice, "will help get the group settled. Try to be nice."

A grunt answered her that Karsima suspected, given the flicker of amusement in Alayne's smirk, came from Garnath. With that handled, for now, she took Alayne's hand and turned toward the house she'd made into her home. Their home now.

"Come, let me show you our quarters."

Alayne strode along at her side, leaning close to whisper into her ear, "I hope you don't have anything too pressing. This could take a while." She squeezed Karsima's hand.

Almost drunk with elation, Karsima quickened her pace, doing everything she could to get to the building quickly short of breaking into a run.

Some hours later, she watched as Alayne sat naked on a chair next to the bed, re-braiding her hair. Karsima lay on the bed, still naked as well, though she wasn't as comfortable being exposed as Alayne appeared to be. She did enjoy the appraising glances the other woman gave her every few minutes.

"It's really the lap of luxury, isn't it," Alayne said, laughing as she cast a look around at the roughly assembled furniture.

Karsima couldn't stop smiling. It had been several months since they'd been together. Far too long. "That's why you brought the Stonebreakers. No one can build like their masons and carpenters. We'll have luxury furniture in no time."

Alayne arched an eyebrow at her. "They'll want homes first."

Karsima rolled over on her back to stare up at the ceiling. "Details."

Alayne chuckled softly. Such an incredible sound.

"How's Phen?"

Karsima drew a deep breath, her elation dampening a fraction. "He's been doing well. I'm a little concerned about him, though."

Alayne finished the braid and secured it. Then she got up and stalked to the bed. She climbed back onto it like a cat, moving over the top of Karsima. She offered a feral grin and lowered herself down, kissing her long and sweet this time, sending a fresh wave of desire through her. Then she lifted up on her arms and gazed down at Karsima.

"Tell me your worries, my love." She came down for a quick kiss this time and back up again. "I'm here to kiss them all away."

Karsima stared up into her green eyes. They weren't going to be talking about Phendaril quite yet, which was fine with her. She raised herself up on her elbows and kissed Alayne, flicking her tongue out to touch the other woman's lips. Alayne made a soft purring sound in her throat and opened her mouth to the kiss.

Raven considered backing out. When she'd reached the well before dawn that morning, Marek had been waiting alone. A few minutes later, Darus and Calin joined them. Both human. Both men. She clung to her resolve and hiked out of town with the small group, struggling not to cast a hopeful glance toward the house Phendaril was living in, longing for rescue.

Once they were outside town, she moved off from the group as she usually did, always looking interested in something else in the hopes that they wouldn't try to engage her in conversation. It worked for a time, then Marek, who had been indulging the two men in tales of his work as a fancy mercenary, glanced over and came her way.

Whatever questions lurked behind the curiosity in his eyes, she decided it was best to head them off. As soon as he fell into step beside her, she asked, "After this long, there can't be enough flesh on the corpses in the crypt to sustain the corpse eaters. Why haven't they moved on."

The glimmer of amusement in his eyes combined with his subdued smirk told her he knew she was trying to distract him, but he went along with it. "Corpse eaters are attracted to crypts and burial grounds because of the pre-ripened meal selection, but they still kill most of their meals. If a kill is fresh, they drag the corpse into a food store in their den and let it rot for several days before eating it."

"Pleasant," she muttered, trying hard not to let her imagination explore that information.

"Why Raven?"

The question jarred her, taking her back to when Eamon inquired about her name. A potent dose of grief and bittersweet longing still laced those memories.

"I'm sorry. I can see you're not ready to talk about it."

The reversal pulled her attention to him. It wasn't what she expected from a man who would ask to borrow a hammer he didn't need just to insert himself in her conversation with Phendaril. Nor from a man who would declare her very existence a crime. Perhaps he was changing his mind.

She met his silver eyes, knowing too well how perfectly they mirrored her own. "Thank you."

He answered with a nod and continued to walk with her in indulgent silence until Darus joined him to discuss the route.

It wasn't a strenuous hike. Unlike the climb to the harpy nests, this trip followed relatively level terrain along an old road that had been substantially reclaimed by the forest. When they reached the edge of the trees near mid-morning, a meadow of gold and green grass stretched before them, leading up to the base of a steep mountainside. A dark hollow opened at the bottom of that mountain, ready and eager to consume them.

When they were close enough, the stink of the corpse eaters wafted from the opening. They smelled of rot and death. Bones around the entrance looked like they had been flung from the shadows. Corpse eaters were sensitive to sunlight, so they rarely ventured out during the day. It appeared that they did like to get rid of their trash once they were done cleaning off the rotten flesh, however.

Marek stopped them outside, and Raven took the opportunity to drink water from the skin she carried. The stench made it hard to want food, but she forced herself to eat a handful of nuts. The work ahead would be exhausting.

"You two will wait out here," Marek stated, indicating Darus and Calin in turn with his stern gaze. "Some may try to bolt once we start clearing them out. I expect you to deal with them. Don't get complacent if you don't see anything right away. It will take us some time to get to the back, and I don't want anyone getting killed."

He turned to Raven and gestured for her to come closer. When she did so, he pulled a parchment from his pack and crouched down, spreading it on the ground for them to look at. It was a map of the mine. The passages weren't as complicated as she had feared they might be. He pointed to a circle near the farthest end.

"This is where they broke through into the crypts. The passage back to there is relatively straightforward. I'm going to guess that their sleeping dens are concentrated in some of these dead-ends." He pointed to several spots on the map. "If we work our way back to here first, we run less risk of driving them back into the crypt and, through that, toward the town. They hadn't broken through again at the last check, but digging could be heard, which means they are probably close to doing so. A little panicked digging might put them through."

She nodded, catching on to his plan. "So, we try to make it back there without causing too much of a stir, then work our way out toward this entrance? Drive them out instead of in."

He gave an answering nod and glanced up at the two men again. "Don't come into the mine. Let the ones that flee come to you. They can see a lot better than you can in that darkness."

He waited until both men agreed to their role, then backed them off a short distance to take a rest. Raven pushed away the threatening panic at the thought of being in there alone with him. If they were going to succeed, they would have to work together, or one of them would pay the price. She'd never seen a corpse eater, but she had read about them. They were scavengers and opportunistic killers. Under normal circumstances, in a solitary encounter, they were unlikely to attack an armed person. Anyone foolish enough to go looking for them where they lived would have a different experience.

When they were ready, the other two men moved off to a distance where they could pick off any fleeing beasts with their bows and hopefully avoid close combat. Raven and Marek stood before the entrance. She had left her bow behind, though she hated letting it out of her sight. In these tight quarters, the longbow would be useless. Marek did have his crossbow, but that weapon was more useful in close quarters.

"How much are they paying you for this?"

He adjusted one leather gauntlet. "Not enough."

She glanced over at him, watching as he tugged the other on tight. "Then why are you doing it?"

"I would have thought that was obvious." He finished his adjustments before meeting her eyes. "I'm keeping myself busy while I decide what to do about you."

"Why do you have to do anything?"

His brow furrowed at that as if the question troubled him. "I've sworn my life and my service to the Brotherhood."

Raven decided to leave it at that for now. No matter the myriad complications that marked their relationship, they had a task to complete right now that required cooperation.

"Shall we?" She gestured toward the entrance, wishing the stench coming from the mine didn't already make her want to vomit.

He peered into that darkness and crinkled his nose in distaste. "Not nearly enough," he muttered.

They both drew their swords and headed in. The worst part was the entrance, where the sunlight fought to maintain its rule. Once darkness folded completely around them, her eyes began to adjust, scaling to the lower and lower light. They were near-perfect predators, she realized, tuning her sharp hearing to the sounds of water dripping and the shuffle of movement from someplace further in. With their magic enhancements and the use of weapons that had long allowed humans and elves to kill things much faster and stronger than themselves, they were uniquely suited to hunting and fighting in this way.

They kept to the left, moving toward the back corner that met up with the crypt passages. Every now and then, the sound of something moving nearby would stop them in their tracks, making them both freeze at the same instant, as if they shared one mind. He wasn't wrong about them being the best team for this job.

They crept forward, time creeping by with every careful step. At one point, a corpse eater came shuffling into their passage. When it became clear the beast was going to spot them, Marek dropped it with a crossbow bolt to the throat.

He started to move on, whispering, "The blood might draw others. We need to get away from this spot."

Raven nodded, but she was staring at the beast, taking in the power in its thick shoulders and the slope of its back to smaller but equally muscular hindquarters. It had four tiny eyes above massive jaws lined with sharp teeth meant to rend rotting flesh. Three long prehensile tongues splayed out on the ground between those teeth.

The backswept horns on its head appeared more for display than functionality. It was easily twice the size of the fell rats they'd dealt with in the town and had no fur, just a mottled, skin stretched tight over its body, looking like it might tear over the sharp joints. Its front paws held her gaze for several seconds. The elongated digits, though tipped in thick claws, had an unnervingly human shape to them.

"Raven," Marek hissed.

She startled and followed him from the area, heading ever back into the black depths of the mine. It was an eternity in darkness, waiting to be attacked, before they reached the end of the mine where the tunnel was intentionally collapsed to cut off access to the crypt. They weren't alone when they got there. A couple of corpse eaters were sniffing around the rubble, one of them starting to paw at a spot where it looked like they might be close to breaking through.

Marek shot the one near the top of the rubble, and Raven stepped in fast, driving her blade into the chest of the closer one when it spun and charged him. She glanced over at Marek, and he nodded his appreciation. He yanked the crossbow bolt out of the corpse eater, and they dragged the two dead beasts out a little farther from the rubble pile. Then Marek encouraged her to move down the tunnel a short distance so he could spread the stench of humans in the most efficient way possible. Raven did her best not to imagine him pissing in the chamber behind her as she waited.

It made sense. If some fled this way once they began working their way through the rest of the mine, the dead corpse eaters and the stench of human urine might drive them back the other way. Rather than dwell on what he was doing, she chose that moment to contemplate how her senses were somehow becoming accustomed to the reek of the corpse eaters. Or perhaps her sinuses had been paralyzed by it.

Marek rejoined her, and they started down a new passage. The corpse eaters were natural denizens of the darkness. They had few predators in their habitat, so they were sound sleepers. That made it easy to get close to the first group of beasts, huddled together in warm sleeping piles in one of the dead ends, where Marek had suspected they would be concentrated. He shot one that was gnawing on a bone at one side of the room, and the pile of beasts in the back surged to life, coming apart into more creatures than she would have thought possible.

Raven charged in, not giving them time to get their bearings. Marek discarded his crossbow and waded in beside her, far enough away to provide them both fighting space. With his heavy two-handed sword, that required a reasonable amount of space. The beasts attacked with frenzied rage, ready to tear apart whatever had dared to invade their haven. Raven focused on every second, striking, slashing, and dodging the flying teeth and claws. At one point, she found herself staring down the gaping maw of one lunging beast, its strangely long, thick tongues reaching for her face, only to have it fall short when Marek swept in with a slash that partially decapitated it.

The only sound left when the last beast fell was their labored breathing. Warm, damp bits of blood and gore spattered her face and the rest of her too.

"Did any escape?"

Marek swept his blade out with an abrupt slash to shake off some of the blood, then retrieved his crossbow. "I'm not sure. If so, it was only a few. We should move on to the next corridor."

She swept her blade like he had, sending a spray of blood across the pile of dead beasts, and followed him out. "I don't like it," she said softly.

"What?"

"Killing these beasts. It feels wrong. It felt wrong when we killed the rats too."

He glanced over at her, though she couldn't make out the finer nuances of his expression in this darkness, even with her enhanced vision.

"But not the bear?"

She shrugged. "The bear served a purpose. It fed people for several days."

"So, you don't like wasteful killing?"

Raven thought about it a moment, then nodded. "I suppose."

"That's probably a good thing."

She looked at him, wishing there was some light by which to read his features. "Do you like it?"

The outline of his shoulders lifted in a shrug. "It's work."

"But it doesn't bother you?"

"We should probably be quiet. We have at least three more chambers like that to get through," he evaded.

It seemed like an affirmation to her. She suspected it was all the same to him. Whether he hunted beasts, humans, or elves—whether their deaths served a purpose or not—it was just a job.

The next chamber was nearly empty, not because they weren't using it, but because it was the storage area Marek had mentioned, where they put fresh meat to let it rot. The stench was almost enough to knock them over. Still, they forged ahead to the carnage-filled chamber and dispatched the three corpse eaters feasting within.

The chamber after that was much like the first, though the beasts here had neatly sorted themselves into two piles, making it easy to divvy them up in the slaughter. They ran into a few others along the way to the final chamber. Raven's arms were heavy from the fighting, but she had at least one more run in her.

As they crept to the last chamber, she could see the fight here would be a little different. The room was larger, with broken-down crates piled in some corners. An old storage area, it appeared. The corpse eaters were spread out more as well, collected in five different piles around the room.

Marek gestured to the right, using two fingers to indicate that they should both go the same way this time. Raven nodded. They began to move in that direction, making their way toward the nearest pile. They hadn't gone more than a few feet from the entrance when a corpse eater sat up suddenly on the other side of the room. At the same time, Raven heard a noise behind them, coming from the chamber entrance. She didn't have time to turn before something heavy slammed into her back, and she pitched forward.

CHAPTER TWENTY SEVEN

Raven caught herself on her hands, barely keeping her face out of the soiled dirt and managing to keep hold of her sword. Her shin struck a rock when she hit, and pain blasted through it.

She twisted around on her back, ready to strike the beast that had plowed into her. Marek was already there, standing above her, one corpse eater dead at his feet as the rest of the room surged awake. He glanced over one shoulder, checking for additional threats as he held a hand out to her. She grabbed it, gritting her teeth against the pain as she let him help her up. She was confident that the leg wasn't broken, but the pain was still excruciating. Forcing it to hold her weight, she positioned herself with her back to Marek's, ready to face the pack.

The beasts charged them, emboldened by their numbers and enraged by the invasion. Raven swung, catching the first beast through its open mouth and coming up hard against its skull. The next, she stabbed through the ribs. It pulled the blade down as it fell, and she grabbed her dagger, driving it into the throat of the next beast the moment its jaws started to close on her other arm. She let the weapon go with that beast, using both hands to pull her sword free in time to cut down the next corpse eater. A sharp sting in her side told her that one of the creature's claws had found a gap in her armor before it fell.

She swung and struck repeatedly, wishing she had some idea of how the battle behind her was going. The cloying stench of blood thickened the air so she could barely breathe. Pain nagged at her from various injuries. Her weary shoulders trembled with each swing of her blade, and she was boiling hot, insulated by gore as much as by her clothing and armor. Then the attacks stopped. Marek shifted back into her, leaning a little. She did the same, letting the mutual lean support them both, and rested her head back against him, too exhausted to care if she trusted him or not.

"Well done," he rasped.

Raven was a little surprised when she chuckled in response. "Which part, the face plant or the not dying?"

His exhausted return laugh vibrated against her back. It was a strangely intimate sensation that drove her to step slowly away, giving him enough time to retake ownership of his own weight.

He faced her. "You fall with extraordinary flair, but I think the not dying was the part that most impressed me."

He sucked in a breath then, wincing.

"You're hurt?" She asked, struggling with the puzzling sensation of being concerned for him.

"No worse than you. We'll deal with it when we're out of here."

That was probably true. The sting in her side and the warmth of blood trickling down told her at least one wound was deeper. The intense throb in her shin was insistent, though she doubted it was more than a severe bruise. Digging into the pile of dead corpse eaters around her feet, she found her dagger and pulled it free. Then she gave him a nod, and they began to make their way out, both limping.

"Did any run?"

He nodded. "I saw at least a few bolting, though I was too busy to keep count."

Raven turned her attention to walking. When they finally reached the entrance, the daylight was dimming. The evening was creeping in. Her gut twisted at the thought of staying out here alone with the three men. There was no way around it, however. They needed to see to injuries before they tried making their way back. Even if that weren't the case, they would be hiking into the night at this point.

Seven corpse eaters lay dead near the entrance. The two men outside obviously had a much easier time, given they lacked the gore that covered her and Marek. It earned them disgusted looks from the other two.

"What did you do, roll in the dead bodies when you were done?" Darus asked, earning a laugh from Calin.

Calin turned and pointed out over the meadow. "There's a stream just inside the tree line on the north side of the road where you can get cleaned up. We'll set up camp and see what we can put together for a meal."

Marek nodded, his lips turning in a faint smirk. "That is the main reason I brought you two along."

Darus returned the smirk. "If you smell like this, we aren't letting you into the camp." His expression turned serious then. "Any injures to deal with?"

"Nothing serious," Marek answered.

Raven had already turned her attention north and was heading that way, her legs dragging with exhaustion. She wanted nothing more than to clean the gore from her hair and off her face and her new armor. Her shin still screamed at her, but she did her best to subdue the limp, not wanting any of them to insist on looking at it. She'd seen Calin helping the healers, but he wasn't a trained healer himself, and the idea of being touched by any of them left her slightly nauseous. Or perhaps that was the stench that clung to her clothes.

The wound in her side hurt. Getting cleaned up would let her take a closer look at that. Marek was still limping when he came up behind her. Where his injury was, she couldn't tell with all the gunk that clung to his black and silver armor.

When they found the creek, Raven crossed to the other side so one of them wouldn't be using the other's dirtied water, then they both peeled off their leather armor in silence. She splashed water over her hair until she no longer felt the weight of the grime in it, then she scrubbed her face and began working her way down, getting her clothes good and soaked while still wearing them. When that was done, she peeled up the side of her shirt to rinse the wound there. It was deeper than the numerous other cuts and punctures she'd sustained in the fighting but still shallow enough not to need extra care once it was clean.

Marek pulled open the long tear in his pants, exposing a deep gash in his thigh. He cleaned it out in silence, grimacing as it continued to ooze blood.

"That should be wrapped," she commented.

"Probably." He glanced up from the wound. "How's your leg? I saw you hit it when you went down."

Raven pulled up the pant leg, revealing a large darkening lump over her shin. He winced in sympathy.

"On the positive side, we're both Silverblood. By morning, these will be significantly improved."

Raven nodded and turned to the task of wiping down the leather armor. She didn't want to think about what she was. What they both were, but only he was allowed to be.

When they arrived at the camp, it was getting dark. Darus or Calin had hunted down and cooked a large pheasant. Calin helped wrap the wound in Marek's leg, then they dug into the meal. The meat was delicious, though she found everything tasted better lately. She suspected it had something to do with how hard she had been working since coming here. When she finished eating, she wandered away from the fire and the conversation the men were having. It was warm enough that her still damp clothes weren't much of an issue.

They had made the camp in the trees not far from the meadow's edge. She wandered back to the meadow and sank down to lean against one of the trees along its perimeter, gazing up at the star-filled sky. The brief peace didn't last long.

Marek walked out of the trees and looked up at the sky. After a few seconds, his gaze moved to the ground a few feet away. "Is this spot open?"

She considered saying no. He would ask her about herself. That was reasonably certain, but with all the open space here, she could walk away if he made her too uncomfortable. She gestured to the spot in invitation, and he sat cross-legged there. He was marginally less intimidating when he wasn't wearing the black and silver Brotherhood armor, though he was still dangerous.

"Why are you here, Raven?"

Straight to it then. "To clear out the corpse eaters."

"You know that isn't what I meant. Why are you here in Amberwood? This isn't where you were planning to go."

Raven let her gaze wander back to the stars, letting their brilliance and calm soothe her. "No. It isn't, but I can't go where I was heading."

"Why not?"

She cast him a wry glance. "You, of all people, should know the answer to that."

He had the decency to look somewhat chagrined, though it didn't stop him from trying another line of questioning. "How were you made?"

She turned it back on him. "How were you made?"

"I almost wasn't."

Now he had her attention. She shifted to look at him, picking his thoughtful expression out effortlessly in this incomplete darkness. "What do you mean?"

"About four years ago, five of my friends and I decided we would apply to the Brotherhood together. We were arrogant and foolish. We walked into the temple, certain we would all be Silverbloods by day's end. Only two of us passed the initial testing process. My friend, Jathus, passed with much better marks than I did, so they moved him through the process faster. His ritual was set three days before mine." A hint of sorrow subdued his expression as he gazed out over the dark meadow. "I waited for hours outside the ritual hall. I was jealous of him, but he was my best friend, and I was eager to congratulate him. When they brought him out, he was on a stretcher. His skin had turned black, and blood ran from his eyes, nose, and ears. Blood that had a metallic silver cast to it. His body tried to reject the magic, but the magic was much stronger than his flesh. It killed him. I almost left that day." He pulled some grass in front of his boot and twirled it in his fingers.

The gesture was so ordinary and oddly vulnerable that Raven wanted to comfort him. She wasn't all that good at such things. Jaecar had rarely let his guard down, so she hadn't gotten much practice at dealing with the emotions of others. She settled for simply prompting him. "But you didn't leave."

"No. One of the newer Silverblood warriors took me out, and we sparred together. He showed me the speed and agility being remade had given him. He took me to many of the training rooms, showing off his strength and enhanced vision. That night, he took me drinking and gave us each a small matching cut so he could show me the next morning how much faster he healed. I know it was all just manipulation to keep me from giving up. The rigorous entrance tests and the risk of dying in the ritual tends to limit the number of applicants they get. They didn't want to lose two in one day. It worked. I wanted what he had, so I stayed."

Raven drew her knees into her chest and wrapped her arms around them. A bat danced through the darkness, twisting and diving, catching insects she could barely see. She clasped her hands in front of her legs, wincing when she accidentally brushed the bruise on her shin, then moved them up to rest on her knees. With a light breeze blowing south, the smell of decay from the mine drifted away from them. The air was fresh and sweet with the scents of green grass and the nearby stream.

"My mom remade me the day she died. She used her own life and that of my father," Raven said softly.

"I'm sorry." Marek lowered his gaze, setting aside the grass he'd twisted into the semblance of a tiny rope. "Thank you for telling me. She was elven?"

Raven nodded, tightness in her throat discouraging her from talking.

"How did she know the magic?"

Raven swallowed the lump in her throat. She kept her gaze out over the meadow so he wouldn't see the tears in her eyes. "Your guess is as good as mine. Since my father died the same day, I couldn't ask him, though I don't know if he knew either."

He placed a hand on her arm then, and she flinched. He didn't take it away immediately as Phendaril would have done. Instead, he gave her arm a gentle squeeze and left it there.

"I am sorry."

After the initial shock, there was something pleasant about the warmth of his hand and the sincerity in his voice. When he took the hand away, the spot was much colder for the absence.

"This will sound insane to you, but maybe you should come to the Brotherhood with me. I don't think they would punish you for something your mother did, and they can't punish your mother. One of the priests might be able to offer insight into how she would have known the magic, though."

Raven slid her hand up, covering the place on her arm where his had been, making it warm again. Her gaze followed another bat flitting low across the meadow.

Marek stood up when she didn't say anything. He placed a hand on her shoulder. She managed not to flinch this time.

"Think about it."

The cold started to creep into her shoulder when he left to return to the camp. She placed her hand over that spot now, trying to keep the warmth in.

CHAPTER TWENTY EIGHT

They were on their way back soon after sunup. Raven's shin ached, though the bruising and swelling had improved significantly overnight. Marek's leg still caused him enough grief that, between them, it made for a slower return trip. Marek lingered close to her as they walked, but he hadn't resumed asking her prying questions. Eventually, when their injuries put them far enough behind the other two to be out of easy earshot, she looked over at him. His shoulders hung, and his steps were heavy, as though the weight of his world had become overwhelming.

She drew her hair back to weave it into a braid as she walked, giving her hands something to do to distract her from the anxiety of initiating conversation. "Do you still want to know about my name?"

A slow, weary smile eased across his lips. "I do."

"I was told that I started trying to climb trees as soon as I could crawl. My parents would be out tending the garden or the goats and lose track of me. When they found me, I would be perched in the branches of some tree. The lowest branches of small trees at first, but it apparently didn't take long for me to start making my way up higher in bigger trees. They started calling me Raven because my mother loved birds and said I liked to perch like a bird and watch them."

His smile broadened. It had a pleasing warmth to it when he wasn't too busy scheming up ways to manipulate the world around him.

"What was your birth name?"

Only her parents and Jaecar had ever called her by her birth name, typically when they were irritated with her. What harm could there be in telling him, as long as she made it clear she didn't want him using it? Still, her chest tightened when she opened her mouth to say it, and she hesitated.

"It's fine. I don't need to know." His smile faded. He turned his attention to the road ahead.

Raven breathed in and out. Soft, even breaths that eased the tightness in her chest. She focused on the way her fingers moved, weaving the braid. "My birth name is Aneiris, though I'd rather you not use it."

Marek chuckled. "Aneiris. Doesn't that essentially mean little bird in elven?"

Raven flushed, a self-conscious smile tugging at her lips. "As I said, my mother had an affinity for birds."

"Don't be embarrassed. It's a beautiful name, though I think I like Raven better. It suits you."

Her flush grew warmer. She focused on using a leather tie to secure the braid in place. Letting out a few of her secrets, with Phendaril the other night and now with him, chipped away at the suffocating walls of her isolated childhood. It was liberating and petrifying. Telling him her birth name brought up a surge of dread that drove her to keep her distance from the three men for the remainder of their hike. When they reached the town close to noon, her anxiety skyrocketed at the sight of all the new inhabitants that had arrived since they left the previous morning.

They came into town from the eastern side, opposite the upper residential district where the initial reclamation efforts were focused. New groups of dark-skinned men and women worked industriously on this side of town, clearing debris from salvageable buildings and starting demolition efforts on those that couldn't be saved. The further in they went, the more unfamiliar people there were. All of them paused their work to watch the party passing through, staring long at Marek and even longer at her until Raven's stomach was a mess of knots. The air grew heavier, harder to breathe, and the sounds of all their voices murmuring made her nerves scream. How humiliating would it be to throw up with them all watching? Worse, how terrifying would it be to be that vulnerable in front of them?

She stopped in the middle of the street.

Marek, who had moved closer as soon as they entered the town, stopped with her. "You needn't worry. I won't let anyone bother you."

Raven shook her head. "I can't breathe," she gasped.

Fear of looking like a coward and a fool couldn't overpower her terror of these people. She stared at him, willing herself to forget the crowds and focus on her breathing. Her chest tightened more, her vision darkening around the edges. She shook her head again and broke into a run, sprinting up a side street she hoped would lead her out of the occupied area faster. Her shin protested, but pain she could deal with.

"Raven!"

She ignored his call. Too many new faces. Too many eyes staring. She wasn't ready for them all.

•

Karsima kicked back in her office with her feet up on her desk. Alayne sat across from her, elbows on the desk, bright eyes shining with fascination as Karsima recounted the challenges they had faced since beginning their work in Amberwood. She'd told her the previous night that Phendaril's interest in Raven concerned her. As she tried to tell the tales of their efforts here, she found that Raven came up in all the most notable events. She could see in Alayne's smirk and the slight cock of one eyebrow that she wasn't the only one noticing a trend.

"I'm curious," Alayne began after Karsima finished another tale, "I understand why Raven could be a danger to the community because she's an unauthorized Silverblood. But is there a point at which the things she's done for–"

She cut off at a knock on the door.

Karsima took her feet off the desk. "Come in."

Jenner opened the door enough to lean in. "Adept Marek has returned, milady. Would you like to speak with him? He's waiting in the front room."

Karsima glanced at Alayne, whose grin held a glimmer of mischievous enthusiasm. "Oh yes," she rubbed her hands together, "let's have him in."

Affection bubbled up in Karsima's chest. She couldn't stop a chuckle as she looked back up at Jenner. "Yes. Please show him in." When he nodded and closed the door, she shook her head at Alayne. "You're incorrigible."

Alayne's grin didn't falter. "It's why you love me." She bounced to her feet. "Should I sit somewhere else? I could stand at your shoulder like an advisor or guard."

How she wanted to take the woman back upstairs and channel that glorious energy to a better purpose. "Sit, or stand, where you please."

Alayne stepped around the desk to stand near her chair, testing out expressions from a stern scowl to a welcoming smile and stances to go with them. Karsima turned to watch the process, wondering if she had time enough to slip in a passionate kiss before Jenner returned with the adept. Another knock came on the door. Alayne threw up her hands, unable to settle on a presentation. Instead, she grabbed a chair and placed it alongside the desk, facing the door. Karsima arched one brow in question to see if she was satisfied with her decision. A playful grin answered her.

Karsima forced a severe expression, something she might have failed at if Alayne hadn't chosen that moment to do the same. "Come in."

The door opened. Jenner stepped aside to allow Marek in. "Adept Marek, milady," he announced.

She nodded, and he shut the door behind the Silverblood warrior.

Marek strode in, looking and smelling like he could use a good scrub, though not as desperately as she would have expected given what he'd been doing. She caught a slight limp in his step, but he appeared otherwise unharmed. He greeted her with a polite enough nod before his shrewd silver-eyed gaze shifted to Alayne. She stood and offered a hand.

"Adept Marek," Karsima offered as both greeting and introduction. "This is Alayne. She brought the new folks you may have noticed outside to help with our endeavor."

He accepted Alayne's hand, giving it a firm shake. "Stonebreakers. You have interesting friends."

It wasn't clear whether he meant the comment for Alayne or herself, so she simply moved on. "How did your mission go?"

No knock came before the door swung open this time. Phendaril stormed in, a dismayed-looking Jenner trailing behind, one hand outstretched behind the elf as if to stop him. Jenner stopped in the doorway, deflated. Karsima gave him a nod. He frowned after Phendaril as he stepped back and pulled the door shut.

"I don't recall sending for you, Phendaril," she let a bit of ire come through in her tone.

He had the nerve to ignore her, turning a burning glare on Marek. "Where's Raven?"

Karsima cast a look at Alayne to mark the moment

that Phendaril proved he was more than casually interested in the half-elf. Alayne shrugged in response. Then Karsima turned an expectant gaze on Marek to convey that if Raven was missing, she too would like to know why.

"Raven's fine." Marek's eyes narrowed as he matched Phendaril's glare with one of his own.

"Then why didn't she return with your party?"

Marek's answering sneer brought a palpable tension to the room. She reached under the desk for the dagger she kept there. It was debatable how much good it would do against a Silverblood if Phendaril lost his temper with the man. Still, it offered a marginal level of comfort. As did the fact that Alayne's hand had shifted closer to her sword.

"You're a smart elf," Marek snarled, "I'm confident you could figure it out if you looked around out there."

Phendaril's glare faltered, and concern rose in his eyes. He started to glance toward the window, then caught himself as though he didn't trust Marek enough to look away from him. "Where is she?"

"I don't know. She got overwhelmed coming into town and bolted. I suspect she'll be back in the evening when things quiet down."

"I'm sure she'll be fine, Phen." Karsima softened her tone to try to defuse the bitter rivalry between the two. Phendaril was one of the best fighters she'd ever seen, but against a Silverblood warrior like Marek, he wouldn't come out in good shape if he survived at all.

Phendaril relaxed back from Marek. Only by about an inch, but she could see the effort that minor concession cost him in the tightness of his jaw and the lingering burn in his gaze. Marek turned away, dismissing him, and focused on her again.

"The mine is cleared. Raven and I both took a few wounds, but those are already healing. One of the benefits of being what we are."

His faint smirk told her he deliberately pointed out the similarities between himself and Raven to dig at Phendaril. Judging from the way the elf's jaw muscles twitched, it was working.

"Darus and Calin?" She tapped a few fingers on the top of the desk to keep Marek's attention on her.

"They're fine. They stayed outside to pick off corpse eaters fleeing the mine."

Phendaril's posture went a little more rigid, though she would have thought that impossible a moment ago. "Just the two of you went in?"

Marek slowly turned his head to meet Phendaril's gaze. "Yes. As I mentioned a second ago, we're both Silverblood. We were uniquely suited to handling that problem together."

All the emotion leached from Phendaril's features. She knew he wanted nothing more than to punch the smirk off Marek's face. The fact that she no longer saw that desire in his expression told her he was dangerously close to acting on it.

Karsima stood. "Thank you, Adept Marek." She slid a pouch of coins she had been holding for him across the desk. "I appreciate your efforts. That should be all for this evening."

Marek took the pouch and gave a slight nod. He turned toward Phendaril, taking advantage of the opportunity to give the elf one last taunting smile before leaving. "I see why you take her with you so often. I learned a great deal about her on that little adventure."

The hint of suggestiveness in his tone drove Karsima to reach for the dagger again. Phendaril didn't even look at the adept as he sauntered out the door.

"That was fun," Alayne commented, her tone belying the sentiment. "Why don't you have a seat, Phen."

He stared at the closed door. "I should see if I can find Raven."

"Don't be a fool." Karsima sank back into her chair. "You're not going to find her until she's ready to be found." She put her feet up on the desk again. "It'll be nice when he finally leaves."

"Tell him you have no more work for him." The fact that Phendaril wouldn't look at either of them when he spoke told her exactly how much Marek's words had gotten to him and how strong his feelings for Raven were becoming.

Alayne gazed thoughtfully at the closed door now. "If she is what you say she is, he'll try to take her with him when he goes."

Karsima cast an irritated glance at the other woman. That line of conversation wasn't helpful. Alayne turned, catching the look, and shrugged as if to say she was only speaking the truth.

"I don't think she'll go with him." Karsima offered, hoping to ease her friend's mind. Although, Marek probably wouldn't give the young half-elf a choice. "Relax, Phen. Have a drink with us."

"I've got work I'd like to finish up today." He left the room, shutting the door harder than necessary behind him.

Alayne moved back to the chair on the other side of the desk and sat down. "He is falling for her, isn't he?"

"It's my fault." Karsima inwardly cursed herself. "I encouraged him to help her because I could see how terrified she was. I knew when I did it that she was likely to become a problem for us. I just failed to see how many ways she might do that."

"It's nice to see that he is moving on from Lysanna."

Karsima grabbed the wooden pitcher on the corner of her desk and refilled her mug. She tipped it up and drank it all before slamming the mug down. Then she met Alayne's curious gaze.

"What do you think it will do to him when Marek

drags Raven back to Pellanth and the Brotherhood executes her?"

Alayne swirled the mead in her mug, gazing into it as though it had prophetic qualities. "He'll go back to hating everyone."

"If he doesn't get himself killed trying to take revenge like he nearly did with the men who raped Lysanna." Karsima's gut curdled at the memory, and she suddenly regretted guzzling the mead.

Alayne cocked an eyebrow at her mug. "With the Brotherhood, the outcome would be fairly certain."

"Exactly." They had both been there to see Phendaril struggle with Lysanna's death and watch it nearly destroy him. The more time he spent around Raven, the more she saw him openly smiling in a way she hadn't seen in a long time. The very thing that was healing him might also destroy him.

CHAPTER TWENTY NINE

Raven slunk back into town after dark fell. Many newcomers were in camps between the town and the river because there simply weren't enough houses ready for occupants yet. Those that weren't already sleeping were focused on food or conversation. Slipping past them was easy enough. From there, she made her way up to the roof of the healer's building. It struck her as one of the more likely places Phendaril might look for her, and she did want him to find her.

She considered sneaking to the house he was living in. The others staying there had moved out a while ago. But he might not show up there for some time. Supper rarely got served before dark since they worked until last light most days. Seeking him out that directly was a little too bold for her comfort anyhow. Still, she wanted to see him. Somehow, he had become her anchor in this strange place. She wasn't entirely sure how it had happened. They hadn't started on a positive note, although he had advocated for the return of her dagger back before he knew anything about her. Not that he knew a great deal yet. Maybe she owed it to him and to herself to change that.

The square below her was far more crowded than usual, even with many newcomers out in their camps. The number of individuals eating, talking, and laughing in the communal space made her skin tighten with unease.

She finally spotted Phendaril wandering across the square alone before he vanished from sight. For about fifteen minutes, she waited, wondering if she might have to seek him out at his house after all. Then she caught the distinctive sound of his footsteps as he climbed onto the roof and came to join her.

He looked her over once, his brow furrowing slightly. "Are you all right?"

She nodded, hoping he might come and sit beside her there as they had done a few nights ago. She wanted that again.

"Have you eaten?"

"Some." She begged her stomach not to betray the truth with a grumble.

He breathed a soft laugh and crouched next to her, looking her in the eyes. "Meaning a few nuts and berries?"

Her cheeks grew warm, and she kept silent, struggling not to look away.

He was quiet for a few seconds, staring into her eyes as unspoken thoughts raced behind his. Then he broke the contact and straightened. "You know the house I'm staying in? On the edge of town?"

Raven nodded, a twist of excitement or apprehension in her chest. She wasn't sure which. Maybe both.

"Meet me there. The door's unlocked. I'll bring us both something more substantial to eat."

Her voice deserted her, so she merely nodded and watched him disappear down the ladder before getting up to follow. The trip back to the edge of town and the two-story home he had made his was quick enough. She hid in the shadows the first few times someone else came along until she discovered that they barely looked her way if she simply strolled by with her hood up and her head down. She lingered in the shadows at his house, waiting for a moment when no one else was around to see her, then ducked inside.

The upper floor of the house still needed repairs, so he was living in the lower rooms. With all the debris cleaned out, there wasn't much there. Some craftsmen were cobbling together passable furniture for occupied homes as fast as they could. Phendaril had two chairs and a simple round of wood set on a block serving as a table. A fire burned in the hearth.

Is that what he had been doing those fifteen minutes before he came up on the roof? Planning for company.

Her gut clenched. This was a mistake. She turned toward the door just as it opened. Phendaril entered carrying a loaded trencher and a large pitcher of mead. He pushed the door closed with one foot.

"This place isn't much." As he set the trencher and pitcher on the table, his crooked, self-conscious grin crushed her desire to leave.

The crumbling keep she'd grown up in rushed to mind. A wistful smile stole across her lips. "Add a few threadbare carpets, and it'll feel like home."

Phendaril cast a delighted grin her way, and her pulse started to race. He disappeared into what she suspected had been the original kitchen, taking away the pressure of his presence. She only got a few seconds to compose herself before he returned with two mugs and gestured to one of the chairs in invitation.

Raven piled her weapons along the wall and settled into the chair, watching his hands as he poured the mead. The many scars took nothing away from the strength and elegance of his movements. They shared food from the single trencher in silence. When the selection had been thoroughly picked over, he carried the empty trencher off to the kitchen while Raven refilled their mugs.

"You said you grew up with your parents?" He

asked, moving his chair closer to the fire.

Familiar anxiety swelled in her, though she noticed that the more mead she drank, the less severe it seemed to be. She took another swallow before giving a nod and moved her chair next to the fire, angled toward his.

"They were in love?"

Raven glanced at him, trying to extract from his expression the point of this line of questioning. His face told her nothing. "Yes. They always struck me as very much in love, though I was young. They moved into the woods when my mother became pregnant with me. Trying to hide from people like the men who stumbled upon our home when I was eight and murdered them. An older warrior lived in an abandoned keep near there. He had become something of a family friend. I ran to him for help when the men came. He made it back in time to kill the men who killed my parents, but we didn't get there fast enough to save them." Regret tightened her throat. "Eight-year-olds have short legs." She swallowed more mead before finishing. "After that, he took me in and raised me himself."

Phendaril's expression turned dark for a few seconds, old anger rising there. When he looked at her, sympathy pushed through that anger. His smile was gentle. "That explains your fighting skills. How did you become a Silverblood if you were hidden away at some keep in the woods?"

Her nerves danced. The urge to leave surged up. Raven took another swallow of the mead, following it with a few slow, careful breaths as she would when preparing for a difficult shot. She wasn't going to run. Not this time.

"My mother made me this way when she and my father were dying."

He was silent, staring into the fire as he took a few drinks. Raven watched him, appreciating his profile and how the firelight brought out the red in his dark hair. Somehow, focusing on those details eased the fear around talking about herself, though it created a different kind of jittery sensation in her chest.

"You were eight when they died?" he asked, breaking her out of her quiet contemplation of him.

"Yes."

"I want to believe you, though I've only just learned to accept the previously impossible fact that a half-elven female could be a Silverblood. How did an eight-year-old child survive being remade?"

Raven stared into the fire. She could see her mother's blue eyes turning black then silver, strange words flowing from her mouth. A shudder swept through her. Phendaril's hand touched her arm, offering comfort, and, for once, she didn't flinch.

"I don't know. I think the evidence suggests that the Brotherhood is built on many falsehoods." The venom in her own voice surprised her a little.

Phendaril said nothing. He waited in silence for her to continue when she was ready.

Raven took a deep breath, still staring at the fire, trying to focus on something other than the warmth of his hand on her arm. "I remember that I thought I was dying. The pain overwhelmed everything. I thought my mother was going to take me with her... and I was glad. I didn't want to live without them." She winced inwardly when he took his hand away, wishing he would have left it there.

"I'm sorry."

"At least you know now why I'm so broken."

She set her mug on the floor and stood, needing to move. She yanked the tie out of her hair and started unraveling the braid. As she did so, she took a few steps toward the door and then stopped. As surprising as it was, despite the difficult conversation, she wanted to stay. Behind her, she heard Phendaril's chair slide back a little as he also stood.

"I don't think you're any more broken than the rest of us." He took a deep breath and exhaled heavily. "And I owe you an apology. It didn't occur to me to warn you that the Stonebreakers were coming."

She forced a small laugh. "Why should it have?"

"Because you needed it to."

Raven pulled out the last of the braid as she turned to face him, letting her silvery-black hair fall in a cascade of liberated waves. He had come up behind her and was standing a couple of feet back. A powerful fluttering spread through her chest as she realized how badly she wanted to kiss him and be kissed by him. And why not? If she could throw herself in front of a wyvern, she could do this. Couldn't she?

He watched her with burning intensity, his eyes widening slightly when she stepped closer. Her heart raced now, and she was trembling, but she forced herself to look up, her gaze lingering on his lips for a second before moving to his eyes. He caught that brief hesitation and bent down, meeting her halfway as she came up on the balls of her feet, doggedly ignoring the protesting pain in her shin.

The touch of his lips lit her on fire, burning through her with the same intensity as the Silverblood magic, but without the pain. A little gasp of surprise escaped her when his hand slid around her waist, pulling her closer. Their bodies touched, and her balance faltered suddenly, her knees growing wobbly. She focused on the taste of mead on his lips as the kiss became more demanding. Then his other hand came up, fingers caressing her neck lightly as he brushed her hair back, igniting lines of fire in their wake.

Raven stiffened and jerked away, the barrage of sensation and emotion opening the door for panic. He took his hands away instantly and started to step back.

No. It wasn't going to go this way.

Raven caught his arm, and he stopped, neither touching her more nor pulling farther away.

"I'm sorry." His voice was tight with the pent-up desire that burned behind his dark eyes.

Something about knowing he wanted her that much eased a little of her anxiety. She shifted forward and leaned her head against his chest, closing her eyes as she inhaled the scents of wood dust and hard work on him. He stood perfectly still while she calmed her breathing, trying to make sense of the tempest of longing that burned through her. It was different with him than it had been with Eamon. More intense. Not so much an exploration as a choice.

She drew another deep, trembling breath and found her voice. "I don't know how to... to be with someone."

She shifted back a little to look up at his face, puzzled by the glimmer of relief in his smile. He leaned in to kiss her once, then twice, a delicious shiver sweeping through her as he caressed her cheek with one thumb. He pressed his forehead to hers, their breath mingling.

"If you want, I can show you," he whispered. "But only when you're ready."

"Can I stay here tonight?" she asked, drawing back to look into his eyes.

Phendaril nodded, and she kissed him on her own this time, relaxing against him as he slid his arms around her and pulled her close.

•

When dawn came, she lay in his bed with her back against his chest and his arms around her. They both still wore their shirts and pants, though her leather armor lay discarded on the floor. His lean archer's arms wrapped warm around her made her feel safer than she could ever remember feeling. She didn't want it to end. He reached up one hand to brush a lock of hair behind her pointed ear. A shiver swept through her, bringing a smile to her lips.

"How did you get that scar?"

He stilled, and she thought for a second that she had made a mistake. He rested his arm back over her side and slid his fingers through hers. "I challenged a group of men to a fight to avenge the elven woman they had raped. I nearly lost an eye for it."

Something inside her twisted unpleasantly. "They won?"

His soft laugh had a bitterness to it this time. "No."

The continuing stillness in him told her it might be better to move on to a less emotionally charged subject, but curiosity nagged at her. "What happened to the woman?"

"Her name was Lysanna." His arms tightened a little around her. "We were supposed to be life-bonded. After the rape, she became pregnant. Rather than bring a half-elven child into the world, a child that would always remind her of what had been done to her, she decided to kill herself."

Raven rolled onto her back, shifting to the side so she could look at him. The old sorrow dimming the light in his eyes tore at her. "I'm so sorry. I shouldn't have asked."

He rose on his elbow to look down at her. "It's all right. I don't have any secrets I wouldn't share with you. Besides," something came back to life in his eyes, and her pulse quickened in response, "you've shown me that I'm still capable of falling in love."

He leaned over and kissed her. It was a soft, gentle kiss. When he pulled away, she stared up at him, amazed that all she wanted right then was more of him.

"Show me," she said, the giddy butterflies in her chest going wild as she spoke the words.

He gazed down at her, the dusky desire that rose in his eyes telling her he recalled what it was he had offered to show her. Still, he hesitated, holding her gaze. "You're sure?"

Raven swallowed against her rising nerves and nodded.

Phendaril slid one hand down her side as he leaned in to kiss her again. A more demanding kiss this time. He brought his hand under her shirt, sliding the garment up as he moved it along her skin underneath. Raven helped him, a new and powerful need building in her. She broke the kiss long enough to pull the shirt off and claimed his mouth again, opening hers to his questing tongue. Her body pressed up, seemingly on its own, as his hand slid back down her skin, every second of contact driving her to want more. His fingers moved across her stomach and down to undo the fastening of her pants.

He drew away then, his sultry smile melting her. She watched in admiring silence as he pulled off his shirt, his torso rippling with lean muscle and a few more scars she might ask him about later. The gentle, respectful way he removed the rest of her clothes, kissing the skin as he exposed it, helped desire overpower her apprehension. His hand slid to the crux of her thighs, where his attentions had made her wet and wanting. She didn't have experience being with someone this way, but her body didn't seem to need it. Her legs opened to his touch, and her hips pressed up in response to his caresses. She gasped in delicious surprise when he leaned down between her legs and began her first lesson in what it was like to be with someone.

Karsima waited in the early light, leaning against a building down the street and across from Phendaril's house. Other residents moved along the roadway, carrying cartloads of debris or construction materials into or out of the town. Most of Amberwood was awake and hard at work. It wasn't like him to sleep in this late, but no one had seen him in any of the usual places. She was about ready to go over and knock on the door to see if he was really still in there.

There was a sinking in her chest when his door opened, and Raven appeared in the doorway. Phendaril stepped into view behind her. The half-elf turned back to him, and they embraced, sharing a long, passionate kiss. The kiss of two individuals who had spent the night and morning intimately enjoying one another. The fact that Raven had her armor on and was carrying her weapons made it obvious she never made it back to her own room last night.

Alayne, who leaned against the building next to her, offered a low whistle in response to the display. "I'd say any hopes you had of heading off a romantic entanglement have been thoroughly demolished."

Karsima exhaled heavily. She glanced away, uncomfortable watching, and spotted Marek a little farther down the street where he had been helping with a supply cart. He had also noticed the pair. He stood staring at them, a dark scowl pulling down the corners of his mouth. After a few seconds, he spun and stalked toward the square, abandoning the cart to the other two men.

Karsima's gut twisted. That wasn't the reaction of a man who only cared about Raven's status as a threat to the integrity of the Brotherhood. That was jealousy. She cursed under her breath and pushed away from the building.

"Come on. I'd like you to meet Raven," she growled.

Alayne trotted to keep up with her quick strides. "Is now really the right time?"

Karsima ignored her.

Raven was turning back toward the street. She and Phendaril spotted them coming at the same moment. Raven blanched a little, though she held her ground as he stepped out of the house to stand beside her, a hint of protectiveness in his close stance. No shame showed in his expression, only a glimmer of defiance, daring Karsima to question his choice. She was almost mad enough to turn it into a scene, though part of that was a response to concern over Marek's reaction to them. Taking that out on them wasn't going to improve the situation.

"Raven, I was hoping to run into you this morning," Karsima stated, forcing a pleasant tone. She even managed a smile as she pointedly ignored Phendaril's stern look of warning.

That silver-eyed gaze darted around as if searching for an escape route, lighting briefly upon several of the busy folk moving up and down the street. Her face paled even more if that were possible. She settled for staring in Karsima's general direction, looking like she might be sick at any moment. Karsima almost felt guilty for placing her on the spot. Still, if the young half-elf intended to keep a low profile, she should have chosen someone other than the future town marshal to sleep with.

"I wanted to introduce you to Alayne."

Alayne offered a hand with her usual unfaltering composure. "A pleasure to meet you. I've heard about the wonderful things you've done to help Amberwood." She glanced over her shoulder at Karsima, a hint of reprimand in the brief pinching of her brows. "Karsima and I are life-bonded."

Raven's hand trembled slightly as she reached to take Alayne's, though she looked tentatively interested now.

"A pleasure," Raven stated softly.

Then Alayne did what Karsima, knowing her as well as she did, should have expected her to do. She seized control of the situation. With an open and disarming smile, she stepped back and gestured toward the town square. "Why don't you two join us for some lunch in a couple of hours. I'd love to catch up with you, Phen, and learn more about you, Raven."

Phendaril placed a reassuring hand on Raven's shoulder. "There's a lot of work to be done."

Alayne knocked the argument aside. "It'll be a few years before any of us can stop saying that. You've both earned a break. I insist."

Karsima fought the urge to point out that they had clearly spent the morning taking a kind of break. Phendaril caught her eyes, his narrowing slightly as he gave a tiny shake of his head. He knew her well enough to predict her need to make such a comment, and he expected her to keep it in her head.

She sighed and relented. "Yes. We'll meet you in the square in a couple of hours."

•

When they escaped Alayne and Karsima, Phendaril accompanied Raven to drop off her armor and weapons at the medical building and pick up clean clothes. Together they strolled out to where the new bathhouses were assembled. Along the way, he told her about Amberwood before its destruction, pointing out specific details. He kept the conversation safe and comfortable. After the way they had spent the morning, it struck her as a little indulgent to waste more of the day with bathing, but she needed it. She couldn't get out of her head that she smelled strongly of him and their intimate activities. Breathing in that scent gave her a giddy rush of pleasure, but she didn't want everyone else to notice it.

Phendaril stayed by her side throughout the remainder of the morning, helping her give her armor a proper cleaning to get the rest of the grime from the corpse eaters off. While they worked, he told her about the Stonebreakers Alayne brought with her. The Stonebreaker clans were renowned for their warriors but also for their smiths, masons, and woodworkers. This clan lost their lands in a wildfire that burned out of control. Alayne invited them to help rebuild Amberwood with the long-term goal of making it their new home.

That led the conversation to Karsima and Alayne. The two women met during Karsima's second year at the university. They were, according to Phendaril, the most convincing case of love at first sight he had ever seen.

Talk of love sparked a flutter in Raven's chest. Something more intimate shone through in the way Phendaril smiled at her now. It made her want to return to those lessons about how to be with someone. If only they hadn't agreed to meet with Karsima and Alayne. When they finished the armor, he helped her carry it to her room and stood in the doorway, watching her lay it out neatly in the corner.

"You could move into the house with me."

The comment caught her by surprise. She turned to stare at him. The idea struck a chord of longing deep inside her. That part of her that desperately missed having a home and someone to share it with. It would mean accepting that she would stay here, which was still a frightening idea. More so now that the population had grown significantly.

She set down the last piece of armor and met his eyes. "Is that what you want?"

He approached her and placed his hands on her waist, pulling her a little closer. She drew a quick breath, trying not to think about the morning. Trying to focus on this moment and how he looked at her like he had found something dear that he had lost.

"I would love to have you there. It might inspire me to fix the place up some more," he added with a playful grin.

That look made her yearn to make him happy. "We'll move my things later then."

She lifted onto the balls of her feet to lay a light kiss on his lips. He slid his arms the rest of the way around her, pulling her into a more ardent kiss than she'd intended. Any other thoughts became lost before the heat that burned between them. She slid her arms around him, delighting in the definition of his lean muscles under her fingertips.

"Raven are... Oh!"

Raven startled free of his embrace and stepped to the side to see Synal in the doorway, her cheeks as bright as Raven imagined her own were. Phendaril glanced sideways at her, offering a scoundrel smirk before schooling his expression and turning around to face Synal.

"I'm so sorry. I didn't realize..." Synal chuckled softly to herself. "Hello, Phendaril."

He inclined his head. "Synal. Did you need something?"

"I..." She glanced between them, and her flush brightened. "I honestly don't remember."

Phendaril reached down and took Raven's hand, giving it a reassuring squeeze before releasing it. "If you remember, we'll be out front with Karsima and Alayne for a bit."

Synal's gaze followed the movement of his hand. She nodded and stepped back to let them pass. "Enjoy the day."

"Thank you." Raven forced the words out. If she was going to consider staying here longer, she would have to learn to talk to the people of Amberwood in various situations. This was as good a time as any to start working on that.

Near the well in the center of the square, Karsima and Alayne were laying claim to a group of chairs near one of the fire pits. The fires themselves weren't lit yet, since it was warm enough out that the heat wasn't needed. They still provided something to gather around, even during warmer daylight hours.

Several others gathered in the square as well. Now that most of the buildings around it were passably functional, it had become the social hub of the expanding reclamation project. Raven focused on the two women and Phendaril beside her, doing her best to tune out everyone else as they walked over to join them. They hadn't even sat down when Veylin strode up to them, her intent gaze on Phendaril.

"I'm sorry to interrupt, Phen," she glanced around at them apologetically. "Jael asked if you might be able to join him near the falls this afternoon. He wanted to show you some things and discuss the giant hornets out there."

Phendaril looked at Raven, a hint of regret in his dark eyes. "It takes a good hour to get out there. I should probably get going now if I'm going to get back by dark."

The urge to flee surged up in Raven. If he left, she would have to stay here alone with them, expected to make conversation. Perhaps she could go with him. Although, if he didn't need her, it would be wasteful for her to go rather than help here. Anxiety began to wrap its suffocating hands around her throat.

"Aneiris."

In that instant of near panic, it was Jaecar's voice she heard in her head. Raven spun, her heart in her throat, but, of course, it was Marek who came sauntering up to her. Jaecar was gone. A faint smirk touched his lips as he glanced at Phendaril next to her, and she was suddenly aware of how still the elven male had become.

She stepped forward, closing the distance and giving the Silverblood adept a withering look. "I asked you not to use that name," she hissed in a low voice.

"Apologies, Raven. I didn't mean to upset you."

She wanted to lash out at him. He couldn't have known that she had never shared her birth name with Phendaril. The vaguely tormented look in the elf's eyes now was enough to make that apparent to anyone paying attention. Phendaril looked at her for a second, the dark depths of his eyes a tempest of indecipherable emotion.

He turned to Karsima. "Excuse me. I have some work to attend to." With a nod to Veylin, the two strode away.

Raven stared after him. Anger that he would leave like this warred with guilt for the hurt Marek's antics had caused. Below it all, and growing stronger, was the dread that came with being here amidst all these people she barely knew.

"What did you want, Adept Marek?" Karsima asked, a discouraging edge to her tone.

Yes, what had he deemed urgent enough to come wreak havoc upon her fledgling relationship? Raven turned to look at him, cocking her head to one side in silent inquiry.

He kept his attention on her, ignoring the town's leader. "I was hoping to speak to you alone for a few minutes."

As annoyed as she was, Raven yearned to get away from the crowd, even if it meant going with him. She made herself face Karsima and Alayne, using Phendaril's departure as a model for her own. "I'm sorry. I need to excuse myself as well."

Karsima nodded. "Of course. We'll talk later." Her shrewd gaze was drilling into Marek, though he appeared oblivious to it or simply not interested enough to acknowledge it.

"I guess it's just you and me," Alayne said, giving Karsima a smile and wink.

Raven turned to Marek. "Lead the way."

Neither of them spoke as she followed him down the street and out of town past the Stonebreaker camps. Once they left the camps behind, he continued slightly downhill toward the river. A glimmer of unease nagged at the edge of her awareness as they dropped out of sight of the town and camps.

"You wanted to talk to me?"

He nodded, glancing over at her, a tightness and distance in his regard that hadn't been there the last time she talked to him. "I'm leaving soon. Have you considered what I said?"

He was asking her if she would come to the Brotherhood with him. Raven cast a glance back in the direction of the town. Pellanth was many times the size of Amberwood. She'd already proven she couldn't handle the numbers here yet. Besides, Phendaril was in Amberwood. The idea of leaving him right now, before she had a chance to discover how far their relationship might go, was unthinkable. Especially leaving with Marek. That would be a death sentence to whatever was building between them.

She faced forward, watching her step as the hill cut

more steeply down toward the river. "I'm not ready for a city like Pellanth yet. I'm sorry, Marek. Maybe you could talk to them and come back."

Marek stopped at the edge of the low cliff. It was the reason the docks were further upriver near the original camp. She glanced down the ten-foot drop to the river. There, in the bushes at the edge of the water, someone had tied a small wooden raft. It struck her as an odd place for it.

"I expected you would say that."

Something about his voice, the edge of anger with an undertone of sorrow, spiked the unease building in her. She looked at him in time to see the silver flare in his eyes. His hand closed on the back of her neck. Then her body went limp, refusing to hold her up. She tumbled over the edge, water rushing up to meet her seconds before the darkness did.

CHAPTER THIRTY ONE

Karsima sat staring into the fire after supper that evening, an insidious dread creeping up her spine.

Alayne reached over and touched her arm. "What's wrong?"

Nothing. Nothing was wrong that she knew of, and yet... It bothered her, the look she had seen in Marek's eyes earlier, that glimmer of victory as he turned to leave with Raven. She had left it up to the fact that he had gotten to boast knowledge of Raven that Phendaril clearly hadn't had, judging from the look on her friend's face at the time. Still, something about the moment continued to eat at her.

Phendaril had not returned yet, though she expected him to show up soon, given that dark was falling. She hadn't seen Raven or Marek since then either, though that wasn't unusual. They could have joined a work crew anywhere in town. Now the second shift of the evening meal was being served. They'd had to implement another shift to accommodate the Stonebreakers. The fact that she still hadn't seen either of them fed into her growing unease.

"It's nothing. I..." She spotted Synal walking toward the tavern. "Synal!"

Synal changed direction to walk over to them. "Milady, Alayne, Jenner." She greeted each of them with a nod and smile.

"Have you seen Raven?"

The sudden flush in the healer's cheeks told Karsima she had seen Raven, probably earlier with Phendaril, in an affectionate display of some kind. "Not since before noon."

"Would you be willing to humor me and see if her things are still in her room?"

Synal nodded and hastened back toward the medical building.

"You think she bolted?" Alayne asked.

Karsima frowned and turned to Jenner. "Could you go check Adept Marek's quarters for me? Send him my way if he's there. If not, see if his things are still there."

Jenner was instantly on his feet. "Milady," he said as he hurried off.

Alayne brushed off the concern. "Given what I saw this morning, even with the little incident at lunch, I can't see her leaving Phen to go with the Silverblood."

"No, not willingly. I'm not convinced Marek would care if she wanted to leave or not, however. His first loyalty is always going to be to the Brotherhood."

Alayne looked troubled now, her delicate, lightly freckled brow furrowing.

Karsima could no longer sit still. She got up from her chair and motioned to Calin and Darus, who were seated nearby. They both got up, but she didn't wait for them to walk over, closing the distance with Alayne hopping up to follow.

"You two have been working with Adept Marek. Did he say anything about leaving?"

Darus's nod deepened the pit of dread growing in her gut. "Yeah. He's been saying he was going to leave any day now. Soon as his ship arrived."

"Can you two go out to the outer edge of the Stonebreaker camp and ask if any ships have been seen on the river today?"

"Yes, ma'am."

Karsima watched them go, then she glanced at the group still sitting around the fire. "When they return, can you let them know I'm in my office?"

After getting satisfactory affirmations, she turned toward home and started walking, her strides fast enough that Alayne had to trot to catch up.

"How can I help?"

"Tell me I'm wrong." Dread weighed heavy in her stomach, bile rising in the back of her throat.

The other woman was silent, and Karsima glanced over at her.

Alayne shook her head, her usual positivity absent. "I don't mean to add to your concern, my love, but something tells me you're not wrong."

Back in her office, Karsima paced behind her desk while Alayne sat and tried to offer supportive commentary. Most of it fell flat on the fact that Alayne knew as well as she did what it would do to Phendaril if Marek had taken Raven. She expected Synal to return first, but it was Jenner who rushed through the door without stopping to knock. He had his hat in his hands, wringing it hard enough that she suspected it might not survive the experience.

"Milady, Adept Marek's things are gone. Also, I ran into Calin on the way here. He said to tell you that the Stonebreakers saw a ship heading upriver earlier this afternoon."

Everything in her abdomen seemed to twist into one giant, painful knot. Why hadn't she done something earlier when she saw that look in Marek's eyes? She could have insisted she needed to talk to Raven. "Go keep an eye out for Phendaril and send him to me the minute he shows up."

Jenner nodded and hurried out, dropping a quick

"milady" as he vanished through the door.

Ten minutes of pacing later, the door swung open, and Phendaril stepped in. He glanced from Karsima to Alayne and back again, his features darkening like a thunderhead had rolled into the room. "What is it?"

"Sit with me." Karsima gestured to the unoccupied chair in front of the desk.

Phendaril narrowed his eyes. "You're not sitting."

He was right. She started to sit, but his scowl stopped her.

"Just tell me, what's going on?"

She straightened, catching a sympathetic glance from Alayne, who had taken to pacing up and down that side of the room in her stead. "Marek is gone, and I think he took..."

She trailed off when Synal stepped into the doorway Phendaril had left standing open. She held a leather case gripped in both hands as she gazed around at them. She met Karsima's eyes and walked into the room, her steps small and tentative. When she got to the desk, she set the case on it with an air of gravity.

"I'm sorry it took so long. I found this in Raven's room."

Karsima slid the case closer. "So, her things are still there?"

Synal nodded, casting an anxious glance in Phendaril's direction. "Everything. Even her swords and bow."

Phendaril's expression had turned to stone. He gave a curt nod toward the case. "What's that?"

Karsima unfastened the buckles and pulled out a collection of folded parchments with the seals all broken. She recognized the seal of Darrenton as she opened the first one. "They're written in Alumen."

Alumen was a written language initially developed by the nobility in Pellanth before it was more widely adopted. It was used primarily for legal documentation, mainly to render those documents unreadable by the lower classes. It made it easier to keep knowledge of important matters that required legal documentation out of their reach.

She opened all of them and skimmed through the contents, not sure how to feel about what she was reading. She set two pages on the desk and tapped them with one finger. "These are legal adoption papers making our Silverblood half-elf, Aneiris *Raven* Darrenton, the legal daughter of Lord Jaecar Nathan Darrenton." She set several more pages down on top of those, smoothing them out when they tried to fold in on themselves. "This is a will, bequeathing all of Jaecar's possessions and holdings to his daughter, the woman we know as Raven. And this," she dug through the parchment and pulled another signature page out to set on top of the others, "is the legal deed making Amberwood the property of Lord Jaecar Nathan Darrenton." She met Phendaril's eyes. "If she had these papers, then I'm guessing Jaecar is dead, which means that Raven was the legal owner of Amberwood."

"Then she wasn't here by accident," Alayne stated.

"I don't know," Synal glanced around at them. "Veylin told me Raven had asked her if she could read. I know Raven could read Thedan and some elvish, so why would she have needed someone else who could read unless it was for these?"

"Can we stop referring to her in the past tense?" Phendaril growled. "Did Marek take her?"

Karsima forced herself to meet his eyes. "I believe so."

CHAPTER THIRTY TWO

Raven woke several times, for a few seconds each time, before Marek finally allowed her to stay awake. Most of those times, she thought she was on a ship, though it was hard to be sure with the disorientation caused by whatever he had done to her. This time, she curled over and vomited violently before she could look to see where she was. The heaving continued for several minutes past when she no longer had anything left to bring up. She crawled a few feet away from the mess across a cold stone floor and sagged against iron bars. With her eyes closed, she could hear two others breathing somewhere to her left. The ache in her skull begged her to keep her eyes closed a moment longer.

"When she's stable, clean her up and bring her to my study." A deep voice; strong, melodious, and unfamiliar.

It was incredibly dark when she opened her eyes, but her enhanced vision adjusted, letting her focus on Marek. The man who had spoken was vanishing up a dimly lit stairwell. She caught a glimpse of black boots disappearing behind the wall.

Her head throbbed, and her stomach roiled threateningly. She put a hand over her gut and closed her eyes again. "What did you do to me?"

"A little magic they teach us here. It's designed specifically to take down other Silverbloods, but you must be one to use it. The headache will pass in an hour or so. I'll be back for you then."

She opened her eyes and saw him walking away. As much as she hated him now, she didn't want to be left alone in this dark cell of stone and iron, surrounded by the stench of her vomit. "Marek. Don't leave me here. Please."

She got up to her hands and knees to reach for the bars, but the sudden motion made her skull roar with agony. Her stomach responded, wracking her with more dry heaves. By the time it stopped, she was alone in the dark. Even what little light had come in from the stairwell was extinguished.

An hour passed with agonizing slowness. The stone was damp and cold, and her shivering made her head-ache worse for a while. Eventually, it did begin to fade along with the nausea. The stench of her vomit drove her to the opposite corner of the cell, where she sat shaking when the door opened, letting dim light back in. Marek entered with two other Silverbloods, both of whom she suspected were recent recruits—acolytes of the Brotherhood—given how young they looked.

One of them stepped up with a key to unlock the cell. Raven waited, conserving what little strength the shivering hadn't stolen from her. The other man walked in and took her arm in a painful grip, jerking her to her feet. She let him do most of the work.

"We'll get you cleaned up before you meet with Father Mallebron." Marek's tone and expression offered her no insight into his thoughts.

They didn't bind her in any way as they led her out, the two acolytes flanking her up the stairs behind Marek. She considered attacking him, if only for the pleasure of perhaps drawing a little blood with her teeth. The memory of what he had done, of how easily he disabled her, was too fresh in her mind. Besides, she had no real weapons. For the moment, she would simply try to appreciate that she was leaving behind the wet, reeking cell.

"Why?"

Marek didn't look back at her. He led the way down a long, dimly lit hallway of dark grey stone. With their magic-enhanced vision, she supposed keeping all the passages well-lit was wasteful. They eventually turned a corner into a more brightly lit section. He stopped before an open doorway, gesturing for her to enter. Within, two modestly dressed serving women waited next to a steaming tub. Raven could smell the perfumed water the second she reached the entrance. A vanity table stood off to the right side of the room with a worn cushioned stool in front of it. On the left side, an old wardrobe closet with crooked doors was pushed up against the wall.

"They'll help you get cleaned up."

"I don't need help," she hissed, yanking her arms free of the two men.

Marek's gaze turned icy. "They'll help you, or we will."

Her stomach clenched in response to the threat and the faint smirks of the other two men. "I'll take them," she answered, gesturing to the women with a slight jerk of her head.

He gave a curt nod and turned away. One of the two acolytes slammed the door shut behind them, sliding a bolt firmly into place. She faced the women. One of them came around the tub toward her.

"Don't fret, milady. You'll feel much better after a warm bath."

"Please don't call me that."

The woman drew back, confusion furrowing her smooth brow. "Milady?"

"Yes." Raven struggled not to snap at her.

"As you wish, milady."

Frustration ran electric through her, feeding on her fear and anger. She gave the woman a sour scowl. "Did you do that on purpose?"

The woman looked puzzled again, then her cheeks grew pink. "Sorry, milady. Habit."

Raven drew a breath, grasping for a calm that evaded her, and shook her head. "Nevermind."

The other woman patted the edge of the tub. "A bath will help."

"Right," she growled, "nothing makes me feel better than getting cleaned up to meet my captors."

The women weren't entirely wrong, however. The warm bath rid her of the clinging stenches of river water and vomit. It also eased her aching muscles. The woman who washed her hair gently massaged her scalp, calming her nerves a little. Then the other woman pulled open the wardrobe and brought out a full-length black and silver gown.

Raven sat up rigidly. "I won't wear that." She scanned the room, noticing that some things had gone missing. "Where did you put my clothes?"

"In the laundry chute, milady. They smelled awful."

She glowered at the elegant gown. "I'm not wearing that. Go get my clothes."

The corners of the woman's mouth pulled down, and she glared at the door before looking at Raven. Pity and anger tightened her voice. "I'm sorry, milady. Adept Marek said you had to wear the gown, or he'd throw you back in the cell for three days just like you are," she leaned closer and whispered, "nekked."

A shudder swept through her at the mere thought. The darkness. The cold. Cut off from everything without even her clothes to ward off the chill and the fear. Exposed to whoever might come down there. She folded her arms around herself, remembering Phendaril's arms holding her not so long ago. How long ago had that been? Hours? Days? She brushed angrily at a tear that slipped down one cheek.

The sorrow and fear were too much. Raven almost screamed, but she caught herself. What would Jaecar tell her now?

He would tell her she was a blind fool for trusting a Silverblood.

She curled her hands into fists, her short nails digging at her palms.

No. He would tell her to breathe. To focus on her target. She needed to be calm and collected if she wanted to find a way out of this. Not that she thought she could escape them, but screaming out her rage and frustration was unlikely to help.

She relaxed her hands. "Fine. I'll play their game for now."

The woman nodded, a hint of relief and approval in her eyes.

The simple bodice and skirt of the gown that they slid over her head were a glistening dark silver. Sheer black fabric was shaped over it, splitting open in the front at the waist to reveal the silver underneath. More black fabric was held in place by silver and diamond clasps across the bosom of the dress. Two more clasps topped her shoulders, holding in place panels of the sheer material that cascaded down both sides of an open back.

They didn't stop with the gown once they had her situated correctly in it. After another brief, pointless argument, they darkened around her eyes with kohl and added a silver shadow above that. Then they styled her hair, placing a low sitting silver tiara on her brow with vine-like tendrils tipped in silver leaves that wove through her hair. A teardrop-shaped diamond hung down over her forehead.

The odd preparation made her skin crawl. Wearing a

dress was insufferable enough. Combined with the rest, it made her feel like she was being prepared for an arranged marriage. It made no sense that they would bother with these excessive adornments just so they could declare her an abomination and put her to death. The possibility that they might have something else in mind didn't bring much comfort.

Eventually, Marek returned, not bothering to knock before opening the door. He stood in the doorway for a moment, staring at her. Raven glared back, unsure how effectively fierce hatred came through with all the makeup and decorations. She could only hope it was even more poignant than usual. He clenched his jaw, and she caught a flash of something in his eyes that might have been regret. Then he cleared his throat and gestured for the two men from earlier to get her.

Raven twisted, evading their grasp, and darted ahead of them toward the door and Marek. If he could see the terror in her eyes, he did nothing to acknowledge it. He simply gave a brusque nod and turned, leading her down the hall and up a spiral staircase. The ascent on the narrow steps made her appreciate that they'd given her flat dress shoes rather than a pair of the dangerous-looking heels she had seen noble ladies wearing in books. It wasn't much to be grateful for, but it was something.

They walked down another hall, this one well-lit and adorned with decorative carpets on the floor. An occasional wall mirror or polished table with flowers on it occupied alcoves along the way. The first time they passed a mirror, she glanced over and almost froze at the sight of the elegant, elven-looking female who gazed back at her. After that, she made a point of not looking. Seeing how they had changed her only made the near-crippling dread stronger. It was bad enough that she felt naked in the dress, with no pants covering her legs or shirt hiding her shoulders and back. Knowing they made her look like a stranger suggested a power over her that didn't settle well.

They started up another staircase, and she thought of Jaecar–of him crouched beside her, reminding her to breathe as she drew back her bowstring.

"Why, Marek?" She asked softly, trying not to let the men behind her hear.

"You know why," he answered, matching her volume.

The anger and hurt in his tone disagreed with the implication of his words. He would expect her to blame his loyalty to the Brotherhood, but his tone told her there was more to it. She considered the last few days for several silent strides, then a sickening realization burst in her gut.

"Phendaril," she murmured.

His shoulder's tightened, giving her all the confirmation she needed. Somehow, he knew about the two of them, and jealousy had decided his course of action for him. How was she supposed to reason with jealousy?

"Marek."

He increased his pace, forcing her to focus on keeping up with his long strides in the awkward attire they had given her. She did her best not to see herself in the numerous gilded mirrors lining the next hallway as they hurried past. He stopped abruptly and turned, knocking on a door that looked like all the others.

"Come in." It was the same voice from earlier, masculine and yet disconcertingly melodic.

Marek opened the door and gestured for her to enter ahead of him. Raven dug deep into herself for the nerve to step through that doorway. Unexpectedly, her first reaction was one of awe. The room was two stories high, bigger than the old keep's main room. Books lined the walls. Hundreds, perhaps thousands of books on shelves four levels high, with elevated walkways around the side for perusing the upper levels. Raised chandeliers cast brilliant flickering light around the upper shelves. Wall sconces and fancy candelabra on the few tables set around the room added to the warm glow.

Then that voice spoke again. "Remarkable."

She spun to look at the man who now approached from the other side of the room. He wore finely made black clothes with elaborate silver embroidery tastefully added to the lapels and cuffs. It was the liquid silver color of his long hair and the intensity of the silver in his eyes that made her breath catch in her throat. His features were distinguished, with a definite air of nobility and power. His strides were swift, and he carried himself with confidence.

Marek had entered with her, leaving the other two in the hall. He sank to one knee beside her, bowing his head to the man. "Father Mallebron," he greeted, unrestrained reverence in his tone.

Raven's legs trembled, threatening to give out on her. She fought the swell of panic as the priest stopped in front of her. For a few minutes, Father Mallebron simply stood gazing down at her, his head cocked to one side, his eyes narrowed in thought. She couldn't bring herself to meet his eyes, so she stared at his chest, which was more at eye level.

"I'm Father Wayland Mallebron. It truly is a pleasure."

He slid his fingers under her chin as if to make her look up, but Raven jerked back with a hiss, the flash of anger giving her enough courage to meet his eyes, if only for a few seconds. In that time, she caught the glimmer of cruel amusement in his smile, and she quailed inside, the hair rising on the back of her neck.

"Her birth name is Aneiris, though she goes by Raven."

Raven glared at Marek for yet another betrayal of her trust, but he kept his head bowed.

"Perfect," Wayland purred. "You may go, Adept

Marek. Complete your contract with that insufferable lord."

Marek did look up then. "It's not urgent. I can..."

He trailed off when Wayland lifted a hand to silence him. He hesitated a second before getting to his feet and starting toward the door. Raven's anger at him faltered. No matter how much she hated him for what he had done, she would rather have his company than be left alone with the priest.

She stepped after him and grabbed his arm. "Marek?"

He looked at her hand, then at her face, and his expression darkened. He jerked his arm away and stalked out the door, shutting it firmly behind him.

CHAPTER THIRTY THREE

I thought my daughter's dress would fit you well."

Raven whirled to face Father Wayland, hating the smug look that reminded her again how much of a fool she was for trusting Marek.

"She can have it back," she growled.

He chuckled. "You have spirit. That's good. It shows that the magic can still be trusted to cull the weak, even if it should never have been used on someone like you. As for the dress, my daughter is dead, so I doubt she cares much who wears it."

A twinge of guilt tempered her anger. No one deserved to lose a child. "I'm sorry."

He waved a hand dismissively, and she caught a glimpse of fingernails as silver as his hair. "She was sixty-four when she died. A decent lifespan."

Raven peered up at him in earnest confusion. He looked no more than thirty himself. It might make sense if he had been an elf, but he was human. How could he be old enough to watch a child die at sixty-four?

"You really are naive of the gift you've been given, aren't you?" He cocked his head at her, a glint of scornful amusement in those bright silver eyes as he continued without allowing a chance to respond. "Adept Marek said your mother made you?"

"Yes."

"How old were you?"

"Eight," she answered, trying to avoid saying more than she had to.

She had no warning. One second, she was standing. The next, she was pressed back against a pillar between two sections of bookcase with his hand around her throat, her feet dangling above the ground. She clawed at his wrist and tried to kick at him, but his strength was stunning, and the dress restricted her reach. The pressure of his grip already caused splashes of darkness across her vision.

"Don't lie to me!"

She would have told him she wasn't, but she couldn't speak. His gaze burned into her. It took a few seconds for her struggles to weaken, her limbs growing heavy. Then her feet touched down, and he let go. Her legs refused to hold her, buckling under her. She sank to the floor.

"Maybe it is true." His knuckles cracked as he closed his hand into a fist and then opened it, stretching his fingers. "I don't see the lie in your eyes. Who died to make you?"

Her first effort to speak came out as a barely audible rasp. She stared at the ground, fighting the tears that stung her eyes. She didn't want him to believe that he was breaking her, though she wasn't sure he would be wrong if he did think it.

A crystalline goblet full of water appeared in her line of sight, his silver fingernails taunting her, reminding her that his power was much greater than hers. She wanted to refuse the offering, but she needed it. Still, the thought of taking it, of knowing that she couldn't do so without touching his hand, held her back. When he relented and set it on the floor, she took it.

After a few drinks, she said, "My mother and father."

"Your mother used her own life. That's unusual." He crouched next to her, taking a strand of her hair between his fingers. His brow furrowed as he considered it. Raven no longer had the will to pull away. "This is more than two lives. Who else died?"

She found her gaze moving to the liquid silver hair that draped down over his shoulders. If more than two had to die to give her hair the amount of silver it had, how many lives had it taken to make him the way he was? She shuddered. He exhaled a soft sigh, a sound of pleasure that made her stomach clench.

"There were others there," she murmured. Raising her voice was too painful. "The men who killed my parents. They were all dead or dying when she used the magic."

He nodded as if he had suspected something like that, but he didn't move away as she had hoped he would when he got his answer. He continued to stroke the lock of her hair between his fingers with his thumb.

"If you're going to kill me, why dress me up like this?"

"Because I like beautiful things, and you, my dear, are extraordinarily beautiful. The perfect marriage of elf and human. The exquisite blend of femininity and Silverblood power. To adorn you in this way is merely to celebrate what you already bring to the moment."

He offered her a hand, and she accepted it, unwilling, for the time being, to suffer the potential consequences of refusal. The ease of his strength as he raised her gently up reminded her of how dangerous he was. He took her elbow to steady her when she wavered on her feet. She placed her hand against the bookcase for support and stepped back from him. He watched, silent and patient now, while she took a minute to recover her balance.

"I'd like to show you something." He strode to the side of the room opposite the entrance and pressed the wing of an elegant bird carved into one of the pillars. Two sections of the bookcase swung inward, and sunlight spilled into the room.

Curiosity lured her away from the wall, and she walked to the opening. The room beyond the hidden doorway was octagonal. The upper half of the far wall and the roof were made entirely of glass panels that let in the daylight. Around the room stood bloodwood pedestals and glass-topped cases with books and various other items displayed in and upon them. In the center, a stuffed bronze wyvern reared up, its vast wings extended and held in place with chains attached to the roof's metal framework.

"Beautiful things," he commented as he strolled inside, gesturing to the wyvern. "That was one of my proudest conquests. The beast put up a fierce fight."

She glanced behind her as she moved into the room and saw a set of wings with gold and blue feathers hanging high above the door.

"Straigh Mountain harpy," he offered, following her gaze. "That color is a rare mutation."

Raven scanned the room. Creatures of all kinds were frozen in time in displays around her. The screaming head of griffon here, a collection of exotic butterflies pinned in place over there. The hand of a dryad wrapped in vines and somehow preserved as it looked in life lay in a case under one wing of the wyvern. Perhaps a hundred or more rare and extraordinary creatures were celebrated in a morbid display of death.

Her stomach turned, and her head spun. She stumbled, catching herself with one hand on the edge of a glass case. Glancing down, she saw a pair of elven ears in the case she had fallen against, preserved as in life like the dryad hand. She pushed away and recoiled into Wayland, his solid figure providing an immovable wall against her back. He caught her arms in his hands and turned her, directing her to a different display.

This pedestal, made of bi-colored amberwood instead of the deep red bloodwood, had an open tome set upon it. The innocuous object sent a dizzying wave of relief through her. The lettering on the pages was strange and unfamiliar, but at least it was just a book. Something ordinary. Something safe. She stepped closer, out of his grasp, and placed a hand on the pedestal, focusing on the book while she remembered to breathe.

She cringed when Wayland moved up beside her, but held her ground. She could not hope to escape him in her current state.

"This tome is an accounting of the Acridan. More specifically, of their magic." His tone picked up an air of reverence as he regarded the book. "Your mother was elven, correct?"

She peered at the strange characters, written in a sweeping hand that conveyed an air of respect and devotion. Focusing on following the progression of those peculiar symbols down the page helped calm her. She nodded.

"The Acridan were an isolated race that once lived in this region near Amberwood. An area I believe you are quite familiar with."

She nodded again, swallowing back the painful longing that rushed up with the mention of Amberwood. She would happily take on the overwhelming population of the recovering town if it meant she didn't have to be here. Amberwood dangled the possibilities of a home and a future before her, but they were foolish dreams. The Brotherhood wouldn't be letting her leave here alive.

Wayland's voice became distant, as of someone reminiscing upon the past. "The Acridan were somewhat elf-like in appearance, but longer of limb and with an external bone growth that provided armor to portions of their body." He moved a hand over his upper arm and shoulder to indicate where some of that armor would have been. "The magic was originally theirs. When our human scouting party came to the region, we encountered the Acridan. They welcomed us into their village and their homes. They shared with us their customs and even started to show us their magic.

"We discovered too late that we carried something with us, something in our bodies, a virus perhaps, that was lethal to the Acridan. The entire species was wiped from existence within six months of our arrival. Before that happened, as soon as they realized they were dying off too fast to stop it, they tried to preserve as much of their culture and knowledge as possible through books and sharing with us. One of the things they passed to us was this tome containing the secrets of their magic. Some feared the magic collected in these pages, but a few of us saw its potential. We banded together and took whatever they would teach us about it. We used that knowledge to form the Silverblood Brotherhood."

"That doesn't explain how my mother knew the magic."

He turned a few pages of the book, running his fingers across the strange characters the way he might caress the skin of a lover. "According to the Acridan, any one of them could use the magic without issue. Male or female. Young or old. Humankind, however, was different. Just as something relatively harmless to humans turned out to be lethal to the Acridan, so did magic that was harmless to the Acridans turn out to be often fatal for humans. The act of making a Silverblood quite often proves fatal to the magic's user, and the subject if they are attempting to change another. The Brotherhood's warriors, and priests like myself, are the elite few who survived the remaking. We learned that once you are transformed by the magic, you are far less likely to suffer ill effects from using it. We don't teach our warriors how to use it, other than a few skills like the one Adept Marek used to subdue you, because we don't want them trying to make more like themselves. The magic must be contained and controlled."

For profit. For power. She held her tongue, waiting to see if he would address the matter of her mother.

"You're not the first rogue Silverblood we've had to put down, and you won't be the last. One of our warriors occasionally figures out how to remake someone, often in a moment of heightened emotion, such as losing a loved one. Then we must put them and their creation down. Early on, when the Brotherhood was just starting to gain power, we found a few Silverblood elves that we eliminated. We didn't realize then that they might be our last chance to translate this book.

"You see," he tilted his head to one side, his expression darkening, "a community of forest elves lived near the Acridan village. They shared crops and participated in one another's festivals, but the Acridan insisted that was the extent of the relationship. Lies, we believe now, to protect that elven community. They vanished soon after our arrival. One day they were there. The next, their village was empty. Every now and then, when the magic shows up in the hands of elves – elves like your mother – we assume they must be descended from those elves."

The severe look he gave her drove her to back up a few steps, but curiosity demanded satisfaction. "Why, if it isn't true, do you tell people the magic can't be used by women or elves?"

His condescending smile chilled her. It was all she could do to keep from scrambling back from him when he moved close to look down at her. He placed a hand on her shoulder, partially cupping her neck with his thumb and forefinger. A casual warning or a promise? She stiffened, barely able to breathe past the constricting of her throat.

"Because they shouldn't be allowed to use it." He

brought his hand up and brushed his fingers lightly over her cheek. A hind of fondness warmed his smile, forcing her to swallow back the bile that rose in her throat. "Sometimes, in nature, there are rare mutations. As beautiful as they can be, it's best to cull them for the good of the species."

Aldrich Darrenton twirled his sword a few times, considering the two battered practice dummies in the sand sparring ring. After a few minutes, he turned to look at the Silverblood warrior. Something about the man today, a heightened tension, made Aldrich warier of him than usual.

"They have a clan of Stonebreakers?"

Marek responded with a curt nod.

"Inconvenient, but useful if they're willing to accept new leadership. And you said the current leader is a woman?"

Marek nodded again. "She seems well-liked."

Aldrich waved a dismissive hand at him. "She's a woman. Well-liked or not, the Stonebreakers will see sense in having a real leader with experience in battle and politics."

Marek's answering silence grated at him. Aldrich turned abruptly, channeling his rage into a couple of fierce swings that left the nearest dummy wavering on its post. When he glanced back at Marek, expecting the respect he deserved, he was met with a derogatory sneer.

"I've paid you. Get out," Aldrich ordered.

Marek lunged forward, his sword appearing in his hand so fast Aldrich had trouble tracking the motion. He took a few steps back to his former position and sheathed the weapon. The dummy's head bounced on the ground a few feet away. Without another word, Marek gave an abrupt nod and strode from the courtyard. Aldrich looked at the head as it rolled to a stop, a strange discomfort in his bowels. His vision turned red, anger exploding through him, scalding away that moment of panic and vulnerability as he laid violently into the other practice dummy.

It seemed like mere minutes had passed, though the exhaustion and the sweat told him it had been longer when one of his servants entered the courtyard and bowed to him.

"Milord."

"What," he snapped, enjoying how the young man flinched.

"There's a woman out front who wishes to speak to you. Lady Alayne Valassian of Chadhurst. She has an elf with her and a Stonebreaker warrior."

That uncomfortable sensation in his bowels returned. What glorious timing. Had the Silverblood bastard betrayed his plans to these people? Why else would they be showing up at his door now? He would prefer to avoid the audience. At the same time, he itched to know how King Navaran's niece was involved in something regarding a territory on the border of Saldin's kingdom, assuming this was about Amberwood. Technically, Amberwood existed in neutral territory between the two kingdoms, so it could be of interest to either side.

"Offer them some refreshments and bring them to my public council hall in twenty minutes. I can't receive them dripping with sweat."

The servant bowed and left to do his bidding.

Closer to twenty-five minutes later, clean and appropriately dressed, he seated himself in the heavy, carved chair that served as his personal *throne* for holding formal audiences. The thick, solid wood seat curved around him, giving a sense of strength and security. He liked the feeling of power that sitting there gave him.

The servant led in his unexpected guests. "Lady Alayne Valassian of Chadhurst and company."

Aldrich appreciated the abbreviated introduction. He hated having too many names to remember. When Alayne walked through the door, he stood and went to meet her halfway across the room alongside the council table, hoping to set the audience off on a positive note. He offered his hand out to accept hers so he might lay a kiss on it. The fiery-haired woman took his hand, turning it into a firm handshake and releasing it back to him.

"A pleasure, Lord Darrenton. It has been some time."

Aldrich hesitated a moment, trying to recall when he had ever had a chance to meet her in person. It was hard to say with noble gatherings. He offered a generic smile. "It has indeed. Please, have a seat."

She accepted the offer, selecting a chair to the right and two places down the council table where she could angle to face him easily. Like all the chairs around the table, it was smaller than his, putting him above her, though her height mitigated the difference. The Stonebreaker and the intense-looking elf took positions near the wall close to where she sat. Aldrich did his best to pretend they weren't there.

"To what do I owe the pleasure of your visit?"

"I come about a matter of land. Specifically, the land known as Amberwood. I believe it was your father's holding for a time."

Aldrich stiffened, struggling to maintain his pleasant manner. At least she didn't insist on wasting his time with meaningless pleasantries. "It is still in the family."

"Well," her smile was a little too sweet, "that's what I wanted to discuss. The land has lain dormant for a long time and gone to ruin–"

He cut her off. "It was bestowed upon my brother, Jaecar, by our father, but he chose to do nothing with it. Now that he has passed, of course, the land falls to me as his closest kin and–"

Amusement shimmered in her eyes when she cut him off in turn. "Actually, because the land was dormant for so long with no one coming forward to assert their claim, I petitioned King Navaran to grant me ownership of the land. A deed has already been written up and sent to King Saldin requesting the placement of his seal next to King Navaran's."

Aldrich was faintly aware that his mouth was open, but he had difficulty mustering up the care to close it. The clever little harlot was stealing his land and resources, and she was getting the blessings of both kings to do it. If what she said was true, he could do nothing to stop it now unless he could convince King Saldin not to approve the deed. But that required securing an audience and finding an argument that would hold more weight than the increased goodwill of the neighboring sovereign.

"Why are you coming to me with this? It sounds like you've already gone out of your way to invalidate my claim." He hated the anger in his voice and how easily she had thrown him into a state of agitation.

"That's where it gets interesting, my lord. You see, I recently met a young lady who can also lay claim to Amberwood. She was raised by your late brother, Jaecar. I've seen the legal adoption papers and the will bequeathing all his holdings to her. She claims to also have the deed to Amberwood. If her claim is recognized, the land would still be in your family."

Cautious hope rose in him. It sounded like the kind of idiot thing Jaecar would do, but if it were true, this woman could be his answer to getting what he wanted out of Amberwood after all. Someone he could generously take under his wing long enough to secure the deed, then send her to university or marry her off while he mined and logged Amberwood's resources. When he had everything he wanted from the land, he could put her in charge of whatever was left, perhaps as a graduation gift or some other such nonsense.

"And where is this young lady?"

"That's the problem and why we came to you. She was taken by the Brotherhood for a crime she didn't commit, and we don't know where she put the deed. If she isn't released, we'll simply have to proceed as if there is no other legal claim. However, we wanted to offer you the chance to keep the land in your family if your niece's claim is valid."

He shifted in his chair, rubbing his hands together to keep himself from gripping the aging wooden arms too tightly. "The Brotherhood has her?" He grimaced at the slight rise in his voice.

"I am afraid so, my lord. Given that she is part of your family, you're likely the only one who might be able to affect her release. I thought it only right to give you the option. She is your brother's daughter."

He narrowed his eyes at her. Alayne didn't have to tell him any of this. She could simply get the seal of both kings on the new deed, which would override any claim anyone else had. However, there was the possibility that she was fond of the girl his brother had taken in. In that case, she might be willing to risk her own claim to help her. Having a friend hold the deed to the land might be enough for this woman. If so, she was a fool, but he could use that to his advantage. Still, none of this would matter if the Brotherhood convicted the girl of some crime.

"The Brotherhood isn't likely to let me waltz off with one of their prisoners without good reason. I didn't know anything about the girl before a few minutes ago.

How can I convince them they should put her in my care?"

Alayne tossed her long red braid over her shoulder and leaned closer. "That's where we come in. If you're willing to present your claim over the girl to the Brotherhood, we can go with you and offer our understanding of her innocence. Together, we might stand a chance."

Aldrich met her eyes. He sensed some catch here but wasn't entirely sure what it was. And did it matter? If he got them to release the girl and took her in, the property would belong to the Darrenton family. He could work on getting the girl out of the way of his plans for the resources from there. If Alayne went through with her claim, those resources would be gone forever. Or he would have to lay siege to Amberwood the way his father had, but that was costly and unpleasant. An option he would prefer to leave unexplored.

"Very well. I'll go with you to the Brotherhood and see what can be done about this young lady. It seems only right to try to honor my brother's dying wishes."

Alayne sat back in her chair and offered a smile that held more secrets than he cared for. "Of course."

CHAPTER THIRTY FIVE

Raven woke in a comfortable bedroom in the Silverblood temple complex. It was still a prison cell. Nothing in the room could double as a weapon, and the two windows had bars over them. The door remained bolted through the night with two Silverblood guards outside. She still wasn't sure why they were bothering to keep her alive, other than her suspicion that Wayland hadn't learned all he wanted to from her yet. He asked her if she knew where her mother was from before sending her here the previous night. He seemed unimpressed by her insistence that she didn't, simply saying they would discuss it another time.

She spent the first half of the day alternating between pacing the room, reading from the one book Wayland had allowed her to take from his study, and practicing sword forms with roses from a vase on the bedside table, all in her undergarments. They hadn't returned her regular clothes to her. A wardrobe against one wall held a collection of five elegant black and silver dresses in different styles. She wasn't sure she could put one on correctly if she wanted to without someone to assist. Since she had no desire to wear any of them, she settled for the undergarments they had given her, keeping her ear tuned for the door bolt so she could cover herself with a blanket if it opened.

For a time, she considered breaking some furniture to create a makeshift weapon. Even if she managed to overcome the two guards outside her door, however, she had no clue which way to go from there. She had woken in the prison cells below. From there, they had taken her to the bathing room one floor up on what she suspected was the ground floor. The study and collection room would be on the third floor if her other guess was correct. This room wasn't far from the study on the same floor. None of her brief trips between rooms had shown her anything that looked like a promising exit.

She abandoned sword forms when the stem of the last rose from the vase broke. From there, she went to one of the windows and gazed out. It was uncomfortable. A steady stream of traffic in the courtyard below sparked her anxiety. Two Silverblood warriors guarded the main entrance to the right and inward of her current location. A few wandered in and out. They were easy to spot in their distinctive black and silver armor. Other people came and went, requiring clearance from one of the guards before they were allowed to enter. Even more stopped at the edge of the open courtyard gates and gaped up at the towering Brotherhood temple, sometimes pointing at the angry spires that tried to pierce the sky above them.

If she pressed her face hard against the window and looked right, she could see some of the glass panes that formed the upper wall and ceiling of the collection room. That meant it lay between her room and the entrance, set up against the front courtyard. Its placement would explain why many sightseers stopped to stare toward that part of the structure. The room, partly walled and roofed in glass, must be impressive from the outside. She wouldn't be surprised if they could see at least part of the wyvern from the ground.

The sound of the bolt sliding free sent her hurrying

to the bed. She grabbed the throw from the foot of the bed and wrapped it around herself. The door opened, and the two women from the previous day bustled in. Raven gave them both a scowl to tell them how she despised what she was sure they were here for. She reserved a feral snarl for the Silverblood in the hallway, who closed the door behind them.

"Milady, are you in your undergarments?" The woman who spoke gave her a startled look while the other, with a puzzled expression, began picking up the broken roses from the floor.

Raven ignored the question. The answer was obvious. "I don't suppose there's a point in asking about my clothes again."

The woman offered a shake of her head, refusing to meet Raven's eyes as she hurried to the wardrobe. "It's better if you don't make a fuss, milady."

"Why? Do you think they'll put me to death more gently if I'm compliant?"

Neither of the women would look at her then. They went about selecting a dress and getting her into it. This one was all layers of shimmering black fabric with a loose silver belt hanging into a low v at the waist, the end of which dangled down to her knees. The snug bodice was enhanced with accents of silver and diamond. A collar of black fabric with a line of diamonds down the front wrapped her neck, extra fabric hanging down past the open back. It hid the bruises around her throat from yesterday, which she suspected was no accident.

She tolerated their ministrations in silence, hating the beautiful tiara they wove back into her hair and the makeup that made her look like someone else. When she peered at the half-elven female in the mirror, she saw the question in her eyes. Was this the way she would look when she died? Was today that day?

The women knocked on the inside of the door when they were done, and it opened for them. A different man stood there now. A man she knew.

She made herself get up from the stool and face him. "Adept Marek."

His gaze flickered over her, his expression guarded. "Come with me."

When she followed him out, two more Silverblood warriors fell into step behind her. He kept to one side of the hall this time, allowing her to walk up beside him.

"Three of you just for me. Are you afraid I'll hurt you?" She asked, hoping to get under his skin, though something in her voice sounded too much like defeat, and she knew he would hear it.

He glanced down at her. "I've fought with you, remember. I know how capable you are."

"I remember," she murmured, hating how the memory hurt. "I remember how we guarded each other's backs. I remember how we cleared the mines together as a team. I remember the lies you told me with your actions."

He looked away. "I wanted to show you something."

It struck her then how few Silverbloods she had seen here. The same two guards had been present every time she was escorted down the halls. She'd heard them switch out with two others overnight, but that only added up to four of them plus Marek and Wayland that she had encountered within the building. Since she hadn't seen the guards outside her door at night, she had no way to know if the ones guarding the entrance were different men. Even if they were, that still only added up to two more. The two serving women were the only other people she'd seen in the halls.

"Is this where you live when you aren't out completing contracts?"

Marek didn't look at her this time. She hoped he

was struggling with guilt for his betrayal, though she had some doubts.

"No."

Not a helpful answer. "Where do you live?"

"Nowhere. Like most Brotherhood adepts, I travel most of the time. When we happen to end up in one of the bigger cities, we stop by the local Brotherhood to present our earnings and receive the blessings of the Priest there."

It didn't sound like a fantastic arrangement, at least not for the warriors, but whether Marek received a fair cut of his profits wasn't her concern. "So, there aren't that many of you in the temple at any one time."

He did look at her then, a hint of warning in the narrowed eyes and pinched brows. "There are enough. If you wish to hasten your demise, feel free to test that."

The route he took brought them to a section of the temple structure she hadn't been in yet. They passed the study and came around a corner, which put them in the vicinity of the entrance. However, it was still on the third floor, which didn't offer much hope as an escape route, though it was at least in the correct direction. He stopped them before a door and held up a hand for the other two guards to wait there. He looked at her and placed a finger to his lips as he opened the door. Curiosity sparked. She stepped through, and he followed close behind her, closing the door gently.

They were on a balcony that ran around the perimeter of a massive chamber. The arched ceiling was lost in the shadows above them. The balcony was also cast in shadow, light from the hanging chandeliers not powerful enough to permeate the darkness. A second balcony stretched around the room a level below them. At ground level, a set of large double doors were opening, letting in daylight from outside. This was the entrance.

The sight of a doorway leading out was sufficient to make her pulse race by itself. Then she saw the group coming through it. A man dressed in noble finery strode alongside Alayne. Behind them came one of the Stonebreaker warriors and an elven male she never expected to see again.

Aware of Marek standing beside her, she did her best to keep her breathing even while she watched Phendaril stalk up the length of the room alongside a dark-skinned Stonebreaker behind Alayne. Her gaze jumped to the dais they were approaching and the man standing there. Wayland wore a long black and silver cloak, his silver hair gleaming in the sliver of sunlight that came through a long narrow window behind him.

The hair on the back of her neck rose, and her hand drifted to her throat, where the lingering pain in her neck suddenly worsened. She stepped back, bumping into Marek, who placed a hand on her shoulder. She would have jerked away from that hated touch in a different moment, but now? She could only stare in terror at the man below them. If she could find her voice, she might have yelled for Phendaril and the others to leave. To get as far from him as they could. Somehow, his mere presence was enough to silence her.

Wayland came forward to the edge of the dais and descended one step, holding his arms over the visitors who knelt a few feet back from the lowest step. "Lady Valassian. Lord Darrenton. Welcome to my temple. How might I help you today?"

Lord Darrenton started to rise, then hesitated, sinking back to one knee. "If I may speak, Father Mallebron." A tremor in his voice told her he either knew how powerful the man before him was or had good enough instincts to sense it.

Wayland made a lifting gesture with his hands before he lowered them to his sides. "You may all rise, and you, Lord Darrenton, may speak if you must."

The four rose. Lord Darrenton cleared his throat. "I've come to ask about a young lady you have here. My late brother, Lord Jaecar Darrenton's adopted daughter, Aneiris Darrenton. She goes by Raven, I believe," he added, casting a glance toward Alayne, who gave a slight nod. "She's family, and I'd like to offer her a place in my home."

Raven caught her breath. Adopted daughter? Was that true? Had Jaecar made her his daughter? Tears stung her eyes even as loathing swelled in her. Eamon said the men she chased to Manderly were Darrenton's men. If that were true, then Lord Darrenton's own men killed his brother, likely at his bidding if he knew Jaecar was dead.

The hint of surprise that touched Wayland's ageless features was quickly replaced by amusement. "I didn't realize she was nobility. No matter. She is to be put to death. You may go."

Phendaril looked like he might come forward, but a low gesture from Alayne stayed him. Lord Darrenton took half a step forward and cleared his throat. Wayland, who had been turning to leave, slowly rotated around to face him again, a warning in his piercing silver eyes.

"Father. I must at least speak to the girl," Lord Darrenton blurted, insultingly quick to scale back his request.

"As I recall, your recently deceased brother was estranged from the family. There isn't a glimmer of concern for the girl in your entire being, Lord Darrenton. What does she have that you want?"

Lord Darrenton wrung his hands. "My brother left her the deed to Amberwood."

Wayland rolled his eyes briefly toward the ceiling, making it clear that he couldn't believe they had bothered him with this. "Which will fall to you when she's dead."

"Not so," Alayne stepped forward. "There is a deed

awaiting Kind Saldin's seal that has already received the approval of King Navaran. That deed grants Amberwood to me. Raven's claim was the only other legitimate claim to the land. If she dies, the new deed will be completed, and ownership of the land will fall to me."

Wayland gave her a brief measuring look. "Congratulations, Lady Valassian, Amberwood is yours."

He turned as if to leave again, and Alayne hurried several steps closer, stopping with one foot on the first step of the dais. "Father Mallebron, Raven has committed no crime."

Wayland spun to face her, his eyes narrowing as he advanced down the first few steps of the dais. The pressure of his power filled the massive room. Alayne and Lord Darrenton both retreated a few feet away from him.

"She *is* a crime, and she will be dealt with accordingly. Take your land and go, Lady Valassian. You will leave here with nothing else."

Again, even with that blood-chilling power sucking the air from the room, Phendaril looked as if he might step forward. Then, for whatever reason, he glanced up instead. His eyes widened. Raven shook her head, pleading with her eyes, hoping he would let it go. Let her go. His expression hardened. He turned away, following Alayne, who was retreating from the room behind Lord Darrenton. She didn't blame Alayne for giving up. It was the smart thing to do, but Phendaril wasn't done yet. That much was apparent in his fierce strides.

Marek guided her into the shadows by the wall to ensure Wayland didn't see them as he turned to leave. When the priest left the room using a passage below them, he ushered her through the door behind them and back toward her room.

"Why did you take me there?"

Marek didn't answer until she was back through the

door to her room. Staring at the door jamb, he said, "I just wanted you to know..." His hand tightened on the handle, and she feared he might leave without finishing. He drew a breath, letting it out slowly before speaking again. "I wanted you to know that you weren't forgotten. That there are many who care for you."

Raven's chest constricted, and she closed her eyes as he shut the door, listening to the bolt slide home.

Whether Marek's intent was to torment her with the realization that her death would hurt Phendaril or comfort her with the fact that she hadn't been forgotten, the brief outing made one thing obvious. She had to force Wayland's hand. Phendaril now knew she was still alive. He had hope. False, foolish hope that she needed to deprive him of before he got hurt.

She waited until after they brought her dinner. Whatever came next, she might need the energy. She had expected Wayland to call upon her before that, but it seemed he was not a man to rush into things. After her dinner had time to settle, she peered out the window, watching until someone lit the candles in the collection room, and they cast a dim light into the courtyard. She dug through the wardrobe and pulled a sheer black shawl from the hanger of one of the other dresses. Thicker material would have been more helpful, but this would have to do. At least everything in the wardrobe followed the same color scheme, so it matched her current dress.

With the shawl draped around her shoulders, she started for the door, but the sound of a carriage rolling up in the quiet evening reached her sensitive ears. It was a little late for visitors or sightseers.

Raven hurried to the window and peered out. A carriage had pulled up in the shadows across the street from the now-closed courtyard gates. Even before the door opened, she knew Phendaril would step out. He slipped quietly across the street, near-invisible in the darkness. A weight dropped in her gut when he jumped over the low gate.

"You weren't supposed to come back so soon," she murmured. A new sense of urgency spurring her on, Raven went to knock on the inside of the door.

"What is it?" One of the guards called.

"I want to speak to Father Mallebron."

After a moment of silence, the bolt slid free, and the door opened. That part had been easier than expected. The two young acolytes stood in the doorway. One of them, his blond hair neatly trimmed, grinned at her. The other, taller and with dark hair that hung down to his shoulders, similar to Marek's in cut, scowled at her, looking less pleased.

She glanced between them. "What?"

"I bet five silver that you'd break today," the blond stated. He elbowed his companion. "He thought you'd last another two days."

She gave a slight shake of her head, still confused. "Break?"

"You're going to beg the Father for your life."

The man's arrogant certainty irked her. She couldn't let it distract her from her goal. "Where is he?"

"In his study. He's always in his study in the evenings." That was the scowling dark-haired acolyte. He got another elbow in the ribs for his trouble.

"You're more of an idiot than I thought," the blond snapped. "She is a prisoner."

"What's she going to do? She's just a girl."

Raven yearned to give him a demonstration, but she wasn't armed and didn't have time for it. Whatever,

Phendaril was planning, he was making his move, and she couldn't risk him getting caught. His presence made things more complicated, but she wasn't ready to let him die for her if she could prevent it.

"And a Silverblood," the blond added. "Not to mention, she's got pointies. You know those elven bastards are quick and sneaky."

The dark-haired acolyte sneered and said nothing. Her apparent breaking had destroyed any respect he might have had for her previously. That was good. It worked into her plan. She needed to speak to Wayland alone, and these two, unlike Marek, wouldn't think twice about leaving him alone with her. Assuming that was why Marek hesitated when Wayland dismissed him the previous day. Regardless, all that mattered now was getting these two to take her to him.

"We're smarter too. And, with a little magic enhancement, generally better at everything." She didn't have to work hard to put disdain in her voice. Ruining the blond's good mood gave her a glimmer of satisfaction. The worst part was that she told them exactly why they had reason to be concerned. They were simply too arrogant to hear it.

The blond glowered at her and stepped back, giving her room to come out. "I hope he makes you beg on your knees and laughs in your freak face."

Freak. She was that, in many ways. A half-elven Silverblood female. She might have agreed with him once. She didn't now. She knew what it felt like to be appreciated and needed. She knew what it felt like to be wanted. Jaecar cared enough to make her his daughter. Alayne had come to try to free her. Phendaril was willing to risk infiltrating a Brotherhood temple to save her. This man might think of her as a worthless freak, but she wasn't worried anymore about finding the truth in his words.

She strode past him, heading down the hall toward

Wayland's study. The two acolytes fell into step behind her, their scowling silence more welcome than their words had been for the short time it lasted.

"Must have one compelling argument in mind at the speed your walking," the dark-haired warrior grumbled as they approached the door.

If things went right, she had a feeling Wayland would find it quite compelling.

She grabbed for the handle, throwing the door open before either of the men could step up to knock. One of them reached for her arm, but she was as quick as they said, and she hoped to throw Wayland off his composure.

When she entered, he stood at a table near the collection room entrance with his back to the door. Raven stopped, her confidence faltering before his disinterest as he flipped a few pages of the book he was holding. The acolytes rushed in behind her.

"Apologies, Father Mallebron," the blond sputtered.

Wayland silenced him with a sharp gesture. "You may go. My business is with *Lady Darrenton*." He sneered the name, mocking her with it.

The two retreated, shutting the door behind them. Raven tried to focus her breathing, making herself take a few steps closer. Given his speed, even being across the room wouldn't put her out of range if he got angry again. There wasn't much point in hanging back. Still, it was hard to get her feet to move.

He glanced over one shoulder at her. "I'm glad you could join me."

It further unnerved her that he acted as if he had invited her here. She drummed up some of Jaecar's favorite curses in her mind, combating the paralyzing fear of Wayland with fond memories. Breathing slow and steady, she walked forward, not to him, but toward the open doors to the collection room. She stopped at the entrance to run her fingers over the carved bird on the pillar, feeling the texture in the wood. She heard the book being set lightly back on the table and the soft scuff of his shoes on the hardwood floor as he turned to look at her.

"Something's changed about you."

"Different dress." It surprised her that the trembling inside her didn't come out in her voice. She'd almost managed to sound flippant.

He was closer when he spoke again, his nearness making her skin crawl. "My Silverblood sons expect you to beg for your life, don't they? But that's not why you're here, is it?"

She moved around the door and into the collection room. This time, she wouldn't let the horror of the death there overwhelm her. Her nerves crackled as he followed her through the doorway. About halfway past the wyvern, she turned and shook her head in answer to his question. Her stomach did a flip as he ran his fingers along the edge of the case that held the elven ears.

"You've accepted your death and have come to ask for it."

Raven nodded. "You won't let me leave here alive. I don't want to live every moment wondering which of your daughter's dresses you'll choose to kill me in. If you mean to kill me, I would ask that you do it sooner rather than later. Why have you not ended this already?"

"Perhaps I want to know more about your mother. Or I might just be trying to figure out how best to preserve you." His smirk and his words sent a shudder through her that she made no effort to hide this time.

"Please. Do it now. Don't drag this on." She walked between two stands, and her gaze found what she was looking for. Something she had known would be in this room in some form. He liked beautiful things. Exotic things. Dangerous things. There was a lock on the case.

A minor inconvenience. She let the shawl slide off her shoulders to drop into one hand.

"You're eager to die tonight. Are you trying to protect your elven friend? The one who looked up at you with such longing in the entrance hall today."

Panic jolted through her that she couldn't have hidden if she wanted to, bringing a metallic taste to her mouth. Somehow, he had known she was watching from the balcony. Did he know Phendaril was here now? Or was he making the connection based on the earlier encounter?

"That *is* it."

His smile tore at her confidence, so she looked away. Taking a few steps closer to the case, she kept her gaze on the head of the bear mounted above it. The beast could have been the twin of the one they encountered in Amberwood. Its muzzle just as scarred and grizzled.

"I've fought a beast such as this one," she remarked, hoping to keep his attention focused up while she twisted her hand beside her leg, winding the shawl around it.

"Adept Marek told me of your battle with the rats and the dire bear. Even the corpse eaters. Did those battles prepare you for this one?" He was moving toward her with slow, confident strides.

The implication behind his question, suggesting he knew she meant to start something, sent a fresh jolt of alarm through her. If she was going to do it, this was the moment, before he got too close to stop her. With her hand wrapped in the shawl, she slammed her fist through the top of the case. The glass shattered, and she grabbed the magnificent elven sword that lay inside it on a bed of blue silk, barely noticing the sharp shards biting at her hand through the fabric of the shawl.

Raven didn't try to attack him. She jumped to one side, knowing he would use his speed to try to grab her. Then she spun, hoping she had predicted correctly. His arrogance, born of so many years without a foe who could challenge him, put him in her range as she swung out with the blade. The magic in him was much greater than that in her. Still, if he expected her to move like one of his warriors, he was forgetting she had an advantage they didn't—elven blood.

The end of the blade caught his upper arm. The cut was shallow. He wasn't prepared for her speed, but his own made up for the oversight. A trickle of blood began to dampen the black sleeve of his shirt. His eyes narrowed, a delighted smile curving his lips. He had to kill her now. She wasn't going to let him get away with anything less.

CHAPTER THIRTY SEVEN

Raven expected him to come at her after that, but he didn't. He took a few steps back and to the left, then reached out, grabbing an ornate halberd from the wall. He spun the weapon in his hands and shifted into a fighting stance.

"I hope you didn't expect me to have no fighting skills because I'm a priest. I started my life as a soldier."

The confidence of his grip on the haft brought her no comfort, but the sword in her hands was like a meal she had been starving for. Now, if only she didn't have the skirt of the dress wrapped around her legs, threatening to trip her. She could not do much about that right now. He wasn't going to stand back and give her a moment to slice off the bottom for freedom of movement.

He lunged. Raven ducked under his attack, leaping not toward him but off to the side and spinning again to face him. Let him think her afraid to engage. It wouldn't be entirely untrue, given the greater reach he now had. But she also needed his overconfidence to work in her favor.

She dodged a couple more times. On the last swing, the haft of the halberd struck the corner of one of the stands and knocked it over, shattering the case that sat atop it. His lip lifted in a snarl. The obstacle not only stoked his anger, it also saved her leg, leaving her with a shallow gash in her thigh that would have gone much deeper if he had been able to follow through. It also left part of the skirt hanging down in a way she hoped wouldn't cause her more trouble. The pain gave her something to focus on other than the expectation that she would die here and had, in fact, started this fight with that end in mind. She wouldn't make it easy for him, though. It wasn't in her nature to do that.

The two acolytes appeared in the doorway. Raven moved away from them, skirting wide around Wayland. Their presence provided an excuse for her to reposition herself deeper into the room again.

"Leave us," Wayland snarled.

The two men hesitated in the doorway. "Father–"

"Leave us!"

They backed away, then turned and left. She heard the door in the other room click shut again.

Wayland smirked at her. "You're very persuasive when you want something. I think I'm going to grant you your wish."

He lunged in with a midline strike this time. Raven jumped back, arching her body away enough that he only managed a shallow gash across her stomach. He pressed his advantage, encouraged by drawing blood again. Raven twisted to the side as he swept the halberd back up at an angle. The breeze of the sharpened steel whisking by her face as she leaned away made her muscles clench. Then the blade lodged in the wing of the wyvern she had led him under.

Raven lunged in and sliced through the center of the pole, eager to shorten his reach. Wayland jumped back from her immediate follow-up attack, leaving the upper half of the polearm behind. His retaliation was so sudden and swift that she hit the ground before realizing he had struck her across the head with the haft. Her ear rang, and the side of her face blazed with agony. Black edged her vision on that side, that eye struggling for focus.

Fighting the injury, she grabbed for the sword that hit the floor less than a foot away, but a powerful kick to her side sent her sprawling in the other direction. She landed on her side and rolled onto her back, struggling to breathe past the searing pain in her ribs. Wayland picked up the sword. She needed to act fast, but dizziness and pain made her sluggish. He sank to one knee next to her, his other knee coming down heavy on her throat. The tip of the blade he brought to rest at the top of her breastbone, pressing through her flesh until the point struck bone. She would have screamed if she could get enough air to do so, but all she could manage was an agonized moan.

He smiled at her. The silver in his eyes flared brightly. "Thank you for the amusement and for the life you've so generously offered me."

Power swelled in the room as he slowly drew the blade down, slicing a line of agony along her breastbone. His intentions became apparent as his eyes turned black. He would use the magic to add her life to the many he had already taken. When the magic was at its peak, he would shove the blade up under her ribs and end her. Though, the way her head pounded with lack of air and blood flow, she wasn't sure she would last that long.

The magic began moving through her. As it dove into her body, a surge of strength bolstered her. This magic was already part of her, and it recognized itself. Black closed at the edges of her vision. Blood was filling her mouth from the inside of her cheek that split against her teeth when he struck her. She seized the magic that was part of her, using it to grab for what he was amassing in preparation for her death and pulling it into herself. Then she shoved it back at him in one violent thrust.

A deafening boom shook the room. All the glass

around and inside the room shattered, showering shards down like deadly rainfall. His body shielded her face and chest, but fragments sank into her legs and abdomen. He jerked up the sword, bringing it over his head as if to protect himself from the falling daggers of glass. The pressure eased up on her neck. Raven reached out, grabbing a large shard that had landed next to her. It cut deep into her palm as she shoved it into his side below the ribs.

Wayland cried out and twisted away, the end of the shard still sticking out of his side. Raven rolled up to her knees and caught the elven sword as he dropped it. The forward lunge from her kneeling position was almost more of a fall into him. He threw one hand in front of his chest. The blade went through the middle of his hand before driving home up below his breastbone. For a second, she leaned on his shoulder, panting. Her bleeding hand still gripped the sword hilt. It was hard to breathe or focus. She shoved back, spitting blood at him as he fell over, groaning and trying to grab the blade hilt with his free hand.

A pounding sound caught her attention. Looking around, she saw that the inside wall of the collection room was gone. It had blasted back into the study, and debris now blocked the door, which was where the pounding came from. It wouldn't take the acolytes long to break through.

She looked around at the rest of the room, her thoughts sluggish. There were no trees here. She didn't want to die here, another one of his grisly trophies.

The dress's fabric pulled at bits of glass still embedded in her legs as she struggled to her feet. She pulled a couple free, one from her abdomen and one from her thigh. Blood gushed forth in their absence. That didn't strike her as desirable, so she left the rest and stumbled toward the outer wall. A wave of dizziness pitched her forward, and she fell, groaning as the glass cut into her knees. Her stomach turned, but she fought nausea and hauled herself up on the same case that had held the elven sword. On her feet again, she made her way to the outer wall, using the displays along the way for balance. Once there, she climbed on a cabinet and knocked out the remaining glass before heaving herself gracelessly over to the outside.

The elaborate architecture provided numerous hand-holds. More than most of the trees she had climbed. She started to work her way down, hindered by dizziness and pain, along with the slickness of blood from her hand and a nearly overwhelming urge to close her eyes. She spat out more blood, grimacing when she managed to hit her own hand with it, not that it made much difference. Little of her body didn't have someone's blood on it now, primarily her own.

One foot tangled in the fabric of the dress. With her wounded, slippery hand, she couldn't catch herself. She fell. Only one floor of the building remained between her and the ground. A prickly but shockingly springy hedge broke her fall. She rolled off it, trying not to notice the trail of blood she had left down the side of the structure. She lay on the cool ground for several seconds, trying to remember why she needed to keep her eyes open.

The clash of steel on steel drew her attention. She crawled out of the garden alongside the building, sucking back against the pain as shards of glass ground deeper into her legs. When she was clear of the shrubbery, she saw Phendaril crossing swords with one of the guards. An absurd glimmer of pride ran through her as she watched him drive the man back. His skill, along with his elven speed and agility, were a match for the Silverblood's enhancements.

The guard tried to twist away, but Phendaril blocked

him, driving him closer to the temple entrance. Somehow, she struggled to her feet one more time. Her legs didn't want to hold her, but she made them take her several steps into the open. Then she caught the glint of silver eyes near the building entrance seconds before someone burst from the shadows. She tried to cry a warning, but her voice came out as little more than a hoarse whisper. The newcomer lunged forward behind the Silverblood guard and, to her surprise, cracked the man across the side of the head with his sword hilt, dropping him instantly.

"Marek." She managed to croak out his name as she sank to her knees.

Phendaril spun toward her. He sheathed his sword as he ran over, catching her when she slumped forward. Worry tightened his eyes as he looked her over once. He lifted her in his arms.

Marek bent down and checked the guard for a pulse before hurrying to them. He looked at Raven, who fought to keep her eyes open. "Get her out of here."

Phendaril hesitated. "They'll come hunting her. She's in no condition to go on the run."

"I'll tell them I saw her staggering out and finished her off, then went to check on things inside. When the guard wakes, he'll mention fighting you. They'll assume you took her body. I doubt they'll waste much effort trying to hunt down a dead woman."

Phendaril lingered a moment longer, asking the question she wanted to ask. "Why are you helping?"

Marek looked down at her and gave a shake of his head. "If you don't go now, the part about her being dead won't be a lie."

•

Karsima, Alayne, and the Stonebreaker, Ehric, sprinted across the street when they saw Phendaril coming toward the gate with Raven in his arms. When they got close enough for him to pass her over the gate to Ehric, Karsima's stomach turned. Raven's tattered black dress glistened wet with blood. One side of her face was swelling, and a trickle of blood ran from that ear. A deep cut down her breastbone bled freely. The dress hid the rest of her injuries, but the amount of blood suggested they were numerous.

They climbed into the carriage, Ehric helping Phendaril lift Raven inside. Then the Stonebreaker closed them in and jumped into the seat alongside the driver. Karsima heard him telling the man to get to the river dock as fast as if a dragon were chasing him. Synal and Talis were on the waiting ship, though she didn't know if that would matter by the time they arrived.

Phendaril held Raven gently, already covered in her blood. Her hand moved once as if she meant to do something with it, but either the effort was too much, or she changed her mind, so it sank back down on the seat, blood streaming from a deep cut in her palm. He brushed a lock of her hair out of her face, and she gave him a weak smile, blood on her lips.

"Why are you here?" Her voice was little more than a whisper, but her gaze was demanding, focused on Phendaril.

Karsima took Alayne's hand. Tears sprang to her eyes as she stared at the two. Alayne's grip was firm and full of the same aching need for contact.

Phendaril leaned down and placed a soft kiss on Raven's forehead. As he drew back, he whispered, "Because I love you."

Raven's smile grew a little stronger for a moment. "Thank you for that," she murmured. Her eyes fluttered shut, and she went limp in his arms.

"Raven? Raven!" Phendaril's voice cracked as he called her name. He pulled her to him and wrapped his arms around her, tears streaming from his eyes.

Tears spilled warm down Karsima's own cheeks. She looked away. Alayne pulled her close, holding her as she wept for Phendaril and for Raven. Perhaps they would have failed to save her no matter how fast they came, but at least they could take her back to Amberwood, where she belonged.

CHAPTER THIRTY EIGHT

It was three weeks before Synal deemed Raven fit to go home. When they reached the ship the night she fought Wayland, Synal had climbed into the coach and sent them back into town to an elven healer's facility she had worked at for a time. They used a blend of modern treatments and traditional elven healing that she believed could save Raven. While they treated her, they kept her hidden in a special wing where her existence was conveniently forgotten by anyone outside the room.

Karsima and Ehric returned to Amberwood once they determined that Raven would survive her injuries. Alayne stayed a few more days, waiting until the deed to Amberwood received the king's seal. Raven persuaded Phendaril to go back with her. Amberwood would keep him busy. He could do little for her here. If he was spotted in the city by the Silverbloods after being seen at the Brotherhood temple the night of her supposed death, they might be inclined to investigate. It was safer if he left, though it took a significant amount of convincing.

Though it should have been big news, no one around town mentioned the incident at the Brotherhood. Synal said it was as if nothing had happened, though she heard talk about part of the temple undergoing renovation. It seemed they wanted to keep the incident quiet. If

Wayland survived or died of his injuries, no one spoke a word of it. No one except Raven and the select few she had told outside the temple even knew there was reason to be concerned about the Brotherhood priest's well-being.

If Wayland survived, she suspected he wasn't as powerful now. None of her companions commented that her eyes, hair, and nails were a little more silver than before. Perhaps they didn't notice. She had lived with those traits so long that the subtle change was evident to her. As was the fact that she was stronger now, despite the injuries she was recovering from. She hadn't absorbed his life, but somehow, when she turned the magic against him, she had managed to take a fragment of his power. It helped with the healing. If he had survived, she hoped that meant he was healing more slowly now.

During those three weeks, Synal sat with Raven often, teaching her how to read the legal documents Jaecar left behind that they had brought with them in case they proved helpful. They had no value. Raven couldn't legally claim noble status or any of the things Jaecar left her because her existence was still in violation of Brotherhood laws. Laws that were upheld by the kingdoms to their north and south. Recent events made that unlikely to change. Synal read them to her, but she wanted to be able to read them herself. She wanted to look at those pages and see for herself that Jaecar wanted to be her father and provide for her future. It would take time to get to that point, but Synal was a patient teacher.

They pulled into the dock above Amberwood in the late afternoon. Raven was strong enough to walk up to the town, but Synal would have none of it.

"You died three weeks ago," the healer reminded her. "You should give yourself a break for a while longer. We'll take a cart up."

Raven shuddered. Wayland accomplished what he set out to do. It just hadn't gone exactly as he had expected it to. Now, if Marek did as he said he would, they should believe her dead. They would have no reason to search for her so long as she managed to avoid drawing their attention again.

She wasn't sure what to think of Marek now. He gave her to Wayland, but, in the end, he helped save her. Perhaps he was as confused by the whole situation as she was. It made her anxious, knowing he could change his mind again and make her life miserable. She could only hope he didn't take that turn.

A few individuals were always posted by the docks with oxen ready to move people and supplies up to town. Raven climbed into the waiting cart. The cuts from the glass and Wayland's attacks were mostly healed, though a few of the deepest one's remained tender. The broken ribs didn't cause her much pain anymore. Even the fractured cheekbone was healing well. Much faster than expected, according to Synal. The other aftereffects of the blow to her head were going away, but Synal wasn't taking any chances.

The sun was starting to set as they reached the Stonebreaker camp. The camp had shrunk, implying that more of the houses in town were occupied. The smells of evening fires and cooking from the camps and the tavern sent a flush of warmth through her. She missed all of this. All these people and elves. The long hard days of work that made every bite of food taste like a king's feast by the end.

This was precisely what Jaecar envisioned for them. This land was the same land he intended to reclaim. She ended up here because she went after his killers, so, in a way, he had brought her here after all. True to his vision, she had started building a life here, though it hadn't been her intention when she arrived. Phendaril,

Karsima, Alayne, and Ehric came to save her when Marek took her as if one of their own had been taken. And perhaps she was becoming just that.

She smiled as the cart started down the road toward the upper residential area square. Synal looked over and raised an eyebrow in question.

Raven sat up and glanced around them. "Do you think I could walk from here just to stretch my legs a little?"

Synal offered a patient smile and relented, asking the driver to stop. Raven climbed out and watched them drive away. When Synal could no longer see her, she made her way over and climbed the ladder up to the rooftops. She walked to the spot where she had positioned herself to fight the fell rats and the bear and sat cross-legged, looking over the busy square.

A delicious blend of boisterous laughter and sated exhaustion rose from below. Raven spotted Karsima and Alayne, the two sitting close, holding hands as they chatted with a group of Stonebreakers. Jenner sat nearby, though he appeared engaged in a separate conversation. It warmed her to see Veylin and several other scouts laughing and chatting at another fire. Were they her friends? If they weren't yet, they had the potential to become such.

Her ears caught the sound of someone coming up behind her. She recognized his footsteps. It never occurred to her that the way one moved could have such a distinctive sound, but not everyone sounded like Jaecar when they walked. No one else sounded precisely like Phendaril either. She would recognize his light, considered footsteps anywhere.

He sank down beside her. His hand touched her arm, and she turned her hand palm up so he could slide his into place against it, their fingers twining.

"I missed you." The tightness in his voice told her

more than his words could.

"I missed you too." And she had. The smell of him delighted her. He had been working with wood again. Working hard, judging by the tang of sweat from him.

She looked at him. His eyes flickered to her lips, but he didn't move.

"It's all right," she murmured, "if you're gentle."

He leaned in and kissed her, a careful, loving kiss that was wary of her injuries. It lit her blood on fire, that brief, soft touch of their lips. He drew back slightly as if he couldn't bring himself to move too far away from her.

"Are you hungry?"

Raven met his eyes and nodded. Then she shifted in and kissed him more deeply, sliding her hand up under his hair and opening her mouth to him to show him exactly what she was hungry for. It hurt her healing cheekbone, but she assured herself she wouldn't push it too far.

They were both breathless when they parted again.

He smiled, his eyes glinting with happiness and desire. "I have a present for you."

He stood up, drawing her up with him. Raven followed in curious silence back to his residence. When they walked in, she was surprised to see that the furniture had been upgraded. She looked around while he went to get whatever he had for her. There were signs of reconstruction in process on the staircase leading up to the next floor. Curiously, the new bed in the adjacent room was the finest piece of new furniture in the building, with an amberwood headboard carved in a forest motif. Her armor and weapons were clean and neatly set out on a matching dresser.

He stepped up behind her. She turned to find him holding up what looked like a piece of bowstring with a beautiful carved wooden arrowhead hanging from it.

"The wood and the string are from your father's bow," he said.

It was the hint of self-consciousness as much as the gift itself that made her love him at that moment. She turned and held her hair up so he could fasten it around her neck. Then she turned back, admiring the rich finish he had placed on the wooden arrowhead. After a few seconds, she let it rest against her skin and slid her arms over his shoulders, stepping closer. Having faced Wayland, this wasn't so terrifying anymore.

She placed a light kiss on his lips, appreciating the careful way he set his hands on her hips, attentive to any injury she might still be recovering from.

"I love you, Phendaril."

He looked too startled to react for a second, then he smiled and kissed her softly. "I love you," he murmured.

She bit her lip and stepped closer until their bodies were touching. His hands slid around her waist to the small of her back.

"I have an idea," she whispered. "I was thinking, maybe you could show me more about how to be with someone."

The fire that kindled in his eyes told her how much he wanted to say yes, but he held back. "I don't want to hurt you?"

Wanting burned through her body like her blood was on fire. Not just wanting, but needing. Right then, more than anything, she needed to be wanted by him. She needed to feel something good.

"Just be gentle," she said, offering a playful smile.

Phendaril kissed her and began slowly backing her toward the bed.

THE END

ACKNOWLEDGEMENTS

After several years spent rebuilding my life—finding a new place to call home and finishing my degree, among other things—I am happy to have found inspiration again with Raven. Her story came to me as I was pondering the effects of pandemic isolation on our social skills (which I had only a bare minimum of to begin with). Those thoughts led me to wonder what it would be like to grow up isolated from other people. Throw in a dash of fantasy, and Raven was born.

As such, I must give a nod of acknowledgment to everyone for surviving in these challenging times. Whatever hardships you have faced over these last few years, I hope you find something in Raven's story to inspire you.

There are a few people I could never leave off this list. That includes my dearest friends and family to my heart, Rick and Ann, my most ardent supporter and loving mom, Linda, and my patient and all-around extraordinary partner, Kai.

As always, I want to acknowledge Robert, my amazing cover artist, and Brian, my fantastic editor and formatter. I value everything you do and the people you are. Thank you for being so wonderful to work with.

To my other friends and family, know that I value your place in my life even if I don't call you out specifically here. Supposedly you aren't supposed to turn your acknowledgements into a second book.

Lastly, I would like to take a quick moment to remember a few of those I have personally lost over the last few years. My beloved Huma, may you find a paradise of books waiting wherever you are now. My friend and fellow author, Jeffrey, who will be so deeply missed by the many lives he touched. My dear equine companion and friend, Cody, who is now running free in a place where his body can once again keep up with his spirit.

AUTHOR BIO

Nikki started writing her first novel at the age of 12, which she still has tucked in a briefcase in her home office. She lives in the magnificent Pacific Northwest with her wondrous cat-god. She feeds her imagination by sitting on the ocean in her kayak gazing out across the never-ending water or hanging from a rope in a cave, embraced by darkness and the sound of dripping water. She finds peace through practicing iaido or shooting her longbow.

•

Thank you for taking time to read this novel. Please leave a review if you enjoyed it.

•

For more about me and my work visit me at http://elysiumpalace.com.

OTHER NOVELS by NIKKI McCORMACK

CLOCKWORK ENTERPRISES
The Girl and the Clockwork Cat
The Girl and the Clockwork Conspiracy
The Girl and the Clockwork Crossfire

FORBIDDEN THINGS
Dissident
Exile
Apostate

ELYSIUM'S FALL
Dark Hope of the Dragons
Dark Savior of the Dragons

STANDALONE WORK
Golden Eyes
The Keeper

Raven's soft boots found easy purchase on the rooftop of the newly rebuilt blacksmith shop on the northeastern edge of town. It was one of the first structures the Stonebreakers finished rebuilding. The clang of hammer on steel and the heat from the now operational forge were comforting. Having a functioning smithy in town was one of several things speeding up reconstruction. She hadn't come up here to appreciate that, however, or even to escape the press of folks working in the streets.

She sank to one knee and watched a harpy circling above the trees at the edge of the forest. They hadn't seen harpies in this close since they drove them from their nesting grounds several months ago. She leveled an arrow at the creature, ready to try to spook it away with a warning shot. After a few more seconds of observation, she lowered her bow.

The beast dipped clumsily in the air, one side losing power with every few strokes of its great wings. As that side dropped low again, she noticed the rust color of drying blood staining the underside of the tan and ivory plumage. The trail of blood extended from the shoulder to the tip of the last feather on that side. The creature struggled to stay aloft.

She didn't turn when someone came up behind her,

recognizing Ehric's solid footsteps. With his height and heavy musculature, it made her uneasy having the dark-skinned Stonebreaker warrior climbing on rooftops. Add to that the weight of the steel and leather armor he wore, and it made sense to her that he should be too heavy to manage such light-footed work. That aside, she found his presence oddly reassuring. He had been there the night she had nearly died–briefly had died in truth–after fighting the Silverblood Brotherhood priest, Father Wayland Mallebron. Ehric had helped Phendaril lift her over the temple gate and get her into the back of the coach. It was irrational, since she had been barely conscious at the time, but she implicitly trusted him now.

His shadow fell over her. "What do you see? Is it a threat?"

"It isn't, but that doesn't mean there isn't a threat." She glanced up at him, smiling faintly at the way he shielded his eyes from the light with one hand and peered hard at the distant creature. Without elven or Silverblood eyesight, he would learn little by looking, but that didn't mean he wouldn't try. "It's injured," she said, sparing him the frustration. "The fact that it flew this way instead of back to the nesting ground makes me wonder if it was hurt there."

"Implying there might be a threat out there we should be concerned about."

Raven nodded. The harpies had found new nesting grounds in the northeastern corner of Amberwood ter-ritory, far enough away that they posed no threat to the population or livestock of the recovering town. They were content to let the creatures live in peace, but some-thing else appeared to be causing them grief now.

She stood, watching the beast in the distance as it found a large branch to land on where it could rest the injured wing. "Perhaps we should get a few more scouts together to investigate."

"I already sent word to Phendaril," he answered.

As if on cue, the sound of approaching horses reached her. Disappointment sat heavy in her chest. If they struck out on horseback, that meant they would be going without her. Until a few weeks ago, she had never touched a horse. Even with Phendaril's patient guidance, the experience was far from triumphant. She'd screeched and almost fallen on her ass when the animal lipped her fingers, looking for a treat. Phendaril laughed so hard while trying to soothe the startled horse that she still hadn't entirely forgiven him for it.

Ehric was heading down off the roof of the smithy via a low shed full of coal that groaned under his bulk. Raven took a more direct route, hopping off the front into the street. She wasn't invulnerable, but she was a Silverblood, which meant she had physical enhancements that gave her skills beyond an average individual with equivalent training. Coupled with Jaecar's instruction and the improved agility, vision, and hearing provided by her half-elven blood, she possessed significant advantages. The last several months had shown her how little those things mattered in some situations.

Phendaril and Veylin trotted up, stopping their mounts in front of the smithy. Veylin led a third horse behind her for Ehric. Raven glanced up at Phendaril, appreciating the way the sun brought out the deep auburn in his long, nearly black hair. She loved his fierce, dark eyes. She even loved the scar that ran down from inside his right eyebrow and down along his nose to his lip on that side. What she appreciated most was the pleasure in his eyes and the intimacy of his smile when he looked at her, that dark intensity calming for a second, just for her.

"Ehric said there was a stray harpy near the town." He held a hand down to Raven.

She resolutely ignored the offer. "There is. It's in the trees over there. It's injured, but it came here instead of going back to the nest."

Phendaril nodded and shifted the horse so that his hand was again in her line of sight. "Come on. We'll get there faster on horseback."

Raven shook her head, staring at his hand as if it were poison.

Veylin and Ehric, who had mounted the third horse, looked away, trying to hide the amusement she'd already seen in their eyes.

Phendaril chuckled, his patient smile lessening her annoyance. "She's a strong, calm mare, and you'll be riding with me. It'll be fine."

Raven took a step back and shook her head.

"We both know you'd rather come than stay here." He moved his foot around in front of the stirrup so she could use it to climb up.

Raven stared at the mare. The horse twitched its ears and turned its head to look at her, soft brown eyes wondering what the holdup was.

"Raven."

His voice–gentle, reasonable, and thick with affection–made her want to please him. Besides, he was right. She would rather go with them than stay here with all these relative strangers. If she climbed up, he would tell her later how impressed he was with her. Then he would love her the way only he could.

She grabbed his hand and put her foot in the stirrup the way she had seen others do. With his pull adding to her own boost, she swung up easily, landing straddled across the animal's back in the saddle behind him. Her heart jumped into her throat with the mare shifted, and she wrapped her arms around Phendaril, squeezing herself against him. He placed one hand on her arm, a gesture meant to comfort, and urged the mare toward the gate out of town.

Raven focused on breathing, the sensation of lean muscles in Phendaril's back pressed against her chest, and the progress made in rebuilding this part of Amberwood since the arrival of the Stonebreakers earlier that year. Anything but the volatile, powerful animal she was now sitting on. The other scouts found it amusing that a female who had faced a wyvern and corpse eaters would tremble before a horse. But she would never throw herself on the back of a wyvern, putting herself at its mercy, especially not to hasten a trip into more danger.

They passed through the gate, and Phendaril gave her arm a squeeze. Then he took his hand away, returning it to the reins.

"Hold on."

Raven did precisely that, pinching her eyelids shut and tightening her arms around him when he urged the horse up from a walk to a trot and then to a canter.

"We're going to fall off if you squeeze me so hard I can't breathe."

There was an edge of laughter in his voice, which told her he could breathe well enough, so she continued to hold on. The animal's motion beneath her was powerful yet smoother than she had expected. It was that power that kept her on edge. All that strength in a moderately intelligent beast. Jaecar shared several stories about how horses could kill you without meaning to because they were so big, strong, and prone to panic.

"They're prey animals," he had told her. *"You have to think like one to understand their fear."*

The harpy shrieked at them as they passed near the tree it had perched in. The cry was enough to compel Raven to open her eyes. She peered up at the beast, her shoulder twinging in sympathy for the wound it suffered. Despite her ongoing fear as the horses kept up their canter into the woods, she made herself study the injured creature, catching sight of what she was searching for seconds before another tree blocked her view.

"There's part of an arrow still in its shoulder. Looks like the rest broke off."

She didn't have to see Phendaril's face to know his anger. She felt it in the slight stiffening of his posture and heard it in his voice.

"Wonderful. We're dealing with trespassing hunters then." He said it loud enough to make sure the other two heard.

Raven squeaked in surprise when he kicked the horse faster.

"Sorry, my love. I just don't want them getting away with this."

Raven said nothing in return. It was hard to be angry with him when he called her his love. She had never been someone's love before. It suited her to be his.

Through the comfort of Phendaril's nearness and the time it took to reach their destination, Raven's horse phobia started to lose some of its power. When they were close to the jagged ravine the harpies had built their new nests in and around, they dropped Raven inside the tree line. They wouldn't risk anyone seeing what she was and reporting her back to the authorities, given that, as an unsanctioned Silverblood, the Brotherhood would put her to death. Silverblood Brotherhood doctrine also taught that elves, women, and children couldn't survive the magical process of becoming a Silverblood. Literally everything about her was an affront to the Brotherhood. Her existence broke their laws and exposed the lies they used to maintain control of Silverblood magic. Still, her need to stay hidden wasn't going to stop her from finding ways to be of use. She simply had to be careful about it.

Raven crept out of the trees, crouching low behind shrubs and a fallen tree, working her way to a spot with a view of the activity below. She drew her bow and knocked an arrow, holding it at rest for now. The others continued down the hill out in the open toward where two men were contemplating the collection of harpy corpses they had dragged out into a flat area at the base of the ravine. At a glance, Raven counted eleven of the creatures. An entire flock decimated for no reason.

Her fingers tightened on the bowstring, and she struggled to keep from sending an arrow down to give them an idea of how she felt about their slaughter. Then she spotted a third man standing in the shadows with his back to her, not laughing or joking with the other two. When her companions approached, he turned. She sucked back a breath of surprise. Even without the black and silver leather armor, his bright silver eyes would have marked him as a Silverblood.

Phendaril stopped his group at the edge of the line of corpses. "What's going on here?"

A tall man with a liberal dusting of gray in his dark hair stepped forward, one hand coming to rest on his hip next to his sword hilt. "We came to clear out these harpies. Lord Darrenton now owns the land north of here, and they're close enough to be a risk."

Raven's anger exploded, her vision going red at the edges. If the two men were Lord Darrenton's soldiers, then they could have been involved in the murder of his brother, Jaecar. It took her several months to come to terms with the idea that the quiet, stern warrior who raised her had been a nobleman who chose to abandon his former life. Then again, if she had a brother like Aldrich Darrenton, she might have gone into hiding too. Her fingers itched to draw the arrow and let it fly, but she held still. Even if either of these men helped kill Jaecar, ending them wasn't going to bring him back.

"The land Darrenton bought is well outside of this flock's range." Phendaril's voice was tight with anger. The scar tugged at his lip, emphasizing his snarl. "I know this because you're well over the border into Amberwood, which is the property of Lady Alayne Valassian. This slaughter," he snapped one hand out to point at the dead beasts, "was unnecessary. It's a mistake we'll allow you to make once, recognizing your ignorance. I suggest you get off this land before we change our minds about that."

Veylin and Ehric both rested a hand on their sword hilts now. Some not-so-subtle support for Phendaril's threat.

The Silverblood showed no interest in their exchange. He was a mercenary. It wouldn't matter to him who did what and where as long as he got paid. His gaze moved up the ravine now, which made her more than a little uneasy, though he didn't appear to have noticed her. She tugged the hood of her cloak further forward, just in case.

"Of course." The younger of Darrenton's two soldiers scratched at the stubble on his chin. The news that this was someone else's land didn't seem to come as a surprise to him. He took a step toward the nearest harpy as he was speaking. "We'll get a move on after we collect the feathers and the–"

Raven planted an arrow less than an inch in front of the toe of his boot as it touched down. He jerked back, casting an angry glare in her direction. The Silverblood placed a hand on his crossbow now. He looked at the log she was hiding behind. She shifted closer to the exposed root ball where the shadows were deepest, her heart beating triple-time.

"We made these kills," the young man protested, still glaring up the ravine. "Those feathers are good for fletching."

Phendaril placed a hand on his sword hilt, and Ehric drew his blades. Veylin changed tactics, pulling out her bow and backing her horse several steps with leg cues as she set an arrow to the string.

"And the breasts and reproductive organs are supposed to make an effective fertility elixir. They fetch a good price on less reputable markets, I'm told." Phendaril made no effort to keep his disgust from showing. He urged his mount a step closer to the nearest corpse. "But you need permission to hunt in Amberwood. Unless you have it, you're poaching. We can take it up with the town constable if you'd like to ride back with us."

Raven aimed an arrow at the younger man's throat. She wouldn't give him the chance to hurt those she cared about if it came to a fight. Phendaril was being more generous than they deserved, offering them the option to leave, unpunished. If they didn't take it, they would get what they had coming.

One of the men glanced at the Silverblood, but he moved his hands away from his weapons and took a step back. They weren't going to get help from him. He apparently considered this outside the scope of whatever they were paying him for.

The older soldier scowled then held his hands up in a gesture of surrender. "No reason to make a big deal of an honest mistake. We'll be on our way."

Raven ground her teeth, shifting her aim to target the man who had spoken. This was no *honest mistake.*

Phendaril absently corrected his mount as the animal started to turn away, not taking his eyes off the three men. "Our patrols will be given your descriptions. Should you choose to trespass again, we'll be sure to give you a proper welcome."

The threat that laced Phendaril's words made her want to kiss him. She would have to ask him later if that meant she could shoot them on sight if they came here again.

"Fuck off," the younger man growled under his breath as they turned to walk to their waiting mounts.

Once they were in the saddle, Darrenton's soldiers kicked their horses to a gallop. The Silverblood held his back, the animal prancing and champing at the bit as it watched its companions depart. He looked up the ravine once more, his silver eyes searching around the end of the log where she was hiding.

"Move on," Phendaril snapped.

The Silverblood glanced over at him, a slight smirk curving his lips before he turned to race after the others.

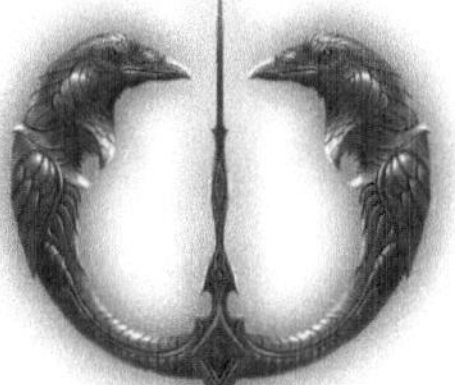